Banged Up

For SACRO.

For Stephen Donaldson, whose invaluable work on the US prison system has yet to be echoed in the UK.

For Ray and Jackie, who have lived with ex-DS Jas Anderson for two novels and will hopefully stick by him for many more.

And for everyone who ever found love in the unlikeliest of places.

GAY MEN'S PRESS

Banged Up

by Jack Dickson

First published 1999 by Millivres Ltd,
part of the Millivres Prowler Group,
3 Broadbent Close, London N6 5GG

A CIP catalogue record for this book is available
from the British Library

ISBN 1 902852 04 4

Distributed in Europe by Central Books,
99 Wallis Rd, London E9 5LN

Distributed in North America by InBook/LPC Group,
1436 West Randolph, Chicago, IL 60607

Distributed in Australia by Bulldog Books,
P O Box 300, Beaconsfield, NSW 2014

Printed and bound in the EU by WSOY, Juva, Finland

One

"Tear the whole rotten place doon, Mr Anderson, that's whit ah'd dae."

Smooth buzzing behind one ear. Jas stared into the mirror.

Terry's clippers continued their progress. So did the chat. "Built tae hold nine hundred. There's ower two thousand in there, these days. Two thousand animals in cells wi' nae plumbin'."

Jas continued to stare into the mirror. He watched as the clippers, clutched in Terry's wrinkled hand, followed the contours of his skull. He closed his eyes.

Terry talked on. "Ken how much ma Billy works fur? Fifteen thousand – oh, ah ken it sounds a lot, but that's wi' the shift-allowance. Turns yer life upside doon, does that. But ah don't huv tae tell you whit like shifts kin be, eh Mr Anderson?"

Jas opened his eyes.

"Under-valued, under-paid... an' under the thumb o' they pen-pushers at the Scottish Office: that's whit prison officers ur." Terry switched off the clippers and produced a comb. "That Inspector o' Prisons' guy's no' livin' in the real world." His eyes never left the work in hand. "Ye couldney pay me enough tae work in the Bar-L, an' they don't pay ma Billy enough, by hauf. It's a dirty joab..."

A strand of blond hair fell from the comb onto an eyelash. Jas blinked it away – "...but somewan's got tae dae it."

Terry met his eyes in the mirror and smiled. "Billy's ma ainly boay – ah worry aboot him."

Jas grinned. "Yer gettin' like an auld wuman, Terry. Billy's a big lad noo." Billy MacKinley was nearly forty. "He ken's whit he's daein'. They aw' dae. The strike'll no' last."

Terry lifted scissors. "Ah'm no' so sure. That security company the Scottish Office huv brought in seems tae be dain' a guid job, fae aw' accounts."

Silence, then snipping.

"Ah wanted Billy tae come in wi' me, Mr. Anderson, make the wee shop intae a family business – ken whit ah mean?" Fingers and scissors moved expertly over the top of Jas's head.

"Ye've bin here – how long noo, Terry?"

In the mirror grey hands continued their work. "Near on forty years." Pride in the ancient voice. "Came straight oota the National

Service an' started up. The army taught me a trade, Mr Anderson. They did me a big favour. Now, if Billy hid even wanted tae join wan o' the Forces..."

Jas switched off. He stared into the mirror, past Terry's busy babbling form, past his own pale face, past the inverted barber's shop. Past twelve years with Strathclyde Police.

Billy McKinley: a screw – a prison officer.

A year ago he'd considered applying. A move from putting them inside to keeping them there. Then reconsidered. He'd fail the medical, anyway.

Under the blue nylon fabric tucked tightly around his neck Jas clenched his right fist.

Nails brushed palm.

Two years ago, the consultant at the Royal Infirmary had told him he'd never use the hand again. He'd proved him wrong. Or partly wrong, at least. The middle and ring fingers still tingled occasionally, and sometimes his grip let him down. But it was far from useless.

After he'd considered then reconsidered the Prison Service?

Six months as a nightwatchman, patrolling the grounds of the derelict cigarette factory with a bad-tempered Alsatian dog. Not a marriage made in heaven. And the work was mind-numbing.

After that? Store detective: three months. Bouncer: three days. Jas had drawn the line at Sheriff's Officer, but the job had been there, had he wanted it.

He hadn't.

Jas scowled. Ex-cops could always find work. But the type of work offered was limited – and limiting. Policing in the private sector. Good references, good body and a hard face: that was all they wanted.

"Ye want gel, Mr Anderson?"

He refocused in the mirror. Terry gestured with a small jar of garish blue gunk. Jas shook his head.

"Short enough fur ye this time?" Laugh. Terry angled a hand mirror behind Jas's neck.

Jas scrutinised the back of his skull. White scalp gleamed through fair bristles. He turned his attention to the rest of his hair. The shorter Terry cut it, the less often Jas had to return – and Terry knew it. Still a bit long on top. Jas smiled. "Aye, Terry, it's great."

The barber untied the blue nylon coverall, removed then shook it over the floor. Showers of fair hair joined a sea of grey and black.

Jas stood up, ran a hand over his head. Stray strands itched under shirt collar. "How much dae ah owe ye?"

The next customer, a white-haired man in a shiny suit, was already in the chair. Terry tied the blue nylon coverall around the wizen neck. "Two fifty, Mr Anderson."

Jas fumbled in his pocket. "Still fifties prices, Terry, eh?" He handed the barber two pound coins and a fifty-pence piece.

Terry grinned. "Well, ye goat a fifties haircut, Mr Anderson. Come back an' see me soon. Ah enjoy oor wee chats." Turning. "Noo, George, how've ye bin keepin'? Ma Billy's oan the picket line the morra, did ah tell ye?"

Jas shrugged on a Levi jacket and moved towards the door. Terry's voice followed him out of the barber's and onto Cumbernauld Road. He looked at his watch. It was just after three-fifteen pm.

'Handy for all local amenities.'

Estate-agent-speak for busy and noisy. He walked the few yards to the M8 feeder road and paused. The man was red. Jas lowered his eyes.

A stream of articulated lorries and cars careered left inches from his feet. Two orange buses carried straight on, up Cumbernauld Road. One stopped ahead. Three women and a dog got off. Jas lifted his eyes.

The man was green.

He stepped off the pavement in front of a revving, impatient car, crossed the feeder road and the railway bridge. From the other side of the road two loud booms were just audible over traffic. The Lanarkshire Blast Cleaning Company was hidden behind a twelve-foot wall. What they cleaned, he had no idea: all he could see from his bedroom window were long, asbestos-roofed sheds. How they cleaned it was audibly obvious. Jas shoved hands deep into pockets and walked on.

He passed the office of the estate agent from whom he had rented the flat. It came with her personal recommendation:

'Friendly area – good close. You'll have no trouble with the neighbours.'

They'd have trouble making themselves heard over the traffic, trains and booms. But she'd been right. He'd been here nearly two years and had only seen, never mind talked to, his neighbours half-a-dozen times.

Changing times.

Cumbernauld Road: Eastercraigs four hundred yards away.

A lifetime away.

Jas quickened his pace. Three closes on was 247. He pushed open the wrought-iron gate, closed it, and jogged up four flights of stone stairs. Green tiles glinted. Outside the top right-hand flat he stopped, located keys, opened the far-from-solid door and walked in.

In the narrow hall-way spiky pink artexing scratched his shoulder, the way it always did. He closed the door and walked the length of the hall, past the freezer and through to the bedroom: one of the flat's plus points. Sunlight blanched gloss-white walls. Jas took off the Levi jacket, threw it on the bed and walked to the window.

Four floors up. East-facing view. He rested his knuckles on the sill's fresh paintwork.

On a good day you could see the sun rise over Coatbridge.

On a bad day you could see Haghill.

Four floors below another bus stopped, disgorged passengers, then continued down Cumbernauld Road into town.

Jas turned from the window and sat down on the bed. The only piece of furniture he'd brought with him.

New mattress, of course.

He reached over and traced the faint handcuff scores on the bars of the brass headboard. Jas lay down, stretched out and closed his eyes.

The phone rang.

He let the machine pick up. His own voice growled through the open door from the lounge: "Anderson Investigations. I can't come to the phone at the moment. Leave your name and number and I'll call you back."

Three short beeps, long beep, then deep, male voice: "Andrew Ainslie here. It's... er, Wednesday afternoon, half past three. Got the report this morning. Your cheque's in the post. Good doing business with you. I'll be in touch if there's anything else. Bye."

Jas smiled. Interviewing nervous prosecution witnesses for MacIntosh and Ainslie, solicitors: money for old rope. He opened his eyes, sat up and rubbed his face. Not exactly Phillip Marlowe stuff, but it paid the rent. He scowled at the lie.

His invalidity settlement from Strathclyde Police would do

that. Or the disability pension...

...or the fifty-four thousand blackmail money, still in a bank book he had no idea what to do with.

He hadn't started working again for the money. Jas got up and walked from the bedroom past the freezer into the other room.

One of the flat's minus points. It looked out onto a permanently sunless, triangular back court. Jas sat down on the cheap, moulded sofa. The ansaphone read '3'. He pressed the replay button and waited.

One beep: rasping male voice, middle-aged. "Er..." Embarrassed, uncertain. "A pal gave me yer number, said ye kid... er, ah need some work done. It's aboot ma..." Noise in background. "Er... ah'll phone ye back, pal." Severed connection.

His... what? Wife? Girlfriend? Boyfriend? Daughter? Son? Dog? The caller had bottled out. A lot of them did.

Another beep: woman's voice, polite, polished. Professional. "IBS. Jean Thompson here, Mr. Anderson. Wednesday morning, nine thirty am. We've completed the company search you required. Stop by the office any time today. Thank you."

Another beep: Andrew Ainslie's message.

Jas picked up a plastic folder from the floor and emptied its contents onto the sofa. Jean Thompson. Office in the Merchant City.

As the machine was rewinding the phone rang again.

Jas sorted through the pile of documentation until he found IBS's address and phone-number.

After five rings the ansaphone picked up. Faint music in the background. Then his voice. Then a laugh: "Whit's aw' this 'Anderson Investigations' shite?" Another laugh.

He laid Jean Thompson's card on the sofa and stared past it.

"Listen, man. Ah ken it's bin a while. Mebbe ye'll no' want tae see me. But ah never goat tae explain proper..."

Jas reached over and picked up the receiver. "Marie."

Forced laugh. "Ah, ye're there, Big Man." Words in a rush. "Look. Kin ah come roon'?"

Marie McGhee.

"How did ye git ma number?" Jas clenched his right fist. Nails hovered an inch from palm.

Harsh laugh. "McGhee Investigations, Big Man! Ah called yer auld number, then Directory Inquiries. Telt them ah wis yer sister, that yer mother wis dyin'." Worried. "She's no', is she?"

"No' as far as ah ken, Marie." He unclenched his fist.

Relaxing. "Well? Kin ah come roon'? Ye wur never wan tae haud a grudge, Big Man. Let me explain, at least..."

"That's aw' in the past, Marie. Ye did whit ye hud tae." Jas closed his eyes. The beating she had facilitated, or his lover's knife: which was more responsible for the damaged tendons in his right arm? "Ah'm busy, Marie. Mebbe ah'll catch ye later..."

Insistent. "Ah really need tae see ye, Jas. It's aboot wee Paul."

Jas opened his eyes. "Paul who?"

Impatient. "Ye ken Paul, Jas. Ma supplier. He drove ye tae London, that summer, when ye went tae see aboot..." – hesitation – "...tae see yer brother."

Jas stared at the grey telephone. Vague memories of a blue Escort, Fila tee-shirt, banana sandwiches and a kid barely old enough to be driving legally. "Ah never kent his name, Marie. Whit's he done?"

"Gone awol, Big Man." Low voice.

"Git yersel' another supplier, Marie. There's plenty aroon'."

No response.

"You still there?"

Soft voice. "Ah'm worried aboot him."

"It's no' like you tae care who ye buy yer gear aff."

Wheedling. "Let me come roon', Big Man."

Jas fingered the phone's coiled flex. Two years ago Marie had been there for him – up to a point. She'd probably saved his life, after almost causing his death. "Ma shoulder's awfy hard, these days."

Laugh. "It's no' sympathy ah'm wantin', Big Man."

"Whit then?"

Soft voice. "Let me come roon', eh?"

He tucked the receiver between chin and shoulder and began to reload documentation into the plastic folder. "Ah've work tae dae, Marie, ah don't ken when ah'll be finished..."

Eager. "Make it fur whenever ye want, Jas."

He looked at his watch. It read three fifty-five pm. "It'll huv tae be efter eleven."

"Sure, sure, Big Man. That's great."

He replaced the plastic folder on the sofa. "Ah'll see ye then, Marie..."

"Haud oan – where ur ye?"

He laughed. "Whit happened tae McGhee Investigations?"

Embarrassed. "BT widney gie me yer address."

He supplied it.

Surprise. "Ye've no' moved far, then?"

Jas frowned. "Far enough, Marie. Ah'll see ye efter eleven." He replaced the receiver then stood up. Lifting the plastic folder, Jas walked through to the bedroom, collected his jacket and left.

It was almost nine when he returned. Jas entered the small flat without turning on any lights: it looked better that way. In the bedroom he took off his jacket and switched on the word processor. A green screen lit up the dark room. He drew up a chair and began to type.

Thirty minutes later two more reports were ready for printing, courtesy of IBS. The first a security check on applicants for manager of a children's home, for Glasgow's Social Work Department. The second an assessment of three dodgy investment managers, for FIMBRO.

Jas stood up, stretched, and pressed P, then Exit. The ancient printer's daisy-wheel clattered into action, filling the silence with noise. He smiled. His neighbours had more to complain about than he did. He walked over to the window.

Below, a group of teenage boys lounged at the bus stop. A bus appeared, stopped at traffic lights. One boy pointed and stepped out into the road. Sixteen-year-old face illuminated under sodium. Freckles. Dark, cropped hair. A single shaved line running from ear to back of head. Black canvas Stussy jacket. No-hips in low-slung jeans.

Jas stared.

The other boys moved to the edge of the pavement and stuck out a communal hand. The lights changed. The bus arrived. Three boys got on. Freckle-face and another waved, then walked up Cumbernauld Road towards the chip shop.

His stomach growled. Jas sighed: he'd eat later.

The printer stopped. He removed the disc, switched off the machine, found and addressed two envelopes. He'd post them in the morning.

In the dark bedroom Jas began to undress. Naked, he peered around the room. An orange light seeped in from street lights below. He looked for a jock-strap, then gave up.

In the narrow space between window and bed he lowered his body onto the floor and braced his arms. He began the press-ups.

At fifty his mind freed itself. A year ago each lift had been an effort, his right arm trembling then collapsing beneath him. Physio had helped.

At one hundred he stopped, resting, elbows locked.

Physio.

Jas grinned.

Recreational physio.

He lay down, forehead barely damp.

He'd wanked his way healthy.

Jas flipped over onto his back. Between iron thighs his prick twitched.

IBS. Merchant city offices. An image of bronzed hands dusted with heavy black hair punched into his brain.

He scowled: not now. He needed a wash. Jas stood up, walked around the bed and opened a sliding door.

'Ensuite shower-room'. More estate agent speak.

Hastily converted bed recess, more like.

Jas switched on the fluorescent strip and stepped into the cubicle. Harsh light blinked twice then blazed into life. Under sub-zero water he shivered, body glowing. He closed his eyes, turning face upwards to meet the icy jet.

The guy in IBS's plush office. Assistant? Secretary? If he'd got the measure of Ms Jean Thompson, the latter probably applied.

Mid-twenties. Six-footish. Dark, glossy hair falling over one eye. Tanned skin. Good body under bad suit.

Fingers brushed prick. Hardening.

Meeting his gaze across a crowded desk. Hairy knuckles. Holding out a brown A4 envelope. Gold signet ring.

His hand gripped his prick. Hard.

Hairy Knuckles naked. On his knees. Dark glossy hair falling over face. Smiling...

Jas's hand began to move slowly.

...on his knees...

Jas's hand moved faster now.

...on his knees...

Frozen water warming on burning skin.

Banging.

...on his...

More banging.

Jas opened his eyes. Voices... or a voice.

More banging. Then shouting.

He looked down. Still hard.

Hairy Knuckles was gone.

The voice. "Jas? You in there?"

He sighed, switched off the shower and grabbed a towel. He rubbed face, hair then threw the sopping towel over one shoulder. Jas made his way from the shower cubicle through the bedroom into the hall past the freezer to the front door. Spiky pink artexing ripped at his skin. "Marie? Ye're early."

Laugh from the other side. "Lemme in, eh? It's freezin' oot here."

Jas sighed, and opened the door.

Two

She was taller than he remembered.

Same pale, colourless skin, matt under the stair-light. Same long brown hair. Same crescent scar above crimson mouth, stretching to just under eye. No leather coat, this time. Light-coloured jacket and skirt. Knee-length suede boots, also light-coloured. Smart. Expensive. In one small hand a bottle-shaped package wrapped in pink paper. The other jammed into jacket pocket.

"Fur fuck's sake, Jas!" Thin body shivering in thin fabric. Stamping on stack heels to keep warm. "Here! Flat-warmin' present." Bottle-shaped package thrust at him.

Jas's shoulder collided with plaster spikes.

Marie pushed past him into the flat. Then paused.

He closed the door behind her.

"Whit've ye goat a freezer in yer hall fur?" Bright eyes in the dark, from him to white formica and back again. "It'll play havoc wi' yer Feng Shui – cold reception, an' aw' that."

Jas shrugged. "Nae room in the kitchen." He pointed to the lounge. "Ah'll be through in a minute."

Laugh. "Dinny git dressed oan ma account, Big Man." Eyes on his shoulder. Broad smile. Eyes from shoulder to groin. "Or huv ah interrupted somethin'?" She poked his chest with a scarlet-tipped finger.

"Only ma shower." He thrust the bottle-shaped package back at her. "Git yersel' a drink." He turned and walked towards the bedroom. The artex-inflicted wounds had started to bleed. He rubbed scratches with wet towel then threw it onto the bed.

Distant voice. "Will ah pit some lights oan? Ah canny see a – Christ! – fuckin' thing in here!" Sounds of stack heels tripping.

Jas smiled, grabbed jeans from a wardrobe and pulled them on. "Switch's oan the left, Marie." Sweatshirt from wardrobe.

Faint clinking of glass. Faint voice. "Yer kitchen's affy wee." Louder. "Who diz yer cookin' noo?" Bedroom light switched on.

Jas pulled his head from a tunnel of black sweatshirting.

Marie stood before him, glass in each hand. Eyes on his wet hair. "Like the flat-top, by the way. It suits ye."

He sat on the bed and pulled on socks then Docs.

She walked to the window and looked out. "No' much o' a view, eh? No' like yer auld flat. Aw' they lovely trees." Wistful.

Jas tied laces then stood up. "Ah didn't move fur the view."

"Naw, ah suppose not." Turning. Face softening. She walked towards him, sipping from one glass. The other extended. "How huv ye been, Big Man?"

He walked through to the lounge. Pleasantries were cheap. Favours usually weren't, when it came to Marie.

She followed. One empty glass placed on a small table.

Jas sat down on the moulded sofa and tried to work out why he'd agreed to this. He reached over, lifted a packet of cigarettes from the floor and raised one to lips.

Tight smile. She sat opposite.

He extended the packet.

Marie took one, produced a lighter, lit her own then held out the flame. As his cigarette neared, she grabbed his fingers. "Ah didney want tae dae it, Jas. Ye ken that, don't ye?"

He lit the cigarette.

She withdrew her hand.

Jas inhaled, then exhaled. "It's aw' water under the bridge, Marie."

Resolute. "Ah want tae tell ye why ah grassed ye up, Big Man."

Jas shrugged. He looked at the cigarette's glowing tip. "Ye wur a snout, Marie. Is that no' whit snouts dae?"

Angry. "They dinny grass up mates, Jas." Sigh. "Ye're ma mate, an' ah let ye doon."

A mate he'd neither seen nor heard from in twenty-four months? He located an ashtray then leant back on the moulded sofa and stared at the ceiling.

The sound of bottle against glass. Pouring. Then drinking. Pause. "It wisney the money, Jas."

"Ah didney think it wis." He struggled to suck some satisfaction from her discomfort. It was all a long time ago.

Fidgeting with jacket button. Head down. "Sloan said he wis gonny help me." Head up. Bright eyes dull now. "Don't ken why ah believed him. Ye ken whit he wis like." Earnest. "Telt me he'd pit a guid word in fur me, tae git the kids back. Ah love ma kids, Big Man..." Eyes reddening. "...ah wid dae onythin' tae...."

"Save it fur the social workers, Marie." He stood up and walked through to the kitchen.

The truth?

He filled a pint glass with water and drank. Then refilled it.

Did it matter?

He walked back through to the lounge and sat down.

Sniffing. "Kin ah use yer toilet?" She stood up, unsteady on four-inch heels.

"First left before the front door."

Marie tottered from the room.

Jas stubbed out the cigarette and lit another.

Marie McGhee. Eighteen when he'd first met her. Flawless face. Heroin addict. Twilight girl. Two kids. His snout. Instrumental in putting away Neil, the youngest of Glasgow's infamous Johnstone Clan.

Twenty-two when he'd last met her. Scarred face courtesy of the Johnstone Brothers. Heroin and temazepam addict. Kids in care. Specialist twilight girl. Friend? Assistant Chief Commissioner Greg Sloan's snout.

Jas drew on the cigarette.

Twenty-four now...

Sound of toilet flushing soft, then louder. Stack heels on lino, then cheap carpeting. Bright voice from the doorway: "Where dae ah wash ma hauns?"

"Bedroom. There's a hand basin in the shower."

Tutting, then turning. "Sno' hygienic, Big Man. These rented places ur fuckin' slums!" Sounds of door sliding, then water running.

Jas inhaled and closed his eyes. The last time he'd seen her: the witness stand. Glasgow High Court. Jimmy 'Mygo' Johnstone was now doing life in HMP Peterhead for the murders of Jason and Leigh Nicols.

Jas opened his eyes.

Leigh – best friend; lover.

Blackmailer. Murderer of Jason Nicols, his own brother.

Jas clenched his right fist. It refused to close.

Marie's flat-warming present eyed him.

He walked into the kitchen and drank more water.

Sounds of heels on carpet.

Jas looked up.

Marie grinned. The scar twitched.

She sat down. Legs crossed. "Well, noo that we've goat that oot the way, ah suppose ye'll want tae ken why ah'm really here." Eyes bright again.

"It wid help."

A sigh. "It's like ah telt ye oan the phone, Jas. Wee Paul's missin'."

Silence.

Jas stood up. "So?" He walked to the window.

Another sigh. "Ah'm worried."

He frowned. "When did ye last see him?"

"September 23rd."

"Ye've a guid memory!"

"It wis oan the visitin' warrant."

"Whit wis he in fur?" Jas stared into the black back court.

"Goat caught at Hanger Thirteen wi' six eccy tablets."

Ecstasy. Class A drug. The law making criminals out of guileless kids. The Paul he'd met was no guileless kid. "He shouldda kent the Force wur crackin' doon oan dealers."

Snort. "He wisney dealin', Jas – no' that night. Widney waste his time wi' eccy." Sigh. "Paul wis there wi' some o' the boays. A night oot. He got done fur possession." Harsh laugh. "Been dealin' H fur three years, then moved oan tae cocaine an' the polis eventually goat him fur carryin' fuckin' happy-pills!"

"How long did he get?"

"Eighteen months."

"Longriggend?"

"The Bar-L."

The bullet-headed kid who had driven him to London was obviously older than he looked. "When did he git oot?"

"September 26th." Pause. "Early release."

It was now the end of October."It's only bin a month, Marie. He'll turn up."

Click of cigarette lighter. Soft voice. "It isney like Paul tae..."

"Why aw' this concern fur a pusher, Marie? His prices that

guid?" He grinned. "Or wur you an' he...?"

Words barely audible. "Me an' Paul? Christ, no, Big Man!" Cough. "His family's worried. Paul eyewis kept in touch." Silence. Then the sound of smoke exhaled. "Folk dinny jist disappear."

Her voice pushed the years away. The window was beginning to steam up. Jas traced a name on the cold glass then rubbed it out.

Hand on his shoulder. "Ah don't ken whit tae dae, Big Man."

Jas turned.

The hand dropped.

He walked past Marie and sat down. "Ye asked aroon' ?"

Irate. "Whit dae ye think ah am – sure ah did! No wan's seen him." Sigh. "No wan kent he wid git early release. Christ! Ah ainly fun' oot when ah tried tae visit him last week."

"Huv ye tried his business associates?"

"His pals dinny ken where he is. They wur keepin' things tickin' ower fur him til he goat oot." Scowl. "Some bastard's taken oan his patch already!" Softer. "Paul didney huv ony really close mates – 'cept his family. Yon wee anorak Hamster's the ainly wan ah kid think o' – an' he's oan remand in Longriggend. Ah thought he mighta heard somethin'." Sigh. "They widney let me in tae see him, cos ah'm no' family." Faraway eyes. "It's like Paul's jist vanished, Big Man."

Jas lit a cigarette. Marie's information sources were legendary. "If you canny fun' oot onythin', whit makes ye think ah'd dae ony better?"

"Ye've goat contacts. Ye kid get permission tae talk tae the guys he wis inside wi', an' Hamster. Mebbe Paul telt them whit he hud planned – him an' Hamster wur as thick as fuckin' thieves." Frown. "Ah've phoned the Bar-L a coupla times, but they'll no' gie me the time o' day." She pushed an ashtray towards him. "If Paul's bin picked up fur somethin' else, you kin fun' oot fae the polis." Scowl. "After the last time ah'm no' goin' within ten miles o' them!" Appealing smile. "Ye kin talk the way they can. They'll listen tae you."

He stared. They'd never listened in the past. Until he'd made them. Jas stubbed out the cigarette.

"Anderson Investigations, Big Man. It'll be easy fur you." Pause. "Ah'll pay the goin' rate, if it's the money..."

"It's no' the money." He exhaled and examined her ashen face.

The scar winked.

Everything about her brought back times he'd rather forget.

"Let me think aboot it, Marie." His stomach growled audibly.

She laughed. "Huv ye eaten, Jas?"

He shook his head. "Ah'll git somethin' later."

Mock stern. Standing. Thin arms folded across chest. "Ye'll eat noo, an' nae arguments!" She walked into the hall. A triangle of light appeared. "Well, at least yer freezer's well-stocked." Rummaging sounds. Small head round lounge door. Hand holding two rectangular packages. "Whit dae ye fancy – lasagne?"

"Whitever." He ground out the cigarette.

Marie stalked past him into the kitchen. Sounds of packaging tearing then microwave programmed. She reappeared. "Pit yer feet up an' relax, Big Man. Yer dinner'll no' be long."

Jas smiled.

Fifteen minutes later he was eating.

She was watching, smoking.

He laid down a fork. "So, Marie. Whit ur ye up tae?"

She poured another vodka. He marvelled at her tolerance.

Proud smile. "Oan a methadone programme." Smile broadening to grin. "Ma key worker says ah've a guid chance of gettin' custody o' the kids, if ah keep ma nose clean." Pause, then flourish. "An' ah'm aff the game, tae."

He raised an eyebrow.

Laugh. "Dinny look so surprised! Ah'm... er, managing human resources, noo."

"So it's Madam McGhee ah should be callin' ye, is it?"

The grace to blush. "Ah'm gettin' too auld fur aw' that masel', Jas."

Over the hill at twenty-four. He laughed.

She continued. "Ah look efter ma girls, pass oan ma experience. Ah treat them like ah'd want tae be treated masel'. They git a better deal aff me than ony pimp."

"Where ye runnin' them oota?"

"Nice place in Wilton Street, up the West End." Uncomfortable. "Ah run a clean hoose, an' we dinny gie onybody ony hassle."

"Ah'm no' polis noo, Marie." He stood up and carried his plate through to the kitchen. "Makes no difference tae me whit ye dae or where ye dae it." He returned to the lounge, sat down and lit a cigarette.

She nodded, then leant forward and winked. "An' whit aboot

you? Who ye gettin' it up these days?"

He looked down at his right hand.

Marie laughed. "Sex wi' the wan ye love best, eh? Ah, well, there a loat tae be said fur wankin'. Ah've no' fucked in three years, an' ah'm feelin' the better fur it."

"No wan keepin' ye warm at night, then?"

Shrug. "When wis there ever, Big Man?" Frown, then smile. "Huv ye hud enough time tae think aboot Paul?"

Something pricked at his brain.

If Marie was off H, why did she need a dealer?

He stared at the small, pale face. "So, this Paul guy goat early release fae Barlinnie an' husney bin seen since: whit's it tae you, really?" He searched her eyes for information. "Ye sure there's nothin' mair tae this, Marie? Nothin' yer no' tellin' me?"

Head shake.

"Ah'm no' gettin' involved in ony drug wars..."

"Big Man!" Mock hurt. "Wid ah lie tae you?"

He locked eyes with her.

She looked away. "It's like ah telt ye. Paul's reliable, disney slip ye ony dodgy gear. Ah kin eyeways fun' him when ah need tae – usually. Noo?" Shrug. "Ca' it curiosity, if ye like."

"Yer curiosity'll cost ye, Marie. Ah don't come cheap."

Sad smile. "Whit diz, Big Man."

She had offered to pay, and money was money. Why not? "Okay, ye've convinced me. Ah'll see whit ah kin dae. Huv ye goat a recent photograph?"

Hand thrust into jacket pocket, then withdrawn. "Taken a coupla weeks before Hanger Thirteen – last year – but he's no' changed that much." A strip of photobooth snaps extended.

Jas took it, scanned five headshots. The first two showed Marie grinning. In the next two a bullet-headed boy scowled into the camera. Jas stared. Young for eighteen. Dark, step-cut hair, one gold ring and a stoned stud in left ear. Sullen eyes.

He looked at the last photograph.

Two faces, cheek-to-cheek. Both grinning now. One with long dark hair, the other with the layers. One with a scar, the other without. Same pale skin. Same sullen eyes. Street eyes. Junkies' eyes.

Jas reached over and lifted a small notepad. "Let's huv some details. Whit's his full name an' date o' birth?"

She stared at him. "McGhee – Paul McGhee."

Three

Jas opened his eyes.

Golden sunshine streamed in through curtainless windows.

His brain raced. A jumble of images pounded at the back of his eyes. He rubbed his face and concentrated.

The jumble faded slightly.

Last night. Marie's request: what would it take – a few phone calls? Jas sat up and stretched.

Marie had a brother. Younger brother.

He pulled the duvet up around his ears.

Two McGhees: brother and sister. Supplier and user.

Keep it in the family?

Jas looked at the clock: 6 am. He closed his eyes and tried to sleep.

Five minutes later he got out of bed.

Ten minutes later he was dressed and leaving the flat.

Fifteen minutes later he was running along Alexandra Parade towards the hospital.

Early mornings. They were the worst. Running helped. His usual circuit took in the Royal, the Cathedral, Duke Street and back up Cumbernauld Road.

Well-padded Nikes pounded on empty pavement.

Rhythm.

Purpose.

At the top of Wishart Street he paused, barely out of breath. He slipped two A4 envelopes into a pillar-box, then looked left. The Necropolis: his former running-ground. He squinted through sun shards. The large cemetery was bathed in autumn leaves.

Jas began to run again.

At seven am he was back at the flat.

At seven-fifteen he was naked, and exercising.

Press-ups. Sit-ups. Burpees. One hundred of each.

Jas stopped and sat on the floor. Sweat dripped from soaking hair. His brain still raced. He scowled, wiped face on arm. The Royal's physiotherapist had recommended yoga: 'Calms the mind, synchronises thought.'

Jas stood up. His thoughts were synchronised. That wasn't the problem. He repeated the routine then headed for the shower.

The cheap plastic cubicle was cramped, but functional. It did the job. Like he had. Under icy power jets he looked down. No hard-on.

For a change.

At eight forty-five he was dressed and sitting beside the telephone. No time like the present. A list of physical characteristics – age, height, weight – and distinguishing features – double-pierced left ear, vaccination scars – sat beside the strip of five photographs. Above them, one name. Paul McGhee.

Might as well do this properly. He punched in the number for Glasgow's Royal Infirmary.

An hour later he replaced the receiver. No amnesia cases or unidentified accident victims answering Paul McGhee's description were at present lying in any of Scotland's twenty-four major hospitals.

The phone rang.

Jas let the machine pick up. Beep. Male voice, young, awkward:

"IBS here, Peter speaking. You collected a report from us yesterday." Pause.

Jas lit a cigarette and smiled. Hairy Knuckles had a name.

Throat clearing: "Er, some documentation has... er unfortunately been omitted from your report. I – I could drop it round to you sometime today, if that's convenient. I'll be out of the office all morning, but if you want to contact me, my mobile number's 0674-109825." Pause. "Looking forward to hearing from you." Beep.

Jas blew a smoke ring, followed it with his eyes.

The company search was complete..

Hairy Knuckles searching for another kind of company?

He looked at his watch: just before ten. Time for the gym. He took a sportsbag from the bedroom and left the flat.

Jas cut along Cumbernauld Road into Onslow Drive. The mist was clearing. As he passed Whitehill Swimming Pool a flash of colour from the notice-board caught his eye.

The naked torso of a man. Tanned. Over-developed pecs. Diaphragm ridges. Blond stomach hair disappeared off the bottom of the picture.

Jas walked on.

The Dennistoun Sports Centre was going up in the world. Big Rab had secured a £10,000 grant for new equipment from the

National Lottery. Deprived area. High unemployment. The poster campaign had followed. Membership had soared.

He turned down Whitehill Street, then left through derelict school gates. In front, two thin boys with 'Head' sportsbags. He followed them through the charred double-doors, paid his £1 and headed for the weights room. It was empty.

Jas undressed down to shorts.

It was early.

A dark head round the door. Asian features. Grin. "No' comin' tae circuit-training, man?"

"No' the day, Ali. It's ma weights day."

Eyes over shoulder. Sigh. "Fuckin' room's still locked..." Dressed in Adidas, the slim figure moved into the room. Rolled-up newspaper under one arm. Ali removed, unfurled the *Record* and leant against a wall.

Jas smiled. "No' like Rab tae sleep in."

Snort from behind newspaper pages. Then a laugh. "Did ye read this? Some wuman fae Cranhill's given birth tae triplets – at fifty!"

Jas stared at the front page headline: 'Third Week of Illegal Strike!' He scanned the rest of the article. "Naw..."

Ali began to fill him in. Enthusiastically.

Jas walked to the weights rack, mind elsewhere. Terry's son. Marie's brother.

The Scottish Prison Officers Association. Technically, they had no union...

He lifted a small cylinder with his left hand and transferred it to his right.

...and no prerogative to industrial action. Technically, it wasn't a strike: cooperative doctors had provided 'stress-related' sick notes for some. Others self-certified...

Gripping the weight with trembling fingers he began to curl then uncurl his arm. Knuckles brushed shoulder.

...the action was a strike in everything but name and made history. Whether it would make any difference to anything else remained to be seen.

"Fuck." A whisper. A single droplet of sweat formed on his forehead. He pushed the strike from his mind and concentrated.

At fifteen: "...unbelievable, eh?"

Jas raised his head. "Aye, Ali."

In the distance, a door opened and closed. Then footsteps. Ali closed the newspaper, shoved it in the back pocket of Adidas sweatpants. Head poking back into hallway. "That's the big bastard noo."

Tendon throbbed in his right forearm. "Mebbe ye'll git an easier time, if he's hauf asleep."

"Aye, an' pigs might fly!" Wry grin. "Catch ye later, Jas."

"If there's much left tae catch..." Tendon-throb shivered up his right arm.

Laugh, then door closed.

He continued. At twenty his fingers spasmed. The weight dropped, rolled across ancient floorboards. A loop of metallic trundling filled the hall. The weight finally stopped under wall bars.

Jas retrieved it and began again.

This time he reached thirty, then paused.

Better. He transferred the weight to his left hand and sat down.

The door opened. A wiry man in sweats walked into the room, nodded to Jas and began to undress.

He nodded back and continued, switching the barbell from hand to hand.

After half an hour he stopped, lowered his head. Voice above him:

"What weight you up to now?"

"Four K." Mouth dry as dust.

"How many of each?"

Jas raised his head.

Wiry man in black jock-strap, crouching. Thighs like pleated rope. Plastic bottle in hand. He held it out.

Jas took it and drank. Fizzy water sparkled over teeth and tongue. He coughed, passed the bottle back. "Four groups of twenty." He clenched his fist. Nails dug into palm.

Slap on the back. Standing. "You'll get there. Just don't push it. Tendon damage's always slow to repair itself."

Jas stood up. "Day off?"

Head shake. "Afternoon surgery." Grin. "No rest for the wicked!"

Jas walked to his sports bag and took out a towel. He rubbed face and hair, then wiped underarms and chest. He turned.

The wiry man was strapping on a support belt. Two 10k weights lay beside him.

Jas pulled on sweats and T-shirt, picked up the sports bag and walked to the door. "Catch ye later."

Grunt. Then: "Look after that arm."

"Sure, doc. Thanks." He left the sports centre and walked back to the flat.

Half an hour later Jas sat down beside the telephone and punched in the number for Glasgow's mortuary.

Training. Procedure.

Fifteen minutes later he replaced the receiver and frowned.

Four unidentified male bodies matching Paul McGhee's general age and description lay unclaimed. An appointment had been made to view them today, at 2 pm.

Jas clenched his right fist. Just what he fuckin' needed. His arm trembled.

He reached for cigarettes, lit one. His right hand cramped. Exercise hadn't helped.

Jas stood up, walked through to the bedroom. At the window he stared over the rooftops at Haghill.

Today was a bad day.

He flexed his fingers, then rubbed them with his left hand. Tingling shot up his arm. He rotated his shoulder. Eventually the tingling subsided. Jas sat down on the bed and rubbed his face.

The phone rang in the other room. The machine picked up:

Beep. Beep. "Mr Anderson? Peter McLaughlin from IBS here. It's, er nearly one o'clock."

He walked towards the voice.

"I'll be in your area this afternoon. Maybe I could drop in with the report if..."

Jas picked up.

1.50pm. On the other side of the road Glasgow Green was a mass of amber and red. Jas kicked a pile of leaves and crossed the Saltmarket into Jocelyn Street. The squat, sandstone outline of Glasgow's mortuary beckoned to him. He pulled open a heavy swing door and walked in.

The familiar smell hit him immediately. During twelve years with Strathclyde Police he had walked along this tiled corridor countless times.

Countless nameless bodies.

Countless waxen faces... or remains of faces.

At least half were never identified or claimed.

Jas knocked softly on a smoked glass door and waited.

Countless deaths unacknowledged.

Husky voice: "Come."

Jas pushed open the door and walked in. Small room. The smell of old leather and formaldehyde. Behind a large desk, a small man. Wrinkly, brown skin. Pickled-looking. Like a lot of his customers.

The pathologist stood up. "Good to see you again, Sergeant Anderson..."

"It's no' sergeant ony mair, doctor. Just plain Jas."

Frown. "So they didn't want you back, then?"

Jas lied. "Ah didney want them."

Old head shaking. "Their loss. You were a good cop. I remember when..."

He stared at a photograph above the pathologist's head. It showed a much younger Dr Patterson in a white coat shaking hands with a grey-haired suit. Jas peered, trying to read the inscription underneath. Too faint. His eyes drifted.

"...was it not?"

He looked at the small man. "Aye, doctor. Now, kin a huv a look at yer stiffs?"

Light laugh. "Still not big on words, are you?" Dr Patterson moved round from behind the desk and opened the door.

Jas followed him into the corridor. "Ah leave that tae you, doctor." He followed the sounds of laughter towards the refrigeration room.

Not as cold as the name implied. But still. Silent. A wall of sixteen shiny handles. The others tiled.

"Like I told you on the phone, we've got four which match your approximate requirements. This one..." Doctor Patterson grabbed a stainless steel handle and pulled, "...was in the Clyde for quite a while before some kids spotted him. He's been here three weeks." He unzipped a black plastic body-bag.

Jas looked down.

Bright, fluorescent light bleached already bloodless skin.

Patterson talked on. "The height's about right. Age approximately seventeen to twenty-five. I've never seen teeth as bad as his..."

Jas stared at the bloated, white flesh of the corpse's face, then into black pulpy pits.

"...and I'm afraid the fish got to his eyes, but from the hair and skin colouring I'd say they were probably brown."

Jas looked at the right ear. One cheap, greening sleeper. He looked away. "That's no' him."

The sound of zipper zipping. Cheerful voice. "Ah, well. Three more to go. You might get lucky." Sounds of heavy drawer closing, then another opening.

Jas withdrew the strip of photographs from his pocket and reacquainted himself with a sullen, bullet-headed boy.

More zipping. "An addict, you say?"

"Dealer..." Jas looked down at a second, lifeless boy. "...though he probably did use, fae time tae time."

"RTA two weeks ago. There's not much left of the head."

Jas stared.

Ears were mush. As was most of the skull.

"...but he's got a birthmark on his left thigh – and old trackmarks around the groin. Want a look?"

"Aye..." Marie hadn't mentioned any mole, but the trackmarks sounded promising.

Sounds of zipper unzipping further.

Apart from the pulped head, the rest of the body was intact. Lightly muscled chest. Thin. Ribs visible beneath parchment skin.

"Here..." The pathologist pulled rigid thighs apart and pointed to a faded brown patch of skin.

Jas stared.

"And here..." Blond pubic hair brushed aside to show faint puncture marks.

Jas rested his eyes on a one-inch, torpedo-shaped birthmark, then looked away. "Wrang hair-colouring."

The pathologist laughed. "A peroxide job! Doesn't match underarm."

Jas frowned, shook his head. "The body-type disney fit. Let's see Number Three."

Zipping, closing and opening of drawers. Then unzipping. "This one's interesting. MDA overdose..."

Paul McGhee had used ecstasy. Jas stared at a peaceful, pale face. Left ear pierced from lobe to cartilage.

"...so at least he died happy!" Zipper fully extended.

The body had the underdeveloped musculature of a teenager. Flawless, ivory skin luminescent in death. Strong, even features. Not Paul McGhee's features. Jas shook his head and looked away.

"The last one's still in the autopsy room. Came in early this morning."

"Let's huv a look."

The pathologist slammed the drawer shut and walked to a small door on the far side of the room.

Jas followed.

"Had five hundred pounds on him, but no ID." Dr. Patterson pushed open the door and held it for Jas. "Baird Street think he was a dealer, that the death was drugs-related – haven't had time to PM him yet..." He walked past two sheeted gurneys.

He sniffed. The smell was strongest in here.

The pathologist stopped at a wide steel table.

Jas walked forward and looked down. Brown, close-cropped hair. A shaved line running from above the right ear. Freckles dotted on still vaguely-pink skin. He closed his eyes. "Ah don't ken how he died, but ah kin tell ye where this wan wis at half-nine last night." He looked at Dr Patterson.

Curious. "Is it...?"

"At the bus stop opposite ma flat. Cumbernauld Road. And it's no' Paul McGhee." He turned and walked from the room.

Back at the flat Jas took off his jacket and sat down on the sofa.

Paul McGhee: not in any hospital, or the city's mortuary. After the obligatory reminiscing, Dr Patterson had agreed to fax the boy's photograph to chief pathologists in Edinburgh, Aberdeen and Inverness.

He lit a cigarette. A freckled face swam before his eyes.

Then three other faces.

All dead.

All between seventeen and twenty-five.

The smell of the mortuary clung to his clothes, seeping through the fabric.

Jas inhaled on the cigarette and concentrated.

At least Marie's brother had not been among them. He closed his eyes and focused thoughts.

Who had seen Paul McGhee most recently, that he knew of?

The staff and inmates of Barlinnie prison.

Who was running the Bar-L, for the duration of the prison-officers' unofficial strike?

Jas lifted 'Yellow Pages', thumbed through, then punched in the number for Hadrian Security Solutions.

A recording told him he had omitted the code.

Jas punched in the code for Livingston, then the number. Waited. Was given another number and an extension. Punched it in. Waited again.

He was still waiting twenty minutes later when the door bell rang.

"Haud oan!" Jas repunched in the original number and left a comprehensive message with a secretary. She repeated it back to him. He replaced the receiver then walked to the front door. He opened it mid-umpteenth ring of the bell.

Six-footish, dark glossy hair falling into eyes. Early twenties. No bad suit this time. Well-cut jeans. Good body under white shirt. Manila folder under one arm. The other extended. Nervous. Two inches of thick, black hair visible between shirt-cuff and wrist. Thicker than the knuckle-hair. Polite voice. Polished accent. Newton Mearns via Glasgow Academy: "Mr Anderson. We met briefly yesterday. Peter McLaughlin."

Jas smiled, ran fingers through sweaty hair. He gripped the extended hand.

Strong, warm, fingers. Palm slightly damp.

Not cold. Not dead.

"The name's Jas."

Hand released. Reluctantly.

Jas moved aside. Strong shoulders brushed against him. Fresh, living smell slicing through formaldehyde. Soap, mixed with...?

The man stopped ahead, blocking out the freezer. Turning. Uncertain.

Jas smiled. "Want a coffee?"

The man turned. Molten eyes relieved.

Jas extended an arm.

Both men walked into the living room.

Three coffees later. "I recognised you straight away. Two years ago – that big court case." Eager. Impressed. "What you did took a lot of guts." Coffee cup placed on floor. Another inch of arm-hair.

Jas walked to the window. He was out of practice.

Peter talked on. "I could never do that – I mean, Jean – my boss – knows, and I've told my sister, but I couldn't tell the whole world. I really admire you."

Jas sighed. A star fucker? He clenched his left fist and turned. This was a bad idea.

One elbow on sofaarm, propping up head. Two shirt buttons undone. Burst of wiry black hair visible. Long, lean thighs, lightly muscled under designer denim.

Jas looked at the face. His prick pulsed.

Shining, molten eyes. Thick, dark lashes. Hint of shadow on upper lip. Large mouth.

Peter smiled, unbuttoned one shirt cuff and rolled up a white sleeve.

Jas scowled. His prick throbbed unbearably.

The smile faded. Uncertain again. Searching for a cigarette. Finding it.

Jas lifted a lighter from the table, held it out.

Fingers brushing hairy knuckles. A hand on his. Jas seized it, pulling the man to his feet.

Arm around his shoulders.

Wet mouth seeking his. Finding it.

Jas closed his eyes, thrusting tongue against tongue.

Then groin against groin. Prick against prick.

Peter moaned, pulled away.

Jas opened his eyes and stared into liquid chocolate.

It had been a long time.

He watched as the man fumbled with shirt buttons, ripping the bottom two. Chest a jet forest. Arms wrenched free from cotton sleeves. Hands moving to belt. Then remembering boots. Glance up. Embarrassed smile. Perching on sofa arm. Clumsy fingers undid Caterpillar laces. The sound of breathing filled the room.

Jas lit a cigarette and moved to the doorway. Still watching.

It had been a long time.

Boots and socks removed. Then jeans. Standing. White Calvins thrown on the heap.

It had been worth waiting for.

Peter walked towards him.

Jas seized tanned shoulders and kissed him again. Coffee-tasting. Sweet-smelling. Oranges?

A hand on his prick, rubbing through sweaty sweatshirting.

Jas closed his eyes and groaned, palms on Peter's bare arse. Smooth, surprisingly hairless, given the knuckles and the arms. He ground hips against naked flesh.

Mouth moving to his ear. Breathy. Hoarse: "Jas..."

Two hours later Peter left.

On the bed Jas plucked three jet hairs from beneath his foreskin and yawned. Then smiled.

Back in the saddle. Thigh muscles quivered. He'd missed the feel of another man's body under his. He glanced at the bedside table.

Business card. Home number on the back.

Jas grinned. Maybe a bit of repeat business. In a couple of days.

He eased himself from damp, rumpled sheets and walked into the shower.

Warm water this time. And soap. He closed his eyes.

A view of Peter McLaughlin's white, hairless arse faded. Replaced by one of a bullet-headed kid driving a blue Ford Escort.

He reached up and turned down the temperature control.

Warm to lukewarm to cool to cold to numbness.

In the distance the telephone rang.

Jas switched off the shower, stepped out of the cubicle and picked up a towel. He had almost reached the lounge door when his own message ended.

Three beeps. Male. English accent. Cool: "Mr Anderson? Geoff Robinson from Hadrian Security Solutions returning your call. Regarding..." Sounds of rustling paper. "...Paul McGhee, the company has no more to add to the original information given to Ms. Marie McGhee. The prisoner was released early, on good behaviour, 26th September." Cooler. "For security reasons, I'm afraid your suggested visits to HMP Barlinnie and Longriggend Remand Institution are out of the question, at the moment." Pre-rehearsed. "Thank you for calling Hadrian Security Solutions. Good afternoon." Beep.

Jas dried his hair and replayed the message twice.

He phoned back.

Engaged tone.

Jas scowled. If Marie was to get her money's worth, he needed to talk anyone who had known Paul McGhee inside.

That was proving difficult.

Next best thing...?

Prison officers. Jas lit a cigarette.

The strike. When had it started? Last month? The month before?

Terry's words: 'Ma Billy's oan the picket line the morra.'

Jas walked through to the bedroom and looked at three unfinished reports.

Three good customers.

Paul McGhee was more than likely holed up somewhere. There would be other days, other picket lines.

He pulled on jeans and sat down at the word processor.

Four

Days passed. Life went on. October slipped into November. November the fifth.

In early morning mist Jas jogged across Cumbernauld Road and into Smithycroft Road. Padded Nikes pounded pavement.

Garthamlock to the north. Springboig to the south.

In between: Riddrie.

Not a bad area.

Residential. Mainly owner-occupied. Couple of presentable bed-sit conversions. Two new housing schemes dotted with Neighbourhood Watch stickers. Small row of shops. Three churches. Circular school and library.

Not a bad area.

Low crime rate.

More criminals per square yard than any other part of Glasgow.

Jas slowed to a walk and turned right into Navers Lee Avenue. Three rows of new houses. He stared. Beyond, Barlinnie's A-Hall raised two, finger-shaped chimneys through grey mist. From behind a dirty stone wall.

Jas lowered his gaze and continued to walk.

A security camera monitored his progress. Yards from the twenty-six-foot wall, to the right of the visitors' car park, a small group of men.

Burly men. Angry men. Hands gloved and clapping.

Cold men.

Jas walked nearer.

He could make out six figures. Pale, bitten faces. He scanned them for Billy MacKinley.

One man stepped forward and walked towards him. Six feet. Heavy. Padded nylon jacket. Woollen hat pulled down over ears. Clean-shaven.

Jas stared.

Terry, but younger. Fatter. Puffy face. Broken veins on cheeks. Frown, then smile. A suede-gloved hand stuck out. Rasping voice: "Well, well! Jas Anderson. How're ye doin', pal? Ma faither said ye wanted a word." Breath condensing in cold air.

Jas smiled and shook the hand. "Ah didney recognise ye, Billy.

Whit happened tae the beard?"

Laugh. Suede hand over suede chin. "The razor slipped. Noo', whit kin ah dae fur ye?"

Jas glanced past the padded jacket. On the picket line a Thermos flask was being passed from gloved hand to gloved hand. He looked back at Billy MacKinley, then reached into jacket pocket. Half bottle of Teachers produced. "Kin ye take a coupla minutes aff?"

Billy eyed the bottle, then his companions. Nod. "Aye, sure. The shift change'll be another oor, yet. Ower here." He led the way into the prison car park.

Jas followed.

In front of a row of cars Billy stopped, leant against the bonnet of a red Jeep Cherokee. August reg.

Jas eyed it.

Billy caught the look. "Visitin' dignitary fae Livingston. Flash bastard! Ah kidney huv afforded wan o' them oan ma wages." Head shake. "Dinny ken how they dae it."

Jas unscrewed the Teachers and drank. The whisky singed his mouth. He passed the bottle to Billy. "Ah'm lookin' fur some information oan wan o' yer former customers."

Billy took a drink, wiped his mouth, then took another.

"Whit kin ye tell me aboot Paul McGhee?"

Billy stared into the distance, bottle cradled in hands. "McGhee... McGhee – whit Hall?"

Jas rested a foot on oversized, chrome bullbars. "C. 5' 6", dark hair. In fur possession of ecstasy."

Laugh. "Goat him, noo. Gallus wee bastard." Another drink. "Due oot aboot noo, ah should think." Head shake. "They'll no' be sorry tae see the back o' Paul, ah reckon. Whit ye wanna ken?"

Jas explained.

Thoughtful. Another drink. "Early release? Ye sure?" Bottle extended.

Jas shook his head.

Raised eyebrow. Shrug. "Ah, well. Aw' the mair fur me." Another drink. Silence.

"McGhee was released on September 26th, Billy. You an' the boays were oot by that time, ah take it?" Jas lit a cigarette.

"Aye, a fortnight intae the strike. McGhee widda bin processed by that shower o' scabs." Turning. Laugh. "Ah hope he made their lives hell!"

Jas followed Billy's eyes up twenty-six feet of stone wall.

"The place is goin' tae the dogs, Jas, ah'll tell ye that fur nothin'. We..."

"McGhee wis giein' ye trouble?"

Laugh. "Trouble? They're aw' trouble, Jas. You should ken that – ye hid a haun' in puttin' a guid few o' them in there!"

"Whit kinda trouble?"

Laugh. "You name it, McGhee had a go at it. Wis intae aw' the minor rackets." Head shake. "Jist a kid, tae..."

"Dealin'?"

Shrug. "In fur possession? Buyin', nae doot. No' dealin', that ah ken..." Pause. Scowl. "...fur aw' his big talk, he'd be way oota his league." Pause. "But that disney mean he wisney huvin' a go at it." Faint smile. "Maist o' the young wans jist want tae dae their time an' git oot." Another drink. Few last drops emptied into mouth. "No' McGhee. Ah canny unnerstaun' him gettin' early release, Jas." Laugh. "Unless they jist wanted rid o' him."

Maybe Hadrian were running a tighter prison by throwing the shite back out onto the street.

Billy bent down and placed the empty Teachers bottle in front of the Cherokee*'s* left wheel. He stood up, eyes back on the wall. "Whit's this tae you, onyway?"

"Ah'm workin' fur his sister. Fur some reason she's worried aboot him. Did ye hear onythin' – onywan he couldda palled up wi' inside, onythin' that might huv made him move on tae pastures new when he goat oot?"

"Ah kidney tell ye. Tae be honest, my heart's no' bin in the joab this past year." He turned. "Christ knows whit's goin' on in that place noo'." Slow head-shake. "Hadrian fuckin' Security Solutions – deliverin' wages an' parcels, til a coupla months ago." Low voice. "Whit dae they ken aboot runnin' prisons? Ye canny cut costs ony mair – no' withoot takin' stupid risks."

"Ony luck wi' negotiations?"

Angry. "The Scottish Office'll no' even sit doon at the table wi' us." Eyes on the picket line. "We're proabably wastin' oor time here – as well as riskin' oor jobs – but we've goat tae dae somethin'." Pause. Eyes back on the wall. "Fifteen years o' ma life ah gied tae Barlinnie." Eyes to Jas. "We didney want tae strike, but what else kin ye dae? Mair officers or less..." Laugh. "...customers. That's aw' we want. That place is gettin' oota haun'. We tried tae warn them, they idiots through in Edinburgh, but they widney listen." Sigh. Suede fist pounded against suede palm. "Oan their ain heids be it, noo'...but it's the poor bastards in the cells ah feel sorry fur." Silence.

Jas ground out cigarette on tarmac, then fished out a card. He handed it to Billy. "If ye remember onythin' else aboot Paul McGhee, gie me a ring – okay?"

Billy took the card, looked at it.

"There's a bottla Teachers in it fur ye."

Billy laughed. "Sure, Jas. Nae problem." Suede hand to pocket.

Behind, the sound of a door closing.

Billy turned. Shouting. "Here's wan o' the dirty scabs noo..." To Jas. "See ye again ... "

Jas walked back onto the road, then stopped.

Billy had rejoined the other five men.

Six angry faces.

Six angry voices. Chanting.

Jas watched as a slight figure made its way from the prison's main door into the car park. Alone. Suit and tie. Receding blond hair. Towards the red Cherokee.

The chanting increased.

The man ignored it.

The beep of car alarm deactivated.

The man climbed into the Cherokee. Started the engine. Moved forward.

The sound of breaking glass, then hissing.

Chanting became laughing.

Engine switched off. Jeep door opened. Irritated face emerging, bending to examine wheel and damaged tyre.

More laughing from the picket line.

Jas smiled, saluted Billy and walked back onto Smithycroft Road.

The green screen was beginning to strobe. Jas got up from the word processor and walked to the bedroom window. In the distance he could see the spasmodic blossoming of fireworks down at Glasgow Green.

Remember, remember...

He looked at his watch: just before eight pm. Marie was due in an hour. A face from the past.

Jas smiled. Peter was due at eleven. Face for the future?

He walked back to the screen, sat down and ran the cursor up two pages.

From all main hospitals and mortuaries? Nothing.

From known associates, according to Marie? Nothing.

From Hadrian Security Solutions? Nothing.

From a former prison officer? Something?

Jas sighed. More to do with disillusionment and bitterness than an awol drugs dealer.

A firework exploded in the street below.

The sum total of ten days' work. Paul McGhee had left Barlinnie at 6 am on the morning of September 26th. He had not been seen since.

Jas rubbed his face, stood up and walked through to the other room. He switched on a lamp. One avenue unexplored.

One last resort. Jas lifted the telephone receiver and punched in the number for D division, London Road. When it was answered he gave an extension number.

Soft purring, then soft voice: "DI McLeod."

"Whit's it like tae be in charge, then – the power gone tae yer head yet?"

Ann McLeod, formally DS McLeod. His partner four years ago. Still his friend?

Soft laugh. "How's life in the private sector?"

"Ah get by. Look, Ann: ah'm after information."

Sigh. "So what's new? I only ever hear from you when you want something."

Jas closed his eyes. "Ye goat promotion the last time ye helped me..."

Angry. "And you nearly got yourself killed!"

Jas opened his eyes. "Don't nag me. Whit kin ye tell me aboot Paul McGhee?"

Pause. "The name means nothing. Has he got form?"

"Eighteen months for possession. Served three-quarters. Early release 26th September. His he bin up tae onythin' since?"

"Ah." Another pause. "Is this a professional or personal inquiry?"

Jas scowled. "Nothin' tae dae wi' me this time – a client's brother."

"Substance involved?"

"E."

"First offence?"

"First time he wis caught."

"Mmm." Pause. "Unusual to get a custodial for first-time possession, even with the crackdown on recreational drugs. What do you want to know?" Another pause.

"Could ye check his record? He's disappeared – or so his sister tells me. Mebbe your lot huv him."

"No problem. Hold on."

Jas held on. Five minutes passed. Then ten. Then Ann:

"Here we go. Wherever he is, he's not in custody – Strathclyde or any other Scottish division. He's not reported in to his probation officer either, I presume?"

Marie hadn't said one way or the other. "Probably no'."

"They usually let it get to three-four missed appointments before we get notified, and even then it'll be left to some..." Pause. "...private investigator to enforce an unenforcable warrant."

Jas smiled wrly: he turned down warrant work every time.

"Want me to check down south?"

"Aye."

"Give me a minute..." Silence, then tapping. Then: "Good news. No mention of him anywhere..." Laugh. "Or maybe it's not good news." Silence.

Jas stared at the telephone.

"Well? Is it?"

"No' really. I've goat a feelin' McGhee's sister wid prefer the idea o' him in custody tae not knowin' where he is."

"Oh... like that, is it? Well, I'm sorry I can't help..."

Jas closed his eyes. "Mebbe ye can."

Surprise. "I don't really see..."

"Access his prison record." Jas opened his eyes.

Wary. "You know I can't do that."

He laughed. "Come oan, Ann. It's me yer talkin' tae, no' some civil liberties group. Ye dae it aw' the time. Ah did it..."

Soft voice. "I'm a DI, now..."

"Aw' the mair reason. Comes wi' the territory."

Silence. Then: "What's his prison record got to do with anything, anyway?"

"Standard missin' persons procedure. Last known address..."

Reluctant. "Okay. Just this once." More tapping. Silence. Then: "Right. Here we go... McGhee, P. Male. Date of birth 18/6/81... that him?"

"Sounds like it."

"Admitted 18th August, 1997... blah blah blah... released 6

am, September 26th, 1998." Pause. "There's an addition, stating that he was fit and well at the last medical. No social work report." Soft laugh. "Seems Mr McGhee wasn't very interested in rehab. No attendance at classes. He requested, and got, a single cell..."

Jas rubbed his face with one hand. "Hmm..."

"What do you mean?" Pause. "Oh, a cell to himself, given Barlinnie's overcrowding problems?"

"Aye."

"Not really. Maybe he earned it. You know how things work inside."

He knew. "Go on."

Pause. "Now, where was... ah yes. No further offences noted. Kept his nose clean. Something of a model prisoner, from what it says here."

Gallus wee bastard.

"Released on good behaviour, accordingly." Pause. "Look, is this helping?"

Jas wrapped the telephone cord around his right hand.

"You still there?"

Jas unwound the cord from his hand. "Anything else? Known associates?"

"McGhee was in for possession..."

"He wis a smack dealer."

"Ah..." Thoughtful. "Well, there's nothing on his prison record to indicate anything of that nature." Pause. "What are you getting at?"

"No' me. His sister canny understand why he husney bin in touch, says it isney like him."

Low laugh. "Regardless of what his record says, McGhee probably made good connection inside. You know what it's like. Minnows grow overnight." Sigh. "Your Mr McGhee could be setting up the deal of the century as we speak. Tell his sister not to worry. He'll turn up – probably the next time there's a raid." Pause. "Want me to give you a ring if we come across him?"

"Ah've done aw' ah'm dain' oan the case, but can ah gie his sister yer name? She'd appreciate a friendly contact."

Impatient. "I'd rather not, if you don't mind. I've got a lot on at the moment."

Jas grinned. "Business still boomin'?"

Softer. "You're well out of it, Jas. The work I can handle." Cagey sigh. "The closer you get to the top of the greasy pole, the more slippery it gets."

Part of him still envied her, nonetheless. "Thanks fur the information. Gie me a ring if ye hear onythin'." Jas gave his number and severed the connection and another link with the past.

He walked into the bedroom to finish Marie's report. His considered opinion? Based on all available information?

Paul McGhee had been released early from Barlinnie, on good behaviour – unlikely as that seemed – and was probably off of his face somewhere, enjoying his freedom.

Jas typed the final sentence, pressed P and waited.

The door bell rang.

He glanced at his watch: almost nine. He frowned. Time to give Marie the news.

She didn't take it well.

In the other room Jas handed Marie the report.

She read it twice, then looked up. Hard eyes. Soft voice. "So much fur Anderson Investigations, Big Man! Ye didney git much."

Jas sat opposite and lit a cigarette. "There wisney much tae get. Ah telt ye, the street's yer best bet."

Eyes back on the report, scanning. Then stopping. "Whit's this at the end?"

Jas exhaled, then quoted. "90 per cent of missing persons disappear through choice, Marie."

Silence, them: "Did ye no' talk tae the other guys Paul wis inside wi'? Mebbe they couldda telt ye if he'd said onythin'?"

Jas stood up. "No' possible." He looked at the small figure. "Ah did aw' ah kid. The ainly way tae git ony mair information wid be tae go inside Barlinnie, an' the security company's widney let me dae that, with wi' the strike an' everythin' – okay?"

Head down. "Ah suppose so..." Silence.

Jas walked into the kitchen, washed two glasses then lifted the Absolut bottle. He returned to the other room.

Marie was folding the report into a small rectangle.

"Ye'll join me, ah take it?" Jas filled two glasses, handed one to Marie.

She took it. Grinned.

He laughed. "Ye'll no' be smilin' when ye see ma bill!" He nursed the vodka.

Marie emptied her glass and held it out.

He refilled it.

She sipped. "Ye wur polis fur twelve years. Where dae you think he is, Big Man?"

Jas looked away. "Ah dinny ken him, so ah canny really say. But fae past experience, ah think he's holed up somewhere with some wuman and half a kilo o' eccy. Remember, Marie – the boay did seven months. He'll huv missed his..." He smiled. "...hame comforts. In his position, ah doubt gettin' in touch wi' ma sister wid be high up the list o' ma priorities!" He drained his glass.

Harsh laugh. "Ye cheeky bastard! Okay, okay! Ah take yer point." Frown. "But ye dinny ken Paul. Him an' me ur... close."

Jas stood up. "Ah never kent ye had ony family, apart fae Chrissie. Ye never talk aboot them." He walked to the window.

Soft voice. "Jist cos ah dinny run aff at the mooth, Big Man, disney mean ah don't care. There's six years between Paul an' me. When we wur fostered oot, ah looked efter him..."

"Long time ago, Marie. The boay's goat a life o' his ain. Let him git oan wi' it. He'll git in touch when he's ready." Jas turned and watched Marie pour more vodka.

"Ye dinny unnerstaun'." Glass to mouth. "We wur close .... really close.

He stared. "Whit dae ye mean?"

Marie looked up. Embarrassed. "Ah've goat a... a feelin' aboot Paul."

Jas laughed. "Ye want a crystal ball, then – no' a PI!"

Hurt, drunken eyes. "Ah'm serious."

He shook his head. "Ah canny act oan feelin's, Marie. Kin ye no' be mair specific?"

Angry. Standing. "Naw, ah canny!"

He sighed. "Sit doon, Marie."

Stare, then bottle to glass.

Jas lit a cigarette. Exhaled.

Resolute. "Ah want ye tae keep lookin', Big Man."

"Sorry, Marie. Ah've done aw' ah can."

Suddenly angry. "Ma money no' guid enough fur ye?"

He shook his head. "Ah'd be wastin' it an' ma time. There's no' enough tae go on."

She swayed, then sat down. Wheedling. "Dae it fur me, Big Man. Fur auld time's sake?"

Old times...

He ground out the cigarette. Even this brief exposure was bringing the years back. "Ye've goat ma report. Ah did whit ye wanted. As far as ah kin see, fur whitever reason, yer brither disney want tae git in touch wi' you, at the moment."

Silence. Liquid pouring. "No' Paul – he widney dae that."

Jas watched her drink. He was wasting his time.

Marie was mumbling into vodka.

Jas walked over and sat beside her. "If ye want tae take it further, git another guy tae look intae it fur ye, ah kin gie ye a coupla numbers." He glanced at his watch: half-ten. Peter at eleven. Jas smiled.

Marie looked up. Scowled. "It's aw' a big joke tae you, isn't? Christ, ye've changed, Jas Anderson! Ye used tae care aboot things. Ma wee brither's Christ knows where an' aw' ye kin dae is smile!"

Jas shrugged. "We're no' talkin' innocent runaways here. Paul's a big boay, fae whit ah've heard. He kin luck efter himsel'..."

Tears.

Jas sighed.

Marie fumbled for a handkerchief. A three-inch cellophane bag fell from her pocket. She dabbed her eyes.

Jas picked up the package: a couple of hundreds' worth, at today's prices. He handed it to her. "Ah see the methadone programme's last week's news..."

"Fur ma lassies, no' me!" She snatched the packet and replaced it in pocket. Then wiped her nose.

He looked at the tear-stained cheeks. "Come oan. Paul'll turn up. Look: ah've left ma number wi' a coupla folk. Maybe..."

"Forget it! How much dae ah owe ye?" On her feet. Swaying. Hand thrust into pocket. Angry.

"Call it five hundred."

Notes torn from a large bundle and thrown on the floor.

Jas looked from the green fifties to Marie.

Her face was flushed. Upset. Very upset.

He lifted the Absolut bottle. "Wan fur the road?"

"No' wi' you!" She turned. Left leg buckling. Heel caught in hem of skirt.

Jas moved forward. Too slowly.

Marie crumpled, head glancing off door-frame. "Ah, ya fucker!" Nails scraping for a hold.

Jas gripped her arm.

She shook him off, staggered to her feet. "Lea' me alain! Ah'm aw' right!" Marie made her way towards the front door.

He grabbed her arm again. "Come on – ye canny go hame like

that!"

Injured dignity. "Ah kin manage!"

"Suit yersel'" He opened the door.

She left, wordlessly.

Jas closed the door and scowled. Another satisfied customer.

He pulled off sweatshirt and walked through to the bedroom. Outside in Cumbernauld Road a final firework fizzled into oblivion.

Five

Tongue traced a line between his nipples. Jas opened his eyes and grabbed a handful of Peter's hair.

Low laugh.

Fingers caressed his stomach. Jas rolled from side onto back and pulled Peter to him. A soft leg thrown across his, prick rubbing thigh-bone, dragging. Velvet skin sticking to silk skin. Wet mouth moving on neck.

His prick twitched. Still hard. Jas buried face in soft, black hair, breathing in the man's smell. Fresh sweat, salt and faint oranges.

Hairy knuckles stroking chest, jet against dark blond. Then slowing. Coming to rest.

His prick twitched again. Jas seized bony wrists and pushed Peter onto his back.

Mild annoyance. Sleepy. "Hey! I was just dozing off!"

Jas pinned wrists to the bed. Elbows locked, legs straddling legs, balls resting on tanned stomach. He stared down.

A man's body...

...a boy's face. Saliva-encrusted lips parted. A scar of dried spunk at the corner of mouth. Skin pale with exertion beneath tan. Peter groaned and thrust upwards.

Jas closed his eyes, holding two wrists with left hand.

The sex had been good, but...

The thoughts came before he could stop them. Jas tighened his grip and opened his eyes.

Yelp. "What..?"

Jas loosened his grip. "Nothin'." Prick brushed navel.

Staring. More awake now. "What is it?"

Jas sighed.

A different time. A different place.

He let go wrists and covered the brown body with his own. Strong arms around him. Groin pushing against him. Rocking.

Rhythm. Purpose.

Jas pulled away. Mouth dry. "Ah need a drink. Want wan?" He stepped from the bed, kicked a Budweiser can and walked through to the hall.

In the freezer, two bottles of mineral water: a present from Peter. Frozen solid: he'd not counted on the sex taking so long. Jas took them, closed the fridge door and walked through to the kitchen. He sat two bottles on the draining board and lifted a glass.

Footsteps. Then voice from the other room. "Thought you didn't drink much?"

Jas filled the glass from the tap, drank, refilled it and walked back to the other room.

Peter waved the Absolut bottle accusingly. It was almost empty.

Jas shrugged. "Fur a client's benefit." He held out the glass.

Peter eyed it, then Jas. "Any lager left?"

"Ye finished it." He sat down on the sofa.

Peter took the glass, drank, passed it to Jas then crouched beside the moulded sofa. He searched pockets of a Paul Smith jacket and produced cigarettes.

Jas watched as the man took two from the packet, lit them then handed one to him. His eyes moved down Peter's naked body. Strong shoulders. A dark band of thick hair sweeping from collar bone down over chest. Pink nipples hardly visible. Hair less dense over stomach, then broadening into a V below navel. Four flaccid inches lying amidst wiry, black curls.

What he could do with that...

Peter met his gaze, blushed and looked away.

Prick throbbed.

Peter inhaled, sat down on the floor. "So who was your client?"

"Just a client." Jas rubbed his face, grateful for small-talk. The thoughts refused to go away.

Intrigued. "Something interesting?" Turning.

Jas grinned. "Oh, aye! Ah've bin asked by a wee guy wi' a foreign accent tae find a Maltese Falcon."

Eyes widening. "You're kidding! I thought you only did missing persons work." Brow furrowing. Thoughtful. "What sort of bird's a Maltese falcon, anyway? Is it a hunting bird?"

Jas traced the nape of Peter's neck. Finger slicked with sweat. His brain dripped with possibilities. "It's the stuff that dreams ur made of."

Quizzical.

"Ah'm showin' ma age!" Jas laughed. "Another private investigator said that – wan in a book. Phillip Marlowe?"

Blank look.

He regretted the reference, even though it took his mind off the thoughts." Chandler – Hammet?"

Eyes wide. "Katy Hamnet?" Impressed. "You're doing work for her?"

He laughed.

Hurt. Understanding. "You're teasing me!" Another blush.

Not as much as he'd like to. Jas ruffled jet hair, pulled the man back against his legs.

Peter nestled between iron thighs.

They smoked.

The head of his cock pushed against the back of a bristly neck. Jas drained the glass, leant over and placed it on the floor. The thoughts made him harder than ever. He took a chance. "Peter?"

Turning. Elbows resting on Jas's thighs. Curious.

Foreskin stretching further. He scowled. Not now. Not yet...

The expression misinterpreted. Peter's eyes lowered. Uncertain.

Jas stroked the glossy head. Words deserted him. Leigh had instinctively known.

Long silence. Then another spoke for him. Throat clearing. "Er... back through in the bedroom – when you... er, held my wrists..." Words floorwards.

He followed the flush of embarrassment as it spread from the lowered face to neck and sholders. Balls tingled. He waited.

"I... er – I kind of liked it!" The rush of consonants and vowels tumbled over each other. "Being... restrained like that, and told what to do, makes me...."

The head of his fully hard cock pushed against the lowered forehead. His mouth was a twisted line of longing.

Peter moved back onto heels. "You think I'm weird, don't you?" Awkward. A hint of self-loathing. Hands returning to own thighs.

Jas almost laughed. "No..." His voice was low.

Glossy black head slowly raised.

"...ah think we've got a lot in common." Jas stared into a scarlet face. Huge brown eyes dominated his vision. A knot of anticipation tightened in his guts. Jas stood up.

Peter remained on knees.

"It's a game..." Jas stared down. "...jist a game." Words came easily now, but did little justice to the thoughts. "But if the game's gonny work, ah need tae ken more aboot whit ye want tae get oota it..." He pulled the man to his feet. "...an' you need tae ken whit ah want fae whit we dae – if we dae onythin'."

Peter's head was bent.

Jas tipped the tanned face upwards. Mouth moved towards another quivering fullness. Peter's breath singed lips. The kiss was slow and gentle.

Arms instinctively moved in the direction of Jas's waist.

He gripped the wrists, pinning them against the man's well-muscled thighs.

Peter moaned. The kiss changed in pitch, deepening.

Jas felt the alteration in every muscle.

Power.

Control.

Forcing the arms gently backwards, he held Peter's wrists behind the man's broad back.

Peter gasped into his mouth.

Three feet below, another hardness poked at Jas's thigh.

Not now.

Not yet...

He broke the kiss slowly. "Okay?"

Peter was breathing heavily now. A whisper. "Oh Jas..."

Still holding the wrists, he pulled the man against his body and listened to a list of fantasies, thought but never uttered.

Fifteen minutes later, his own requirements were whispered into a pink ear.

Ten minutes after that, Jas grabbed the Paul Smith jacket from the floor and led Peter back to the bedroom.

In the corner, an ancient chair. He walked towards it and sat down. The leather was cold beneath sweating thighs. Jas looked at Peter. "Come here."

The man moved forward, stopped in front of him. Head lowered, waiting. Expectant.

Jas let him wait. The man's discomfort hung in the air. Jas's balls clenched and unclenched.

Two minutes.

Four.

He knew it felt like a lifetime to the novice in front of him. Jas stared between bronzed thighs, waiting for the first sign. When Peter's cock began to droop: "Look at me."

Head raised. The man's shaft flexed. Eyes hidden beneath thick lashes.

"Ah'm gonny take ye, Peter..."

Six inches of pale flesh was pushing upwards and outwards.

"...ah'm gonny take ye, an' ah'm gonny use ye..."

Six pale inches quivered.

"...cos that's white ye're for, Peter."

A sharp intake of breath parallel with another twitch of the stiffening, pale length.

Jas laughed. "Ye're a fuck-boay, Peter – whit ur ye?"

Words low, almost inaudible.

A bolt of desire shot through his own shaft. Jas laughed again. "Ah didney hear ye, Peter – whit wis that?"

"I'm a... fuck-boy..." The words moaned. The six inches quivered, fully erect at the final two syllables.

"Louder..."

"I'm a fuck-boy!"

Jas chuckled, eyes moving from the most uncomfortable erection he knew Peter had ever had to the flushed, sweating face. "Aye, that's right – ye're fur other men tae use, when they feel like it – an' ah feel like it noo!" He thrust the jacket at Peter. "Ye ken whit tae dae." Closing his eyes, he leant back on the chair, thighs apart. Rustling, then tearing. Then hands. Shaking hands. On his prick. Then moist rubber encasing dryness. A second skin. Jas groaned.

Peter's fingers pulled the condom tight, smoothing, checking.

Red pulsed on Jas's eyelids. Not yet...

Fingers stopped.

Jas opened his eyes, looked at Peter.

The man's pupils were huge: part fear, part desire...

Jas smiled, seized a hairy wrist. He pulled Peter closer, left hand on neck. Face inches from face.

Peter's mouth searched for his.

Jas drew back, eyes never leaving Peter's.

The man's heartbeat filled the room. Nervous. Swallowing. Husky voice. "Er..." Eyes averted. "I've not done... er, anal before

– can we use...?"

A virgin – in two ways. The confession broke the moment. Jas sighed, stood up. He walked into the bathroom and scowled: where was it? At the bottom of a toiletries bag he eventually located a rusty, nearly flat tube of KY. Years old. He walked back to the bedroom.

By the chair, Peter was still waiting. Still hard.

Pleased, Jas laughed.

The man jumped. Naughty-schoolboy face tilted upwards. Blushing.

Jas sat down on the chair. "Come here."

Obedient.

Jas kissed him roughly, teeth glancing off enamel. Then pushed him away.

Peter's tongue probed desperately.

Jas held the man at arm's length and looked down.

Six hard, throbbing inches.

"Turn roon'."

Peter turned, uncertain, glancing over shoulder.

"Kneel."

Peter knelt.

Light from the other room blazed in Jas's eyes. He unscrewed the KY, squeezed, then coated condomed prick. He scowled. More layers. Another skin. He paused and ran a hand over Peter's white, hairless arse.

A shiver shook soft flesh. Shoulder heaved, lungs inhaling sharply.

Jas squeezed again, rubbed cold jelly between hot fingers and began to lubricate.

A groan. Resistance.

Jas kissed the small of Peter's back.

Another groan. Less resistance.

One then two fingers. Then three.

Smooth. Slippery. Warm. Jas dropped the tube, removed fingers and gripped Peter's waist. He stood up and leant forward. Hands under ribs, steadying. Two misses. Too slippery.

Peter was panting.

Jas let go, seized his prick and guided the head slowly into Peter.

A sharp inhale.

Hands back on waist. One then two inches. Then three. Slick.

Easy. Then five.

Peter gasped, moved back against Jas.

Then six.

He dug fingers into firm flesh, bracing thumbs against ribs. Jas thrust upwards. Seven. A warm, moist vice welcomed him.

Peter made a low, animal noise.

Jas pressed his face against the man's spine, gripped bronze legs. He sat back on the chair and pulled Peter up onto his lap.

A bare foot braced against his thigh.

Jas moved hands to under Peter's armpits, lifting. Supporting. He withdrew, shifted, adjusting to the weight. Then lowered the tanned body. Jas thrust again.

Controlling.

Using – and being used.

Arrows of pleasure pierced his prick.

Peter's arms at each side of his head, fingers clutching the back of the chair.

Jas closed his eyes and scowled. His right arm trembled. Not yet...

Two bodies slid into sync.

Rhythm.

Purpose.

Peter limp in his hands. Heavy. Sweat-slippy.

Moving together. Slow to begin with. Then faster. Red faded into black. The pressure was almost unbearable. Jas pressed teeth against Peter's skin.

Now...

His brain exploded.

Later.

A noise?

Jas opened his eyes. Mucus and sweat clogged lashes. Too hot. He tried to move. Pins and needles tingled in the fingers of his right hand. On his chest Peter moaned softly. Jas smiled, wrapping arms more tightly around the sleeping figure.

Peter mumbled.

Jas brushed lips against damp forehead then glanced at the alarm: 3 am. Eyelids fluttered.

Peter stirred, nestling head under Jas's chin. A baby. A novice.

Jas grinned. The grin slipped into a scowl.

Like chess, The Game was best played with someone known.
Intimately.
Distant ringing. Door bell? His, or a neighbour's?
Jas ignored it. Peter...
Good body. But no mind-sync – yet. He rubbed semi-numb fingers over a pink nipple. Then tweaked.
A low moan.
Jas licked his lips. The smile returned. Breaking in a novice. The ten brief, intense minutes before The Game had degenerated into fucking lingered in his mind, promise of longer sessions to come.
More ringing, then banging.
Fingers pausing mid-rub.
Definitely his door bell. He waited.
More banging.
Jas sighed, easing out from under Peter.
Annoyed. More mumbling. Then light snore.
He got out of bed, grabbed combat pants from floor and pulled them on. Then frowned.
Marie – back for a re-match?
More banging.
Jas walked to the front door. "Okay, okay. Take it easy wi' ma paintwork." Buttoning fly. "Who is it?"
Not Marie. "James Anderson?" Male voice.
Hand pausing on bolt. "Aye. Who wants tae know?"
"Police, Mr Anderson. We have a warrant to search these premises."
Jas drew back the bolt, opened the door an inch. "Whit ur ye talkin' aboot? There's bin some sorta mistake..."
The door hit off the wall. Five uniforms pushed past him into the flat.
He turned. Lethal artexing scraped his shoulder. "Where dae ye think...?"
"You are James Anderson?" Voice behind. Cool. Professional.
Jas spun round.
Warrant card in one hand. Folded paper in the other.
He looked at the pale face on the card, read the name DS Michaels. Stewart Street.
"Let's go inside, Mr Anderson, eh?"
Jas took the folded paper, unfolded it. Half-open eyes scanning.

His name. His address. The words 'Class A drug' shimmered on the white paper. "Whit...?"

"Let's go inside, Mr Anderson." Unemotional.

Jas sighed and walked into the other room.

Six

Jas stared.

In the dimly lit room two uniformed officers were already sifting though books and papers.

He turned. The other three...?

Thin, sandy hair framing a pink face. Cold eyes staring into his. DS Michaels tried to smile. It didn't work.

At least he'd tried.

Shouts from the bedroom. Anger. "What...?" Then fear. "What's going on?" Then Peter emerged from bedroom, duvet round waist. Pale, sleep-stained face. Glossy hair sweat-plastered to head. Rubbing eyes. Duvet slipping. Sounds of harsh male laughter from behind. Whistles. Peter clutched the fabric more tightly and staggered past Michaels. He looked at Jas. Confused.

Amused eyes moving from man-in-combat-pants to man-in-duvet and back again. "And this is?"

Peter sat down on the sofa and pulled duvet around shoulders. Confusion slipping from the pale face, to be replaced by terror.

Jas scowled. "Never mind him. Whit's aw' this aboot drugs?" He regarded the man facing him.

DS Michaels. He hadn't noticed the first name. Mid forties. Not local, from the accent. Tall. Thin. Looked human.

Another laugh from the bedroom.

"Your name?" Procedural.

Jas sighed.

Brave words from the sofa. "Peter McLaughlin."

Heavy footsteps.

Jas looked past Michaels into the hall.

Young uniform. Male. 6' plus. Overweight. Flushed face grinning. Waving Marie's bundle of fifties. At Michaels, then Jas. "Where did the likes o' you git this?" Leer to Peter.

Michaels: "Shut up, Bennett!" Fingers clicking. "Give."

It was handed over. Another leer.

Michaels flicked through the bundle. To the uniform: "Carry on." To Jas: "This yours?"

"Aye."

"Can I ask where you got it?"

"Ah earned it."

Laugh from the bedroom, then: "Or the other guy did!"

Michaels frowned. "Keep it down in there!" To Jas: "By what means?"

Jas clenched his right fist. It trembled. "Whit business is it o' yours?"

Whisper from sofa. "Er, is it okay if I use the toilet?" To no one in particular and everyone in general.

Another uniform clutching evidence bag paused mid-search of telephone directory. Female. Sympathetic moon-face. Eyes to Michaels. "Want me to go wi' him, sir, make sure he disney... dispose o' any evidence?"

Laughing from bedroom. "No' your type, Eileen, hen. Ye'll be wasting yer time..."

Michaels. Angry: "Shut up!" To the WPC: a smile. Then eyes on duvet-clad figure.

Peter shivered, and looked at Jas.

Jas rubbed his face. "There's nae drugs here. Christ, let the guy huv a piss!"

Michaels nodded. Shout: "Toilet been searched?"

Returning shout: "Aye, sir. Clean."

To Peter: "Away you go, son. Leave the door open."

Jas watched figure-in-duvet scramble from the room and almost collide with another uniform.

Sound of light switched on, then urinating.

The side of the moulded sofa hit his shin. Jas moved back as a hatless uniform tipped the couch forward.

Four sets of eyes stared at the small, cellophane package which had slipped from between upholstered folds.

Michaels crouched, picked it up.

Jas watched a press-seal edge pressed and opened. "That's no'..."

"Let me guess – you've never seen this before." Fingertip into white powder. Fingertip licked. A frown.

He remembered an identical package, dropped hours earlier. One of two? "This is a mistake. Ah don't do drugs. Tell me where ye goat yer information." He looked at Michaels.

"Tell me where you got the £ 500." Ten fifties now encased in polythene. Michaels re-sealed the press-seal edge and handed it to a uniform.

"Ah telt ye, ah earned it." He sighed. "Ah dae a bit o' investigative work. Sometimes ah git paid in cash. Ah did the night."

Silence. Then sound of toilet flushing.

Then: "Your client's name?" Patient. Procedural.

Work in the private sector also had its procedures. "That's confidential." On the periphery of his vision, a small cellophane package now double-encased.

"Don't be so quick with your loyalty." Less patient. "One plus one, Mr Anderson..." Both evidence bags held out. Eyes from drugs to money. " ...equals...?"

Jas frowned at the simple equation: possession was one thing – dealing was something else. "This is ma place o' business as well as ma hame – in this line o' work, ye get aw' sorts o' visitors, but the five hundred wis earned, fair an' square."

Peter appeared.

Jas met his eyes.

Frightened.

Jas shrugged: casual was the best reassurance he knew.

Michaels, to the officer. "Keep an eye oan them." He walked from the room.

Peter stood in the doorway, uncertain. Tufts of dense black chest hair sprouted from behind the duvet. Panic drenched the tanned skin.

Jas looked away.

Voice from the bedroom. Michaels: "Anything in here?"

Mutters of angry disappointment. Then: "Coupla used johnnies, but nothin' else, sir."

"Bag them, and keep looking."

Resentful. "Ah'm no' touchin' them, sir, no' even wi' gloves..."

"Don't show your ignorance, man!" Irritation. "Just bag them, and get them to the lab with the other stuff – oh, and make sure the SOCO boys dust the vodka bottle through there." Turning.

Jas stepped forward, stood beside Peter. "Kin he git dressed, noo? He's goat nothin' tae dae wi'..."

"Maybe." Michaels walked past Jas and Peter into the other room. To the WPC. "Take Mr McLaughlin into the bedroom, Eileen. Get his details."

"Jas...?" Worried. At his side, Peter shivered.

He knew the feeling. From years ago. Court appearances.

Witness statements. Private matters aired for public gaze. Jas rubbed a hairy hand through padded fabric. "It's okay. Don't worry..."

Michaels again. "Now, Mr Anderson..." As the moon-faced WPC ushered Peter through to the bedroom, DS Michaels closed the lounge door. He re-righted a moulded armchair and sat down.

Jas stood.

"James Anderson, I am arresting you for possession of a Class A drug and on suspicion of selling a Class A..."

"Ah'm no' dealin'." Marie's distraught face floated before his eyes. He wondered vaguely if she knew one of her girls would be going short, tonight.

Michaels continued the formalities. "Do you understand, Mr Anderson?"

Jas frowned. "Ah'm no' dealin' an' ah've never seen that stuff before the night." The truth – of sorts.

Sceptical eyes from his face to pocket. Notebook produced. "Possession of a Class A drug, plus an unusually large amount of cash can only be read a limited number of ways, Mr Anderson." Cellophane-wrapped fifties fingered. "Give us your client's name – if he can corroborate the source of this, that'll be something." Eyes to Jas.

The source of a small, clingfilm-wrapped package swam in his head. He clenched his left fist.

Nod to the bedroom. "Your... friend's?"

Jas frowned. His mind cleared. "Where did ye get yer information?"

Michaels stared at him. "That's not your business, Mr Anderson." Two cellophane packages replaced on the moulded sofa. "Do a little dealing on the side, to augment the income from your other business?"

"No! Ah..."

"So tell me who gave you the £500." Notebook flicked shut. Nod to the bedroom. "Or maybe I should talk to your friend..."

"Marie McGhee." Jas closed his eyes: his problem. Peter's fear-streaked face filled his mind.

Pleased. "That's better..." Sounds of notebook re-opening. "...address?"

Jas eased eyelids ajar. "Ah don't huv it."

Michaels didn't look convinced.

It didn't sound convincing.

Radio fished from pocket. Switched on. Michael turned away.

Low voice. "Can you do a PNC check on a... Marie McGhee?"

Jas rubbed his face. "Ah really huv nae idea whit her address is – she moves around a lot." It sounded lamer by the minute.

Pause. Crackles.

Michaels listened. To the radio: "Thanks." Turning back. Less convinced than ever."So Marie McGhee was here last night?"

"Aye, but..."

"And she gave you the £500?"

"Aye, but let me finish..."

"Are you aware Ms McGhee has a string of convictions for drug misuse as long as your arm?"

Jas rubbed at his shoulder.

"You do a lot of business with junkies, Anderson?"

Jas scowled. "She's clean, noo."

Surprise. "You know her well?"

He followed the implication. "Aye, but..."

Michaels talked through him. "You admit to an association with a known user; a quantity of a Class A drug has been found in your possession, plus five hundred pounds in cash..."

"Maist o' ma clients pay cash – it's that kinda business!"

Michaels talked on. "We can do this the easy way, Anderson, or we can take Mr er McLaughlin into custody and..."

"No!" He rubbed his face. Marie – fuckin' Marie!

The door opened. Overweight uniform clutching evidence bags in one hand. Behind, sounds of patient female then low, confused male voice.

Michaels turned. Annoyed. "What is it, Bennett?"

Scowl. "That's us done, sir." Staring at Jas. Nostrils wrinkling. "Fun' this in the other wan's jaicket." Small, smoked-glass bottle produced from pocket.

Fingers clicking, then hand out-stretched.

Bennett placed the bottle in Michaels' palm.

Michaels unscrewed the top, sniffed, then moved back.

Amyl nitrite fumes filled the room.

Michaels replaced the top.

Jas leant against the wall. "Poppers ur legal, when ah last looked!"

Michaels ignored him, gave the bottle back. "Bag it. How's Eileen doing with Mr McLaughlin?"

Harsh laugh. "He's greetin' like a wee lassie, noo, sir!" Disgust. "Be wantin' his mammy next."

"Whit's goin' oan through there?" Rage pulsed in temples. Jas pushed past them into the hall.

A pair of strong arms gripped his, pulling him back. Stiff serge dragged on bare skin.

Cool voice. "Let him go, Bennett!"

Arms reluctantly disengaged.

Jas walked through to the bedroom, scanned.

Harsh overhead light. Wardrobe door open. Clothes covered the floor. Mattress askew, pillows slipless. The duvet's cover had been removed. Several ragged slashes decorated the duvet itself.

In front of the word processor a uniform was going through diskettes. Two others were smoking at the window. In a corner, on the ancient chair, Peter sat, head in hands. White Calvins, Paul Smith jacket around shoulders. Moonface was writing in a notebook.

Cool voice behind. "Get those cigarettes out!"

Jas picked up a pair of black jeans from the mess and moved towards Peter.

The man looked up. Eyes swimming. Out of his depth.

Jas handed him the jeans. Smiled. "Aw' right?"

Peter nodded, looked away.

Jas turned to Michaels, right fist clenched. "He wisney here when Marie came roon'. He kens nothin' – kin ye no' see that? Let him go hame."

Moonface unsure. To Michaels: "Ah've no' got a proper statement yet sir, and there's the prints tae get, yet."

Jas stared at Michaels. "He'll come tae Stewart Street the morra, gie it then. Ye kin get his prints then, tae." He searched for humanity in the professional face.

And found it.

To Peter: "We've got your address, Mr McLaughlin?"

Peter nodded, scrambling into jeans.

Radio crackle. Unintelligible voice.

Michaels turned away and replied softly.

Radio crackle subsided.

Michael turned back. "Do you still deny this..." Double-wrapped white powder brandished. "...is yours?" Humanity tinged with the job.

A deal. Him for Peter. Jas rubbed his face. "Ah wanna talk tae ma solicitor."

To Peter: "Any time tomorrow will be fine, then. Ask for

WPC Morrison." Michaels to Moonface: "See that Mr McLaughlin gets home then bring Mr Anderson up to the station." Michaels left the room. One of the uniforms went with him.

An overweight shape reappeared in the doorway. Eyes to hall. Disappointed: "Whit aboot the body search, sir? They kid both huv drugs up their..."

"Leave it, Bennett – we've got what we came for." Sound of front door opening then closing as DI Michaels left the flat.

Jas spun round, inner arms held out for inspection. "Dae ah luck like a user?" Biceps pulsed. Eyes to Peter: "Dis he?"

Harsh laugh. Bennett seized Jas's right wrist and twisted it up behind his back. "The tip-aff said ye were dealin', no' using, ya bastard! Guid veins means nothin'." He pulled Jas's arm further up his back.

A disabling hold.

...the tip-aff...

...the tip-aff...

Through the first indication of where the police had obtained their information, the hold's effectiveness kicked in. Knuckles pressed into spine. Pain throbbed in damaged tendons. Vision blurred. He closed his eyes.

"Leave him alone!" Low growl from Peter.

Laugh. Dismissive: "An' whit ye gonny dae aboot it?"

Pressure on arm increasing. Sound ebbed and flowed in his ears. Voices faded. Then returned. Shouting. Female voice placating. On the edge of consciousness his arm was released. Jas gasped, shook his head and opened his eyes.

More shouting.

Jas blinked and focused.

Peter. Pinned to the bedroom wall. Bennett's arm against his throat. Moonface pulling at a serge-covered back. Unsuccessfully. Two other uniforms standing against the closed door. Watching.

Then silence. Then the sound of laboured breathing.

Slow motion though star-spangled vision. Jas stared at Peter's face, white beneath tan. Then bluish around mouth. Hairy arms flailing, then slowing...

More shouting. Bennett: "Hit an officer, wid ye, ya wee..."

Jas pushed past Moonface and grabbed flabby shoulders.

"Whit the...?"

He pulled Bennett around. Knee contacted with groin.

Scream, then moaning. Bennett doubled up and fell forwards.

Jas pushed him away.

Bennett fell sideways.

Peter slid silently down the wall and slumped to the floor, head lolling.

Jas knelt beside him, two fingers on neck. Weak pulse. He smoothed glossy hair back from face and slapped one cheek lightly.

No response.

Moonface at his side, worried: "He okay?"

Jas lifted the limp body in trembling arms and laid Peter on the mattress.

Eyes still closed. Shallow breathing. Broad reddening line across adam's apple.

Jas turned to Moonface: "Git an ambulance." He slapped Peter's face again, harder.

Radio crackle. Lowered voice. More radio crackle. Frowning.

He stared at the imprint of his palm and cursed radio-blackspots. "Phone's in the other room."

Quivering Moon-voice: "Come on, boys, let me past."

He turned away from the reddening handprint, watched as the two uniforms reluctantly opened the bedroom door.

On the floor, Bennett was still writhing, clutching groin.

Jas stood up, walked over and kicked the overweight figure twice. In the kidneys.

Bennett gasped, then fell silent.

On the mattress, Peter groaned.

Jas turned and crouched beside him, stroking hair.

Eyelids fluttered open. Pupils unfocused. Croaking words: "You okay?"

The concern flushed his face. Jas leant over and brushed purplish lips.

Behind, three sets of eyes bored hate-holes into his back.

"Aye, ah'm fine. How aboot you?"

Trying to sound brave. "Sure." Head raised inches. Pain flashed across face. Peter sank back onto the mattress.

"Lie still." Jas reached down and picked up the Paul Smith jacket. He draped it over Peter's tanned chest.

Sounds of unsteady breathing. Then curses from Bennett, in the background.

Jas tucked the jacket more tightly around the inert form.

Outside, a siren broke the night.

Good response time. The Royal was close. His eyes brushed

over the alarm clock, which lay inches away: almost five. He looked at Peter.

Eyes still closed. Breathing laboured.

Moon-voice above him, whispering. "Look: ah saw whit happened. Put in a complaint. Bennett's hid it comin' fur a while. Ah'll back ye up."

Jas stared at Peter. "If he's hurt, Bennett'll huv mair tae worry him than a disciplinary hearin'!" He stroked the tanned forehead.

Bell ringing. Jas looked up.

The two uniforms at the door moved into the hallway, half-carrying Bennett.

Ambulance crew appeared. Low voices.

Jas continued to stroke. Then a hand on his arm.

Moonface: "Come on. Let them dae their joab."

Jas stopped stroking and stood up.

Moon-voice to ambulance man: "His name's McLaughlin..."

"It's Peter..." He frowned as the green-overalled figure located a pulse.

Moonface talked on: "Neck injury, but ah don't think onythin' broken. He's bin conscious, off an' oan." To Jas: "Right. Let's git you up to Stewart Street."

Jas watched as a brace was placed round neck, listened as the ambulance driver talked soothingly, reassuringly. As Peter was moved onto stretcher the Paul Smith jacket slipped to the floor. He picked it up and placed it across the matted chest.

Eyelids flickered, then opened. Confused. "Jas? Where...?"

"Ye're goin' tae the hospital, jist til they check ye ower." He smiled.

More confused. Too confused to be brave. "Come with me?" Pupils tiny.

Jas looked at Moonface.

Sigh. "Sorry. Ah've goat ma orders." Placating. "Ye kin phone the Royal later, find oot how he is."

He watched as Peter was carried from the bedroom.

Soft Moon-voice: "Get dressed. Ah'll wait in the other room." Tactful. Understanding.

Jas scowled. She was a minority. He walked towards a heap of clothes and located an Adidas tee-shirt. One of his Docs was under the window. He found the other beneath a heap of shredded bedding. Jas laced boots, then stood up and looked out.

Outside, an ambulance pulled away from behind a white and

pink squad car.

He lifted a leather biker's jacket and walked through to the other room. It was empty, apart from Moonface on the re-righted sofa. She stood up when he entered.

"Ready?"

Jas nodded and led the way to the front door.

Seven

He knew the room, had seen dozens similar...

Jas zipped up the biker's jacket and stared at the small, metal hatch. The alkaline stench of ingrained piss and sweat twitched his nostrils. He moved his eyes around three bare walls. Beyond, sobbing. In a more distant cell, someone was singing.

... from the other side of the door.

He raised his left fist, pounded the metal hatch for the eighth time. "Oi! Where's ma breakfast?" Hunger was the last thing on his mind, but he'd given up asking if his solicitor had arrived.

In the distance, the singing stopped.

Other pounding. "Aye!" A distant, drunken echo. "Whit kinda establishment is this?"

Jas smiled wryly and walked to the back of the cell. The smile faded. He walked to the door, pounded again.

The alter-echo. "A wee paira kippers wid go doon a treat..."

Left fist lingered on scarred metal. Jas tilted it, looking at his wrist for the watch which was no longer there. He frowned.

Approximately four hours ago, Moonface had driven him to Stewart Street Police Station. His personal possessions were now in a another cellophane envelope, behind the Custody Sergeant's desk.

Approximately half an hour later, he'd sat in another room. On another desk, three smaller cellophane envelopes. And a tape machine. And DI Michaels, plus a uniform whose name he hadn't caught. Not Moonface.

He'd been asked if he wanted to make a statement.

Jas had confirmed his name, address, reiterated the request to phone his solicitor...

He thumped again. Several cells up, the breakfast demands increased in number and volume.

... and eventually got it. Andrew Ainslie had sounded sleepy.

And surprised.
Approximately three hours ago, he'd been returned to the cell.
Since?
Jas kicked the door. "Breakfast, eh? It's an EU statute!" Metal vibrated under the sole of his boot. From through the wall:
"Aye, an' none o' yer continental shite: full fry-up – wi' kippers."
His boot hovered. "Come on..." He kicked again. Somewhere beyond:
"Keep it doon, eh? Summa us ur tryin' tae sleep!"
He recognised the Custody Sergeant's voice. Jas frowned. Four hours: even without legal advice, he should have been bailed and released by this time. A different approach raised itself. "Ah wanna see Michaels – git Michaels doon here!"
Distant disinterest. "Gie it a rest, eh?"
Jas stepped back, thumped the door with the heel of his boot. "Noo!" Peter's pale face superimposed itself over the scored surface of the door. He'd asked three times that they phone the Royal, three hours ago, then parrotted the same question to a half-awake Andrew Ainslie. Jas blinked.
Full, blue-tinged lips refused to leave his mind. He kicked metal and watched ancient iron shimmer.
And again.
And again.
From beyond the door, nothing. The breakfast requests had either been satisfied or abandoned.
Jas walked to the back of the cell, turned then walked to the door...
Marie.
...and walked to the back of the cell...
Class A drugs. An ex-junkie trying to go straight.
....and walked to the door. A kick. Jas paused, rubbed his face. A statement from Marie would explain everything. And leave her open to prosecution.
He frowned. Regardless of any statement she gave, possession was nine-tenths of the law – but at least the five hundred pounds could be explained, and the Intent to Supply aspect dropped.
Sounds of scraping metal.
He moved away from the door.
The hatch lowered.

Jas peered. "At fuckin' last."

A round, disembodied face peered back at him. Cropped hair.

Not Michaels.

Not the Custody Sergeant.

Not Andrew Ainslie...

...the hatch closed. Then more scraping. Key scraping.

Jas retreated further. "Ah hope this breakfast's hot."

The door opened...

He sat down on the bolted-to-the-floor bench, scanned the four men in serge trousers and white shirts moving into the cell.

No breakfast.

...and closed. Cropped-hair flattened himself against the scored surface. One large hand held keys. The other gripped a side baton.

Jas' eyes flicked around the other three. He stood up.

"So you're Anderson..."

He focused on the source of sneering words: blond curly hair. Pink face. Mouth tilting downwards. Blue, narrowed eyes boring into his.

"...we've heard aw' aboot you...."

Another voice. To his left. Jas turned.

Smaller than Curly. Older. More solidly built. Eyebrow scar.

Jas scowled.

More hours ago than he cared to remember. The bedroom. The same foot which had kicked the cell door impacting with a more yielding subject. "Four against wan – ye're affy brave, boays..."

Behind the trio, in front of the door, Cropped-hair threw the keys into the air and caught them.

"...it's aw' roon' the station, Anderson..."

The third voice came from an inch away, brushing his ear. Jas's head jerked right. He stared at a thin figure in white shirt/ black trousers, remembered another, flabbier figure...

...and a code of tit-for-tat camaraderie. "Bennett wis askin' fur it, pal – ye..."

Harsh laugh. "This isney aboot Bennett."

A gob of spit struck his skin. He felt the hate dribble down his right cheek and thought of last night, with Peter.

"Ye're a fuckin' disgrace, Anderson..." Curly.

Jas clenched his left fist. The old hate. "Whit ah dae in ma ain hame's none o' your..."

"...how they ever let ye wear the uniform, Christ only knows!" Something behind the voice.

Jas moved forward. This wasn't about now.

This was about then. "Bent cops ur a disgrace tae everywan..."

Snigger. "Ye're wan tae talk aboot bent, Anderson!"

The words shivered on his skin. The spit continued to trickle. Jas ignored both, tried to keep track of the voices. They moved around him, circling then easing away. "Sloan lied – he withheld evidence. He falsified confessions – he wis the disgrace, no'..."

The first blow came from behind, caught him across the right shoulder and off-guard. Breath on his lowered face:

"He wis wanna us, Anderson..."

Something solid impacted with his kidneys. Jas made a grab for the weapon.

"...an' you grassed him up, ya bastard!"

The side baton swept upwards, taking his left arm with it. Someone grabbed him from behind. The creak of leather filled his ears as his arms were wrenched behind his back.

"Ye stood there, in open court, an' grassed up wanna yer ain – ye're scum!" Curly's features contorted with rage.

A blow to the back of his knees made them crumple. Jas inhaled sharply.

"Dirty, grassin' scum!"

Kneecaps met the stone floor. Blows designed for maximum pain/minimum damage rained onto his body from side batons. The sole of a boot met tensed abdominals. "Dirty fuckin' scum..."

He closed his eyes against rising vomit, slid sideways and wrenched an arm free. A satisfying gasp filled his ears as his elbow contacted between vulnerable, serge-covered legs.

The grip on his arms was replaced by fingers in his hair.

Jas cursed Terry's too-long haircut and twisted away. Fist impacted with solid skull.

A howl.

Leathered shoulders ground against bare brick. Knuckles stinging, he staggered to his feet. And stared.

Curly was holding crushed genitals, hissing through teeth.

Blood from a forehead tear trickled down towards an eyebrow scar .

A panicked, thin figure was glancing between its two injured companions.

In front of the door, Cropped-Hair scowled. "Finish him aff – go oan!"

Pain burned in the pit of his stomach. Jas glowered, raised

lead arms and beckoned. "Come oan, then – fuckin' try it." The burning moved lower. He winced through the scowl.

The cell pulsed with wordless breathing and the smell of frustrated violence.

Then footsteps. Two sets.

Through blurring vision, he watched Cropped-Hair resheath the side baton and hastily edge open the door. The other three moved quickly towards it.

Jas lowered aching arms. He brushed what felt like solidifying snot from the side of his mouth. "This ma breakfast at last?" The words were thick. Jas cleared his throat.

The door opened completely.

Four dishevelled figures in rumpled white shirts sloped out. Eyebrow-Scar was holding a handkerchief against a dripping scalp-wound.

Jas stared, rubbing kidney area with a leathered elbow.

In front of a frowning Custody Sergeant, Andrew Ainslie's sparsely covered head swivelled:

"What's been going on here?" Eyes in the direction of the departing foursome.

He could still smell the animosity. "The boays jist dropped in tae talk aboot auld times." His word against theirs.

Disbelieving stare.

Jas ignored the scepticism and walked gingerly to the floor-bolted bench. The burning in his kidneys ignited into flares as he eased himself onto it.

Andrew Ainslie looked at the Custody Sergeant, who shrugged. "Any complaints, Mr Anderson?" The title grudging.

Jas unzipped the biker's jacket. "Aye – where's ma breakfast?"

A snort. To the solicitor: "Gimme a shout when ye're through."

Then Andrew was opening his briefcase and the cell door was closing.

Breakfast arrived half an hour later. Jas stared at the underdone fried egg. "So he's aw' right?"

Sigh. "Like I said, Mr McLaughlin was released from the Royal at six-thirty..." Running out of patience. "...I think we can presume he's out of danger. Are you sure there's nothing more you want to tell me, regarding the search of your flat and..." Pause. "...your four visitors?"

Jas shook his head. The burning in his kidneys had died to dull embers. He'd managed the rest of the breakfast, but the egg was defeating him.

A sigh. Then. "About your bail..."

Jas sliced into runny yoke with a plastic fork. "Ah should git it oan ma ain recognisance, aye?" He scooped it into his mouth: nothing like adrenalin to boost an appetite. It was cold. Jas chewed slowly.

The question ignored. "I have a proposition for you."

He stopped chewed, stared at the pink, shiny face.

Andrew Ainslie pushed a lank shred of greying hair back from a creased forehead. "DI Michaels is willing to do a deal."

"Whit sorta deal?" The yoke slid down his throat, coating soreness.

"Plead guilty to possession and they'll drop the supply charges."

The yoke hit his stomach. "In his fuckin' dreams!"

"Come on – this..." Flicking through notes. "...Marie McGhee may or may not explain the five hundred pounds, if I can find her, but I doubt she'll cooperate over her – the – heroin. Possession's undeniable. Plead guilty and..."

"An' ah'll huv a record." He pushed the plate away and stared at his solicitor. "Naw, ah'll take ma chances wi' a jury." Jas wiped his mouth on the back of bruising knuckles. "Jist get ma bail organised an' ah kin spend fae noo til the trial workin' oan Marie." He stood up.

Pain flared in his side.

Jas frowned.

Andrew Ainslie mirrored the expression. "You know the way the courts are cracking down on pushers..." One hand over a sparsely greying head.

"Ah'm ex-polis, ah've got a job, ah've never bin in trouble before an' ah've nae history o' usin'. Nae Sheriff in his right mind's gonny pit me oan remand." He grabbed a mug of lukewarm tea, drained it.

Andrew's brow creased further. Eyes to notes. "As your solicitor, I must advise you to seriously consider DI Michaels' offer – it's generous, considering the amount of heroin and the five hundred..."

"Michaels kens he's no' gotta leg tae stand oan, wi' intent tae supply.." He replaced the mug on the bench. "...that's the main reason he's bein' so generous." Jas rubbed his face: he needed a wash. "An' he kens ah've a fair chance o' beatin' the possession charge – wi' or withoot Marie's cooperation."

Eyes from notes. "Think about this carefully."

"Whit ye think ah've been daein' fur the last four hours?" He frowned. "Ah'm no' huvin' a record fur somethin' ah didney do. Michaels thinks he's gotta case? Let him fuckin' prove it in court."

Resigned sigh. "This is against my advice – you understand that?"

Jas nodded. He'd talk to Marie himself...

Hairy knuckles and a boyish face edged into his mind.

..after he'd checked on Peter. "Ah ken whit ah'm daein'." Twelve years working with the courts, a year working for them had taught him something. He cocked his head towards the door. "Is there a chance ah kin appear before the Sheriff this mornin'?" The sooner the trial date was set, the sooner...

Weary nod. "I'll see what I can do." Notes-folder closed. " And I'll arrange bail, if recognisance is denied."

Jas zipped up the jacket, flexing shoulders. "Ah'm no' user – an' the Sheriff'll agree wi' me." Another ache sprang into life.

"I wish I had your confidence." Andrew Ainslie stood up, gathered the briefcase against a skinny chest.

Jas laughed. "You're a solicitor – lookin' oan the black side's part o' yer job!"

Somewhere in the distance, someone was singing again. In tune. Jas grinned at the scored, metal door and thought about Peter.

The day could only get better.

He was wrong.

Jas sat on another metal bench. Different room...

Gyproc'ed walls. Off-white emulsion souring by the minutes. He focused on a red, Magic-Markered red dot within a red circle, and the ironic words: 'Press twice for room service'.

...different building.

His first mistake had been ever agreeing to do business with Marie McGhee.

His second was placing any faith in the criminal justice system.

Resting head in hands, he gazed at scuffed concrete and tried to take in what had happened.

Ex-Strathclyde police... should know better.... should be ashamed of yourself.

Jas closed his eyes against the Sheriff's condemnatory words. Andrew Ainslie's badly hidden *I-warned-you* face appeared before him. Then another face. Supported by a white neck brace above broad, soberly suited shoulders.

A boyishly naive smile of solidarity glinting down down at him from Court Fourteen's public gallery.

Jas opened his eyes to get away from it.

Words swarmed in his head.

Recognisance denied.

Bail denied.

Trial set for December 4th. Six weeks away.

He rubbed at a mark on the scuffed concrete floor with the heel of his boot.

Remanded to HMP Barlinnie.

Jas waited for the Sheriff's words to sink in. They floated on the surface of his brain.

The sound of keys jerked his head up.

Door opening. Andrew Ainslie's weary face. The *I-warned-you* expression now back behind professional mask.

Jas looked away.

Throat clearing. "The Fiscal's office are under a lot of pressure to make an example of what few dealers the police can come up with – and that means holding on to them. Nine out of ten jump any bail set. You know that."

He knew, and didn't blame them. Jas looked up. "Ye get in touch wi' Marie?" One face had been noticeable by its absence, back in the courtroom.

"Left three messages – if she doesn't return them, I'll get someone onto it."

Less than twenty-four hours ago, he would have been that someone. Now?

"Don't worry, Jas – we'll argue the heroin is circumstantial. You work from home – you can't be responsible for... contraband dropped by your clients."

He looked beyond Andrew Ainslie's sparse grey hair. Now?

"I'll get Jim Duncan briefed on your case – he's a good barrister. You'll get the best possible legal..."

Reassurances faded. Jas stared at the door.

Now?

Six weeks.

Six weeks in Barlinnie.

The Bar-L. The Big Hoose. One of the toughest penal establishments in the country. The animosity from Curly and co. shrank in the face of six weeks in Glasgow's infamous prison.

Andrew Ainslie's professional tones rumbled on in the background.

The hair on the back of his neck sprang to attention.

The Bar-L.

A voice crept through the shiver. "...with a bit of luck, you'll go straight to Isolation – the prison authorities are usually sympathetic to the plight of ex-police officers in their custody."

They might be: 'ex' wasn't a prefix with much meaning for the others amongst whom he was to pass the next six weeks. He refocused on the suited figure.

It tried a smile. "They'll do everything to ensure your safety."

Jas almost laughed. As well as a good few petty offenders with long memories, the Bar-L was now home to someone with a sharper axe to grind...

...who had sworn to bury that axe between Jas's shoulder-blades.

The sound of tentative knuckles on the half-open door.

He followed his solicitor's eyes.

Tentative hairy knuckles. A similar smile, inches above a white padded neck brace. Above that, large tear-filled eyes.

"Ah, I think your...friend wants a word..."

Commiseratory hand on his arm:

"...I'll be in touch – and don't worry. We'll sort this out."

Worry wasn't an emotion his mind had room for. Jas listened to the sound of leather-soled shoes on concrete and continued to stare at the boyish face.

Then Andrew was gone and hairy-knuckled hands were on his shoulders, damp eyes pressing against his neck.

"...Jean's given me the rest of the week off, but I feel fine..." Croaking voice. "... bruised larynx, or something – I'm not much use around the office like this...."

He wasn't doing a lot of good here, either. Jas leant back against the wall, inhaled the orangy aftershave with its bitter undernote.

Peter had eventually stopped crying...

Jas patted a broad shoulder and opened his mouth.

...but would not stop talking. "And she says if there's anything she can do, don't hesitate." The new, hoarse delivery was at odds with the boyish face.

Jas exhaled, closed his mouth.

"I'd like to... er, help too. Since I won't be at work, maybe I could... keep an eye on your flat – tidy up, forward your mail and that sort of thing."

A hand squeezed his. Jas stared at the hairy knuckles linked between his own grubby fingers. Beneath combat-pants and the Adidas tee-shirt, his unwashed body still smelt of last night.

Last night...

...only last night. Tonight?

Jas tried to return the pressure. Barlinnie beckoned, inevitable and terrifying.

"Oh, I... brought you some things..." One hand removed from his. White-rope handles slipped from blue-suited shoulder.

Jas focused on the name on the side of the carrier bag and tried not to think about the strong, male body beneath the blue suit.

"...your solicitor told me what you might need..."

A head rested on his shoulder. Jas flinched: not this. He stared at a carton of cigarettes, watched as three polythene bags and a fourth, crinklier-wrapped package joined them.

"...is there anything else I can bring you?"

Jas picked up the packet of Bic disposable razors. "They'll no' let me take these in." He replaced the razors beside three packs of expensive designer underwear and lifted the cigarettes. "But thanks fur..."

"Oh Jas..." Blue-suited arms around his neck again. "...I'll come and visit you – just let me know when. I want to do whatever I can to..."

"Peter?" He gently gripped hairy wrists and eased them away.

Expensively cut head raised from his chest. "You're innocent, Jas..." Huge eyes brimming again. "...I'll be here, when you come to trial – I'll wait for you."

There was a good chance there would be nothing to wait for – in every sense of the word. Jas stared at the packet of Bics.

He was as disposable as one of the razors: the odds on him ever leaving the Bar-L alive were slimmer than those thin blades, safe behind their plastic guards.

Something twisted in his stomach, overshadowing the pain in

his side. Brain searched for words.

Brave smile. Then an open mouth moving towards his.

The twisting curled into a knot of affection he couldn't afford. Jas released hairy wrists and stood up. He walked to the door.

"What's wrong?" Confusion from the metal bench. "What have I...?"

"Sno' you." Jas turned, rubbed a hot face.

More confusion. "Did I bring the wrong...?"

"Ah said it's nothin' tae dae wi' you!" The shout echoed around the tiny, stinking space.

His fight.

His problem.

Peter had a job, a life...

...Jas turned.

Red-rimmed eyes shone, beacons he couldn't afford to reach out to. Peter stood up. An uncertain step towards him.

Jas backed away, fingers clenched. Left fist thumped on the door. "Okay!" Ears strained for the footsteps of the officer who would take Peter out of this cell and out of his life.

Other footsteps. "Jas..." Pleading. "...I know prison's awful, but we'll..."

"We?" He hurled the word at the handsome face. "There's no we, pal!" The pain and confusion in the red-rimmed eyes pulled at his heart. "Ye wur an okay fuck, but that wis it!"

Peter flinched.

Jas capitalised, moving in for the kill. "Wan night, pal – that's aw' it wis. You ken nothin' aboot me, an' ah don't wanna ken onythin' aboot you!" He couldn't look at the confused, hurt face so he stared at the wall behind it. "Get oot, Peter ..."

A limp body in a blue suit was motionless.

Silence pulsed between them.

Jas pounded on the door again. "C'mon – get this wanker oota here!"

Seconds later, a white-shirted police officer led Peter from the cell. He didn't look back.

Half an hour later, the cell door opened again. One of the Bic razors now lodged between underwear and pubic hair, Jas walked from the holding cells and out into the yard.

Eight

Wet, grey dusk threw itself against already darkened windows. Glasgow twilight flicked past outside. The smell of unwashed clothes and cigarettes seeped into his nostrils.

At the rear of the half-full bus, Jas looked up from cuffed wrists and surveyed his fellow passengers.

All equally restrained, courtesy of the new rigid handcuffs. Jas stared at the back of a Zero-crop, then a greasy, balding head.

All types.

Most already ensconced in the ancient vehicle when he'd boarded: transferrees and remand prisoners from the High and other regional courts.

Most on their own.

With the occasional exception. Jas stared at a trio of sportswear-clad teenagers, bodies squashed together on a seat meant for two. Barely-broken voices bonding with engine vibrations.

Groups within groups.

Eyes brushed a small, hunched figure in a padded jacket across the aisle. Alone.Younger-looking than the trio, but had to be at least eighteen. Step-cut hair skimming earphones. Sleeves hung down over cuffed wrists. Stubby fingers waggled rapidly above something Jas couldn't see. A cardboard Kwik-Save box sat on the double seat beside the boy.

The bus changed gear.

Jas refocused down the aisle to the front.

Leaning against the dashboard, a slight figure in grey blouson jacket and matching trousers. Blond. Looked barely older than the kids in the sportswear. The uniform sat uneasily on narrow shoulders. Clipboard in one hand, mobile phone in the other. Chatting to the driver. The black embroidered brickwork of Hadrian Security's insignia glared at him from breast pocket.

Jas frowned. The Scottish Prison Service never transported prisoners with anything less than a five-man escort, excluding driver.

The mobile phone burred.

One of the teens sniggered.

The blond Hadrian officer curtailed his conversation. Face lowered to mobile. Jas refocused beyond the tinted window.

The bus idled at traffic lights.

Traffic was heavy on George V bridge. Umbrella'd and raincoated figures scurried along slick pavements.

Shoppers.

Schoolkids.

Office workers.

Fingers tightened around Peter's Armani shoulder-bag.

Ordinary people doing ordinary things...

Ahead, wet red light slipped through amber into diluted green. The bus moved slowly forward.

...ordinary people homebound. Jas rested his face against the tinted window and tried not to think about his home, for the next six weeks. Engine vibrations shivered through glass. Then the sound of a throat clearing from the front of the bus:

"Your attention please." Too loud, given the size of the vehicle. Front attempting to compensate for inexperience?

Someone else sniggered.

His eyes swivelled left. He watched approximately twenty-five other pairs do likewise.

Across the aisle, one step-cut head remained lowered.

A name tag was now visible above the embroidered-wall insignia: Jas peered, couldn't read it.

Another throat clearing. "I'm Officer Brodie, and you will address me as that, or sir."

Jas tried to place the accent: educated, middle-class Glasgow – Milngavie or Bearsden.

"Is that understood?"

Mumbled assent. A snigger.

Less uncertain. "Good." Clipboard held at chest height. "Please respond when your name is called, lads."

The title struck another wry note.

Three rows in front, one of the teens found it equally amusing.

"Abbot?"

"Aye..."

He watched a mid-fifties man in a shabby overcoat raise a mottled hand. Jas thrust his own hand into Peter's carrier-bag and fumbled for cigarettes.

"Abernethy?"

"Here!"

A voice somewhere near the front. Jas tore at cellophane, stuck a Benson and Hedges between his lips.

"Adair?"

"Mr Brodie, sir!"

Muffled sniggers.

Jas looked to where Zero-crop was on his feet.

Mock salute. The skinhead was grinning around himself.

"Thank you, Adair." The sarcasm ignored.

Jas caught one cocky eye as the skinhead reluctantly sat down then returned his attention to a pink disposable lighter.

"Adamson?"

"Here, miss!" One of the teens.

Jas inhaled deeply, drawing the smoke into his lungs.

Baiting: part of the routine – part of separating Them from Us. He hoped the rest of the bus was enjoying the fun: once inside Barlinnie's iron gates, there would be little to laugh about.

"Ahmed?"

A silver cuff slid down a coffee-coloured forearm. "Present."

Jas leant back on the worn, vinyl seat. He closed his eyes and smoked, listening as the roll call continued. Then:

"Anderson?"

Jas opened his eyes, nodded.

Frown. "Can't you read?"

Twenty-four heads swivelled on twenty-four necks. Forty-eight eyes stared at him, along with Brodie's.

Jas raised an eyebrow.

Clipboard pointed to a barely visible No Smoking sign on the dashboard.

Jas gripped what was left of the cigarette between thumb and forefinger. "Ye didney tell them tae put theirs oot..." He took a long drag, exhaled ceilingwards.

A snigger from two of the smoking teens.

A deepening frown from Brodie. "Never mind them – do as the sign says, Anderson."

Jas inhaled again, meeting and holding a gaze which for the first time bordered on antagonism.

"Now!"

Jas stood up. "Whit's your problem?" He gripped Peter's Armani bag beneath one cuffed arm.

Brodie was striding up the aisle towards him. Inches away, he stopped, grabbed the bag. "This should have been confiscated."

Jas glowered.

"Now put that cigarette out."

Jas sighed. He stared at the last few millimetres of tobacco, then squeezed the end between thumb and forefinger. The burn on his skin hardly registered as he flicked the filter floorwards.

Another frown. "Not getting off to a very good start are we, Anderson?" Low voice, barely audible over engine rumbles.

Jas flinched. Narrowed eyes met knowing pupils.

Then Brodie turned away and strode back to the front of the bus. "Fisher?"

"Aye..."

Jas rubbed his face with damp palms.

"Gordon?"

"Here..."

Jas ran hands over hair in need of a wash and frowned. Did his reputation precede him, even amongst Hadrian officers?

"Hamilton?"

His reputation as – what? Threat to order? Trouble-maker?

"Hamilton!" Louder.

The change in tone refocused his attention. Eyes swept the half-full bus, then settled on the back of an oblivious step-cut head.

"David Hamilton!"

Jas reached over, tapped a hunched shoulder.

It stiffened under his touch. Earphones ripped from ears. Bouncing to feet housed in giant trainers.

The sound of something falling.

Scared-rabbit eyes darting around.

Jas nodded to where Brodie was frowning again. He reached down, picked up the plastic consol-game,

"David Hamilton?"

"Er, aye – ah mean, here."

"Try to stay awake, Hamilton." Weary sarcasm.

"Aye – yeah, sorry."

The teens sniggered.

Rabbit-eyes scurrying over the floor. The step-cut head raising itself. Rabbit-eyes running to earth in his.

Jas met the scared gaze, held out the console.

The Game-Boy seized by the shaking hands of a very un-game boy. David Hamilton sat down. From the front of the bus:

"MacIntyre?"

"Here..."

Jas watched the step-cut head re-lower itself. Earphones tucked back beneath step-cut hair. Rabbit-eyes once more directed to the small console. He stared at a pink, rabbit ear and wondered vaguely how old the kid was...

The bus slowed. A volley of fists and boots thumped along the side. And voices.

...only vaguely. Through the tinted window, Jas recognised the scowling faces of the SPA picket-line.

He had problems of his own...

A last few thumps on the rear bodywork of the ancient bus. Ahead, large metal gates were parting to admit them.

...problems which were only just begining.

The walls had been re-painted. New carpet. New style...

...new guards.

In the Processing area, Jas moved closer to the man in front. He could smell his own body and those of others around him. The line inched forward. Overhead, whirring.

He looked up.

From the four corners of light grey walls, the red eyes of four cctv cameras blinked back at him.

"Abernethy, Adamson, Fisher and Malcolmson."

Four shuffling shapes broke ranks and alphabetisation.

Jas watched. More procedure: prisoners awaiting trial would be separated off at this stage, remand-wing bound. Transferrees and sentenced men would join one of six Halls.

Behind three more Brodie clones – two with clipboards, one female at a computer terminal – eyes brushed the familiar Hadrian brick-wall insignia. Beneath, one sentence:

Pioneers in Security Solutions. The legend emblazoned wages-delivery vans throughout Scotland

"Morrison, O'Brien, Patterson, Pllu."

Jas focused on one of those pioneers. As another four shapes moved towards a clip-boarded Brodie-clone, he stared at the officer behind the desk. She couldn't possibly be as young or small as she looked.

A gate in the far corner slid noiselessly open.

The Hadrian officer and his four charges walked through.

The gate slide noiselessly shut. New style...

He inhaled.

...old smell. A mixture of generic disinfectant and stale male sweat. He'd interviewed remand prisoners here countless times. The stench of the place stuck to clothes, got into hair, lingered in the mouth and the mind long after the gates closed and the case faded.

Jas frowned. Hadrian could paint the walls, instal computers and oil the gates but they couldn't hide the tenor of Barlinnie. It was foolish to even try.

"Redman, Salmon, Travis..."

A vague buzz in his ears obliterated the final name. Jas watched the three teens and a middle-aged man head off with a Brodie-clone. Eyes flicked over shoulder.

A lowered, step-cut head stared into a Kwik-Save box of meagre possessions.

Jas looked back to the desk. In the corner, a friction-defeating gate was silently sliding open and shut in the wake of the departing fivesome. Brodie peered at the computer terminal with the tiny, grey-clad girl. Peter's Armani bag sat on the desk beside the monitor, Jas cleared his throat. "Scuse me?"

Ms Pepperpot glanced up, glanced away.

Brodie frowned wordlessly.

Jas moved forward. "Ah'm remand – ah should be wi' the..."

"Get back in line, Anderson!"

There was no line to get back into. The rat-faced kid was sidling over towards a grey radiator. Wrists cuffed, Zero-crop lounged against a wall, smoking two-handed.

Jas caught a smile of solidarity. He frowned, eyes noting another two cuffed figures shuffling aimlessly. He registered a white line painted into grey carpeting, walked towards it and away from unwanted camaraderie. "How come ah'm still here?"

His words ignored. Sounds of frantic keyboard tapping. Brodie delivered a slap to the side of the terminal. Ms Pepperpot chewed her lip.

Jas pulled a cigarette from the Bensons packet, stuck it in his mouth. "Crashed oan ye, has it?"

Two lowered heads flicked up. Brodie: "Get back, Anderson!"

Jas almost smiled. Patting biker's jacket pockets, he remembered the lighter was still in the bag. One hand reached across.

The motion registered. "I said back!" Barely concealed panic in the words. "You'll be dealt with in due course."

Overhead, the whirring had stopped. The security gate continued to open and shut, then stuck in the open position. Jas wondered about circuits no longer closed and gates yawning in other parts of the prison.

Pioneers in Security Solutions?

Stepping back from the white line, he wandered over to the lounging skinhead. The rat-faced kid with the box was staring straight ahead, eyes inches from a grey wall. Terror radiated off the boy in waves.

The sight sobered him: somewhere beyond that gate, he'd be dealt with, in more sense than one. Yards away, Brodie thumped the terminal a second time. As if on command, two more Hadrian officers appeared in the gateway, staring blankly at an inch of jammed, visible bars.

Jas watched a huddled conversation around the computer terminal. Movement at his side. He turned.

A cuffed figure with a Zero-crop removed two inches of damp roll-up from between lips, held out the glowing end. A grin.

Jas took in the gesture, then the hard musculature beneath the unzipped Harrington. He was amazed they still made the jackets. Eyes moved downwards to impossibly tight, bleached denims, and the very visible outline at the top of the man's left thigh. Balls tingled. He shook his head, plucked the unlit cigarette from mouth and shoved it back in the packet: he'd have more use for it later anyway.

Shrug. Roll-up back between lips.

Renewed whirring above indicated the system was back on line. As if in sync:

"Hamilton?"

The rat-faced boy flinched beneath padded nylon.

"Get a move on, Hamilton!" The voice of the bus: in command once more.

Jas watched huge-trainered feet bounce across new grey carpet to the waiting grey escort. The boy struggled with the Kwik-Save box, which was seized by a Brodie-clone. Then the sound of the real thing:

"Adair, Anderson, McCann and Miles."

Jas rubbed at one cuffed wrist and followed the skinhead towards another escort.

Steam filled the short leg of the L-shaped shower-room. Jas turned back to the thin, slatted bench. Easing the Bic razor from beneath his curled prick, he peeled off underwear, balling the fabric around the stiff stem.

He fingered the length of plastic, considering options. Following a shower, the medical: internal storage of the razor wasn't a good idea. Jas shoved still-warm underwear into the folds of his combat pants and sat down. Slatted wood dug into skin. Although now cuffless, red rings looped his wrists, stinging reminders.

From the long leg of the L-shaped room, the sound of running water. And low humming.

Jas stood up. He stared at the heap of Harrington and bleached jeans inches from his own clothes.

The other two had showered half-heartedly and rapidly...

Low humming rose into a burst of tuneless singing.

...Zero-crop obviously believed in a thorough wash. At the far end of the L's short leg, a door opened:

"Get a move on, man!"

Jas's eyes moved to the larger, less-Brodie-like figure making its way towards him. Grabbing the threadbare length of grey towel, he walked in the direction of the singing.

"Aw'right, pal?"

Pal: the automatic title, one of an assortment predicated on automatic, meaningless assumptions. Jas nodded wordlessly, braced arms against tiles and let the water do more than its job. Heat seeped into bruised flesh and tensed muscle.

The sounds of soaping and more singing. The smell of coal tar drifted over, erasing the the odour of sweat. Eyes swept the wet floor to another pair of bare, wet feet. Then up thickly haired legs.

The proximity was unavoidable: he'd tried four other faucets before finding one that didn't merely dribble. Raising his head, he let water pour down chest, matting hair. A sour odour rose over the smell of carbolic. Jas rubbed at armpits. Eyes flicked to a curved, built-in soap-holder. Empty.

The out-of-tune singing changed to out-of-tune whistling.

Jas lowered his head, looked left.

Knees bent, skull skimming tiled wall, Zero-Crop ran a block of mushy red over hard white buttocks.

Jas watched the skinhead soap the dark crack between the two solid mounds.

One leg raised itself. Fingers moved down the dark crevice, spreading pinkish suds over small, tight balls.

Jas frowned, moved away and continued his own, soapless wash. He pushed his mind onwards and inwards.

Remand.

Segregated from convicted prisoners.

Safety – of a sort.

Isolation, he knew, would be at the discretion of the governor...

He gripped his prick, hauling back foreskin to rinse beneath.

...Jas wondered vaguely if Hadrian had appointed their own administrator, or if the Scottish Office maintained a presence.

"Want it?" Hoarse voice in this ear.

Jas spun round.

A faded St. Andrew's Cross rippled on a leanly-muscled arm. One large hand gripped a bony knee. Mouthful of water onto the already-swimming floor.

Jas blinked at the seven inches of hardening flesh which swung beneath Zero-Crop's sopping pubic bush. Water ran into his eyes.

"Eh?" Broader grin

He focused on the sallow face.

On the outside...

Those grinning lips stretching wordlessly, his own lips tight around that hardening prick.

Those hair-covered thighs spread and waiting.

Those hard pale arse-cheeks wrenched apart....

...those knuckles white with mounting desire..

A large hand held out a mushy bar of soap. "Afore it fuckin' disintegrates completely!" Watery laugh.

"Thanks." Jas seized the soap and smiled wryly at his own susceptibility. A cluster of curled hairs adhered to the soft, red surface.

The naked man turned back to the faucet. "Gerry – Gerry Adair."

Pink carbolic mushed further between his fingers. He didn't want to know. Jas lathered palms and tried to increase the already yawning distant between them.

"Whit ye in fur?"

Jas soaped pit hair. Gerry's question answered an unspoken enquiry of his own. First-timer: only a novice would ask. In prison, a man made his own reputation, if he had any sense. "Remand." The outside meant nothing...

..inside. Soap slipped from between rigid fingers.

Two hands scooped to retrieve it.

"Me tae – aggravated assault. Fuckin' polis stitched me up..." Gerry got there first, lobbed the bar left.

Jas caught it one-handed. More in common than he'd thought?

"...ah wis oota ma heid, man – too fucked tae assault onywan!" Gerry leant against the wall, one hand scratching at tight balls. "But gimme hauf an oor alone wi' wanna them noo an'..." Threat retreating into a grin.

The thought ricocheted back. Jas stared at water-gleamed stubble. On the outside. Those hands...

...beating the living shite out of him. Gaze moved downwards, glancing to the scratching. Jas tore his eyes away and soaped thighs.

The glance registered.

Jas felt his own body scanned.

Hoarse laugh. "Missin' it awready?"

He continued to wash. If this man knew he was polis – ex or otherwise – he'd never make it to the medical. If this man knew his choice of sleeping-partner?

"Man, ah wis like a fuckin' rock, on that bus!"

The unwarranted, unwanted intimacy rained onto his skin, a less soothing deluge. Jas turned.

Large fingers wrapped around shaft. "Must be the motion, eh?" Head thrown back, eyes upwards. The length slowly stroked. "Whit ah widney give fur a paira open legs right noo!"

Jas looked away, began to rinse. Carbolic receded in the face of raging testosterone. He tried to will himself soft...

..and failed. Face raised to the faucet, water washed the last suds from his glowing body. Somewhere around the kidney area, another unwelcome glow helped refocus his mind.

"Ma lassie'd better no' think aboot gettin' it elsewhere, while ah'm in here!" Suddenly worried.

Where Gerry's lassie intended to slake her desire was the least of his problems. And should be the least of Gerry's. Jas moved out from under the shower-head.

A voice from beyond: "Get a move oan, you two!"

Sudden burst of aggression. "Enjoyin' the show, pal?" A wet, naked shape strutted forward, prick waggled between cocky fingers.

"Shut it, Adair." Weary tolerance

Jas groped for his threadbare scrap of fabric.

The sting of a towel flicked against his arse. Jas grabbed it, spun round.

Stubbly head lowered, then cocked towards the source of the voice. "Watch yersel', pal – these places ur fulla fuckin' poofs an' perverts." Bonding whisper.

Assumptions...

Assumptions...

...the words dissolved what little glue cemented himself and Gerry.

Inside, a single-sex environment.

Inside mirrored outside in the only way it could.

Inside, there was no 'straight', no 'gay'.

Merely 'active' and 'passive'.

'Men', who enjoyed the privileges at the top of prison hierarchy...

...and 'cunts', who were used and abused, in return – if they were lucky – for reflected kudos and protection from their 'man'.

A too-simple over-simplification, governing everything which happened 'inside'.

Jas released the towel, found his own and tied the grey rectangle around his waist.

Ex-polis... poof... pervert..

...one of three attributes was his main problem, at the moment. As he hurriedly dried his bruised body, other bruises formed mentally, in anticipation of injuries yet received.

"Epilepsy or any other form of seizure?"

The Examination Room was old. A wilting begonia drooped forlornly on top of an ancient filing cabinet. "No." Jas returned his attention to the crown of a white-haired head.

The duty GP was older. "Any history of mental illness?"

"No." Jas watched fingers well past retirement age continue to write.

"Any chronic medical condition of which Hadrian Security should be aware?" A slight tremor shivered over the back of a liver-spotted hand.

Jas registered the shake, thought about his own, mainly healed right arm. "No."

"Any special dietary requirements?"

The question made him grin. "Ah'm allergic tae porridge."

The joke unappreciated. The head raised itself, spectacled eyes flicking between the form-in-process and what Jas knew was his chargesheet. "Hepatitis B or C?"

He sobered: Hep-A, yes, but that was years ago. "No."

Spectacled eyes raised further. "Have you been tested for HIV in the past twelve months?"

Jas registered the cursory glance over his naked body. "None o' your business!"

Spectacles removed. "You are here for possession with intent to..."

"Ah'm oan remand..." Jas clenched fists against naked thighs. ".....nothin's been proved!" He scowled in the face of assumptions more professional than Gerry-in-the-shower's.

Sceptical, unspectacled eyes. "Have you been tested for HIV in the past twelve months?" Professional repetition.

A muscle twitched in his calf. Jas inhaled slowly: no point in lying. "Aye."

Happier. "Do you know your result?"

"Negative." He had a standing appointment at the Royal's drop-in clinic.

"Good..." The doctor wrote something on the sheet. "..now, I'm sorry we can no longer offer you any detox treatment, while you are in here, but the way things are at the moment, with the... er, strike..."

"Ah don't dae drugs!" Irritation throbbed in his stomach. "Wanna check between ma toes? My prick?"

Myopic eyes blinked.

Jas took a deep breath. The man had probably heard it all a hundred times before. More protestations would only add to the scepticism. He exhaled slowly.

Spectacles replaced, eyes to a liver-spotted wrist. Then a pair of thin latex gloves eased from a box beside the wilting begonia, snapped on. "Stand on the line, please."

Jas moved to another demarcation more permanent than the one in the induction area.

"Open your mouth."

He complied.

Quivering fingers efficiently explored under tongue, around teeth and up into soft palate.

Jas stared at the ceiling, gagging on talc and rubber.

The fingers removed. "Turn round and spread your buttocks."

Jas thought about the Bic razor at present snuggling in a so far unsearched heap of clothing. He stared at the white line, fingers wrenching arse-cheeks apart.

A pause. "How did you get these bruises?" Fingers on the kidney area.

Jas frowned: it wasn't worth it.

Sigh. "Fighting will not be tolerated in here..." Then another well-greased digit exploring another orifice. "...and no drugs. Hadrian are very strict about that." The digit curled upwards.

Bowels clenched. Mongrel sensations flushed his skin. Jas inhaled sharply. "Ah don't dae drugs!" Finger tips rigid on arse-cheeks.

Sounds of a door opening. Footsteps. Two sets.

The first thing prison took away from you: dignity. Jas scowled.

"Kindly knock in future." Irritated digit removed, gloves pulled off, binned.

Jas straightened up. Blood rushed from his face. He stared into other, younger features.

A blushing Ms Pepperpot looked away from his naked body. Brodie met, held the Armani bag and his stare:

"Finished, doctor?"

Question ignored. "Get dressed er... Anderson."

Jas eyed his heap of clothes.

Ms Pepperpot wandered over to inspect the leaves of the wilting begonia.

Jas scooped up underpants, palming the Bic and hauling jersey over goosefleshed thighs. He slipped the slim section of plastic back beside a now-shrivelled prick and continued to dress.

The medical examination had been cursory – his clothes had never left his sight. Jas struggled into Adidas tee-shirt then combat-trousers.

Pioneer Security Solutions? If he could get a razor past Hadrian, fuck knows what other, more experienced inductees had managed.

Shreds of low conversation drifted over from the Brodie/Doctor huddle:

"There should really be a locum at least on call at all..." Concerned.

"It's in hand..." Placatory.

"You've been saying that for..." Unconvinced.

"It's in hand, doctor." Less placatory.

Sigh. "Like the overcrowding in Remand's in hand?"

Jas paused. Billy McKinley's words reeled back at him: *Two thousand in a prison built fur nine hundred.*

Brodie's response was less certain: "We're doing what we can, doctor."

The responding silence spoke volumes.

Jas turned, picked up Peter's Armani bag. Predictably, the

Bics had vanished, as had the lighter. The cellophane-wrapped underwear and cigarettes were still there. He raised his eyes to where Ms Pepperpot was now relieving the begonia of several withered leaves.

Bespectacled eyes regarded him. Words to Hadrian-grey. "As a former police officer, this prisoner should be segregated for the duration of his remand."

"Don't tell me how to do my job, doctor."

Jas stared at the too-young face. Hadrian had an obligation over and above keeping him here: keeping him alive.

Brodie returned the stare. "Don't worry, Anderson – we've always got room for the likes of you. Come on..." A hand gripped his arm. Wry smile. "There's a cell in Triple-S with your name on it." Joined by Ms Pepperpot, Brodie steered him towards the door.

Triple-S: Strict Suicide Supervision. Better than nothing.

The door opened. Jas walked through. He stared at the back of Brodie's blond head.

Next stop for inductees: the Governor's office.

He continued to walk, inhaling the silent smell of two thousand, unseen men...

...and the sour stench of his own apprehension.

Nine

Ms Pepperpot had departed a while back.

Jas looked at his wrist, then remembered the second thing they took away from you. His watch was in a manila envelope with his name on it, somewhere in the prison safe.

Officer Brodie walked two steps in front.

A bell rang.

He registered the sound. BST. Barlinnie Standard Time.

He was here on remand, not for punishment.

He was here because twelve years on the force counted for nothing.

He was here because drug dealers were the scum of the earth...

...and the courts wanted it seen they believed that.

He followed Brodie along another yellow corridor, past an empty recreation area. Jas glanced at his wrist again, sighed and tried to estimate the time.

Should be late afternoon-ish.

Should be recreation or work duties.

As the slight Hadrian officer waved at another heavy gate leading to another empty corridor, they had the prison to themselves.

No sounds.

No other prisoners.

No other officers.

Just him and Brodie...

...the head of the Bic razor dug into the top of his thigh. Jas remembered their destination: as ex-polis, and therefore high risk, was Triple-S doubling as Isolation? He walked through another gate into a corridor which looked exactly like the first one.

Rows of doors stared at him.

Behind, the gate slid silently shut.

Jas glanced up at the cctv camera perched on a ledge fourteen feet above his head. Its red eye glanced back, then continued its automated sweep of the area.

Officer Brodie quickened his pace and moved in front, heading for the stairs.

Jas stared past the cctv camera and up through the suicide net...

Four floors of B-Block. For some reason, Barlinnie always reminded him of a ship's engine-room. A powerhouse.

...no one stared down. The sound of boots on metal steps told him Brodie was already climbing the stairs. He turned his eyes to the row of locked doors to his left.

Triple-S cells were usually ground level. For obvious reasons.

"Get a move on, Anderson!"

Brodie's attempt at authority drifted down from the first landing.

Jas nudged the Armani bag more securely over his shoulder, and mounted the stairs.

On the second landing, life-signs.

Cursing life-signs.

He paused behind Brodie.

A figure in jeans and denim shirt appeared backwards out of a cell. The figure was holding the end of a single cot. A yard down, neatly stationed against the narrow walkway's yellow-brick wall, a double set of bunks.

So much for single cells. So much for Triple-S.

The figure cursed again, moved back into the cell.

Brodie. Impatient. "Come on – get a move on..."

The man obviously had a thing about speed. Jas leant against the yellow brick wall.

More cursing. Different voice. The figure clad in denim re-emerged, with more of the cot this time. And another figure on the end. Carefully, they manoeuvred the bed out of the cell and along past where Jas stood.

One then two sets of eyes on him, then the Armani shoulder-bag.

He met the gaze and held it.

Brodie ruined the moment. "We've not got all day, lads!"

Jas looked away, turning to the metal railing which surrounded the walkway. He stared down past yards of yellow brick wall...

...scraping of metal on metal behind told him the double bunk was on its way into the cell. The noise echoed around the otherwise silent block.

"Straighten up there, Anderson!"

His hands tightened on the smooth metal bar. Jas gazed around at the appearance of order and control. Maybe Hadrian were doing a good job: he'd never seen a quieter prison.

More scrapings. More curses.

"I said, straighten up!" The voice was louder, partly for the benefit of the two figures in denim. Then words for his ears only. "I've got your number, Anderson. Don't push it..."

Jas spun round. Any number Brodie had was way out of date, long since disconnected. He stared into a pink youthful face desperately trying to maintain its power position. He shrugged and straightened up, eyes beyond.

The men in denim reappeared from the cell, looked expectantly at Brodie's back.

Jas stared over a grey-clad shoulder.

Two sets of pupils, more curious than hostile.

Front was all. Jas stared back.

One of the denimed figures looked away. The other winked.

As he was pushed past the two men into the cell, Jas registered the winker.

Mid-forties. Grey, receding hair. Ruddy face. Small grey beard. Brodie was talking at him. Jas continued to hold the man's stare over a uniformed shoulder.

Another wink.

Another still.

A voice. "C'mon, Twitchy..."

The ruddy face reddened further, then turned.

Footsteps. Away from the cell. Jas threw the Armani shoulder-bag on the lower of two bunks and returned his attention to Brodie. "Ah want tae make a phone call."

"No phone calls for the first two weeks."

Jas stared. "Whit?"

Brodie produced a small booklet from the pocket of the grey blouson. "No phone calls in or out for the first two weeks. No incoming or outgoing mail for a similar period..." He thrust the booklet at Jas. "...no visitors for the first month. Only family and your legal advisor may visit. If you have family, please ask them to put in a request for a visitor's warrant to the Secretary of State for Scotland at least four weeks in advance, in order that Hadrian can process it..."

Jas looked at the booklet, then took it.

"...please read the rules, Anderson. Make life easier for yourself and try to stick to them..." Brodie turned towards the door.

"Oi!" The booklet quivered between his fingers. Jas stared at the back of a neatly cut head: legal visits were a right, at any time. "Ma trial's in six weeks – ah need tae talk tae ma solicitor now, no' in a fortnight's time! Accordin' tae the rules ah..."

"...new rules, Anderson." Turning. Face impassive. "...this is a strike situation. The old rules don't apply." Brodie seized what he thought was the initiative. "Don't make trouble, Anderson. Keep your nose clean and you'll do okay..."

Jas frowned. "Ah should be segregated." He nodded to the double-bunk, leant against it.

"Just read the rules and..."

"Ah want a single cell an' ah want tae see the governor."

"I'll make an appointment for you..." Said without conviction.

"An interview wi' the governor's standard induction procedure – even you ken that..." Jas levered himself off the bunks. "... ah want tae see him now!"

Brodie took a step closer. "What you want doesn't count for much, Anderson. Hadrian..."

"Who's in charge, here?" Something was making sense.

"Centre Control, in Livingston, are responsible for..."

"No one, right?" Jas scowled.

"Hadrian's structure dictates..."

"Aw' forget it!" Jas sat down. No governor on the premises –

it made a kind of sense: had the Scottish Office employee refused to work with Hadrian, or was it cheaper to control from an anonymous building on an industrial estate in Livingston?

"Sir."

Jas looked up.

"Sir!" Brodie was struggling.

Jas tried not to savour the man's discomfort. He feigned ignorance.

Brodie cleared his throat. "Please address me as sir or Officer Brodie!"

Jas grinned, despite himself. "Okay – Officer Brodie!" He watched the man wrap himself in the title.

It was just a title. The real power lay elsewhere. Jas eyed the keys which dangled from the man's belt.

The uniform.

The words.

The trappings...

Jas took in the face.

The face of Hadrian Security Solutions.

A face regulations said he should respect...

...a face tax-payers should trust with their rejects.

Brodie avoided his gaze.

Strike one.

He wouldn't trust this man to run an egg-and-spoon race, let alone a penal institution. Jas scowled, stared at the rule book. Hadrian were a joke...

He waited for the punch-line, listening to the silence in an institution where noise was the norm. Two thousand men in a prison built to hold nine hundred.

Maybe there wasn't a punch-line.

Maybe this wasn't a joke.

"Let me give you some advice, Anderson."

Jas looked up, flicking the pages of the rulebook with one thumb.

Brodie was leaning in the doorway, back in command. "I don't know what you're used to, but things work differently, in here..."

Jas watched the face closely.

"...we don't want trouble. You don't want trouble. We're here to see there is no trouble..."

We?

Jas listened to the silence, then remembered Ms Pepperpot

and a handful of other grey-clad figures: no apparent chain-of-command. No apparent experience. A bunch of kids with pcs and cctv-cameras running the Bar-L like it was Crims-R-Us. New management structures. New rule books. New uniforms.

"...help us to help you..."

Jas blinked. He wondered whether a day or a weekend's training course had qualified him to think he could do this job. "Okay, Officer Brodie."

"Good!" Pale hands rubbing each other. Brodie looked like a scout master after a successful jamboree. How secure were the guy-ropes?

But it wasn't his problem.

His problem was the next six weeks and how to get through them. Jas watched Officer Brodie walk from the cell. The door swung shut. Sounds of locking. Bootsteps trailed along the walkway. When he could no longer hear them, he opened the Armani shoulder-bag and removed a packet of cigarettes.

No lighter.

He sat down on the bottom bunk and took in his environment.

Twelve feet by eight. The space was barely big enough for one man, never mind two. The bunk on which he sat lined one, unpainted brick wall. Opposite, more unpainted brick.

No yellow.

Jas looked towards the small window which punctured the bricks facing the door. His eyes slid down the wall to the aluminium piss-pot under the barred space, then did another tour of the cell.

Barlinnie was short-stay, low security...

...in theory.

Barlinnie had a remand wing, reserved for remand prisoners...

...in theory.

This was Triple S...

...in theory.

Reality, he had a feeling, was something else.

Despite the single bunk he'd seen removed, minutes earlier, this cell seemed unoccupied...

...no magazines, no posters, no radio, no sign this room was inhabited by a living creature.

Where were the porno pics, the desperate indications that another sex existed?

He stuck the unlit cigarette between his lips, leant back and stared at the wall behind him.

A sign.

One sign.

Jas moved closer to the small Polaroid, blu-tacked to bare brick.

A woman. A man. Two children. Boy and girl. On grass. Smiling, the boy held a football. The man held Jas's attention.

Tall. Neatly-cut dark hair. Lop-sided grin. One hand obscured behind the woman's back. The other resting on top of the boy's head...

He scrutinised more closely.

...late twenties... relaxed-looking... an ordinary guy...

...a happy, family group.

He'd been in enough prisons, in a professional capacity, to know memories and connections were hoarded and savoured. Regardless of the pain they caused, or the length of the sentence, those on the outside were necessary to give inside a meaning.

His eyes flicked to the back of the door.

Clothes.

A pair of jeans. A denim shirt. Spare regulation uniform.

Jas stood up. The unlit cigarette bobbed between his lips. He turned and leaned against the opposite wall.

Six weeks.

The small, grey room shrank around him. The unlit cigarette's filter was damp and soggy. He wished he'd asked Scoutmaster Brodie for two sticks to rub together.

Returning to the bunk, Jas stretched out on bare springs and contemplated what he knew about his cell-mate...

Male.

Two kids.

Inside.

...in effect, nothing. He removed the useless cigarette from his mouth, crumpled it in his fist.

A bell rang.

Nothing happened.

Jas stared at the ceiling and waited til something did.

A Hadrian officer – not Brodie – arrived wordlessly with bedding, then a tray of food.

Jas ate something mushy in silence, then unrolled two soiled mattresses the same way.

The officer left.

Jas pissed into an aluminium bucket, listening to the sounds of urine splatter against metal. He lay on his bunk. He walked to the small window. He walked back to the bunk. He walked to the small window. He walked back to the bunk, sat down and wrapped himself in a hard, fuzzy-grey blanket and tried to sleep.

He'd almost managed it when the scraping of keys punctured the silence. Jas opened his eyes, head craning up from the lower bunk.

"Whit the...?" Low antagonism.

"New cell-mate for you."

"Get him oota here!" Lower.

Jas stayed where he was: there was little enough room in the tiny space. He stared up at the broad man, whose head was flicking between the officer and the double-bunk.

An attempt at placating. "Take it easy, McStay. Ah..."

"Get him oot! Now!" Barely audible.

Warning, not placating any more. "Shut it, McStay, or ah'll..."

"Ye'll – whit?" Taunting. "Lock me up?" Finger jabbed into a Hadrian-grey chest.

Jas took in a broad forearm and bitten-down nail, trying to match the hulking form with a Polaroid image.

One other known fact about his cell-mate. This was Triple-S: the man was either high suicide risk or, like himself, at risk from other quarters.

The officer tried a laugh. "Funny guy!" It didn't come off.

His eyes travelled up the body to the face.

An angry face. "Funny, am ah?" No lop-sided grin. "Well, let's see how amusin' ye find this!" Head lowered, the man charged towards a grey-uniformed figure...

"Get used to it, McStay!"

...who neatly avoided the bull-run and stepped out onto the walkway.

The cell door banged, then locked shut.

Jas stared up at the face. Where McStay's body was larger, bulkier than his alter-photo-ego, the features were still angular, well-chiselled. Dark eyes narrowed, looked down at him.

He could hear the man's breathing, almost feel the breath on his face.

McStay moved back a little.

Jas swung legs onto the floor, grabbed a packet of cigarettes and threw them towards broad hands.

McStay caught the gold rectangle, fist tightening.

"Ah'll get them tae move me tae the penthouse suit the morra." Jas examined the face for an area of common ground. He smiled at the large mouth, at present set in a hard line...

...where it remained. The pack of cigarettes crumpled and thrown against the opposite wall. Hard.

Jas lowered his head, ducked out from under the bunk and stood up.

The space was too small. He was closer to this man than he wanted to be.

McStay was at least 6'2", pushing two-fifty pounds. Less than an inch between them in height, slightly more in distance.

He groped for an approach: humour had failed, anything more serious was inappropriate. Jas stared at the crumpled packet of cigarettes. "Can ah cadge a light aff ye?" He waited for an answer to his question.

And waited. He focused on the five o'clock shadow which dusted the square chin and wondered how accurate it was.

McStay turned his face towards the small, barred window. Or the piss-pot. It was hard to tell which.

Jas followed the gaze. He could smell the man – an unfamiliar combination of carbolic soap and heated vegetable oil. He could hear his own breathing now, slow and steady where McStay's lungs seemed to be struggling to breathe at all.

Something else was washing off the man, in great rolling waves. Jas stared at a small vein which pulsed erratically on McStay's neck.

Then a sigh.

Jas tried to interpret the sound. Resignation? Annoyance? Frustration? He addressed the man's back. "The name's Anderson – Jas Anderson." He considered another off-the-cuff joke, but had a feeling McStay wasn't the laughing type. He waited for the introduction to be returned...

His cell-mate turned. "Stay oota ma face, pal, just..." McStay pushed past him and threw himself onto the top bunk. "...stay oota ma face!"

...three silent hours later, at lights-out, he'd had all the introduction he was going to get.

Ten

He woke up to the sound of his cell-mate pissing.

Eyelids sprang open. Semi-darkness. Jas pulled the stiff, damp-smelling blanket more tightly around his fully-clothed body and stared.

Legs.

Bare legs.

Liquid splattered against aluminium.

He eased himself up on one elbow. The tail of McStay's denim shirt hung down over hairy thighs. Jas blinked. Despite the cold in the cell, his clothes stuck to him like a semi-sloughed skin but felt cleaner than the bedding looked.

The pissing stopped. The legs moved closer to the bucket, then turned.

Jas closed his eyes. Damp air was warming with the scent of fresh urine. A bell rang. Jaundiced light flooded his eyelids.

"Ah, fuck!" McStay's voice was thick with sleep and irritation.

Jas listened to the sounds of dressing, waiting for the springs of the bunk above to creak.

The cell was small enough.

He unwrapped himself from the blanket and stretched. The bruises around his kidneys throbbed a little, but nothing major. He frowned, unhooking toes from beneath the metal rail at the bottom of the bed. His feet had hung over the bottom of the cot all night. Whoever manufactured the frames evidently had 5' 7" slender builds in mind. Jas rubbed his face, running a hand over his bristling chin. His mind returned to the Bic razor still nestling at his groin.

A second bell.

He listened beyond its echoes for evidence of doors unlocking.

The bunk above creaked.

Jas opened his eyes.

A pair of bony ankles were attempting to cram themselves into work-boots, above his head.

He swung legs over the edge of the cot and stood up.

Harsh fluorescent lighting did nothing to improve the accommodation. Limbs stiff and tense, Jas glanced at his cell-mate's lowered head as the man laced up boots.

Dark, tangled hair tied back in a pony-tail. Last night's five o'clock shadow etched the jaw-line like a sketcher's smudge.

Jas cleared dawn sludge from his throat. Good morning was inappropriate.

The head snapped up. "Whit you lookin' at?" Narrowed eyes nailed him, then returned to the laces.

Jas sighed. He crouched, reaching under the lower bunk for his own boots.

Keys scraping.

The door ricocheted against his shoulder as it swung inwards. He was still registering the shudder in his arm as a pair of booted feet landed beside him. Then sloshing sounds. Crouching, Jas moved back against the bunks.

McStay grabbed the piss-pot and a towel which had appeared from somewhere. Large feet stepped over him.

"You too, Anderson!" Something crisp and rough hit his head.

Jas got up, grabbed the grey towel and a pair of Peter's cellophane-wrapped underwear, moved out onto the landing.

He had no idea what time it was, but BST told him he was about to meet his fellow inmates.

He shuffled along the walkway, behind a figure dressed in denim and in front of a figure dressed the same. Three in front, he recognised the back of his cell-mate's head.

Every second man held a piss-pot.

On the walkway opposite, a mirror-image line of denimed men shuffled in sync. Below, the landings and stairs teamed with a sea of blue, punctuated by the occasional Hadrian-identified grey serge.

Dry men and full piss-pots moving west.

Damp men with empty piss-pots moving east.

Jas slung the stiff, grey towel over one shoulder. He scanned the lines for a break in the denim, for other remand prisoners...

...and spotted one. T-shirt, bleached jeans. No Harrington. Large hands hugging goose-bumped, wiry arms and blotting out the St Andrew's cross tattoo. Gerry from the showers was laughing and joking with the denimed men around him, zero-crop bobbing cockily.

He frowned, eyes moving away to...

...on the other side of the walkway, at the far end of the block, a smaller figure. Still wearing the padded, Puffa-jacket. And earphones.

He walked on, watching the rodent-faced boy. The only sound was the thump of boots on metal. The boy kept his head down, ignoring all glances.

Jas did likewise.

Steam from the shower block leaked out into the corridor. He stared through a haze of condensation and a mist of murmured conversation.

In front, men were starting to undress. Over the low hum of words, water and the occasional shout from an officer.

The Bic razor dug into his thigh. Jas ran a hand over his chin. He felt like using it, but knew one would be provided. He watched a pale, pockmarked back appear from under the denim shirt in front. He'd lost track of Gerry and the rodent-faced boy from the bus.

The line inched forward.

Jas peered into a tiled area, identical to the one in which he'd showered yesterday. He thought vaguely of a St Andrew's cross and the sharing of a slim bar of carbolic soap.

Then killed the thought.

Shower time had other functions. Non-washing functions. Jas pulled off the Adidas T-shirt and did what he was good at: he watched. And he waited.

In front, man after man emptied his piss-pot, rinsed it then moved on.

Another thing they took away from you: privacy.

By the time the line reached a long wooden bench, most men were naked. Jas began to unbutton combat pants. The line was remarkable well-behaved. A few were still talking in low voices.

Most stood silently, anonymous cogs in the machine.

Anonymity was the desired state. Jas glanced behind.

Half a dozen men. And one grey, Hadrian uniform, who closed and locked the door from the outside.

He turned his attention back to the shower faucets and those washing beneath them.

Ages spanned late teens to early sixties. Mainly white. Mainly late-teens to mid-twenties. Jas thought about statistics: the main perpetrators of crime were ages 17 to 26. As were the main victims.

The sound of drumming water filled his ears. He filtered out the noise of twenty shower-faucets.

The very old knew the ropes: the very young were too scared to even acknowledge ropes existed.

Distilled to its essentials, only two things mattered in Bar-L life.

Getting through it – and getting out.

Beyond the line of now-showering bodies, at the far end of the shower-block, two Hadrian officers were chatting, backs to the queue. A huddle of dripping men were drying themselves or dressing. An elbow in his ribs:

"Get a move on, pal."

Jas moved towards the vacant faucet without turning. He pulled off the rest of his clothes, slipping the Bic into the pocket of the combat pants. He looked for a dry spot on the swimming floor, then gave up and stepped into the shower.

At least the water was warm. He closed his eyes, tilting his face towards the faucet.

"Anderson!"

He flinched. Eyes shot open. He looked for the grey Hadrian uniform.

Both officers had left the block.

Jas glanced around.

No one glanced back.

He continued to wash. Something slimy stuck to the soles of his feet.

At least the water was clean. He scooped up the slimy remnants of a bar of carbolic from the floor and began to soap his body. The bruising on his stomach had faded to an insipid yellow. Hands skimmed the area, reaching down to groin.

"Jas Anderson!"

He spat a mouthful of water and turned.

A man stood a yard away, arms folded. Clothed and staring.

Eyes flicked to the other faucets.

Thorough, heads-down ablutions were taking place in each. At the far end, two other men stood, watching. They walked towards his facet.

Jas stared at his starer.

5' 10"-ish. Shoulder-length hair. Full beard, enhancing probably twenty-odd years. Prison denims hung on a coat-hanger of a body...

...a long-stayer. Jas watched the two other men join the first. Water ran into his eyes. He blinked it away, stepped forward.

Coat-hanger grinned at his two companions, then looked back at Jas. "Got a message fur you!" The voice was almost friendly.

He looked down at three sets of booted feet, one of which was standing on his towel and clothes, and knew better than to trust an almost. "So gimme the message!"

"Neil sez hello –" Grin. "...an' he'll seeya later... polis!" With a mock bow, Coat-hanger laughed then walked away, messages delivered. His two companions grinned, then trailed after their leader.

Jas followed them with his eyes, water cooling on colder skin.

No threat.

Nothing you could put a finger on.

Nothing that couldn't have been said in front of an officer...

...or a crowd of officers.

A shiver swept his naked body. The shower block was emptying, apart from a drying straggler or two.

They could have had him then and there...

Jas moved out of the shower, picked up a boot-printed towel and tried to dry himself.

...but that would have been too easy.

The visit had delivered two messages: one to Jas, and another to the rest of the prison.

He picked up damp clothes and moved to the other end of the shower area.

Ex-polis.

Ex-polis and disliked by Neil Johnstone, who evidently had acquired clout with the years.

Jas dragged a pair of too-tight Calvins over wet thighs. He thought briefly of Peter and almost smiled.

The smell of over-cooked food churned his stomach.

As he held out his breakfast tray, a man in kitchen whites dumped a portion of beans on top of two greasy rashers of bacon. Then a grinning mouthful of phlegm.

Jas stared at the smear of greenish mucus: the Bar-L grapevine was as efficient as ever. He moved on. As he filled his coffee cup at the urn, his cell-mate's eyes flicked from beyond the serving hatch, then flicked away.

He turned to the dining-hall and searched for a vacant place.

Three then four empty seats drawn into the closest tables.

On the periphery, one Hadrian uniform strode up and down, a solitary guard over four hundred men: seeing everything and taking in nothing.

Jas walked on, drinking black instant coffee as he walked. Every head turned away. Every spare seat was studiously pulled in. He scowled.

"Mr Anderson?" Questioning half-whisper.

The tray shook in his grip. Jas walked on.

"Mr Anderson!" Insistent.

He turned to the direction of the voice.

Head and shoulders above the seated masses, a stocky, bald man with the familiar full beard of the long-stay prisoner who had better things to do with a razor. Unfamiliar smile. Beckoning.

Jas shrugged, weaving his way over to the figure.

This table was half-empty.

The bald man pointed to one of the vacant chairs.

Jas eyed the face. More a type than a face. The broken veins of a heavy drinker tracked cheeks like B roads.

"Ah thought it wis you." An edge of urgency. "Sit doon, eh?"

Jas sat.

The balding man resumed eating. "Whit you doin' here?" Said between munches.

Jas gripped the coffee cup. The question sounded strangely casual...

...like meeting a vague acquaintance, on holiday. He sat his cup down on the table. "Takin' a rest cure!"

Choking laugh. "Ach, Mr Anderson – that sense of humour of yours!"

Jas drained his coffee cup.

The choking subsided into a cough. Then subsided into seriousness. "Ye don't remember me, dae ye?" Hurt.

Jas stared. "Ten oota ten, pal! Gimme a clue."

The offended face smiled. "1989. Easterhoose Polis station."

Years ago. Jas blinked, then shook his head. He'd processed hundreds in his three years with E division: why did they always expect their face to remain with you? "Bigger clue, pal!"

Small, yellowed fingers extended a packet of cigarettes.

Jas accepted.

Yellow fingers lit it, then his own. "Disney matter, ah suppose..."

Jas stared at the face. It did. This man obviously remembered him, and he was down far enough already, in the information stakes. He tried to think, waited for a bell to ring. The nicotine helped. Drawing the smoke into his lungs, he smiled. "Telephone, right?"

Coughing laugh. "Ye dae remember!"

Jas re-examined A. Graham Bell. In for petty theft, handling on top of breach of the peace. A drunk who'd made the mistake of throwing up over his arresting officers. A drunk who'd narrowly avoided a beating. Jas remembered his first realisation that 'enforcing the law' was a phrase with many meanings.

"You saved ma bacon, Mr Anderson – the only polis tae ever dae that. Ah still owe ye."

Jas frowned. It was a debt he may need to call in.

Telly continued to talk. "Ah kept tabs oan ye, Mr. Anderson – knew ye were a good'un, even back then..."

Jas looked up from the table. Three sets of eyes stared at him. Eyes bordering on friendly.

"...ah followed the court case, afore they took away ma library priviledges. Grassin' up another polis canny have bin easy..."

One of the easiest things he'd ever done. Jas rubbed his face. The consequences of the action were another matter.

"...there canny be wan rule fur them, an' another fur us – right, Mr Anderson?"

Jas felt himself wilting under the weight of the spontaneous tribute to his moral righteousness. "Right, Telly." He flicked cigarette ash onto the pile of snot. "Now tell me aboot the rules in here!"

The ruddy face stared at him, paling beneath the broken veins. "Only wan rule, noo that lot ur in charge..." Puffy eyes darted to an oblivious grey uniform and back to Jas. "...keep yer heid doon, Mr Anderson, an'..."

"Cut the chat, lads!"

Jas looked up.

The grey uniform stared down at him.

Jas frowned. "Ah want tae see the governor!"

Impassive face. "Your request will be passed on and..."

"Ah wiz telt that last night! Ah need tae see whoever's in charge – an' ah want a single cell."

"Your request will be passed on! Now eat!"

Jas stared at his ruined food. "Ah'm no' hungry." His eyes flicked back to the impassive face. The lump of snot was obvious.

So was the silence that now surrounded their exchange.

The officer shrugged. "Suit yourself! Now, keep the chat down." He strolled away.

Jas stared after him. Tugging on his arm:

"Lea' it, Mr Anderson. Ye'll get no sense oota that lot." The voice lower.

Jas turned.

Telly took a deep breath. "When's yer trial?"

"December 4th." That was the least of his worries.

Telly worried for him. "Things ur bad in here, Mr Anderson."

Jas laughed. "Tell me something ah don't know!"

"There's a book sez ye'll no' last the week."

Jas sobered. Odds on, it was a distinct possibility.

A sigh. "The things some people'll bet oan..."

Jas thought of the showers: Coat-hanger and co. had opportunity and means. Their motive had been something other than physical violence.

"...relieves the boredom, what wi' twenty-two hour lock-up an'..."

Jas stared.

Telly elaborated. "Cos of the strike. Nae reccy, nae exercise, nae visits, nae further education classes – an' ah wiz daein' that well wi' ma conversational Italian!" Disappointment fading into a cough. "They goat ye in Isolation?"

Jas shook his head.

Surprise. "Who're ye sharin' wi'?"

"Some clown wi' a ponytail an' an attitude problem – McStay?"

The ruddy face stared at him.

He clarified. "Works in the kitchen. Whit's he in fur?"

"Why ye wanna ken that, Mr Anderson?"

Jas stubbed out his cigarette on the pile of phlegm. "Cos ah'm in Triple-S wi' him an' ah need tae ken whit ah'm dealin' wi'!"

Small hands covered the ruddy face, obliterating a yawn. "McStay's no' a bad guy, Mr Anderson..."

Jas stared at wrinkled knuckles. A voice from the other side of the table:

"...mair o' a danger tae himsel' than onywan else, far as ah kin see."

A bell rang.

"He in Triple-S fur the usual reasons?" The scraping of hundred of chair legs almost drowned his words. The more he knew about his cell-mate, the better things would be for both of them.

"McStay jumped a coupla poofs in Strathclyde Park, Mr Anderson – that's how come he's in here. Then tried tae aff himsel'." Uncomprehending head-shake.

"File out!"

Telly stood up, as did the other three.

A gay-basher: out of all the cells in all the world, he had to...

...Jas continued to sit until small, surprisingly strong fingers hauled him upright and pushed him towards the already forming line of men:

"Ye got onythin' tae trade wi', Mr Anderson?" Eager.

Jas turned his mind to the cigarettes, then the Bic razor, now more precious than anything Telly could offer. Then he thought about the one friendly face he'd encountered so far, and the need to keep it that way. As they walked from the canteen, he leant forward and aimed for a red ear. "Maybe."

Telly's head moved slightly. "Ah'll seeya later – git ye sorted oot."

Eleven

Doing time.

Jas sat on the bottom bunk, staring at three walls and a metal door. For the first time, the phrase sank in.

Doing time.

Doing a stretch...

...struggling with seconds, working with minutes which elongated and refused to turn into hours. The only accurate gauge was night and day – and perhaps the bells, which seemed to be still programmed to mark the start and finish of activities no longer permitted.

He stared at the door. There had been a brief period – he had no idea how long – when it was open, following his return after breakfast. Then a grey arm had stretched in, fingers clutching keys. The door had been locked ever since. He turned his head and stared at the wall opposite.

Twenty-twohours a day.

Twenty-two hours doing nothing.

Correction – doing time.

'On Remand' ceased to have any meaning, apart from the

dubious privilege of wearing his own clothes and standing out as such.

He lay back on the bunk, staring at the underside of the bed above. Activities like building scale models of the *Cutty Sark* from spent matches suddenly made sense. Jas focused on the pattern of springs, at the sections of mattress which bulged down between metal coils. He tried to immerse himself in the design, see beyond the surface into the distance. Unblinking eyes bored up at the bed-springs, then began to water.

Jas frowned. Maybe he should have paid more attention, when the physio-consultant at the Royal had suggested yoga. Somewhere transcendental to retreat to would be welcome...

He stretched up his right arm, tracing the outline of one of the metal spirals with a forefinger.

...but the Bar-L was all too real, all too concrete. Meditation was an escape he couldn't attempt...

The rounded edge of the bed-spring dug into the soft pad of his finger.

...couldn't risk the damage which might be done to his body when his mind was otherwise engaged. He reached up with the other hand, curling eight digits around eight metal ellipses. Gripping tightly, he relaxed the muscles in his arms.

Then tensed.

And pulled.

A sharp crack. He paused, relaxed, then tensed again.

No sound.

He did ten pull-ups. The cot above began groaning before he did. Jas released the springs and ducked out from beneath the bunk.

The small window was set high in the wall opposite the door.

He gripped the bars, pulled himself up. In his right biceps, a tremor. Jas glimpsed the roofs of a row of houses, before fingers cramped and he was forced to let go.

Back on terra firma, he rubbed his arms and waited for his heart to slow.

Seeing the outside was worse than imagining it. At least in the realms of imagination, there was distance.

In reality, Riddrie was less than five hundred yards away. Barlinnie wasn't the Shotts: no new, modern prison set appropriately in the middle of nowhere.

The Bar-L was a grim, Victorian reality, yards from normality.

He sank to a crouch. An odour drifted into his nostrils. Jas glanced at the newly washed and as-yet-unused piss-pot, and moved away.

Reality pressed in. And reality had to be dealt with. Jas eased himself to his feet, stripped off the Adidas T-shirt and began to exercise.

A bell rang.

He completed one hundred press-ups, flipped onto his back and rested for ten breaths. He breathed out for longer than he breathed in, slowing his heart rate.

Sit-ups. He moved back, hooking boots under the rail of the lower bunk. Forehead blistered with sweat, after forty.

After sixty, the concrete beneath his back was both warm and wet.

After one hundred, he could taste sour, black, instant coffee. Jas unhooked his feet and stared at the ceiling. Pounding in his ears, which slowly subsided as he watched a spider tramp its way around the fluorescent light's blackened sparker.

The sour coffee taste was burning his throat. No way to put out the fire. Suddenly, running water had become a luxury.

Jas rubbed his face and scowled. Last he'd heard, there had been plans to install plumbing in all Barlinnie's cells...

..and that was probably the last anyone had heard of it. Stomach muscles throbbed as he rolled on his side.

No cell sanitation.

No running water.

No telephone calls.

No letters.

No visits...

He levered himself up onto his left elbow.

...no basic human rights. Jas tried to smile.

No big deal.

But it was, and he knew it.

The first thud made him jump.

Jas stared at the heavy metal door. From outside:

"Room service!" Low laughter.

The second thud made him angry:

"Settlin' in, polis?" Louder laughter. The door hatch opened.

Jas stared at the grinning face which appeared and tried not to rise to the bait.

"Need onythin'?" Two more thuds...

...then a volley.

Jas clenched his fists. The cell shrank around him.

"Change yer bed, polis? Change yer..." Guffaws. "...face?"

He bit back a retort. Twelve years in Strathclyde police and thirty-five as a gay man had taught him threats hurt but didn't mark.

Boots marked.

Knives marked...

...he slipped a hand into the pocket of the combat pants and fingered the disposable razor.

"No' gonny open yer door, polis?"

The thudding had become rhythmic, beating in sync with his heart. Jas frowned. Where the fuck were Hadrian? Twenty-two hour lock-up usually extended to all prisoners. He watched heavy metal shudder under the impact of at least four sets of shoulders.

The grinning face disappeared from the hatch-space.

Then silence. Then:

"Well, we'll jist huv tae use oor pass key!"

The words turned his blood to ice-water.

Instinct kicked in. He moved towards the door, fingers tight around the Bic razor.

Metal scraping...

Adrenalin careered around his body.

...a bell rang...

...and the door heaved inwards.

Jas stared at five men.

Men he didn't know, had never seen before...

...but who knew him as one thing only. Three pushed past him, the other two blocking the doorway. One held a crudely-fashioned sliver of metal. "An' how ye findin' the accommodation, polis?"

Jas frowned. "Ah'm no' polis..." A laugh behind.

"...no' noo, maybe, but wance polis always polis – eh, boys?"

"An' ah don't want ony trouble." He moved to the side wall, eyes flicking between the doorway and the three men at present rifling through the Armani bag. "Get oota ma cell!"

Chuckles. "Ye're no very hospitable, ur ye?"

"Get oot!" He knew it was a test. He knew five against one was no competition.

Shrug. "Jist goin'..."

He focused on the denimed figure doing most of the talking. Late twenties. Shoulder-length red hair. Skinny – no presence. No beard.

Long-termers were more settled, less antagonistic. New boys had something to prove. To other new boys.

"...but we'll be back." Wink.

A finger jabbed at his chest:

"...an' we'll expect a friendlier welcome."

Jas noticed three packets of Peter's Bensons slipped into denim pockets. He let them go. "Tell me when ye're comin' an' ah'll bake a fuckin' cake!"

More laughter – some of it genuine-sounding.

The skinny red-head pulled the door behind him, then paused: "Have a nice day, noo."

Then slamming. And the sound of makeshift key scraping.

Sweat trickled from his pits, tracking a rapidly cooling trail down his sides. Grabbing a damp-smelling blanket, he pulled the fabric around himself and sat down on the lower bunk.

Some things you never got used to...

Adrenalin slowly receeded.

...like fear, and what it did to your body.

A couple of bells later, more scraping.

He unwrapped himself from the blanket and stood up, well back from the door...

...which swung gently inwards.

Jas looked at Telly.

Telly looked back, then placed the tray of food on the bottom bunk.

Jas peered beyond, out onto the walkway. Nothing. No one.

"Settlin' in, Mr Anderson?"

Jas looked from the walkway to the food, then at Telly: action replay?

Offended. "Prepared it masel', Mr Anderson. Ye can eat it."

Jas remained where he was. Suspicion was a dangerous friend to lose.

Telly poked his head out into the corridor, looked both ways, then slowly shut the door. The ruddy face regarded his. Deft fingers unbuttoning the denim shirt.

Jas tensed.

"Okay, Mr Anderson..." Beneath the work shirt, fingers

unfastening a large bag, suspended from neck. "...whit ye got tae trade?"

Jas laughed. "Telly, don't do that!"

Confusion, then a shrug.

Jas lifted a fish-cake from the food tray and began to chew. "Ah've goat fags – that's aboot it." He wondered which part of a fish was the cake.

Telly eyed the heavy leather biker's jacket, at present draped across the pillow of the lower cot. "Whit aboot that?"

Jas shook his head.

"Sure?"

Jas repeated the gesture.

Grin. "Okay – it's Supermarket Sweep time!" The contents of the bag emptied onto the mattress.

Jas regarded the cache. Four sample-size bottles of cologne, complimentary books of matches, a variety of underwear, a toothbrush, a trial-size Head and Shoulders, a small tub of petroleum jelly and numerous knotted condoms containing smaller, cellophane-wrapped packages. His throat burned. "Got ony water?"

Telly shook his head. "Naw, but ah kin get ye an empty bottle. Fill it up at slop-oot."

Jas pulled the toothbrush, two books of matches and a pair of red briefs towards him. "How much fur this lot?" He stared at the broken veins as Telly's brain began to work. A pause. Then:

"Forty."

Jas leant down, scooped the Armani bag from under his bunk. "It's Bensons..." He pulled two gold packets from the larger carton, then rummaged. "..an' ah'll trade these..." He pushed two pairs of cellophane-wrapped Calvins towards Telly. "..if those..." He pointed to the red briefs. "...ur a bigger size."

Liver-spotted fingers seized the underwear, turning them over, examining the label. "New?"

"Of course they're..." He stared at the red briefs, then plucked them from the bunk and searched for the waist size.

L.

"Fur new drawers an' the carrier-bag ah'll throw in a quarter gram o' whitever gets ye through the night, Mr. Anderson!"

Jas stared at the condomed packages. "No thanks. But ah'll huv the other knickers."

They exchanged underwear. Telly seemed pleased with his part of the deal. Jas smiled. "Ye missed yer vocation, shouldda gone intae retail!"

Smile returned. "Ony orders, Mr Andreson? Ah kin get ma hauns on maist stuff." The bizarre Tupperware party continued.

Jas shook his head.

"Take the smack, Mr Anderson – trade it oan, if ye dinny want it yersel'."

Jas scowled. "Thanks but no thanks." Bad enough he was on remand for possession: caught with heroin in here would only add to the prosecution's case.

Sigh. "Ah well, you ken best, Mr. Anderson. Noo..." Rummaging in trouser pockets. "...ah kin spare ye a couple, but it'll cost ye another forty Bensons."

Jas stared at the two foil-wrapped condoms.

"Ma supply's sorta dried up, since they stopped hame visits." Laugh. "The doctor used tae gie the boays dozens o' johnnies, fur weekend leave..." The laugh fading. "...as if hame leave wiz wan long shag!" Eyes from the bunk to Jas. "...but you're new, Mr. Anderson. Ye'll..." Gnarled fingers gripped the tub of petroleum jelly and pushed it towards him. "..need this tae."

"Ah'm oan remand, 'member?" Jas stared into baggy eyes. "Ah'm no' plannin' on any romance, pal."

Baggy eyes narrowed. "Who's talkin' romance, Mr Anderson?"

Jas blinked, picked up the condoms and shoved them in his pocket.

All sorts of power...

He swept the petroleum jelly over to his own cache. Protection took on an extra meaning: power came in as many forms as muscle did. Tipping a cigarette from one of the remaining packets, he stuck it in his mouth.

The sound of flint on flint, then roaring.

Jas lowered the cigarette's end to the flame of the lighter, then inhaled.

The smoke scorched his already-burning throat. He drew the nicotine deep into his lungs, coughed.

"A dirty habit, Mr Anderson – ye should give it up 'fore it kills ye."

"Ah've already had the safe-sex lecture, Telly – gie it a rest, eh?" The first nicotine hit always made him irritable.

Telly shrugged. "Huv it your way, Mr. Anderson..." Baggy eyes again on the jacket. "...sure ye'll no' trade that?"

Jas almost laughed, then remembered the past day of endless

bells and no sense of time. "Maybe – kin ye get me a watch? Or a clock?"

The bald head shook slowly. "Naw, but ah've got the next best thing..."

Jas stared.

Telly winked. "...trade the jaicket an' ah'll git ye a job!"

Jas looked at the biker's jacket: they'd been through a lot together.

"...an' ah'll throw in a coupla jumpers, if it's the cold yer worried aboot."

It wasn't. The jacket was a link to the outside. "Whit dae ah want wi' a job?"

A rasping, racking laugh. "Six weeks 'til yer trial?"

Jas's head flicked up.

"...it's a long time, Mr Anderson..." Baggy eyes held his. "...the mind diz weird things, when it's left tae its own devices..."

He blinked. He could deal with his mind.

"..an', tae be honest, Mr Anderson, ah dinny fancy yer chances, hangin' aboot in here. Yer odds are goin' doon by the minute."

Jas lifted another fish-cake, smeared it in congealing beans and took a bite. As he ate, he glanced at the unlocked door, then back. He met Telly's eyes:

"Ah've no' got half the clout some people huv, Mr Anderson. A wee nod the right direction an' yer aw' theirs..."

He chewed the last of the fish-cake.

"...keep on the move – that's ma advice. If ye're no' in the wan place fur long enough, they canny find ya." Eyes narrowing. "But jobs ur hard tae come by..." Glance to the biker's jacket. "...an' they cost."

He swallowed, still tasting sour coffee.

"...Big Tim owes me – he'll gie up the cleaning fur, say, four weeks. How's that sound, Mr. Anderson?"

Like the strangest job interview and offer he'd ever attended. Jas grabbed a slice of cake from the other plate. He glanced around the cell, munching on surprisingly light sponge.

The surprise registered. "Yer cell-mate made that!"

Jas choked on a fragment of cake.

Telly thumped his back. "Whitever else he is, McStay's a guid cook, eh?"

Jas flinched, swallowed the sliver. He coughed. "Aye, a regular Delia Smith!" He wiped his mouth. "Why's he in Triple-S onyway?" Last time he'd looked, kicking the shite out of gay men didn't merit special treatment.

"Nae room in Solitary." Frown. "Ah don't like laggin' oan guys, Mr Anderson, but.." Pause. "...Stevie got intae a bitta trouble, a wee while back..." Sigh. "...ah'd offer ye a weapon, but ah doubt it wid dae ony good..." Slow head shake. "...chib the bastard when he's in wanna yon tempers an' he disney feel a thing!" Telly lifted a morsel of cake. "His ain recipe tae – guid, isn't it?" Munching.

Jas sighed, mind back on the visit from Room Service. "Aboot this job..."

Swallowing. "Great! Ah'll fix ye up." Telly whipped off the denim workshirt, struggled into the biker's jacket, then replaced the denim. He grabbed the Armani bag, two pairs of Calvins and four packs of cigarettes.

Jas let him: he was the novice here.

The jacket provided the bulk Telly had always lacked. Carefully folding the Armani bag, he slipped it under the shirt, then stuffed the rest of his cache back into the neck-pouch. "Ah'll be in touch, Mr Anderson. Guid doin' business with ye." He seized the empty tray, pulled the door open and left the cell.

Seconds later, the sound of keys in locks.

Jas finished the cake, stared at the large metal door. Power came in various forms: when demand was high and supply was low, the commodities trader had muscle of a different sort...

He eyed the jar of petroleum jelly, patting the two condoms in his pocket.

...there was one commodity every man in the Bar-L possessed: a body.

Jas knew it was a buyer's market. He shoved the lube under his bunk, then stretched out on the lumpy mattress. No offers so far, but no guarantee it would stay that way.

Sometime during Telly's visit, the light had faded.

Sometime during that time, the caged, fluorescent light had flickered into life.

Jas stared up between more bars at a flickering, humming cylinder.

The spider circled a couple of times, then disappeared into the sparker.

Jas closed his eyes.

He was using the piss-pot when keys scraped again.
Jas shook his prick, zipped up and turned.
McStay's large form instantly shrank the cell.
Jas nodded a greeting.
The gesture was ignored. McStay vaulted up onto the top bunk.
Jas watched the man lie back, clasp hands behind head and stare at the small photograph. "Yer kids?"
"Whit's it tae you?" Angry brown eyes fixed his.
Jas shrugged, pulled the packet of Bensons from his pocket and held them out.
The gesture ignored. McStay's eyes were back on the photograph.
Jas frowned, stuck a cigarette between his lips and lit it. He leant against bare brick, watching the way his cell-mate's chest rose and fell with each breath. Anonymous hate he expected.
Hate for the uniform he no longer wore.
Hate for the laws he no longer enforced...
Jas flicked ash into the piss-pot.
...but this felt...?
He flicked more ash, listening to the sizzle as it hit the piss. Jas turned.
Brown eyes met his, then immediately glanced away.
Fingers tightened around the cigarette's filter. Anonymous hate was cold, clean. What came off his cell-mate in crashing waves was something else, something more threatening and less easily identifiable.
But identifiable, nonetheless.
Two men. One cell. A power balance needed asserting.
Jas turned back to the window, stuck his hand into the pocket of the combat pants...
He remembered Telly's warning.
...and removed the only weapon he had.
The cell was silent.
Jas took a last few draws from the cigarette, then dropped it into the piss-pot.
A still-glowing end extinguished itself in three inches of yellow liquid.
He pulled the T-shirt free from waistband, slipped the disposable razor between two layers of fabric and applied pressure.
The lower plastic blade-guard snapped off easily. He removed the jagged shard, tucking it into back pocket.

A sound. The sound of worn bed-springs. Then boots on concrete.

Jas moved away from the piss-pot and turned round slowly.

Inches away, his cell-mate unzipped, pointing his prick towards the aluminium bucket.

Jas stared at the cell door, fingers still gripping the now-exposed razor blade. On the periphery of his vision, a stream of urine splattered into the pot. The rational part of his mind told him McStay was merely taking a piss.

Another part of his mind felt the closeness, smelled an enforced intimacy...

...Jas edged past the bulky body and walked to his bunk. Throwing himself onto it, he stared at the small window above a tangled, ponytailed head.

Peter was out there. Marie was out there.

His solicitor was out there...

He moved gaze from bars to stone.

...what was left of his detective business was beyond that wall.

Peter was something he didn't want to think about. Marie was another matter. Jas narrowed his eyes.

His solicitor had her name, her occupation, her approximate address. Everything the police had on him was circumstantial. Jas blinked.

The tangled, ponytailed head had moved, exposing more brick.

Jas sighed. The wall erected between himself and his cell-mate was was more solid than anything hewn from stone.

As he lay fully-dressed on the narrow cot, boots hanging over the end and eyes closed, Jas knew he was far from sleep.

Tweve

Only after lights-out did he realise how far.

The first scream stopped his heart.

Eyelids shot open.

The second scream sent the organ into overdrive.

The third helped him place the screamer. He stared at the bunk above.

Not this cell. Not the next. Ten, maybe fifteen yards away, a voice not long broken wailed like a wounded animal.

Fingernails dug into palms. Jas waited for the corresponding shouts of annoyance, then the sound of boots on metal and the scraping of keys.

Nothing. Just more screams.

He propped himself up on one elbow and listened.

From the bunk above, muffled snores drifted down.

He fingered the exposed razor, then shoved the blade under the mattress and pulled the pillow over his head. It didn't help much.

But it did help.

Just as dawn's grey light seeped in through the bars, the screams stopped.

Jas wondered if the screamer had grown hoarse...

He stared up at the fluorescent light casing.

...or merely screamed himself to sleep.

Time played its tricks. What seemed like minutes later, keys scraping. Jas scrambled from his bunk, grabbed the towel and was first out of the cell.

As he filed past an open door three cells down, a loose noose drooped from window-bars.

The screamer had found a more permanent oblivion.

So much for Strict Suicide Supervision.

He looked away.

None of his business.

Five yards in front, a familiar jacket.

Jas threw his still-damp towel over one shoulder and stared at the stranger in his biker's jacket. He vaguely remembered Telly's trade: a job would get him out of the cell during the day. Nights were something else...

...he walked on.

Snatches of disturbed sleep stuck to his skin, lingering in his brain like broken cobwebs, dreams half-spun. Jas rubbed his face, fingers running up over scalp.

He moved with the snake of figures towards the shower block. A hundred pairs of booted feet rang in his ears.

The makeshift noose hung in his brain, suspended from shreds of some kid's screams.

Some kid with parents, or parentless?

Some kid with someone to worry about him?

Some kid with worries of his own?

None of his business...

...his head flicked left. Jas stared across the anti-suicide net to the opposite walkway, searching a line of denimed men for normality...

...Gerry or the rodent-faced boy from the bus.

Boy... kid...

Jas followed the denimed serpent down two flights of metal stairs. He glanced up at the cctv cameras and wondered about the non-red eyes and ears which patrolled the corridors at night.

Cries for help that long and that loud were hard to miss.

So much for Strict Suicide Supervision.

Running a prison meant more than keeping them here: keeping them alive was part of the contract too.

The line of men seemed to be moving more quickly...

Jas walked through a doorway which was flanked by two figures in grey uniform. He paused, staring at a face almost as young as that which had produced the ersatz lullaby. No eyes met his. Someone behind bumped into him. Jas walked on.

...or maybe he was merely getting used to the way time worked in the Bar-L.

The way everything worked in the Bar-L.

Inside the shower block, he stripped off.

"Oi! You!"

Jas recognised the voice but couldn't place it. He didn't need this. Tomorrow he'd skip showers...

...the washing did everything but get him clean, anyway.

"You! Anderson, or whitever yer fuckin' name is!" The voice was closer, now.

Jas clenched his fist, spun round.

McStay. Out of line and holding the piss-pot, which he thrust at Jas. "Your turn!"

The half-full bucket hit him in the stomach, splashing its contents over the flimsy lid.

Jas glared into large brown eyes with pupils the size of full stops. He gripped the pot with wet hands, watched as McStay thundered wordlessly away, then turned back to the showers.

Following the two men in front, he made his way to the stalls, emptied the pot, then rinsed worn aluminium under a tap in a large sink. He could smell piss and the scent of stagnant water on his hands.

When he returned to the queue, someone else had taken his place. Jas frowned, watching a back view of his cell-mate. Large hands moved the ponytail then lathered shoulders. His eyes flicked away to beyond, and a St Andrew's Cross tattoo.

Gerry's naked wiry body filled his eyes...

...then pupils stared back into his. The smile from Induction gone. Mouth set in a hard line, the skinhead held the gaze, then removed a hand from around a soapy cock.

One finger extended. "Whit you lookin' at, polis?"

Jas looked away and cursed the ever-efficient grapevine. On the edge of his vision, in the drying area, denimed legs. Three pairs. He tensed.

Denimed legs walked on past...

...and stopped in front of Gerry.

Jas stared, saw everyone was staring.

Under the faucet, skinhead bravado was being tested...

Two clothed men grabbed a wiry arm each and pulled the naked man from under the faucet. Another seized the strong chin, forcing Gerry's head back against tiles.

"Hey, boays, come on." Worried and trying to sound otherwise.

...and found wanting.

Other words. "Think ye're a big man, eh son?"

Jas's gaze flicked to between wet, ropy thighs. Gerry's balls were trying to hide inside his body.

One of the three men leant forward, whispered something Jas couldn't hear.

The light went out of Gerry's sparkling eyes. A zero-cropped head shook from side to side in fervent denial. The rest of the body merely shook.

Hands released narrow wrists.

Gerry slid down the tiled wall, eyes never leaving the heavier of the three men.

Jas watched the St Andrew's flag waver in surrender, watched the heavy-set man crouch down. The large face was inches from Gerry's down-tilted head. Which nodded.

Laughter.

The three men moved away.

Gerry continued to cower against tiles.

The humiliation had been public and undeniable. Jas compared the slumped figure to the swaggering man of minutes earlier.

Gerry was out of his depth and league, and had just been reminded of that fact.

Power had been exerted...

A faucet became free. Jas dumped clothes and piss-pot on a wooden bench and stepped under the shower, three down from the crumpled skinhead.

...had gone unchallenged. Gerry wouldn't open his mouth again for the duration of his remand.

Maybe his arse would be a different matter.

Jas located what was left of the soap and looked away.

Not his business...

...nor his problem. Eyes moved to the drying area.

Telly. And two others he didn't recognise. Beyond, a skinny, underdeveloped form was attempting to drag dry clothes on over a still-damp body. Head lowered, constantly flicking over shoulder.

Jas met the eyes of the rodent-faced boy from the bus.

Half-dressed and holding large trainers, the kid was making for the door.

Telly's cronies beat him to it.

Beside the two older, larger men, the rodent-faced kid was slighter than ever.

A rat in a trap. Would he bite or flee...

Jas lathered up the soap and washed his pits.

...or accept, as Gerry had done?

The kid stared up at one of Telly's cronies, shook his head.

The man shrugged, ruffled step-cut hair. He and his mates moved away. Rodent-face scurried from the block, dropping one trainer. Someone picked up the large shoe and hurled it after the departing boy.

The refusal had been good-naturedly accepted. Jas rubbed soap between his palms and continued to wash.

None of his business...

He washed legs and arse, scanning the room.

...but business nonetheless. Jas tried to wash last night's screams and rat-faced terror from his mind. A layer of grime and sleep was swept from his body in a tide of carbolic.

Everything else stayed.

Eyes darted to exit then entrance and back again, noting Gerry was slowly pulling on bleached , skin-tight jeans. His mind returned to his own skin...

...wherever Neil Johnstone was housed, it wasn't B-Hall, unless washing with the riff-raff was below the dignity of someone already at the bottom of the heap.

Despite or maybe because of what had just happened, his body began to unwind under the warm water. He turned his face up to the faucet and closed his eyes.

Neil Johnstone: youngest of the Johnstone brothers. Seventeen when Jas had arrested him, mid-twenties now. Where older brothers Liam had the front, Michael the style and Jimmy the gall, Neil was an unknown quantity.

His last image of the teenager was in the High Court's dock, the judge passing a two-year sentence for vehicular manslaughter. The expression on the hard face had been harder to read.

The expression of the key prosecution witness's face, after a knife had slashed her from eye to mouth, had been an open book.

Marie McGhee had received her letter of thanks promptly.

And Jas?

He soaped belly and chest, trying to enjoy the feel of the soft lather on his goosefleshed skin.

There was a postcript outstanding – a postscript Neil was now in a position to write.

"Git a move oan, yeah?"

He shook water from his face and opened his eyes, head flicking to a heavy, red-haired man who was stamping his feet and hugging tits large enough to be female.

Jas stepped out from under the faucet. "Sorry, pal." He brushed the large, freckled body as he reached for the towel. Low words:

"Ye're no pal o' mine, polis!"

Jas ignored the remark. Drying himself, he rejoined the previous train of thought.

Unknown quantity...

...maybe brains sank to the bottom, in the Johnstone family. In an environment where everything was certain, veiled threats and concealed anger were unusual weapons.

Did Neil Johnstone put the psycho in psychological warfare?

He pulled on clothes that felt too tight, grabbed the piss-pot and headed for the door.

He would, no doubt, find out.

In the canteen, a different cook served him and didn't spit in his breakfast.

A large, anonymous foot hit the back of his right knee as he walked from the serving hatch.

Breaking the worst of the fall with forearms, Jas scowled up from the concrete floor. He ignored the laughter and scanned for officers.

None looked in his direction, and he knew better than to seek them out: like Gerry and rodent-face, he was being tested.

He was still picking bits of congealed egg from the Adidas T-shirt when he located Telly's table.

Concerned, ruddy face. "Here, Mr Anderson." A chair was pulled out.

Jas sat down.

Telly plucked a rasher of bacon from his own, then each of his companions' trays, placed the meat on a spare tray and pushed it towards him. "Gotta keep yer strength up!"

Jas almost laughed.

Telephone stared at his stained T-shirt. "Ah'll get they jumpers tae ye the day sometime."

He munched on the bacon. The hatred of polis was easy to understand: Telly's attentions were harder to fathom.

"Sleep well, Mr Anderson?"

Jas looked up into baggy eyes. "Did you?" He frowned.

Blink. "Ah'm at the far end o' the hall. Ah didney hear him..."

Jas glanced to a line of four grey backs which stood at the door.

Telly talked on. "...an' they widney, nice an' cosy in their wee control-room wi' the cameras switched aff!" Something in the voice. More than anger.

Pity.

Jas flicked back to Telly. Baggier eyes:

"Ah tried tae tell the wee bastard, clue him in – ye ken?" Baggy sigh. "The pretty wans git it worst..." Telly fiddled with a plastic fork. "...an' they could huv it best, if they'd only wake up an' smell the – " Sigh. "Ah, whit the hell! Ye dae whit ye can, right Mr Anderson?"

Jas crunched a piece of over-cooked bacon. He had no intention of doing anything except getting through the next five weeks. But he nodded.

"Aye, ye're a guid guy, Mr Anderson."

Jas chewed, swallowed. "The feelin's mutual, Telly..." He remembered other feelings – the feeling of being trapped in a cell to which many seemed to have easy access. "...so when dae ah start this job?"

Telly slid a half-full cup of coffee sideways, and lowered his voice.

An hour later, Jas dunked his mop into a bucket of scummy water. He'd turned down the chance to buy back the biker's jacket in return for delivering three condomed packages to locations on the other side of the Hall.

But at least he'd got the jumpers. And out of his cell. He squeezed excess water from the mop and continued to wash the corridor.

Occasionally, men in denim strolled past, carrying trays. Or nothing. Or similar buckets and mops.

Barlinnie had never been so clean...

Occasionally, other men exchanged objects and packages he couldn't see, but didn't need to.

...or so dirty.

If visits had been suspended, the mail routinely searched, how were the drugs getting in?

Someone else's business. Not his. Jas swabbed at the edge of a yellow-brick wall.

Time passed. He took a break, smoked a cigarette.

A group of denimed men walked quickly past. No one talked to him. No one even acknowledged his presence. Knotted muscle began to relax into anonymity.

Jas looked up through the suicide net at the strutted, concave ceiling.

The place was eerie.

Approaching a locked gate, he paused, scowled up at a cctv camera...

...a red eye which saw no evil, night or day.

A buzz. Then a scraping. The gate slid ajar.

Jas lifted his bucket and walked through.

Heavy iron slid shut behind him.

Pioneers in Security Solutions?

Hadrian's presence was shadowy, unreliable.

In the Bar-L, visibility was all. Sophisticated surveillance techniques were for cop shows and science fiction.

Visibility was all. In the reality that was Barlinnie, shows of strength were important.

Like the Gerry Shower-show.

Like Neil's veiled-shows.

Like...

...noise shattered thought. Wet, metal noise.

"Oops! Aw, willya look at that – he's spilled his water!"

Jas glared up from the rolling bucket.

Three well-muscled, denimed torsos. Three unknown faces. Three mouths grinning. One moving: "Whit dae ye say?"

Jas held the stare, then glanced down. "Ah say watch where ye're puttin' yer fuckin' feet!" Water the colour and temperature of fresh sewage formed a pool around his docs. Tutting. then:

"Wrang answer, polis!" A hand knocked the mop from his.

Jas slowly raised his head, fists balling. Cold seeped from the wall behind, penetrating Telly's fuzzy acrylic. He stared at a face he didn't know, but which evidently knew him.

Thin lips twisted further into a sneer. "Right answer: sorry, sir."

Jas took a step back. "Fuck off!" He bent to lift the mop.

A booted foot on his fingers. "Don't think you're gettin' the hang of this, cunt..."

Pressure on his fingers. Jas winced, staring at denimed knees...

...which bent to a crouch.

Breath on his face. "...only wan thing worse than polis ..."

Spittle struck his face. He blinked it away, shivered as the hot bile cooled on his cold skin. The pain in his fingers was hotter.

"...an' that's queer polis!"

Every muscle in his body quivered. A vein pulsed in his neck. Jas narrowed his eyes, but didn't break the gaze. Sweat was another matter.

The booted foot removed, impacting with the bucket.

The corridor sang with the sound of rolling aluminium on concrete. Then: "Clean it up, Queer-boy!"

Jas didn't move.

Mock sigh. "Ah still don't think you've got the hang of how things work here..." Parody of a smile.

His eyes raced around the three faces. Where the bodies were muscled and over-exercised, the faces were grey-tinged. Despite the appearance of health, none looked well. The one which talked and mock-smiled looked least well.

"...see, we like to keep everyone happy – an' we think you'd be happier if ye dae whit we tell ye."

He felt the knee before his eyes registered movement. Air rushed from his lungs. Jas doubled over, hands clutching at his crotch. Over-cooked bacon filled his mouth, as breakfast passed through his gullet a second time.

"We jist want ye tae be happy, Queer-boy...an' here ye are puking all over yer lovely clean floor..." More tutting.

Jas closed his eyes. His balls were on fire. He tried to breathe through his nose, but could only manage low, liquid moans. Slumping to the ground, the wet floor was comforting against his burning face.

"...now there's even mair tae clean up..."

Fingers gripped his cheek, twisting viciously. Jas managed to raise his head.

"...but – as luck wid huv it – ah've got the time tae stay here an' make sure ye dae it properly."

Jas wrenched away and hauled himself to his feet, teeth clenched again the ache in his groin. He grabbed the mop, sliding in the mixture of vomit and filthy water.

A laugh. "Hope we can develop a guid working relationship..."

"Oi! You lot! What's going on down...?" Rich baritone. Bootsteps.

"Nothin', Mr Dalgleish! We're jist helpin' this..."

"Back to your cells..." Closer bootsteps. "...you know the rules..."

"Aye, Mr Dalgleish..." A change in tone. Bordering on respect. "...just goin'..."

Jas mopped, tasting sour bile. Three bodies bumped against him. Kissing sound. One lowered voice:

"Be seein' you, Queer-boy..." Three sets of feet retreating. "...mind ye don't break a nail!"

Jas ignored the pain in his face and the rage in his head as the bucket was kicked a third time. He listened to three sets of footsteps echo down the corridor, waited for the fourth set to take the usual Hadrian path of least resistance.

It didn't. "Here!"

Jas looked up at the handkerchief held in a large fist, then at the figure behind it.

A big man – more bulk than height – in Hadrian grey. Late fifties, but fit. Darker, iron-grey hair. Gun-metal eyes widening in recognition. "Anderson? Jas Anderson?" Then narrowing.

He took the offered handkerchief, wiping vomit from his lips. Something in the voice. Jas released the mop and nursed his injured fingers.

The large man was staring after the threesome. "You okay?" Said without breaking the stare into the distance.

Jas flinched. The concern was more disconcerting than the antagonism. "Ah'll live." He tried to place the profile.

"That's the difference between you an' them..." Rugged face turned to his. Frowning. "...this place is part-time hospice, part-time psychiatric unit – part-time death row an' general dumping ground..."

Jas stared into gun-metal eyes. Mists cleared in his brain as the face continued to talk:

"...hundred an' fifty HIV positive – that we ken aboot..." Shrug. "...they've nothin' tae lose an' a lotta anger tae work-aff – they ken they'll either die in here, or oan the streets. Their families'll probably no' take them back, no' now."

As voice recognition provided a name, Jas took a step back and surveyed the man. "It's been a while." He wiped his lips.

Dalgleish stooped, re-righted the bucket. "It has that." Words tinged with disappointment.

He looked away as the familiar respect seeped into his brain. "Ye've read ma charge-sheet, no doubt." The years rolled back, exposing memories.

1987: Gorbals division. An eighteen-year-old probationer and a sergeant in his late thirties.

1992: Dumbarton Division. After thirty years' illustrious service, Sergeant Ian Dalgleish had retired from Strathclyde Police, amidst hearty good wishes and a clutch of decorations. Secondment to Lothian and Borders' Police had prevented a now-CID officer attending the party.

1997: London Road. DS James Anderson had resigned from Strathclyde Police. Not dishonourably, but in an equal glare of publicity. And no party.

Jas leant against the wall and took the cigarette offered.

A sigh. "That ah have."

He dragged nicotine into his lungs, flinching at the disappointment in the voice. "You bin with Hadrian long?"

"Four years..." Gun-metal eyes brightening. "...best four years of ma life. Maxwell Fulton's got modern ideas..." Glancing around. "..look at this place – it's crazy! Overcrowded, insanitary. We need new prisons, new approaches – there's eyeways gonny be crime..." Mock-laugh. "... the new growth industry!"

Jas stared at the man beside him, saw Hadrian grey blur into serge. "Aye, ye were always ambitious!"

Sober baritone "Whit happened tae your ambitions, Anderson

– you wur a good cop."

He stared at the pool of sludge circling his feet. "Me an' the polis didney see eye-tae-eye oan a coupla issues."

"Aye, the Force isney whit it used tae be." Snort. "Budgets are tighter than ever – an' they've even got productivity targets noo..." Frown. "...nae wonder corruption's rife."

Jas looked up, remembering a sergeant in Gorbals division who had taught him the rule he'd tried to live by: one law for all.

Criminals carrying warrant cards were still criminals.

"...an' whit is there fur ex-polis, these days?"

He almost smiled. "Retirement no' whit ye thought it wid be? Moira git fed up o' ye hangin' around aw' day?"

Frown. "We...separated two years ago."

"Sorry tae hear that." A thirty-year marriage ending hot on the heels of what should have been Moira and Ian Dalgleish's twilight years.

Shrug.

Jas watched Ian Dalgleish smoke the cigarette, recalling their brief partnering during his probationary period...

The same period during which his personal life had been a mass of unresolved questions and tensions

...and the number of times the man's wife had cooked dinner for an eighteen-year-old probationer who had been too clueless and confused to even feed himself.

"You keep up yer game?"

Jas raised an eyebrow. Another memory pushed itself forward. "Ah'm probably a bit rusty, but ah could still gie yer queen a run fur her money!"

A laugh. The sound was at odds with high yellow walls and low spirits. "Away! Yer pawn defence wis like a string vest!"

Jas felt tension start to ebb from his limbs. "Ah beat ye – how many times?"

"Wance. In eighteen months ye beat me wance..." Rugged face creasing and recreasing. "Christ, Jas Anderson – the last man on earth ah expected tae see in here."

He returned the grin...

...then frowned.

Two ex-polis...

One in combat pants and a scratchy jumper.

The other in Hadrian grey.

More than his own brain became acutely aware of where they

were having this conversation. Authoriative, baritone voice. "Ye'll be treated like ony other prisoner..." Cigarette stubbed out under size twelve boot. "...nae special privileges."

He nodded: he didn't expect anything less from Ian Dalgleish.

Bootsteps.

Frown. Lowered baritone. "Keep yer nose clean an' yer heid doon..."

Bootsteps. Closer.

"...now get this mess cleaned up, Anderson! Ah'll no' tell ye again!" Voice raised.

He grabbed the mop, lowered his head and watched a ramrod figure stride off down the corridor.

Another set of legs came into view. "He giein' ye hassle?"

Jas's head flipped up.

Telly sighed. "Telt ye, ye shouldda taken the smack, Mr Anderson..." Eyes on his cheek.

Jas touched throbbing skin, then leant on his mop.

Telly produced a packet of Bensons, held them out. "How come bastards like Dalgleish got a job wi' Hadrian, that's whit ah wanna ken?"

The ex-polis' flawless record and good references would stand him in excellent stead. Jas took a cigarette and held his tongue.

Telly lit it for him, sighed again. "The ainly qualifications ye seem tae need is wantin' the job..." He blew a perfectly formed smoke ring. "...half of them is kids, wi' no' a clue between them."

Jas thought of Brodie and Ms Pepperpot, of other slight figures in grey who looked inexperienced, to put it mildly.

"...the other hauf is ex-polis, ex-army, ex-fuck kens whit!"

Jas drew hard on the cigarette. At least the last couple had training. But he knew better than to argue the toss. In the Bar-L, there were only two sides. He changed the subject. "You said ah'd be safer oot here, man!" The pain in his groin was a dull roar.

Telly inhaled deeply. "Aye, Mr Anderson: safer – no' safe. Naewan's really safe in here."

Jas exhaled, remembering three gaunt men.

Nothing to lose...

...he shared the memory.

Telly frowned, eyes lowered to the bucket, then back to Jas. "If ye've got onythin' tae buy them aff with, use it, Mr Anderson. If no', just keep oota their way – an' pray they dinny come lookin' fur ye." Telly dropped the dog-end into the bucket and padded away.

Jas watched him go. A throbbing in his head overtook the ache in his balls.

Thirteen

He ate his evening meal in the canteen, with a dozen other cleaning workers. Each had a table to themselves. No one talked.

Behind the serving hatch, the sullen outline of his cell-mate came into and disappeared from view.

Jas drained his coffee cup and lit a cigarette. Face and balls tingled.

A bell rang. He looked at his fellow diners.

No one stirred.

He stayed with the herd, resting an elbow on the table. Thoughts coagulated in his brain.

There was a system within a system here, a wheel within a wheel.

Jas flicked his cigarette into the vegetable compartment of his tray.

Each system had its own rules.

Each system acknowledged the other system.

He thought about Ian Dalgleish's unnecessary warning...

..and his own position as a rogue cog, trying to function within one system while joined by implication to the other...

...then he thought about Brodie, Ms Pepperpot... Dalgleish.

He could visualise Hadrian's selection procedure: you, you and you – off wages delivery, go run a prison! The company had a so-so record in the private-security sector...

...but patrolling building-sites for £1.50 an hour was no preparation for guarding more organic cargo.

His mind lingered on Ian Dalgleish...

...and chess. Slow nights in the Gorbals. Custody duty. Jas smiled at the memory. Two years' probation had taught him a lot...

...including the art of strategy, planning ahead, second-guessing...

...and eventually beating the man who had taught him chess. But only once.

Another bell rang, pushing another name into his brain.

Alan Somerville. The memory was distant but vivid. Staring at his tray, he heard the scraping of chair legs through thoughts of an incident far from forgotten. Jas stood up with the rest of the canteen.

The informal discipline system he was working out...

...the bells would take slightly longer.

"Can ah use the library?" He paused in the cell doorway, head cocked towards a Brodie-clone. It was worth a try.

"Library's closed until further notice." The Hadrian Officer parrotted the answer.

Jas stared at a mere mouthpiece. No physical bulk, no presence, no real authority. The uniform was a sham, and they both knew it. He glanced into the cell.

An empty two-litre Pepsi bottle sat at the foot of his bunk: Telly-delivery.

"Can ah fill this, then?" Jas stepped inside, reached out for the bottle.

The cell door slammed behind him.

Jas stared, then turned. He sat down on the lower bunk, tossed the Pepsi bottle into the air and caught it. He looked at the nine-foot by three-foot section of bare floor.

A work-out would bring back the thirst.

Inactivity would bring back the day.

He slipped the plastic bottle under his bunk, pulled off the scratchy jumper and the T-shirt. Jas dropped to his knees, then stretched out on the floor. Press-ups...

You could never be too rich – or too fit...

Alan Somerville.

...you could, however, think too much.

He'd just finished fifty stomach-curls when the cell door opened.

McStay stepped wordlessly over him and headed for the piss-pot.

Jas hugged his knees, listening as the trickle became a torrent. He could smell the man over the stink of his own sweat and the cold, damp November air which somehow permeated the unpainted brick. He released his knees, stood up and stretched warm muscle. Pressure in his groin.

"Get oot ma way!"

Jas sighed.

"Move!"

Flattening himself against the wall, he turned, just as McStay hauled himself onto the top bunk. Jas didn't look up, didn't need to. He walked to the piss-pot and unzipped. Fingers brushed sore balls.

Flinching, he gripped his prick and tried to piss.

The first few drops were painless enough. Then burning. Jas clenched his teeth, studying the urine through narrowed eyes for any trace of pink or red.

Nothing. Only more burning. His balls felt bigger, harder. Jas focused on bare brick a foot from his nose and finished the job.

As he shook the last few dribbles from his slit, his urethra resembled post-eruption Krakatoa. Jas shoved his prick back in his combat pants and walked slowly to his bunk.

The strip-light had developed a stutter. Yellow flickers strobed on his eyelids. Buzzing in his ears. Jas propped himself up on one elbow and opened his eyes.

At the foot of the bunk, his cell-mate was undressing.

Jas looked away. On the periphery of his vision, slashes of yellow illuminated then hid the half-naked body. He stared at the worn floor.

Over the buzzing, the sounds of unzipping.

He frowned, moved onto his back and gazed up at the bed-springs. He could still hear the drag of clothing from skin, the rub of denim against denim. A trickle of sweat leaked from one pit and made its way down onto his stomach. Jas stared at metal spirals, which faded then refocused with each shimmer of the light.

Then darkness.

His body began to relax. He never thought he'd be glad to be blind.

Springs creaked, then fell silent.

He sat up, unlaced boots and kicked them free of his feet. Combat pants went the same way. The blanket prickled skin which had suddenly become hypersensitive. He stretched out a hand, reached under the mattress and located the razor-blade. Curling fingers around the slim length of plastic, Jas closed his eyes. Sleep was a heartbeat away, kept at bay the previous night by the last beats of a younger heart, two cells down.

Creaking.

Eyelids shot open.

Jas stared up, listening to the rhythmic movement of bed-springs. Fingers tightening around the blade...

More creaking. Faster creaking.

...then untightening, to be replaced by a different tension. He bit back a moan as his prick twitched.

McStay's wank was almost silent, but in the noiseless cell every sound and movement filled his ears.

Jas rolled over onto his stomach.

The creaking stopped.

Shallow breathing. His, or McStay's?

The creaking resumed.

His prick tried to uncurl inside the too-tight Calvins. Foreskin caught in pubic hair, pulling at the roots as the shaft stretched itself in response to the creaks. He moved onto his side, drew up legs against the dull ache in his balls.

His ears strained through the creaks, listening to the drag of flesh on flesh, the urgent caress of damp fist around damper shaft.

Unrelated thoughts darted into his mind. The photograph...a wife... kids... McStay's permanently furrowed brow furrowing further as he jerked himself towards orgasm... the faceless kid last night... Ian Dalgleish...

Jas frowned, drew his knees up further. Thighs brushed balls. He shivered and turned onto his back.

...tomorrow. The day after. The day after that. Neil Johnstone. Marie. Small packages of white powder...

His hand lay over his half-hard prick.

...McStay's hard shoulders. The smell of McStay's piss, his sweat and...

Jas felt the outline of the razor's guard press itself into his palm as a quiet sigh ended the creaking. He sniffed the air, trying to draw comfort from the warm stench of life which drifted down from the bunk above. The dull ache in his balls had subsided into a pulsating discomfort.

Tiredness and arousal fought a battle in his groin.

Rustling.

Then silence.

Sometime later, snoring.

Sometime after that, tiredness won.

Jas stuffed the too-tight Calvins under his bunk and pulled on Telly's red contraband underwear. The roomier briefs felt better against his balls. Scooping combat pants from the floor, he stepped into them, listening to the sounds of his cell-mate's breathing.

No bells...

...dawn had woken him, rays of greying light puncturing the darkness and poking his mind from an uncomfortable doze.

His body was cold and stiff, despite yesterday's work-out. His brain refused to function.

Jas straightened up. He leant back against bare brick and stared at his cell-mate's blanket-muffled outline. Breath condensed in the cold air. Beneath his bare feet, Victorian stone chilled the soles. He struggled into socks, boots then reached for cigarettes, sparking a match in the dim gloom.

The brick was a block of ice behind his shoulders as he smoked the cigarette and stared at McStay's inert form.

Even in sleep, the antagonism was there, radiating up through the thin blanket. Jas thought about the razor blade, back between mattress and bed-springs.

Two men. One cell. A power balance begged to be established.

As he flicked the glowing cigarette-end into the piss-pot, artificial gloom flickered then burst into light above his head.

A bell.

Seconds later, keys scraped at a lock.

Jas grabbed his towel and the piss-pot, brushing past the grey Hadrian uniform and out onto the walk-way. Most prisoners were still in their cells. Glancing across the suicide net, he watched a rodent-faced figure scurry parallel. He wasn't the only one to want to wash early. Frowning, he made his way down metal stairs towards the shower block.

Gerry the Skinhead was nowhere in sight.

Deja vu...

...but the routine was reassuring. Jas undressed in line, staring across the freezing room to where a skinny figure was washing step-cut hair. Leaving his clothes to mark his place in the queue, he ducked into one of the stalls to empty the piss-pot.

The toilet bowl was filled to the brim, grey, stinking sludge spilling over the rim.

Jas tried the other three doorless cubicles.

All similar.

He returned to the queue, glanced around for an officer.

The room was denim and flesh-toned. No grey.

Jas scowled. Even the plumbing couldn't handle the amount of shite which was circulating in the Bar-L these days. He tossed his clothes onto a bench, then picked up the piss-pot and stood patiently with a dozen other naked men, all holding piss-pots.

The smell in the room turned his stomach. Jas focused on the floor in front.

A low whistle.

Fingers tightened, digging into palm, The piss-pot trembled in his fist.

Another whistle, two-note, this time. Laughing. Then pleading.

Jas raised his head.

At the end of the shower area, four figures where there should be one.

Deja vu.

Three dry and dressed. One wet and naked.

The rodent-faced kid backed further into a corner, frantically shielding shrivelled genitals.

Jas moved up the queue as the two men ahead of him slipped under newly vacated faucets.

One of the dressed figures stretched out a hand and lightly slapped the dripping rodent-face.

The kid knocked the hand away and shrank further into the corner.

Someone laughed.

Jas looked over his shoulder.

At least a dozen pairs of eyes were watching. Deja vu. No one moved.

He looked back at the kid.

All three were slapping him now, arms and legs more than face. With each impact of dry flesh on wet, the kid yelped.

No hard slaps.

Force wasn't necessary.

Pain wasn't the object.

Jas took a step forward, remembering the previous morning. Rodent-face had already been on the receiving end of a more polite, less demonstrative offer, which he had stupidly turned down. He remembered Gerry, then Telly's words:

..the wee, pretty ones get it the worst...when they could huv it the best...

Yelps were fading into sobs, low laughs increasing in volume. Face buried in hands, the kid had turned to the wall.

Jas watched two clothed figures grab a skinny wrist each, pinning the arms high above the head. The teenage body had a limp, defeated look about it, step-cut hair plastered to a soaking, lowered skull. He sighed: none of his business...

Then a howl of surprise.

A bare foot kicked backward a second time, catching the largest of the three dressed men neatly in the shin.

Another howl. Rage, this time.

The rat-faced kid was spun round, before his heels could do any more damage.

Jas wanted to look away. Couldn't. He stared as the kid was dragged from the wet to the dry, one denimed arm around his scrawny neck, another twisting his wrist behind his back.

The third dressed figure straightened up from rubbing his shin, balled a fist and aimed it at the kid's cheek.

"Lea' him alone, eh?" The words were out before he could stop them.

Hard knuckles contacted with soft skin.

"Ah said, lea' him alone!" Jas hurled the piss-pot at the far wall.

The sound obliterated the kid's gasp of pain. The faecal matter which drenched the skinny body and two of the clothed ones raised gasps of disgust.

"Aw', fur fuck's sake!" The third figure leapt back. The other two released the shite-slimed kid and plucked at their soiled clothing.

Terrified eyes darted around the tiled room.

Jas strode forward, reclaimed the piss-pot with one hand, a skinny white arm with the other. He shoved the kid in the direction of what looked like the kids' clothes.

"Whit's your fuckin' game, pal?"

Angry eyes glared at him.

Behind, scurrying noises told him the boy was making another hasty exit. Okay, so he'd stink like a shithouse all day, but smells faded.

Jas glared back. "Sorry – ma hand slipped." He dangled the empty piss-pot from two fingers in mock apology.

The door at the far end of the showers opened. Two grey-clad figures, noses wrinkling at the stench.

"What's goin' on here?"

No response.

Jas glanced from the two screws to three piss-stained men and back again. "Ma fault – a wee accident."

Another, bulkier grey figure pushed through. "What the fuck's all this?" Gun-metal eyes bore down on them.

Jas moved closer to the denimed men.

Dalgleish responded on cue. Practised eyes read the situation, then switched to the other three prisoners.

A voice from the denim. "Like he sez, an accident, Mister Dalgleish."

Hoarse laugh. "Get this stinkin' mess cleaned up, Anderson ..."

Jas looked at the brown smears which slid down the tiled wall.

"...now!" Dalgleish turned on his heel and walked from the shower room.

Seconds later, the two other screws followed.

Jas stared at the rodent-faced kid's three admirers, then back at the line of naked men waiting to wash. He didn't risk a smile of solidarity.

He knew how his actions would be interpreted: self-interest. Every action had a reaction.

He also knew there were other times, other places. Jas moved under a faucet and began to wash.

The first repercussion came an hour later.

Today's cleaning duties augmented by shower-block work, he was wiping the last traces of shite from greying tiles.

Eyes. The pressure of a stare.

He spun round.

The boy huddled deeper into the padded jacket and tried to smile.

It didn't work.

Jas frowned. "Whit dae you want?"

A blush spread over rodent-features. "Er... fierce, man – thanks."

Jas scanned the almost childish body. "Forget it!" He turned back to the tiles.

Silence. Then:

"Ah'm David – David Hamilton."

"That meant tae dae somethin' fur me?" He scrubbed at the wall, manufacturing a hardness he didn't feel.

Confusion. "Er... no, but ah..." Fading into embarrassment.

Jas stopped scrubbing and turned. He stared at the kid.

Neither physical...

..nor brain-muscle. Pale, nipped-in face. At the front of the queue when they were handing out cheekbones and lips. The padded jacket quivered. At the end of the line, when it came to suss.

Jas tried a smile.

The expression reciprocated. Feelings gushed out. "Oh, man, ah owe ye – dunno whit ah wid huv..."

Jas dammed up the torrent before it swept him away. "Get a clue, yeah?"

Confusion back in the rodent eyes.

Jas looked away. "Whit ye in fur?" No transferree would be this green.

"Joy-ridin', man, an..."

"Ye're oan remand, yeah? Coupla months?" At eighteen, they were moved from Remand Homes to adult institutions.

"Aye, but..."

"Ken how things work in here... David?" For some reason, using the name made it less personal.

"Naw, no' really – in Longriggend ah..."

"Don't gimme yer life story. You need protection – right?"

Nothing.

"Right?" Jas glowered.

Obedient nod.

"A guy comes oan tae ye, you let him – git ma meanin'?"

Understanding glimmered, sensed but not yet admitted.

"Play fair by him, an' he'll look after ye, yeah?"

The eyes were filling up. A slow nod. Sniff. "Christ, Longriggend wiz a dawdle compared tae this!" A sob caught in a throat barely adult enough to merit the bobbing adam's apple.

Jas frowned. He didn't need this...

...didn't need any of it. But something made him reach over and ruffle the kid's thick, step-cut hair. "Ye'll be okay, David – jist watch yersel', yeah?"

Obedient nod.

His hand lingered, feeling slight tremors from David's scalp.

"Anderson?" The shout echoed in the tiled room.

His hand snapped back. He looked over his shoulder. Another Brodie-clone.

"Visitor! Get cleaned up an' wait at the gates..." Frown. "...an' you, back tae yer cell."

Scurrying behind cut into his surprise. But an order was an

order. Jas washed his hands under a faucet, moved the bucket into a corner and headed for the door.

Fourteen

He waited in his group of six.

Waited while the six in front were body-searched.

What could they smuggle out? Letters? Complaints? Jas shoved hands deeper into pockets and tried not to think about the identity of his visitor, tried not to think about Peter's last words to him, in the holding cells under the Sheriff Court.

Behind, conversation buzzed. Jas considered asking one of the grey uniforms what had happened to the no-visits-for-the-first-fortnight rule, then remembered gift-horses...

...and his solicitor. Maybe the basic right to time with legal representation was still his.

Maybe he wouldn't need to sit opposite Peter's tanned, handsome face and feel ten times worse about returning to his cell.

Maybe he'd actually feel better. Jas glanced up at the cctv camera, then glanced away. Maybe not: solicitors could only do so much.

The sound of metal on metal. A gate slid open. Six denimed figures slouched through.

Metal on metal. The gate slid shut. Jas frowned. The half-dozen on their way through to the visiting suite looked anything but enthusiastic.

Steeling themselves for an hour opposite their own Peters?

He watched as the body searches began again. He watched two grey uniforms tentatively pat down men twice their age, light years apart from them.

A small man with dark curly hair resisted the search half-heartedly. The rest stood passively.

The clever caught on quick.

His mind flashed back to rodent-faced David, then the faceless screaming kid three cells down. He knew it wasn't lack of intelligence which stopped either catching on to the way of the world...

...the Bar-L world.

Parents, girlfriends, wives, mates: no one understood. You had to be here, feel here, and survive here...

Jas raised his arms and spread his legs. Stick-like fingers gave him a cursory search, then moved on.

...and the authorities wondered why prisoners were always harder to control after a visit.

A closed world. In every sense...

...which made nonsense of every other relationship in a prisoner's life.

And when two worlds collide...?

...the sound of metal on metal. The gate slid open.

Jas and five other men filed through, following a Hadrian officer down one corridor, then another.

Peter...

The six paused at a gate. Distant voices.

...his solicitor...

The officer waved his arms at a cctv camera.

...Peter...

Nothing happened. "Yer batteries ur flat, son!" Laughter. Jas smiled at the joke.

...his solicitor...

The officer turned, glared, then waved less vigorously at the camera.

...Peter...

The half dozen exchanged similar, less amusing remarks.

...his solicitor...

Metal on metal. Distant voices becoming louder. Heart pounded. He made his way through the open gate.

Peter. His solicitor. Peter. His solicitor...

Fifteen yards ahead, the dull hum of adult chatter and children's voices leaked out from between the bars of the last gate.

Turn back.

Walk away...

...he couldn't face Peter, didn't want to hear more bad news from Andrew Ainslie.

No sound of metal on metal. Just the scraping of keys in a lock.

Jas walked stiffly through, scanning the large room of tables and chairs and people.

Brown eyes careered into his. The first face he recognised was McStay's. He glanced away.

The second face he recognised was painted porcelain, with a large crack running lip to eye.

"Jas! Darlin'!"

Everyone turned. Everyone stared. Marie was on her feet, arms windmilling. He picked his way between tabled islands of families.

Hands grabbed his, dragging him into a kiss.

Jas flinched, tensing as a tongue prised his lips apart. Then something else entered his mouth...

...something other than her saliva. He pulled away, tasting metal. Foil.

Someone whistled. Then cheering. Then uniformed attempts to subdue the cheering.

Jas gazed past Marie's grinning face and met McStay's eyes a second time. He looked away, down to the child in his cell-mate's lap.

Hissing. "Shove it under yer tongue, Big Man!"

His eyes flicked back to the china-doll face. He sat, noticing Marie was still holding one of his hands, tiny fingers wrapped round his own. "Whit ye...?" His mouth sounded full.

"Shut it an' listen!" Head lowered, a curtain of brown hair falling across the damaged face. "Ah had a hellova job gettin' it in here, Big Man. Keep it under yer tongue."

Jas stared, then did as he was told.

It was becoming a habit.

The small, foil-wrapped package nestling behind his front teeth, he frowned.

Marie squeezed his hand.

"Ma solicitor's bin in touch?" The words were muffled.

Nod.

"Why did ye no' come tae the hearin', Marie?"

Shrug. Leaning closer towards him. "Couldney make it..." Low words. Intimate gestures.

Jas glanced around. He knew how this looked. He knew how Marie wanted it to look.

"...ony word oan wee Paul?"

He stared into hard eyes. "Whit?" The word was louder than he'd meant it to be. Conversation around them ceased... then started up again.

Marie winked. "Well, since ye're in here onyway..."

Something was making sense.

"...an' only on remand, at that... ah thought maybe ye'd..."

"You set me up!" He seized her wrist.

She didn't struggle. A denial equally absent.

"You wanted me in here, so ah could ask aboot yer toe-rag of a brother!"

Small smile. "You're the best, Big Man, an' ah ainly want the best."

He tried to read beyond the smile, then gave up. "You any idea whit ye've done, Marie?" He released the wrist.

She rubbed it. "Don't worry – ye'll git paid fur yer time. Come the fourth o' December, ye'll be back in yer flat a coupla thousand richer an' ah'll huv Paul back wi' me!" She grinned.

He scowled. "You're gonny carry the can?"

Wide-eyed stare. "Well, it wiz ma smack, after aw'..." Wide changing to sly. "... like ah could tell yon wee solicitor o' yours – if ah decide tae return his calls. Aw' ah gotta dae is appear at yer trial, tell 'em it wiz mine an' that the hale thing's bin a misunderstandin'..." She cocked her head. "...how diz that sound?" Cigarettes plucked from pocket, unwrapped and extended.

He ignored the gesture. "Sounds like a fuckin' set-up!" Fury flickered across his skin.

She laughed, stuck a cigarette between his clenched lips, lit it. "Nae harm done, in the long run. The charges against ye'll be dropped..." Voice lowered. "...the minute ye find oot where Paul's holed up."

He inhaled, then exhaled, watching her face through a haze of smoke. Marie held the key to his freedom – a key she intended to hold on to, until it suited her. The powerlessness tugged at his lips. "This is blackmail, ya..."

"That's a nasty word, Big Man – it's mair an... efficient use o' resources."

"So ye'll come tae court, take aw' the blame if..?"

Nod. The curtain of hair flicked behind an ear.

Could he trust her? "An' whit aboot you goin' straight, gettin' yer kids back?"

The scar twitched. "Ah'll handle that, Big Man – don't you worry aboot me..."

He laughed for the first time in four days. It was a harsh, half-laugh.

She frowned. "Whit's so funny?"

Jas coughed, sobered.

His cell-mate. Neil Johnstone. Countless other men. Marie didn't have a clue...

A small hand on his shoulder.

...or did she? His eyes wandered around the room. Marie and he appeared more intimate, more physically connected than most of the other male/female couples in the smoke-filled room. Jas fixed her with his eyes. "You ken whit they dae tae ex-polis in here?"

The stare returned, unflinchingly. "You can handle it, Big Man."

For the first time in his life, he wanted to hit a woman.

She leant over and kissed him again. Hands wrenched them apart after a few seconds:

"No physical contact, Anderson!"

Low chuckles in the background.

Marie wiped red-tinged saliva from his mouth with the back of her hand. "An' that'll put paid tae ony rumours about where ye like tae bury yer face!"

He stared at the ancient eyes, and saw the understanding.

Marie lit a cigarette. "When ah wiz doin' the discipline stuff, coupla years ago? Summa ma best customers wur ex-cons. They git a taste fur the domination, an' their poor wives ur worse than useless – ah ken how things work, an' so dae you."

Jas ground the cigarette out in an ashtray.

They stared at each other.

Marie extended the packet a second time, then tugged at Telly's scratchy jumper. "No' yer usual style, Big Man..." She winked. "...present fae a friend? Goat yersel' a cunt awready?"

He flicked the foil-wrapped package of heroin into his right cheek. "No' funny, Marie."

She sobered, lowered her face closer to his. "Dae we huv a deal, Big Man?" She smelled of cosmetics, cigarettes and cloyingly expensive perfume. A lower, basser note of desperation soured the scent.

It leaked from his own pores. Barrels, and what it felt like to be over one filled his head. Jas sighed. "Okay – jist don't kiss me again."

She threw back her head and laughed .

He watched her light another cigarette and stare over his shoulder:

"Ye're suckin' oan three grams o' high-grade smack, man. Use it – ken how tae cut?"

Jas shook his head, staring to where his cell-mate was frowning, deep in evidently unpleasant conversation with a thin, harassed-looking woman: not the woman in the photograph.

"Shouldda brought talc in wi' me – whit the fuck wiz ah thinkin' aboot?" Self-reproach.

He looked away from McStay and flicked his cigarette. Gallus, bullet-head Paul McGhee slipped into his thoughts. His mind began to work – at least now it had something to work on. "Whit dae ye want me tae dae?"

Elbows placed on the table between them. "You're the investigator, Big Man – investigate!" She stared over his shoulder again.

"Whit you lookin' at?" He watched the tip of the scar edge downwards.

"Somethin' funny goin' on, ower there – naw, don't turn roon'!"

He continued to watch her eyes, which were narrowed in concentration.

"Two lassies... at a table on their ain... no wan's sittin' wi' them... noo they're talkin' tae wanna the screws an'..."

"Which screw?"

Eyes narrowed further. "How the fuck should ah ken? Some big bastard wi' grey..."

A bell shattered the sentence. Shouting shattered the bell. Marie stood up. Jas turned, just as Ian Dalgleish grabbed two overly made-up girls and pulled them towards the exit. A worried-looking Ms Pepperpot trailed in their wake.

A low laugh at his side. "Ah kent there wiz somethin' goin' oan wi' that pair. Aye, well they tried..." She turned. "... ah'll no' tell ye where ah wiz hiding the smack afore ah gied it to you!" The scar twitched.

Before his stomach could respond, a trio of Brodie-clones marched into the room. Another bell rang. Jas watched hastily-conducted farewells before joining the rest of the visited.

Marie lingered.

As half the Brodie-clones manoeuvred a mass of women and children towards the outside world, Jas watched her blow him a kiss:

"Seeya soon, darlin'! You take care, mind – ah'll hear fae ye soon, eh?"

He wanted to laugh.

"Move it, lads."

Jas recognised Brodie's attempt at authority. Nodding at

Marie's disappearing form, he walked from the visiting area.

The small silver package nestled inside the red briefs. Jas looked across the canteen table at Telly.

The ruddy face grinned and munched. "Heard ye had a visitor the day, Mr Anderson." Wink.

Word travelled fast.

Munching. "Yer girlfriend?"

Jas frowned. "Jist a friend."

Nod. "If you say so." Another plastic forkful of something unrecognisable raised to mouth.

Jas looked down at his plate, prodded a heap of soggy vegetables: no time like the present. "Her wee brother wiz in here. Maybe ye ken him..." Eyes to Telly's face. "McGhee – Paul McGhee."

The mouth paused, mid-munch. Brain slipping into gear. "McGhee... McGhee..."

Voice at his side. "Skinny boay? Big mooth?"

Jas glanced left. "Aye, in fur possession: E." He glanced back at Telly for confirmation and reaction.

A frown. "Oh, him..." Chew, then swallow. "...is he no' oot, noo?"

"Aye, but causa the 'nae mail' rule, he wants me tae gie a message tae wanna his pals'..." He stared at the ruddy face. "...wid that be you, Telly?"

Choking laugh. "No' me, Mr. Anderson." Cough, then chewing resumed.

"Who wiz he friendly wi'?"

Quizzical frown. "Why ye wanna ken, Mr. Anderson?" Automatic suspicion.

Jas felt three sets of eyes on him. He shrugged. "Telt ye:ah've got a message fur them – the guys he wiz dealin' wi'."

Telly rubbed his chin. "Nae eccy in here, Mr. Anderson." Eyes over Jas's shoulder.

He followed the look to a group of grey uniforms. "Who wiz his mates, then?" Jas watched Ian Dalgleish's bulky form shake with laughter at some shared joke, then returned his gaze to Telly.

Another shrug. "Nae idea, Mr Anderson."

Jas patted the smack in his briefs. "Ah'll trade."

Head-shake. "You keep yer fags..." Another mouthful of slop. "...an' forget aboot yer lassie's wee brother."

Jas put down his fork, leaned closer to the ruddy, still-eating face. "Whit wiz he intae, Telly? Who wis he friendly wi?" He lowered his voice. "Three grams. Pure stuff..." Jas watched the bait considered.

"Like ah said, nae idea..." Voice lower. "...ah'll git ridda hauf a gram fur ye, but that's it."

Jas stared. "Ye ken maist o' whit goes oan in here..."

Telly crossed plastic knife and fork neatly, then pushed his plate away. "Lea' it, Mr. Anderson – yer lassie'll no' thank ye fur the ins an' oots o' it."

"C'mon, man..."

Slow head-shake. "Ah didney ken him that well, Mr Anderson..."

Jas clenched his fists. "You kent him well enough, Telly."

Sigh. "Make it a gram..." Eyes raised. "... ah really didney ken him that well, but ah ken a guy who did..." Pushing back his chair, Telly got up. "Come oan, then: there's corridors tae be washed."

It was a package-deal. In every sense.

Leaning against the tiled wall of the shower block, he watched skilled fingers unwrap the smack, dab a little onto a yellowing tongue, then nod.

"It's guid stuff, right enough." Telly carefully shook approximately half the white powder into a scrap of cling-film, then returned the remainder to Jas. "Keep that oota sight."

Half an hour later, they both held mops and buckets and a third of the smack he'd traded Telly had been traded on.

Some time after that, Jas found himself on the other side of a heavier gate than usual.

Three Halls away from B.

Segregation wing.

Telly nodded from behind thick, forged iron. "Talk tae Black Bill. He wiz pally with yer lassie's brother..." Frown. "...Christ kens whit they had in common, but..."

Jas raised an eyebrow.

"Go on, Mr Anderson." Telly nodded down the corridor. Faint music drifted up from the far end. "Ah'll come back fur ye in hauf an oor." He lifted his mop and bucket, walked away.

Jas stared after him, then lifted his own cleaning cover and walked towards what sounded like Cole Porter.

He was right. Jas paused outside the final cell-door. It was ajar. 'Night and Day' trickled out. He knocked, surprised at his own courtesy.

"Come." Soft voice.

He pushed the door fully open, and stared.

Painted walls. Pictures...sketches. Single cell...

...his eyes zeroed in on a cheap-looking ghetto-blaster, from which Ella Fitzgerald's rich voice drifted up. "Bill?" He focused on the back of a slim figure, hunched over a small desk.

The figure turned. "Who wants to know?"

Jas rested his mop against the cell door.

The body said mid-fifties. The face said late teens. Blond, wispy hair surrounded youthful, almost child-like features. The denim work-shirt was buttoned to the neck, giving it a formal, white-collar look. Elegant, pianists' fingers protruded from shirt cuffs. One hand held a blackened stick.

"Yes, I'm William Black..." He placed the charcoal on the table, then turned back to Jas. "...and you are?"

"Ah'm a mate of Paul's – Paul McGhee?" His eyes were dragged to the sketches which covered the walls.

"Oh, really?"

Something in the voice pulled his eyes back to the gentle-looking man. Jas thought of the bullet-headed kid who had driven him to London, two years ago. He stared at the intelligent, cultured face, hands clasped loosely in a relaxed lap.

Chalk and cheese?

Prisons threw up strange combinations.

"How is he? Enjoying his freedom?"

Jas stepped into the softly-lit environment, closing the door behind him. "You knew he wiz gettin' oot early?" It was something to say. Grey eyes studied his:

"I knew that was what he was hoping for..." Eyes continued to examine his features. "...Paul a friend of yours, you say?"

Jas flinched under the stare, moved forward. "A friend o' a friend."

"Ah..." Black Bill stood up, met him half way. "...you've got a remarkable face."

Jas stepped back. He tried to laugh. It didn't work.

Soft smile. "Am I embarrassing you? Sorry."

His skin was hot. Jas clenched his fists.

Slender fingers stretched up, traced the outline of his jaw. "That chin's marvellous..."

Jas stiffened, twisted his head away. "How did Paul swing

early release?" He walked to the side of the desk, stared down at a mess of papers.

"Let me draw you..."

Jas stared down at faces. Old faces, young faces, male, female.

"...I'll tell you about Paul, if you like..." More bait.

The voice was close, soft. His eyes flicked up, past the child-like face to a pen-and-ink sketch on the wall above the bed.

A male version of Marie, with step-cut hair stared back at him.

"Agreed?"

Jas nodded, turned.

Black Bill lifted a pad of A3 cartridge paper and the stick of charcoal, moved back a little. As skilled fingers darted and shaded on paper, the small mouth began to move in sync. "He liked to talk, Paul did – he needed to..."

Jas listened, staring at the drawing of Marie's brother.

Black Bill talked easily. "The way things... work inside was all very new to him. He had to..."

Jas shifted uncomfortably.

"...keep still, please..."

Jas complied.

"...to... adjust. Told me about his exploits, on the outside..." Soft laugh. "...about his friends, his cunts..."

The word seemed at odds with the gentle, soft-spoken figure with the charcoal and the Ella Fitzgerald. Jas shifted uncomfortably. "He talked about his mates?"

"That's good – keep frowning, it suits the lie of your face..."

Cheeks began to burn. Jas flinched. "Mates – who wur his mates?"

"We didn't dwell much on the present – more the past, and the future. Balance, you know? Paul confided in me: he was trying to... make sense of what was happening to him, and I like to think, in my small way, I was helping him do that."

The future? "Did he say where he wis goin', when he got oot?"

Blackened fingers pausing, eyes looking beyond his face. "Ah, you're the cop?"

The future? "Ex, an' this has nothin' tae dae wi' polis. Dae ye ken whit Paul's plans were – fur after he got out?" He shuffled his feet.

If Black Bill registered his discomfort, he made no comment. "He was intending to contact a friend of his, in Longriggend." The sketching continued.

"Dis this friend huv a name?"

Soft laugh. "If he did, it escapes me for the moment." Pause. "Paul was a little boy with big ideas..." Chuckle. Blackened fingers moving more quickly. "...I don't know how he did it, but he had something going with one of the officers."

"Whit screw he wiz friendly wi'?" Jas seized on the information, knew Telly would be back soon. He didn't have much time.

Grey eyes raised from the sketch. "Mr Dalgleish."

"An' whit dae ye mean – 'something going with'?" He frowned.

"Judge not, lest ye be judged..." Grey eyes met his. The sketching ceased. "...Paul did what he had to – we all do." A page torn loose, held out.

Jas ignored it. Fists balled, then relaxed.

Black Bill seemed to suck the aggression into himself, neutralise and render it harmless.

Jas scowled. Something about the man made his skin crawl.

Smile. "Please accept this as a gift..." The sketch held out. "...I'd love to draw you naked, sometime. Come and visit again. Soon."

"You keep it..." He pushed the sketch back at the child-like figure and walked from the cell.

"What's your name?"

Jas ignored the question, grabbed his mop and bucket. He wanted away from gentle Black Bill and the cell full of faces.

Telly was waiting at the gate. "He see ye right, Mr Anderson?" Nervous eyes darted as he fiddled with the lock.

Jas considered seeking confirmation of the information he'd just recieved. Then reconsidered. "No' really..."

One fence.

Two sides...

...if Paul McGhee was involved with a screw – in any capacity – it would not be public knowledge anyway.

More fiddling. "Shouldney be in here at aw'..." One hand raised to make circular motions an inch from a balding head. "...Carstairs didney huv the bed space...." Both hands back to fiddling. "...geez me the willies, but if ye're voice's broken, Bill's harmless..." Gate creaking, then swinging open. Telly pushed Jas down the corridor. "...did a rare drawin' o' me fur the wife – fair pleased wi' it, she wiz..." At the next gate, he smiled at a Brodie-clone, walking through into B-Hall.

Jas followed wordlessly.

Fifteen

On the cot, he linked fingers behind his head and stared up at metal spirals. Jas focused on curled springs and knew how they felt. On the periphery of his vision, his cell-mate's thighs stalked into view, turned then stalked away.

The mood in the cell was tighter than usual...

He frowned.

...but he wasn't here for the atmosphere. The frown twisted into a scowl. And he needed to think. Closing his eyes, he thought of Black Bill's neat cell...

...his mind culled news reports from over the past ten years. Then found what it was looking for.

William Black. Lothian and Borders region. Sentenced to a minimum of thirty years for the rape and murder of five boys, none of whom had seen their tenth birthday.

Sentenced to thirty years in a maximum security mental hospital.

The Bar-L was neither maximum security or a hospital, but needs must... when Hadrian held the reigns. It was not surprising Black was here: it was a surprise he was still alive. According to Telly, the man had been transferred from Peterhead, awaiting a bed at Carstairs. He thought about the small, neat segregation cell... the faces... the CD player. Not the cell of a prisoner in transit.

Not the type of prisoner who usually had an easy time of it. Not the type of prisoner to attract visitors to his cell...

...unless they were carrying weapons. Not the type of prisoner he'd expect Paul McGhee to be friendly with.

Jas rubbed his face.

Not the type.

Judge not, lest ye be judged...

Jas tried to relax the muscles in his face.

Ex-polis: possession with intent to supply...

...thinking in types wasn't productive.

Types was meaningless.

He ran a hand through hair: according to Black, Paul was intending to get in touch with a friend, after release and had been friendly with Ian Dalgleish during his sentence. The first piece of information took him nowhere.

The second?

Inside, there were few reasons for friendliness between officers and prisoners. Jas thought about the bullet-headed kid who'd driven him to London three years ago...

"Where is it?"

Jas opened his eyes, poked his head out from the lower bunk. "Where's whit?"

"The fuckin' piss-pot!"

He swung his feet onto the floor and stood up. He didn't need this... not now.

His cell-mate was standing beneath the barred window, face a study in fury.

Jas stared at the semi-undressed man. For the first time he noticed the ridges of scar tissue decorating McStay's chest. "Whit you on aboot? It's..." He dragged his eyes away from the wounds, to the corner.

No piss-pot.

His mind travelled back to this morning's fracas in the showers, and an item thrown but not retrieved. "Sorry, ah..."

"Fuck sorry, pal!" McStay took a step towards him.

Jas held his ground. Animosity crackled through the air between them.

Two men. One cell. A hierarchy as yet unestablished.

"Look, it's no' lights oot yet, there'll be somewan still around..." He turned, to the locked door and thumped twice. "Oi! Mr Brodie? Ah need..."

The forearm around his neck stifled the end of the sentence. Jas inhaled sharply, thrusting back with both elbows, then following their motion against the body behind him.

The movement took McStay by surprise. He staggered, then toppled, loosening his grip in an attempt to break his fall.

Jas twisted around, pulling free from the grip. "Whit's your problem, pal?"

"You're ma fuckin' problem!" McStay cleared his throat.

Head flicking left, Jas avoided the bullet of phlegm. He seized his cell-mate's naked shoulders.

Tremors darted up and down muscle. He could smell the violence, smell...

"Ya fuckin'...!"

Fingers gripped more tightly. He held McStay steady, brought up his knee and...

...something hit him in the stomach, something hard and round. His knee impacted with McStay's nose, missing the intended target in the face of the vicious head-butt. Jas fell back against the cell door, skull glancing off rusting iron, hands still gripping cold shoulders.

Fingers clutched at his face, thumbs gouging at his eyes.

He twisted away.

Hands scrabbling for a grip. Someone was breathing hard and cursing. Gasping, Jas raised his knee again.

The other leg hooked from under him, he fell backwards, spine jarring against the lower bunk. "Fuck, ya...!" Fingers dug into hard flesh.

McStay lunged forward, crushing him. Jas gritted his teeth, tasting blood in his mouth. He strained, bucking his hips against the heavy form.

Nothing.

He buckled again, muscles rigid, and rolled.

Movement. Pulling him upright.

Strong arms pinned his to the side of his body. Stronger legs pressed against him.

His spine glanced off bare brick.

Breathing in his ear – heavy, laboured breathing.

Using his weight, Jas swore and pushed forward, using McStay's motion to topple the man a second time.

An elbow came loose. He rammed it into a soft stomach, felt the rest of the body go limp. His guts ached, his head spun from the glancing blow of the bunk's edge. Jas grabbed a flailing fist as it zoomed towards his face, fingers tightening around a tensed wrist. With the other hand, he shoved his cell-mate back onto the floor.

The man's head landed with a thud.

Jas registered the stunned look on McStay's face, but didn't stop.

This wasn't about piss-pots...

...the faceless, innocent victims of this man's homophobia floated in front of his eyes. He flattened McStay's right arm on the stone floor, threw himself on top of the snarling body and grabbed the other arm.

McStay bucked and heaved, roaring.

His knees slid off a fleshy abdomen. Jas straddled thighs and glanced at the fine white lines which encircled the man's wrists like bracelets. It took every ounce of his strength and weight to hold

McStay there.

The body beneath strained upwards, lips frothed with pink spittle, frustration contorting face.

Two men. One cell. A power balance asserted.

Jas scowled down, then lowered his head, stopping inches from his cell-mate's bleeding nose. His stomach brushed a hardness.

An unexpected hardness.

Heart thumping in his ears, Jas moved his eyes from the enraged face to the crotch of the man's regulation denims. He continued to grip McStay's damaged wrists, staring at the raised outline.

The arms in his grip tried to flex.

Jas tensed, flicking eyes back up to his cell-mate's face.

McStay turned his head away.

Beneath his chest and stomach, Jas could feel laboured breathing. His own groin ached with a new pain.

McStay twisted in his grip...

...and brought back Telly's words: '*...disney feel onythin' when he's in wanna they tempers..*' He thought about the razor, at present lurking in the mattress, then disregarded the thought. Moving down the erect, cursing semi-naked man, Jas nudged thighs apart and forced a knee against McStay's balls.

"Ya bastard! Ah'm gonny..."

"Ye're gonny – whit?" Jas released one wrist, then regripped both with strong fingers. He waited for his damaged arm to let him down: it didn't. He stared at ridges of white scar tissue and the blush which was spreading over the pale face, trickling down onto neck and chest.

There was more here...

...more than he wanted to deal with. With his free hand, Jas seized a chin, held the thrashing head steady.

Then slapped.

And slapped again.

No punches. Pain wasn't the object.

The pale face reddened further but didn't flinch.

Jas scowled, hand stinging. "Open yer eyes!"

Lids clenched firmly shut.

Beneath denim, vulnerable flesh flexed. Jas pressed his knee more firmly into the man's groin.

Eyelids shot open. Glazed amber glowered up at him.

Easing himself off quivering flesh, Jas replaced his knee with his hand.

The blush extended under jeans' waistband towards the hard outline.

Jas cupped tight balls, squeezing. "Forget the fuckin' piss-pot, eh?" Instinctively, he rubbed the root of the hardness with a thumb. Blue eyes never left brown.

Inches above his fist, the outline twitched.

"Eh?" Jas squeezed again.

"Aye – okay!"

He released the wrists.

McStay's arms remained above his head. A gesture of defeat.

Jas closed his eyes, feeling a man in the palm of his hand. The smell of two sweating bodies drifted into his nostrils. Jas scowled.

His own prick itched against the zip of his combat pants. He opened his eyes and looked at the spoils of the fight.

McStay's chest was still heaving, the broad shoulders pushing down against the cold stone floor.

Jas stared at the ridges of dead skin. Some looked old, some relatively new. Fingers tightened. He knew what he should do. Unzipping, he hauled his prick free from combat pants.

McStay should be broken completely.

The shaft flexed against his palm. His left hand still gripping the man's balls, Jas stared at bloodied, swollen lips.

He should take what was rightfully his.

McStay would respect him for it.

Word would shinny up the Bar-L's grapevine. His position in the hierarchy would be established.

Jas released denim-and-jersey-coated balls, moving up the defeated body. Knees in the hollows of his cell-mate's armpits, he ran a hand down his own pulsing length. Eyes floorwards.

McStay's nose had stopped bleeding. A crust of crimson snot outlined the upper lip, frosting dark growth...

...then Jas shoved prick back inside compat pants and pushed himself to his feet. A flicker of surprise on the angular features.

He continued to stare as McStay hauled himself upright.

His cell-mate stared back, skin flushed from exertion.

Jas hoped the show was enough. Just in case it wasn't...

...turning away, he reached under lumpy bedding. Fingers brushed what was left of the heroin, then the steel of the denuded Bic. He drew the blade out. Voice behind:

"Whit did ye dae wi' that fuckin' piss-pot, onyway?"

Different sounding. Jas slid the blade back between bed-frame and mattress, and turned.

A lop-sided grin. The expression rearranged the man's features more than any beating could have.

Jas tried to ignore the throbbing in his groin, and grin back. Semi-success. "Ah canny remember!"

A laugh.

He watched as his cell-mate reached towards the denim shirt which was draped over the end of the bunk.

Fingers into pocket, two hand-rolled cigarettes produced. One extended.

Jas took it. He lit both cigarettes, remembering tight ball-sac warm in his grip.

His cell-mate inhaled, sighed. "Christ, ah needed that!" He sat down on the lower bunk.

The smoke?

But at least they were talking.

After lights-out, each lying on his own bunk, they were still talking. Or one of them was.

Jas glanced silently from the glowing tip of his cigarette to the McStay-shaped dip in the mattress above.

Steven. Stevie.

"Aye, that wiz ma sister, Carol – she took Sam an' Haley, when ah got sent doon. She comes when she can, but it's no' easy – ah don't like the kids seein' me here, but."

The mattress-shape changed position. A sigh, then: "You got kids?"

Jas frowned, flicked cigarette ash onto the stone floor. His mind was back with what he knew about Stevie McStay: the fights...

And what he didn't.

...the scars, the frustration which had hung over the man like a storm cloud.

None of his business...

A point had been made. A hierarchy had been established.

...he wanted to ask. None of his business. He wanted to...

"...Sam an' Haley's mother walked oot oan us – oh, don't get me wrang – ah don't blame her, ah'm no' the..." Half-laugh. "...easiest o' bastards tae live wi'!"

He stared up at the dent in the mattress. The storm cloud had burst, releasing a deluge. Ears drifted beyond the words.

"...but me an' the kids get by okay..." Defensive. "... they're both at school noo, so ah could still work. Carol's been guid, helpin' oot an' stuff..."

The voice was husky from the cigarette. Smoky, like the thick haze floating down from above. It seeped into his ears, flooding his body in a soft, unwanted glow.

"...she's got three o' her ain, says another two disney make ony difference." Laugh.

The sound was warm, good-natured. Jas responded in kind and managed a parody of humour. It was all he could do. His silence had been double-edged: the refusal to talk about himself had given Stevie more scope. The details only served to bite deeper than any razor blade.

"Ye're oan remand, eh Jas-man?"

The title sent a shiver over his body. He leant out of the bunk, stubbed his cigarette on the cold stone floor and watched sparks fly then die. "Ten oota ten, pal!"

Another laugh. No resentment in the sound.

Jas stretched out on the cot and tried to ignore the throbbing in his groin. One tension had been replaced by another. He had to get his mind of it, he had to talk. "You?"

The mattress-shape moved.

Jas stiffened as a head appeared over the edge of the bunk above him:

"Two years..."

He stared through smoky gloom at glowing brown eyes.

Two more roll-ups extended downwards.

Jas reached up, took one.

Light flaring in the darkness.

He moved towards the flame like a moth. In the yellow matchlight, Stevie's face was very close. Jas stretched up his head, singed the tip of the cigarette, inhaled then moved back. He gripped the filter between thumb and forefinger, searching for a change of subject. "Kitchen-duties – that yer trade? Ootside, ah mean." He lay back on his bunk, hoped Stevie would do likewise.

The head continued to dangle, roll-up held between full lips. Frown. "Aye – they let me keep ma hand in." A drag. An exhale.

A cloud of smoke drifted across the air between them. Jas blew a grey oval. It swam towards the upside-down face.

The frown slid into a scowl. Cigarette removed from lips, ash flicked beyond onto the floor. "An' it keeps ma... mind aff stuff, ken?"

Jas knew. Hardness flexed against the fly of the combat pants.

Stevie took a long draw of the cigarette. "Eight months left o' ma sentence..." Upside-down eyes stared towards the barred window. "...shouldda been six, but they added another two."

Something else in the voice now – the voice which refused to let blood leave his aching prick: sadness.

Sleep pressed against his stinging eye-lids, seeping into his tired brain.

"Ah, well..." Sadness replaced by a philosophical yawn. Then more practical consideratons."Fuck, ah need a piss!"

Jas smiled in the darkness. "Tie a knot in it!"

A laugh.

Jas frowned, remembering the feel of Stevie's balls in his hand. "Git some sleep, eh?"

"Aye – guid night, Jas-man."

He pinched the cigarette between thumb and forefinger, felt the burn. "Night, Stevie."

Sixteen

By the time a Brodie-clone unlocked the cell door, Stevie was clutching his groin and swearing.

Jas watched his cell-mate dash past the grey uniform. He listened to the thump of work boots on metal.

"No running!" An order delivered without conviction. Or effect.

The bootsteps faded, but kept up speed.

Jas grabbed his towel, moved out onto the walkway. For the first time in six days, he didn't feel tired.

Six days – only six days. More like weeks. Or months...

...or minutes.

BST. Barlinnie Standard Time. Time stretched could also contract.

Telly.

Black Bill.

Gerry.

Alliances formed swiftly...

Stevie.

...and viciously. Jas frowned.

Time wasn't the only constant to blur and bevel within the

Bar-L's stone walls. He had just acquired status – unwanted, but much needed....

The queue moved more quickly. Jas glimpsed the back of a step-cut head, four men in front. He peered beyond, into the shower block, and caught sight of a figure already under a faucet, washing vigorously.

Stevie grinned and beckoned.

...with all the privileges that status carried. Jas glanced at the five men ahead of him in the queue, then broke ranks. He walked towards the middle shower.

Stevie's naked body shimmered, scars like Alps white and wet under a layer of lather. "It's still there!" Soapy head nodded.

He glanced at the errant piss-pot, and laughed, moving to retrieve a piece of Her Majesty's property.

"Naw, lea' it, Jas-man – that's ma job."

He nodded.

Jas-man.

The title was strange, but was growing on him. He watched fingers scrub ruthlessly at face and body, taking in the man's bulk. Stevie seemed more relaxed, even under his obvious gaze.

He glanced from one naked man to a queue of others.

Several pairs of eyes glanced away.

One rodent set stayed.

Jas frowned at David Hamilton, who was watching him with a mixture of fear and confusion. He looked away, over towards where his cell-mate's towel lay. Walking to the bench, Jas picked up the length of grey fabric, then returned to his previous position.

He'd watched dozens of men shower.

Men with whom he had just spent the night.

Men he made hard.

Men who made him hard.

Men he had chosen, who had chosen him.

All types of men...

He stared at Stevie's back, eyes tracing the long line of flexing sinew between shoulders and the swell of solid buttocks.

...never men he had just fought with.

Stevie leaned forward, chasing a sliver of soap along the wet floor.

Jas stared at the dark crevice between slick mounds of flesh. His cock twitched, remembering the frustration of last night.

Stevie straightened up, turned. He began to rinse his body,

closed eyes raised to the streaming faucet.

Men moved past him and around him. Jas ignored the activity, continued to watch his cell-mate. He thought of other intimacies, of friendships, working relationships...

...rubbing Stevie's towel between thumb and forefinger, he frowned. "Christ, get oota there! Ye'll use aw' the hot water!"

Brown eyes flicked open.

Jas threw the towel.

Stevie caught it easily, began to dry himself.

Jas strolled to where his cell-mate's clothes lay in a crumpled heap. He stood silently, watching Stevie dress.

The other side of status...?

Jas stared, noting his cell-mate's small, shrivelled cock.

...control. A response he could handle. He waited until Stevie was fully clothed, then caught a brown eye.

Stevie returned the stare. "Seeya at breakfast." Fingers securing still-damp hair in ponytail, then turning.

His eyes followed the man to the corner of the block.

Stevie lifted the aluminium bucket, looked back once, then walked from the steam-filled room.

Jas smiled, resumed his place in the queue. Voice in his ear:

"Yer loony bum-chum canny be with ya aw' the time, Anderson..."

He shivered. Breath against his lobe.

"...Neil sez tae tell ye he'll be in touch."

He stared at the tiled wall ahead.

Stevie: one threat down...

...a multitude to go. He stood motionless. The faucet was still free, unused after Stevie. Jas knew the vacant shower was implicitly his for the taking – there would be no argument. He undressed quickly, then stepped under lukewarm water.

An extra slice of bacon was piled on his plate.

Jas glanced from his tray to the pale face.

Tangled ponytail hidden beneath a white, hygiene cap. Brown, friendly eyes.

Behind, the breakfast queue waited impatiently. He nodded.

Stevie winked. "Fancy a spell in the kitchen?"

Jas stared over a white-clad shoulder, through a serving-hatch into a hot, steam-filled room.

"Ah can get ye in – if ye want."

Jas returned his gaze to Stevie.. "We'll talk aboot it later."

Nod. "Sure. Enjoy yer breakfast..."

He filled his coffee cup from the urn and headed for Telly's table.

The familiar chair was pushed out in anticipation, with more gusto than usual. Jas blinked. The other three men at the table fed on his presence, his new status: he knew Telly would trade on it, later.

"Mornin', Mr Anderson!" Cheerful.

Jas sat down.

Telly leant forward. " Ah see ya've dealt with McStay."

The acknowledgement took him in a direction he didn't want to go. Jas tucked into his breakfast, surprised at his appetite.

"Ah..." Disappointment badly hidden at the lack of details.

Information was highly prized. But some things were private. Jas continued to eat.

The desire to flex his newly acquired muscle was tempting. He paused, set down his knife and fork and turned to Telly. "Ken that jacket ah traded ye?"

The ruddy face was eager to please. "Ah huvney selt it on yet, Mr Anderson – kent you'd be wantin' it again."

Jas recalled the man he'd spotted two days ago, the bikers' jacket slumping badly on thin shoulders. "That wiz nice o' ye, Telly. Gie it tae..." Eyes flicking to the serving-hatch. "...Stevie. He'll see it gets tae me."

Eager nod. "Ah'll dae that, Mr Anderson." Telly did a fair impression of an over-enthusiastic, if badly trained, puppy.

Jas almost smiled, then remembered the whispered threat in the showers.

Neil Johnstone. At the moment, in another block, but with contacts everywhere.

He resumed his meal.

Shouting. A buzz of conversation sank to a low hum, then evaporated.

His head flicked up, then left.

Over by the wall. At the table, five denimed men pretending to eat with gusto. The sixth hidden by a large, grey shape.

Jas cocked an ear. The low, baritone was audible. Ian Dalgleish's words escaped him, as did the voice of the prisoner under intimidation. He continued to stare.

Telly lived up to his name: relayer of messages. "That stupid wee nyaff's rubbin' too many folk up the wrang way..."

Jas watched as Dalgleish's bulky form moved back, exposing his victim.

A small rodent-face poked up from black nylon padding. It was hard to tell if David Hamilton's head shook in denial or fear.

Jas frowned: the boy's refusal to fit in would cause ripples in every direction.

Telly snorted. "Fuckin' kids – shouldney be fuckin' in here at aw'. That wan's ainly just turned eighteen..." A head shake, disbelief the motivator. "...if he disney git himself sorted oot soon..."

Jas turned, an eyebrow raised in encouragement.

Telly blinked. "Me?" Coughing laugh. "...too much trouble, Mr Anderson."

A squeak of panic refocused Jas's eyes beyond the ruddy face.

Dalgleish blotted out David completely.

His table-mates ate furiously.

Jas sighed. Trouble followed the kid like a bad smell. The panicked squeak echoed in his head and brought back the screams of two nights ago. He scowled, did the only thing he could and swept his breakfast plate onto the floor.Clattering echoed in silence.

Abruptly, the bulky grey figure released a now-bobbing Adam's apple and turned.

"Sorry, Mr Dalgleish..." Jas stood up. "...ma hand slipped." He stared past quizzical gunmetal eyes to where a rodent-hand was rubbing a rodent-neck.

Professional baritone growl. "Accident-prone, are ye, Anderson?"

On the edge of his vision, Jas saw looming grey. Dead ahead, a rodent face managed a smile of thanks.

"Pick it up!"

Jas ducked down. Large boots planted inches from his face. Fingers collected shards of shattered plate. He stood up. "Sorry, Mr Dalgleish, it'll no'..."

"Ye're right it'll no' happen again!" Ian Dalgleish shook his head and strode back towards a group of Hadrian grey.

Wisps of conversation rose, condensing into a thin mist of whispers.

Jas looked across to David Hamilton's table. The rodent-face was wet, blotchy. He moved his gaze to the back of Dalgleish's outline.

A bell rang. Around him, men rose reluctantly to their feet. Jas joined them. Lifting the broken plate and cup, he filed towards the serving hatch behind Telly. With two hundred other men, he placed his breakfast dishes on one of three trolleys, then turned to file out.

As he approached the barred gate, he caught sight of a tear-stained rodent-face.

David Hamilton scurried towards him.

Two grey uniforms ignored the motion.

Padded nylon closed the gap.The step-cut head flicked up to meet his frown with a wan smile.

Jas nodded to beyond the gate, paused. He wondered about his own motivation...

The kid scuttled into a space in the queue.

...then gave up wondering. Jas watched the attempt to shrink into the mass of denim. David was new, fresh, young and unattached.

At least one of those attributes needed changing.

Beyond the gate, the slender shape in the padded jacket waited against a yellow brick wall.

Jas raised his eyes to the cctv and walked on.

David fell in step with him. "Fierce, man..."

"You okay?" Said without turning.

"Aye, ah'm fine." Sniff. "Yersel'?"

Normality kept up at all costs. Jas glanced ahead. Grey uniforms were chatting idly. He steered the kid to one side, down towards the area where the cleaning-materials were kept. One last chance – after this, it wasn't his problem.

Away from the crowd, David began to sob.

Jas flinched. The kid's misery twisted at his guts. "Look, ye..."

"Oh, man, this is fierce – ah canny stand much mair an'..."

"Who ye in wi'?"

Head raised. Quizzical look.

"Who ye sharin' a cell wi'?"

Understanding. "Ah'm no' sharin' – no' ony more! Ah'm gettin' a cell tae masel'."

"Since when?" Cells were doubled up, even in Triple-S. The Bar-L was too overcrowded to permit such luxuries...

...free of charge.

Sniff. "Since this mornin' – Mr Dalgleish is arrangin' it."

Maybe it was worth it, for the smoother running of good ship

Barlinnie – damage limitation? Jas remembered the roughly fashioned key which had facilitated entry to his own cell.

"Fierce, this is wan scarey place!"

A single cell would cut down on daytime harassment. Nights were another matter. "Listen David..."

"Aw, it's Hammy, man..."

Jas raised an eyebrow.

"Hamster." Shadow of a smile. "Cos ah look like a wee rat!"

The name echoed in his mind.

The smile waned. Whining. "Whit am ah gonny dae?" A hand through step-cut hair.

Jas closed his ears. The plea resounded in his head. He thought about the screams, three cells down, two days earlier. There would have been a build-up to that final, desperate act: had indications of that build-up fallen on equally closed ears?

The rat-mouth was moving, babbling on, rising in volume.

"Keep it doon!" Jas glanced behind, then moved closer. He tried to think. Nothing for nothing, in the Bar-L: single cells meant many things.

Trouble-maker.

Favouritism.

Patronage...

"If Mr Dalgleish is bein' nice tae ye, it's no' cos he's wantin' yer arse, Hamster." Jas stared at the pale face, watched the implication sink in.

Step-cut hair whipped from side to side across the pale face. "No way, man – no' fuckin' way!"

Jas almost smiled: barely eighteen, but the kid already knew which side he was on. As Dalgleish's snitch, Hamster would have the officer's implicit protection. But if implicit knowledge became explicit, the kid would have no chance amongst the other men.

Screws were hated, par-for-the-course.

Grasses were despised...

...a hand gripping the sleeve of the scratchy jumper:

"Help me..."

"Shut it, will ya?" Jas scowled.

Lips clamped together, mid-syllable, eyes making up for lack of words.

He scanned the pale face, then the rest of the body, shrouded in padded nylon and over-sized jeans. He didn't need this – he didn't need the responsibility, in a world where taking charge of his own survival was difficult enough.

He didn't need the hassle of treading on Ian Dalgleish's toes.

Jas moved his eyes from a terrified face and stared at the yellow brick wall behind the step-cut head. Through the thoughts, rushed words:

"...yeah, man? Whit aboot it?"

Jas refocused.

Hamster was staring hopefully up at him, the rodent face scarlet. "How's aboot it?"

Jas blinked.

Hammy glanced down at huge trainers. "Ye want me?" Words barely audible.

Jas frowned. He had been wrong. Telly had been wrong. David Hamilton knew the ropes all too well. The boy had misinterpreted a few meagre shreds of humanity. He ignored the offer...

Hands on the belt of his combat pants, inexperienced fingers unzipping him.

...and felt his cock stiffen. Arms rose to push the boy away. Eager words:

"Ah'm guid, man – aw' the boays in Longriggend said so..."

Jas stared down at the top of a step-cut head. Cold air brushed thighs. Nimble fingers wrenched Telly's contraband briefs further down. The waistband dug in beneath his balls.

Hamster knelt on cold stone.

Then experienced, lip-sheathed teeth over the head of his half-hard shaft.

Jas gripped padded nylon-clad shoulders and pulled the boy to his feet. This was getting complicated. "Ah've goat a cunt, and ah'm no' in the market fur another."

Bemused expression.

Jas tried to keep his mind off his hardening prick. He stared into the childish, high-cheekboned face: Hamster had already received two offers – powerful offers.

A step-cut head against the arm of the scratchy jumper. "Tell me whit ye like..."

Jas flinched, lowered his voice. "If ye dinny want tae be a guy's cunt, ye gotta buy him aff – ye got onythin' tae dae that wi'?"

A negating sniff against his sleeve.

Bootsteps.

Moving instinctively in front of the smaller figure, Jas turned, hands pushing cock back beneath Telly's contraband underwear.

Stevie. Wearing the bikers' jacket. Narrowed eyes registering his open fly.

Jas zipped, moved back.

Stevie approached. The bikers' jacket fitted him well – almost as well as its owner.

Jas nodded. "Ah see Telly got it tae ye?"

Laugh. A broad hand rubbing the worn leather sleeve. "Aye, it's the gemme..." Laugh cut short. Stevie stared beyond him. "...he botherin' you?"

Jas shook his head. "Hamster's no' botherin' onywan." He looked at the once-more shivering kid, remembered the last gram of Marie's H.

The path of least resistance...

...and the other, ever-stable currency in the Bar-L. Digging a hand into the side pocket of the combat-pants, he located the foil-wrapped package. Stevie's disapproving eyes bored into his back. Jas held out his hand.

Hammy stared at the closed fist.

Jas frowned. "Take it..." His voice was low.

Step-cut head raised. Eyes met his.

Jas sighed. "Take it, pal! Buy yersel' some protection."

Hammy looked confused, shuffled his feet. "Ah thought you an' me wur...?"

"Ken Telly?"

Slow nod.

"Go find him. Tell him ah sent ye..." Jas seized a scrawny wrist, prised open fingers and crammed the H into Hammy's hand. "...he'll help ye oot."

Telly knew the ropes.

Telly knew who was in the market for a cunt.

Telly knew who would ask least and provide the most, if the H failed to cut it.

He watched a small hand disappear into the pocket of oversized jeans:

"Fierce, man, ah..."

"Ye owe me – ah ken..." Jas smiled: nothing for nothing..

"Oi!"

Jas stiffened. Inches behind, he felt Stevie's broad form flinch.

"McStay! Anderson!"

He stepped out from behind Stevie, shoved Hamster in the direction of the dining-hall. "Whit?"

Over-sized trainers slapped along the corridor and out sight.

He stared at the four officers. Jas hoped the transaction had passed unnoticed. Half-heard words:

"Cell search..."

Stevie. Protesting. "Why? Whit ye think...?"

"Come on, lads..."

Two grey uniforms moved behind, trying to herd.

Stevie. Still protesting. "There's nothin' in oor cell – why dae ye...?"

Jas found himself walking.

Flanked by grey, they were marched back to B-Hall.

As he climbed the stairs to the second floor walkway, Jas thought about Hamster, and the H, and the unwitting favour the kid had just done him.

Seventeen

A cell built to house one now held four.

Jas stood on one side of the doorway, a grey uniformed hand gripping his arm.

On the other side, Stevie was a surly reflection. Noise: metal on metal, fabric ripping and tearing, boots on stone, laboured breathing. The sounds of frustration.

Jas clenched his fists.

Stevie's anger wasn't as easily contained. "Whit ye lookin' fur?"

The two screws flanking them didn't answer. A third appeared from inside the cell. Eyes to Jas, then Stevie:

"We have reason to believe Class A drugs are secreted in this cell. You're in for dealing, Anderson. Thought you could do a bit more while...?"

"Ah'm only accused o' dealin', pal! Nothin's bin proved." He stared past the officer into the bomb-site of a cell.

Stevie: "There's nae drugs in there! Lea' oor stuff alain!"

Jas glanced at his cell-mate.

Anger didn't come anywhere near the expression on the furious features.

Jas sighed.

The officer stared at him. "Well, Anderson? I don't hear you denying the charge..." Blink. "...make it easy on yersel', lad. Tell us..."

"Bingo!" Voice from inside the cell. A grey figure. One hand holding two halves of the disposable razor. The other gripped condoms and the jar of Vaseline.

Jas glanced across at Stevie, met confused brown eyes.

"Who does this belong to?"

"Smine!"

Two voices. Jas watched Stevie's face redden.

The officer frowned. "This is a fuckin' first! Ye both want put oan a charge?"

"The blade's mine..." Jas continued to meet Stevie's eyes. "...the johnnies ur his."

"Right – come on, the paira you!" Hands gripped his arms.

Jas bucked against the movement, watched his reaction mirrored in Stevie. "Ah said the blade's mine! He's got nothin' tae dae wi' it – there's nae law against johnnies, is there?"

Unamused laugh. "If yer usin' them tae spread drugs around this prison, there's lotsa laws against it!"

Three officers focused on Stevie. One spoke. "Whit ur the condoms fur, McStay? You've no hame visits scheduled..."

Jas blinked.

A low laugh. "...an' even if ye did, ye've nae wuman tae fuck, isn't that right, McStay?"

Another voice, taunting. "Walked oot on ye, didn't she? Widney stay wi' a fuckin' loony an' his two loony kids..."

"Shut yer fuckin'...!" Stevie lunged forward. Two pairs of hands grabbed his arms:

"Want assaultin' an officer added to the charges, McStay?"

Jas scowled. "Lea' him alain!"

The hands on his arms regripped. "Ken whit the penalty is fur huvin' a weapon in yer cell?"

He twisted in the grip. "Ah lose ma privileges?" No response. Then a flushed face inches from his. Low voice:

"You'll lose privileges ye never knew ye had! Now, get a move on – ye can tell yer tale o' woe tae Mr Dalgleish!"

Jas continued to frown as he was propelled, with a struggling Stevie, down a metal staircase.

"Thanks, Jim – ah can handle this."

Jas stood in front of a large desk, in a small room. He watched the officer who had taunted Stevie exchange glances with Ian Dalgleish, then reluctantly leave. He returned his gaze to the broken Bic, the condoms and the Vaseline, which lay on a pile of blue folders. "That lot's mine – all o' it: McStay had nothin' tae dae wi'..."

"Why?" Gunmetal eyes bored up at him. Disappointment and frustration shone from both barrels.

Once, this man's approval had been everything to him. Jas felt himself struggling to justify present failure. "Ah didney ken whit ah wiz walkin' intae, comin' in here – the razor's fur protection..." He frowned. "...so's the condoms!"

Ian Dalgleish stood up and strode over to a filing cabinet. "Ah should put ye oan a charge – you ken that..."

His eyes focused on the small, intricately carved chess-set which sat on top of the filing cabinet, game in progress.

"...but ah'm more interested in the heroin ye've bin flashin' around: where ye bought it, and where ye've stashed it." The bulky figure turned.

Jas stared. "Who tipped ye aff?"

Ian Dalgleish lifted the black knight from the chess board and stroked its rigid mane. "Cell searches are routine – we try tae dae it with all new prisoners..." Gunmetal eyes cocked. "...for their ain safety."

Jas raised an eyebrow.

"Where did ye get the H?"

Jas bit his lip: grassing Marie up would do no one any good, himself most of all.

Gunmetal eyes blazing. "Don't even think aboot dealin' – Barlinnie is a drugs-free zone."

He remembered Telly's offer, the other transactions he'd witnessed while washing corridors. Jas' eyebrow arched further. "Aw', come oan..." He wanted to laugh, but knew this was no laughing matter.

Dalgleish walked back to the desk, still holding the black knight. "Ah want a list o' yer customers..."

He knew Officer Dalgleish had put two and two together, and made the usual four. "Ah'm no dealer."

The statement ignored. "Hadrian are taking a very hard line oan drugs." The bulky man sat down. "Barlinnie hud a serious problem, when we took over fae the SPS..."

Jas stared.

"...aw' prisons have – you ken that. Maist fights are over drugs, and ma men have enough tae dae, withoot constantly drug-busting." The black knight placed on the desk between them. "Eradicate that problem, and maist others go too – it's oor primary mission statement."

Jas stared at the chess piece. "Ground Control tae Hadrian – come in Hadrian!" He wondered what world Ian Dalgleish was living in. Then remebered two sides of one fence. Opposite sides.

Gunmetal eyes narrowed. "Control the drugs..." Dalgleish leaned across the desk and looked up at him. "...an' ye control Barlinnie."

Jas stared from the black knight to the contraband. "The condoms aren't fur transportin' H. Ah'm no'..."

"Dae ye understand what I'm saying?"

He glanced up. "Are ye askin' me tae believe there's nae drugs in...?"

"We're workin' oan it – an' we're getting there. Barlinnie's a lot cleaner – an' safer – a place tae be than it wis."

Jas recalled the screaming boy, three cells down, the threats he'd received...

...was still receiving. Drugs were only part of the problem. But arguing the toss was pointless. He repeated the truth. "The johnnies urney fur transportin' drugs."

The implication acknowledged. "Ah should still pit ye oan a charge." Broad fingers picked up a condom, turned the foil package over, the held it out. "Ye ken the official Scottish Office line on male-tae-male sex?"

Jas frowned.

"...it disney happen – because if it did, it wid be criminal activity, since prison is defined as a public place..."

"Well, that policy's no' exactly been a roaring success." Jas scowled. "Needles and fuckin' have already got ye 150 HIV positive men..."

Dalgleish stood up. "...who are isolated, and will be given condoms if an' when they ur released."

Jas clenched his fists and thought about the three well-muscled men he had encountered while washing corridors. "Ah' whit good does that dae onywan they take a dislike tae, in here?"

"Ah'm no' saying we've solved all Barlinnie's problems..." Gunmetal eyes blazed, then looked away. "Rome wasn't built in a day..."

"Aye, but it burnt doon in wan." Everyone knew drugs had a place in prisons: cannabis helped relieve the boredom and calm things down. Failure to acknowledge this fact, let alone attempt to eradicate drugs completely, was tantamount to idiocy.

Ian Dalgleish was no idiot: did the order come from above? Livingston?

He stared at iron-grey hair: doped-up or otherwise – acknowledged or otherwise – tensions would continue to simmer in any prison. He watched Ian Dalgleish pluck the black knight from the desk and replace the piece on the chess-board:

"Let me give ye a bitta advice, Anderson: don't..." Turning. "...get involved in onythin'..."

David Hamilton flashed into his mind. "Whit makes ye think ah want tae?"

Gunmetal eyes stared back. "You huv been observed..."

Jas blinked. Cctv? Hadrian officers? Or snitches?

"...an' if ye have ony heroin left, get rid o' it."

The truth. "Ah've done that..." More truth. "...an' ah've no' intention o' either usin' or dealin'." He searched the face for belief.

Gunmetal eyes focused on the contraband. "Did ye buy this lot wi' the H?" Eyes raised to his.

He looked away and let silence lie for him, remembering the present destination of the remainder of the smack.

A sigh. Something like relief. "Aye, well ah canny blame ye fur that, ah suppose." Dalgleish flicked open a folder, picked up a pencil. "This isney the safest place fur you tae be." Pause. "Yer trial's – fourth of December?" Eyes raised.

Jas met the gaze. Paul McGhee and the Black Bill-sourced information shot into his mind. "Hadrian in the market fur grasses?"

Curious smile. "Ye'll only be here – whit, another five weeks?" Smile slipping. "...and ye'll be doin' well if ye..."

"Ah'm no' volunteerin' – ah'm wonderin' aboot a friend o' a friend. He got oota here, coupla months ago."

Quizzical iron-grey eyebrow raised.

Jas supplied the name.

Gunmetal eyes narrowing. "McGhee?"

Jas nodded.

Stare, then slow headshake. "The name means nothin'." Frown. "You ony idea o' the administrative chaos Hadrian walked intae, when the SPA called that strike?" Quizzical again. "Whit's yer interest in this guy?"

The truth? "His sister used to snitch fur me, years ago. We keep in touch..."

Understanding in the gunmetal grey. "Ah – the lassie wi' the scarred face? Yer visitor, yesterday?"

Marie had made her usual impression. Jas nodded.

Dalgleish stood up. "Pretty lassie – shame aboot that scar..." He walked around the desk.

"So her brither wisney grassin' for ye, then – or ony o' yer men?"

"Like ah said, the name means nothin'..." File flicked shut. "...noo, keep yer nose clean ..."

Jas turned towards the door.

"...and ah'll see whit ah can dae aboot gettin' ye a single cell."

Jas paused. Him and Hamster both?

"There's nae room in Isolation, but ye should at least be moved. McStay's..."

"...ah'm fine where ah am." Jas turned.

Surprised. "You didney waste ony time!"

Jas savoured the respect: at least he'd got one thing right.

"Watch yersel' wi' McStay, though." Dalgleish talked on. "The guy's goat problems. They ainly tolerate him in the kitchens cos he's an excellent cook..." Laugh. "...make someone a lovely wife!"

Jas flinched under the innuendo. "Ah ken whit ah'm doin'."

"Do ye, now?" Vaguely amused. "Aye, well ah suppose ye do." Black knight re-plucked from board. "Ah was thinking about the auld days earlier..." The carved piece held between thumb and forefinger. "...knights were your downfall, if ah remember correctly – ye eyeways underestimated their ability to move around the board." Dalgleish reached past him, grabbed the door handle and pulled. "McStay! In here – noo!"

Jas edged out of the office.

Stevie's glowering form pushed in, flanked by Hadrian grey. The door reclosed.

As he stood, flanked by similar officers, Jas's mind returned to the black knight...

...and a Gorbals sergeant's skill at chess.

Door slammed shut. Keys scraping. Early lock-up as punishment. Stevie had lost kitchen privileges.

Silence.

Jas stared at the small, barred window then turned.

Stevie scowled, eyes scanning the debris of the recent cell search. Then focusing.

Jas followed his gaze. A heap of blankets, pillows and stuffing littered the floor. One of the mattresses was ripped beyond use. On top of the pile, a small, Polaroid-coloured rectangle.

Stevie crouched, picked up the photograph.

Jas watched the movement.

Waves of antagonism radiated up from the lowered head, directed outwards, to beyond the locked door.

Jas grabbed the mineral-water bottle, unscrewed the top and took a slug of Eau de Bar-L. He wiped his mouth, staring at two clenched fists: one held a connection with outside...

...the other was a way of life inside.

Silence.

He took another drink. The water was cold, at least. Jas stared at the kneeling man.

Then Stevie balled the torn photograph in a hard fist and slammed his hand against bare brick.

And slammed it again.

And again.

Jas gripped the arm just before the fourth punch. Tremors rippled through a pulsing biceps, travelling up fingers, wrist and ending in his guts.

Stevie's body was rigid and shaking. Blood poured from knuckle grazes, trickling down the back of the quivering hand and onto the sleeve of the bikers' jacket.

Jas knelt behind, his other hand gripping Stevie's shoulder. He watched his fingers tighten on hard muscle, felt the resistance.

It took all his strength to lower the fist.

It took more than strength to pull the man back against him, holding tight around the solid pectorals. Jas trapped Stevie's arms against his sides.

No resistance.

Stevie sank back onto his chest.

Jas could feel hard sinew, still tensed and trembling. Maintaining his grip, he stared at the well-worn leather of his own bikers' jacket, staring at the scars on the man's wrists.

They sat in silence, on a bed of ripped mattress, tangled bedding and Telly's contraband underwear.

He inhaled the smell of sweat and something less easily identifiable, but deeply familiar.

Anger and frustration he knew only too well...

...knew how they ate into everything.

After a while, Jas slackened his grip, turning Stevie's broad form around to face him.

The brown eyes lowered, refused to meet his.

Jas didn't push it.

Time was one thing he had plenty of.

Bells rang.

No meals arrived.

Stomach grumbling, he grabbed one end of a ripped mattress. Together they heaved the remnants of bedding onto the top bunk. The knuckles of Stevie's right hand were bound in a pair of contraband underwear.

The photograph had been meticulously flattened, the creases pressed out. A faintly rumpled woman and two smiling children again beamed down at him from bare brick.

He kicked the empty piss-pot, then lit a cigarette, sinking to a crouch against the wall.

"Can ah cadge wan?"

Jas extended the packet and fumbled for matches.

Stevie inhaled, then blew a smoke ring. "Bastard!" The word rang hollow, inadequate.

"Who?"

"Dalgleish!" Smoke flaring from nostrils.

Jas exhaled. Hating screws was par for the course.

Stevie leant against the re-righted bunks. "Telt me this wis ma last warnin'..." Scowling lips blew smoke over his head.

Jas stared up at his cell-mate. Darker red was seeping through the scarlet underwear.

"Did me fur assaultin' an officer, six weeks ago." Voice tightening. "Wiz a fuckin' accident – ah didney... ken whit ah wiz daein' – jist tryin' tae get away an'..." Voice almost inaudible. "...wish noo ah really had assaulted him, the number o' poor bastards Dalgleish's fucked over since!"

He gripped the cigarette between thumb and forefinger.

"Ah ken aboot you, Jas-man..." Words slow, deliberate. "...you fucked the polis back, eh?" Head lowered.

Jas stood up. "They returned the compliment!"

Snorting laugh. "Ah kent you wurney a druggy – yer lassie bring in the H fur ye?"

He eyeballed the man inches away. No sign of the earlier anger – no sign of the rage which had nearly broken the bones in

Stevie's fingers. He wanted to keep it that way. Too many tensions already. Jas knelt, began to unlace boots. "Aye..."

The hardness beneath his jeans was a surprise, uncomfortable in every way.

He didn't want to think about Paul or Marie McGhee...

Boots kicked free.

...he didn't want to think about Neil Johnstone, and other antagonisms he didn't need...

Socks dragged off, stuffed into boots.

...he didn't want to think about Dalgleish, and whether Hadrian had or had not been using Paul McGhee as a grass...

T-shirt pulled off, draped over the end of the bunk.

...he didn't want to think about the way the head of his cock rubbed against the fly of his jeans.

He didn't want to think at all. Jas crouched, then stretched out, arms braced. "Count fur me, yeah?"

"Whit?" Surprise.

"Jist count."

"Sure, Jas-man." The voice was closer.

He stared at the floor.

Stevie's boots entered his line of vision.

He closed his eyes and began the push-ups.

Stevie's voice punctured the sound of his breathing...

...then a fist beneath his chest. He felt the dampness, hoped it was sweat and not bloody underwear.

At twenty, he was skimming skin.

At forty, the bone between his pecs was impacting hard on the fleshy marker.

At sixty, he was back in the gym, and the fist belonged to Ali, Jimmy – one of any of a dozen men with whom he trained regularly.

At seventy, low words in his ear:

"Jeez, Jas-man!"

Elbows locked in the raised-arm position, he opened his eyes. Heat rippled up and down bi and triceps. Three inches below, Stevie's undamaged fist was strong and steady.

"...fuckin' impressive!"

Jas scowled, sank back onto knees. He didn't want to impress. Wiping face and chest with the T-shirt, he lay down on his back, knees raised. Jas clasped hands behind his head.

Pressure on his ankles. Warm pressure.

He flinched.

Stevie held his feet tightly. "Wan..."

He touched forehead to knees, eyes closed.

"...two..."

Forehead to knees.

"...three..."

Forehead to knees. Cock against thigh.

"...four..."

Forehead... knees... cock... belly...

"...five..."

Forehead... knees... cock... stomach muscles trembling...

...somewhere between twenty-five and thirty, a bell rang and the lights went out. Fingers gripped ankles, tighter than ever.

Jas opened his eyes, continued the sit-ups.

Through the darkness, he met Stevie's luminous gaze every five seconds. He tried to slow down, lengthen the gaps.

The counting continued, maintaining the pace.

At fifty, one hand released his ankles and reached behind his head, holding him upright.

Throat burning, chest hammering, guts churning, prick aching, Jas stared through the darkness at the face inches from his.

Breath on his cheek...

...on his eyes, his forehead, his...

Soft laugh. "Take it easy, eh? Ye'll damage yersel'!"

Jas ducked out from under the hand behind his neck and stood up.

Damage... the sobs of a desperate boy, three cells down... David Hamilton's terrified face...

He walked to the window, gripped two iron bars and hauled himself up.

...the ridges of scar tissue which crossed Stevie's body like battle-lines...

Jas stared out at the night lights of Riddrie, then straighten his arms and gazed at brick.

...all types of damage.

He bent his elbows. Riddrie appeared.

He straightened his arms. Riddrie vanished..

Movement in the darkness behind.

Jas continued the pull-ups, trying to ignore the closeness of Stevie, trying not to listen to the lowering of a zip. Sweat trickled from his pits, the hair on his chest was damp and cold. Head lowered, he stared at his bare feet. Moisture dripped through eyebrows, stinging his eyes. He closed them.

The sound of pissing flooded through his labouring breath.

He squeezed his eyes shut. Heat sizzled through sinew, the heat of exertion...

...and the hot feel of his cock hard against his belly.

The pissing stopped.

Jas dragged himself up to the window and hovered there, listening to the metal drag of zipping over the thump of his heart. He waited for the pad of retreating footsteps, for the creak Stevie's body would make as he hurled himself onto the top bunk.

Nothing.

Flashes of other times erupted in his mind...

...of the physical closeness of changing-rooms, the shower room at C Division's rugby practice... men he had worked with, men he had known...

...of parks, toilets, beaches... men whose faces he barely registered and would never see again, but whose bodies he would know intimately.

Young men. Old men.

White men... occasionally Asian men.

Married men.

Men with boyfriends, girlfriends, wives... kids... homes... lives...

A clanging sound. Then: "Fuck!"

One of Stevie's hastily discarded boots impacted with the aluminium piss-pot.

His cell-mate was close – very close. Jas could no long feel the muscles in his arms, but at least they were functioning. The smell of his sweat was strong and salty: sea-salty. Mixed with the scent of piss and a faint odour of disinfectant, the stink took him to another, equally unwanted environment...

...early teens. Family summers at the beach. Ancient lavatories with a whispered reputation his thirteen-year-old mind could make no sense of. Adult warnings versus teenage curiosity...

Something burned in his right arm.

Jas released the bars, felt his feet touch the floor. He turned, groin aching with the need to piss and the hard-on which made that impossible.

A hand on his arm. Fingers tightening.

Eyelids shot open. Jas blinked into amber.

A laugh. "Work oot regularly?"

The fingers on his biceps were acid, burning through to the bone. Jas pulled away. "Aye..."

One last squeeze of muscle, then his arm released. The Stevie-shape turned away. "Ah huvney got the patience..." The Stevie-shape picked up a boot.

An arm brushed against his groin. His heart stuttered, then found a louder, heavier voice.

"...maybe ah'm just lazy – workin' oot's too much trouble..."

In his mind, the arm was still there, became a hand... the hand that made excuses to be there. Jas closed his eyes and thought of his curious, thirteen-year-old prick in the grip of older, equally curious fingers.

...swimming-trunks couldn't hide what his mind had tried to. Standing in damp darkness, he thought of other damp darknesses, of his faceless lover's dry hand inside the trunks on his sea-wet, sandy balls. He remembered the confusion, the vague tremors of fear mixed with unbridled pleasure as the man had caressed him to orgasm, while his brothers and sister ate sandy banana sandwiches, yards away.

Sweat cooled rapidly on his burning skin. Jas shivered, damp Barlinnie air erecting every hair on his body. His heart sank. His cock leapt. His balls tensed, a thin film of sweat shimmering on the skin.

Twice more, that summer, he'd gone to other toilets, hung about and waited for the same thing to happen.

It never did...

...and when he'd finally summoned up the courage to risk a fumbling hand towards a stranger's prick...

He rubbed his face, remembering the look of revulsion in the man's eyes, the push which had sent him sprawling backwards onto the wet toilet floor and the sight of a rapidly departing sports jacket.

"Show me a coupla exercises, Jas-man? The morra, maybe?"

He pushed hands back over hair and stared at the Stevie-shape. Those hands holding those ankles, the closeness, the feel...

...Jas reached out into darkness, fingers settling loosely on a heavy shoulder. He rubbed the bristly line at the back of Stevie's neck.

All types of power...

...he'd never felt so powerless. "Aye, maybe." He aimed a playful fist at the approximate area of Stevie's mid-section.

A laugh. His cell-mate dodged to one side, then batted the side of his face. "Wanna take me on, Jas-man?" Half taunt. Another test?

Jas scowled. His dominance in the cell had been asserted by fists and bulk. He wanted nothing else from this man...

...not like this. He gripped the strong chin. "Gie it a rest, eh?"

Flesh flinched in his grip. Stevie's laugh died, replaced by something else.

Jas's cock flexed. He released the chin, moving away.

Pupils expanding in the dark, he watched the Stevie-shape vault onto the upper bunk.

"Whit wiz aw' that wi' the boay?" Curious.

Hand paused on zipper. "Whit boay?"

"The wan wi' a face like a rat – the wan you gave the H tae."

Jas frowned. "He wiz gettin' hassle – ah couldney jist stand by an'..."

"Aye ye could..." Low voice. "...it's none o' your business."

Stevie was right. He pulled off combat pants, boots, then the red underwear. His business was finding out the possible whereabouts of Paul McGhee...

He walked towards the double bunk.

...and doing that was proving difficult enough. An arm through the darkness:

"Fancy a smoke?"

Jas shook his head. Every muscle in his body ached with the force of the work-out.

The sound of a match stroking, then smoke drifting down through the darkness.

As he crouched, pulling back the thin blanket, another muscle made itself known. "Good night, Stevie."

"'Night, Jas-man!"

Eighteen

The cold woke him.

And stomach cramps. Jas levered himself off the cot and padded across the stone floor.

Dim, lunar light spangled off aluminium and bleached the skin on his legs. He held his prick loosely, sighed with relief. His balls tingled, but the cramping in his stomach lessened as he continued to piss.

Soft snoring behind.

Jas listening to the sound of liquid on metal, thumb and fore-finger tightening around his shaft. He glanced over his shoulder at the Stevie-shaped hump in the top bunk.

A spurt of urine hit the wall behind the bucket as his prick began to harden in his hand.

He turned away, clearing his mind and willing himself soft. As the last few dribbles dropped from his cock, a shudder rippled over ashen skin.

Sleep was the furthest thing from his mind.

Jas turned back to his bunk, fumbled for a blanket and...

Keys scraping. Turning. The cell door swung open.

Bright light in his eyes.

Not moonlight.

Jas froze.

From the top bunk: "Whit the...?"

"Shut it, McStay!" Two sets of hands grabbed his bare arms, pulling him off balance.

Jas wrenched himself away.

Hands regripped.

He ducked his head, peered beyond the torch beam to a group of figures on the dark walkway, eyes blinking. Another cost-cutting measure by Hadrian flashed into his mind, just before Neil Johnstone did.

"Oi! Whit's this? Lea' him...!"

"Keep oota this, McStay!" Fingers tightened.

Someone grabbed his waist, trying to hold him there.

Fingers pulled harder, dragging him towards the doorway. Voice in his ear:

"Move it, Anderson – or yer bum-chum comes tae."

Seconds later, his bare feet scraped the hard metal of the walk-way. He tried to focus on faces. Failed. He tried to assess numbers. Failed again. Pushed against the railing, he was held there, a hand on the back of his neck.

The sounds of relocking...

...then banging. From the inside. Stevie's shouts and the thump of his feet faded as Jas half-walked, half-stumbled blindly towards the stairs.

"Whit is aw' this?"

No response.

He didn't really expect an answer, but it was worth a try.

Pause. Unlocking.

His eyes were getting used to the gloom. Four men – two holding him, one walking behind. In front an outline hauled the gate open. Jas looked upwards.

No red eye logged their progress.

Hands pushed him forward.

He'd considered breaking free a good two blocks back. Then disregarded the idea: where could he go? The gate was relocked behind. Keys rattled. He flicked his head left, then right.

Faces were dark silhouettes, occasionally illuminated by a rogue beam from the torch. Features unreadable.

No one talked... no one had talked since the brief sentences, back in the cell. Even then the voice had been unfamiliar. And familiar.

Male.

Adult.

Glasgow accent.

Jas stumbled on. "Whit's this all aboot?"

Another no response.

His brain was working too fast. Thoughts sprinted past. He clutched at their tails and held only confusion...

...and the unmistakable beginnings of fear.

Abruptly, he was pushed sideways.

No scraping of keys. This corridor was unlocked.

Light blinded him. Hands propelled then released him. His face impacted on polished wood.

Jas shook his head, raised himself onto all fours, then turned.

This corridor wasn't a corridor...

The large, open space of a gymnasium loomed around him.

...and it did have a lock. Jas focused on the back of a denimed figure, at present inserting and turning a key which dangled from a large, official-looking bunch. The gym was huge after the smallness of his cell, smelled vaguely of sweat and an odour which reminded him of schools. His heart speeded up, keeping pace with his racing brain. He staggered to his feet, swaying slightly. Fists clenched, Jas examined his captors, trying to ignore the disorienting effect of his surroundings.

Faces...

...faces he didn't know, but who evidently knew him. Three remained at the door. One began to circle.

Jas followed the movement with his naked body.

No one spoke. Over the sound of measured bootsteps, the silence pressed in on him. Jas frowned: he knew the technique...

...continued to mirror the circles, trying to ignore his vulnerability. He registered ancient wall bars, a couple of limp-looking punch bags and a vaulting horse which should have been put out to pasture years ago.

Instinct told him the four men in the room were not into subtlety.

Instinct told him the intimidation would be brief.

Instinct told him there was little he could do against four.

He scanned floor and walls for visible weapons.

Nothing.

Eyes flicked to the door.

The three men had moved.

Panic surged through his veins. Adrenalin joined the brew. His balls tightened, drawing up towards his body. Eyes darting, he searched for the rest of...

...and found them too late. Arms grabbed him from behind. A dull thud to the side of his head, heard more than felt.

Jas reared backwards, as he'd done wth Stevie two nights ago. The trick didn't work this time.

Hands held him firmly. A dull thud in his stomach.

The blow heard and felt. Jas buckled, air rushing from his lungs.

Something hit him again.

Lower.

He crumpled, eyes watering. He fought the instinct to curl, clutch his genitals and go fetal. His brain careered out of control and towards things he didn't want to think about:

A screaming boy in the cell three-down.

The well-muscled figures in a corridor.

Neil Johnstone...

A hand grabbed his hair, pulling his head back.

Rage diluted the pain and rendered it useful. Jas cleared his throat and spat.

The man leapt back, wiping phlegm from his cheek.

Bracing himself against those behind, Jas drew up his knees, then kicked.

Bulls-eye!

Fingers briefly loosened.

Jas pulled knees back to belly, felt his own thigh against his injured groin. He gritted his teeth, doubled over and tried to throw the men behind.

It half-worked.

Then pressure on his throat.

Jas tried to twist away from the hand. The movement was useless.

Watery green eyes fired into his.

His own eyes refused to focus.

The hand on his throat tightened and squeezed.

Something buzzed in his ears. Spangling on the edge of his blurry vision. A tingling in his fingers. Then he was moving again. His feet hit the ground, legs buckling beneath him.

The hand released his windpipe.

Jas gulped in air. Knees scraped along worn, wooden floor.

Something impacted with his belly.

Not a fist.

Bigger... more solid. He tried to kick. His legs wouldn't work. Then someone worked them for him.

Coldness around his ankles... then wrists.

He prayed for the pain to return and bring the adrenalin.

The prayer went unanswered. His body was numb and limp.

Leather-encased hands cuffed his legs and wrists to something cold and hard.

And heavy.

Vision stabilised. Jas blinked at the worn surface of the vaulting-horse, inches from his face. Icy air brushed his thighs and arse. Muscle clenched instinctively as unwanted sensation returned to his body. Pressed against padded leather, his balls ached.

Good with the bad.

Shreds of strength returned with the pain. He hauled against the metal restraints, then gave up. Another useless instinct: the vaulting-horse was bolted to the floor. Through the buzzing and pounding in his ears, he fought to make sense of the sounds behind him...

...then something that needed no explanation. Blood rose in his face as strong hands gripped the cheeks of his arse, wrenching. Jas tried to relax. His mind fought the clench of his sphincter and lost the battle.

Fingers pulled harder.

Instinct fought on...

...he heard rather than felt tearing. Then something hit the side of his head:

"Come on, Queer-boy – ya ken ya want it!" Laughing.

His body floated away, released by another blow to his head. Through the numbness, hands gripped his shoulders...

...and hot hardness drove into his arse.

Wetness on his face. Scarlet skin heating salted water. Jas closed his eyes. He concentrated on the sounds around him, then pushed them away. Voices crowded in on him. Pressure...

...building, thudding, stretching pressure.

He knew the pain in his arse was a cock when it came inside him. Jas tried to breath normally, but his body wouldn't stop shaking.

Then something made it.

The cock was pulled out. His arse-hole gaped, then was immediately refilled.

He pressed his burning face against the worn nap of the vaulting horse. He could smell them, smell their bravado and the sour stench of his own terror.

Someone grabbed one ear, wrenched his head up and grabbed the other,

Jas rode the pain like the cock rode him: awkwardly.

Another show...

...words in his ears. "Ye've got a big mooth, Anderson – but no' as big as yer arsehole's gonny be when we've finished with ye."

Not the voice of the man fucking him: too calm...

...he bit through his bottom lip.

"Guid cunt, eh boys?"

Laughing... and panting and... something hot and salty leaked from his eyes and cooled on his hot face...

The cock inside him jerked, then slid out.

Jas spat blood. Hand released his ears. Two down...

...two to go.

Somewhere on the edge of sensation, movement. Against wrists and ankles, removing the cuffs. Hauled from the support of the vaulting horse, he fell against someone.

Who caught him, laughed and pushed him away.

Jas slumped back against someone else, limbs lead and cotton wool at the same time.

Hands held him tightly, pushed him forward. He broke the fall with aching arms.

Pressure on his fingers. Boot pressure.

Another cock bumped off his arse-cheek, stabbed twice more then hit home.

He fell, hot cheek pressed to the gymnasium floor, knees dragging. An arm under him, hauling his body onto all fours.

More wetness, beneath skin rubbed raw by friction.

He vomited bile. Someone growled in disgust. A boot left his right hand and hit his cheek...

...then a voice: "Keep yer nose oota whit disney concern ye, Anderson..."

Pain in his head.

"...or next time we'll no' be so nice aboot it!"

Laughter zeroed in, then pulled away. Raw tingles inside him...

...then emptiness. And darkness.

More words. Hauling him up from a dark, quivering tunnel. Shouted words:

"Bastards! Fuckin' animals! You're fuckin' dead, ya..."

Jas flinched. Something tight around him. He fought it, fought the journey from numbness into sensation.

It retightened.

He stopped struggling against the arm. It relaxed a little.

A hand on his face. He flinched again.

"Oh, Jas-man, whit the fuck...?"

He tried to move. Coughed. The dregs of someone's spunk oozed down the back of a thigh. And something less viscose. Jas opened his eyes. Semi-darkness. Flesh pulsed and stung. Everywhere. He could smell ammonia and his own blood.

The hand moved from his face. "Hold oan..." Sounds of rummaging. Then swearing.

He moaned, reclosed his eyes and sought the black. "How long..." The words came out as a formless mumble. Jas coughed again. Warmth trickled from his nose. "How long...?"

Coldness against his hot lips. Then wetness.

He gulped down water, choked on a metallic taste. A hand behind his head, holding him steady. The liquid burned. He swallowed it desperately. "How long have ah been...?"

"No' long, Jas-man..." The sound of splashing.

The black on his eyelids turned bright red.

Jas shivered against the light.

"Oh fuck!"

He tried to move. Failed. He tried again, hauling himself upright. He opened his eyes, blinking against fluorescent glare.

Stevie's stare was wide, horrified: the dark had hidden the worst.

Jas inched towards the wall, stared through half-shut eyes.

His cell-mate was holding a bloodied T-shirt and an empty mineral-water bottle. Kneeling beside an aluminium bucket, Stevie dipped the rag into the piss-pot, squeezed excess out, then brought the make-shift sponge down above Jas's right eye:

"Stay still – ah've tried tae clean ya up a bit... wanted tae keep the water til ye came round." Dabbing. Surprisingly gentle.

Ammonia tingled in his nostrils. "Kills all known germs, eh?" Desperation brought the humour.

An attempt at a laugh.

He needed to focus, he needed to stay with it...

Jas zeroed in on Stevie's face.

...needed to fight the urge to roll into a ball and shut everything out. His visible cuts and bruises were the least serious. His guts throbbed, balls swollen and sore – immediate damage. The long-term variety worried him more. Inside, his body gaped from the intrusion.

Desperation brought the thoughts – the reckless, irrational thoughts.

Jas pushed them away. His brain thrust them back at him. His body pulsed with the illogical need to be clean, when any infection was a foregone conclusion, occurring in seconds.

The trickling on the back of his thighs was moving more quickly. He stared at Stevie's furrowed brow and willed his mind to stop functioning.

Panic rose before him, smashing out everything he knew and leaving only unsound, wishful thinking. "There much left?" Voice was a croak. He eyed the piss-pot.

The hand paused. "Enough – get ye tae the showers soon an'..."

"Pour it intae ma arse." He eased himself onto his right side, muscle twisting and tearing as new sections brushed the stone floor. If there had been acid, he would have bathed in it willingly.

"Whit?"

Jas inhaled sharply, then managed to manoeuvre himself onto his belly. "They came in me..." Every movement was agony. "...an' ah'm fuckin' bleedin'!" Raising himself onto one elbow, he glanced over his shoulder. "Do it, man! Come on!" He gripped quivering flesh, pulled against insitinctive clenching.

Confusion, hesitation painted the pale face.

He watched Stevie lift the aluminium bucket with both hands, then looked away.

The piss burned like acid.

Stevie poured carefully.

Fingers clenched into fists, knuckles scraping raw on the stone floor. "If it wiz good enough fur the Romans tae bleach their togas wi', it's good enough fur me!"

"Whit?"

"Nothin'! Keep pourin'!" Coldness through the burning heat. He tried to draw the liquid up into him, hold it there.

To cauterise.

To seal...

...to...

...rings of fire tightened.

He clenched his arse-cheeks. Then clenched higher, and became aware of new muscle... raw, searing muscle.

Jas closed his eyes, felt the scream build in his lungs. He held it like he held the piss. Scorched tissue seemed to soak up the stinging liquid. He began to shake...

"Oh fuck... oh fuck..."

...he staggered backwards on all fours, then squatted. Hands on his waist, guiding. The rim of the piss-pot dug into thighs. Sweat poured from his brow, his pits. Stevie's arms tight around his waist, his head on Stevie's shoulder, Jas released his sphincter.

The cell was filled with splattering. The stink made him gag. The relief made him shake more violently. Jas lowered his head and hugged himself. A blanket around his shoulders. Arms around the blanket. He slumped forward onto his knees.

The shivering subsided as something warm and gentle dabbed and wiped at his arse and thighs. Then a cigarette between dry lips.

Match struck. Stevie held the roll-up still as he lit it.

Jas sucked smoke into his aching lungs, drawing the nicotine deep into his brain. It mixed with shimmering adrenalin and helped keep alive what he wanted to forget.

The bleeding stopped. Eventually.

By the time keys scraped on metal, he'd managed into T-shirt and a pair of Stevie's briefs. The cell door opened. Jas stared at the grey uniform, watched a snub nose wrinkle in distaste then anger:

"Ya dirty bastards! Get this shitehole cleaned up straight after slop-out!"

Stevie took a step towards the rapidly disappearing grey back.

Jas caught a rigid arm. "Ah canny prove onythin' – an' who would ah try an' prove it tae, onyway?" At least he could talk.

Cold brown eyes.

Jas rubbed Stevie's biceps.

Brown eyes thawing a little. "Aye, well..." Unconvinced.

Jas eased himself off the wall, picked up jeans and made his way to the door. Behind, he heard the clang of the empty piss-pot.

At least he could walk. Jas inched slowly towards the shower-block.

All sorts of power...

...all sorts of privileges.

Neil Johnstone had just exercised one of his.

Jas stumbled past the queue, stopped under a vacant faucet. He pulled off the T-shirt, turned his face up to the shower-head and drank in the soothing heat.

He closed his eyes.

He didn't move.

He didn't wash.

Water flowed over him. Warmth seeped through his skin. He let it soothe and try to heal the unhealable.

Hands on his shoulders.

Jas opened his eyes, levelled his head.

Stevie.

Naked.

Holding a larger-than-usual bar of carbolic.

Jas glanced right, then left.

Nothing. No eyes – no grey uniforms.

His gaze returned to Stevie...

...and saw only tiled wall. But felt fingers. Jas lowered his eyes.

Soapy hands eased down soaking briefs and began to lather his thighs. He stared at the man who knelt before him and thought of other men...

...Jas tensed.

The hand stopped abruptly. Soft brown eyes looked up. "Sorry! Did ah hurt ye?"

He gazed down. The gentleness and concern made his guts turn over. He shook his head.

Vague, reassured smile. Then head relowered. The soaping

continued. As Stevie washed every inch of his bruising body, Jas's mind focused.

Last night...

...the pain was lessening, making room for anger. And curiosity. He remembered what that impulse did to cats. Amidst the jumble of taunts, one comment lingered:

...keep yer nose oota whit disney concern ye...

Stevie's fingers moved into his hair, rubbing vigorously.

He moaned, tried to relax into the movement, fists clenching.

Hands wiping sudsy water from his face. Jas blinked his eyes open. A bell rang.

He turned his head and watched a pudgy man demurely pass Stevie a remarkably fluffy-looking towel. He stepped out from beneath the faucet, caught the towel handed to him, and began to dry himself.

Another bell rang. He shivered, needing longer, needing more time... the warmth was bringing back the ache...

...and the desire to curl into a ball and stay there. Jas tossed the towel, watched it snatched one-hand, mid-air. Walking to the bench, damp men moved to give him room. He leant against the wall, muscle and sinew loosening and stiffening by turns. Awkardly, he pulled on combat pants, his cell-mate's thigh inches from his face.

Cell-mates...

...Jas frowned up at his ersatz nurse.

All sorts of power.

All sorts of relationships...

...one of which was being tested by another source?

He eased feet into boots, which had appeared from somewhere. Jas straightened up.

The room swayed.

He clutched at a shoulder solid and reassuring, brought his mouth close to Stevie's ear and thought about other, more short-term damge: to his reputation. "It'll be aw' roon' the Hall, that ah wis..."

"They'll ken ye wur worked over – nothin' mair." Tight words. Tighter hands on his shoulders:

"Who did this tae ye, Jas-man?"

He felt himself held, then pushed back a little. Fingers gripping:

"Wiz it over that wee toe-rag ye gave the H to?"

Jas raised his head. "Neil Johnstone." He stared into angry brown eyes.

"Mystic fuckin' Meg?" A headshake. "Whit's he got tae dae wi' you?"

The truth? Jas scrutinised the eyes inches from his.

Confused brown eyes.

His own head was in a parallel state. Jas cupped a hand behind Stevie's neck, ruffling stubbly hair. The gesture was affable, affectionate – inadequate.

Brown eyes acknowledge the deficiency. Stevie frowned, twisted away.

Jas stared at Stevie's naked back: "Neil an' me go way back..."

Stevie spun round. "Whit ye wanna go pokin' aroon' in other folk's... private business?"

The question took him by surprise."Whit ye oan aboot?"

Stevie looked down. Face dried with towel.

There was something else here. Jas snatched the towel away. The sound of running faucets and unspoken words. "Tell me!"

Pink face raised to his. Fingers gripped his shoulders again. "You tell me whit's between you an' Johnstone, Jas-man! An' ah want the truth."

"Break it up, you two!" Voice from the end of the shower block. "...an' should you no' be in the kitchen, McStay?"

Jas refocused, saw the shower block was empty, apart from himself, Stevie and a Brodie-clone.

"Jist goin'..." His cell-mate moved away, then turned. Eyes still narrowed. "...tell me, eh?"

Jas could only nod. Stevie had more than earned his trust.

Nineteen

Telly and the rest of the table maintained a stony silence.

No eyes met his, although several hands refilled his coffee-cup several times.

Jas chewed on over-cooked fried egg. Grease slicked and soothed the cut on his bottom lip. He pushed the plate away and leant back on the hard, plastic chair. The food hit his stomach like a punch.

Three hands offered him a cigarette. Two were roll-ups. He accepted the one that wasn't.

Another hand lit it for him.

Jas inhaled, scanned the room.

A greyer presence than usual.

He stared at three uniformed faces, knew they registered his. If his injuries were half as bad as they felt, the bruising should not go noticed.

Hear no evil, see no evil...

Jas exhaled a cloud of blue-grey smoke. He examined the features of a Hadrian officer he hadn't seen before, caught and held a tentative grey gaze. Which immediately flicked away.

...led to all sorts of chaos. He continued to scan the room. At yesterday's table, David Hamilton's seat was occupied by a scraggy, bearded man who seemed more intent on listening to his food than eating it. Jas examined the yellow egg-yolk which decorated the man's cheeks like war-paint.

He was right about the war...

Details of his nocturnal visit crouched in his mind.

...the enemy was less easily identified. Last night, four men had gained the keys to his cell: keys, not a makeshift jemmy like the last time.

Jas's eyes circled the room.

All sorts of crimes.

All sorts of criminals...

...facilitating the theft of keys was little short of criminal neglect. Jas pushed pointless anger from his mind and listened to the sounds of subdued men eating.

Men subdued by fear and boredom.

Something had to give.

Eventually, something would...

...and Jas hoped to hell he was beyond these walls when it finally did. A hand on his shoulder sent shudders through his body. A voice in his ear neutralised the shiver:

"Mr Dalgleish wants to see you, Anderson."

He pushed back his chair and followed the Hadrian officer towards the gate.

A room full of eyes bored into his back.

The intricately carved chess-set sat in the middle of the desk.

Gunmetal eyes glanced up as the officer led him forward. A nod...

...then the sound of a door closing.

Jas examined the arrangement of chessmen. "Yer queen's under threat."

Sounds of standing, then a voice close. "When did this happen?"

He continued to stare at the checkered board. Accusations minus proof were no good to anyone...

...as was lagging on their basis.

"Who did this?"

Jas focused on the one remaining black knight, which languished at the other end of the board. He flicked his eyes to the face at his side. "No' like you tae waste a valuable piece."

"Tell me..." Barely restrained irritation. "...Sergeant Anderson – an' that's an order!"

The authoritative tone tugged at polis training. But they were on different sides of the fence now. Jas looked back to the board. "Ah wiz locked in ma cell from when ah left here last night til they opened the door this..."

"McStay?"

Jas stared at the chess pieces: three days ago – another, less damaging but equally illicit visit. Last night had been – different: more organised, in every sense of the word. "Naw, but either somewan in this place has an unauthorised set of keys or..." His mind drifted to Brodie, Pepperpot... and the man in Hadrian grey who had taunted Stevie yesterday. "...wanna your officers let four men intae ma cell tae beat an'..." His voice rose then cracked at the memory.

Barely restrained denial. "Ma men ur..."

"Yer men ur young, badly trained an' fuckin' useless!" He knew he was shouting.

A firm hand on his shoulder. "Sit down..."

He flinched, remembering other hands. His legs began to shake. Jas staggered towards a chair, knocking the chessboard aside as he tried to steady himself. He watched the black queen roll from one end of the board to the other.

Sound behind. Then a glass thrust at him. "...drink this..."

Jas took the glass, swallowed the water and wished it was something stronger. "Sorry aboot yer game..."

"Ye don't need tae tell me." Calm voice. "Wi' the bad blood between the two o' you, this huz Johnstone's signature aw' over it."

Jas stared at his empty glass.

"Ah warned ye aboot dealin'..."

He could hear the sounds of bootsteps on nylon carpeting as the man paced. Jas strained to make sense of the remark.

"...ah shouldda said mair." Sigh. "Christ!" Pause.

The empty glass shrank then came back into focus. Ian Dalgelish's words swam as the man began to talk:

"Ah'm tellin' ye this fur yer own guid – an' cos ah'd hate tae see ye gettin' mixed up in onythin." Pause. "Johnstone's the biggest dealer in here. He's organised, the drugs ur top quality..."

His mind raced.

Neil Johnstone...

...from hot-wirer to drugs baron in three years? His brothers would be proud of him.

"...an' he obviously thinks ye're tryin' tae muscle in."

Jas frowned. "Whit happened tae Hadrian's nae-drugs-in-Barlinnie line?"

"They huv their function in penal establishments. We're never gonny eradicate the problem, so we're tryin' tae limit it."

Jas stared at the glass. "Tae heroin?"

"It's whit they want."

"A drugged prisoner is a happy prisoner?" He tried to keep the sarcasm out of his voice. He raised his head.

Gunmetal eyes narrowed. "If supply can be restricted tae wan dealer, it can be controlled..." Dalgleish leaned across the desk. "...it took a while, an' a lotta work, but we're gettin' there..."

He glanced up. "You're turnin' a blind eye to criminal activity..." The phrase made him flinch, bringing back twenty-year-old memories. Alan Somerville.

"There ur... degrees of criminality."

The justification only served to heighten his recall. Jas pushed the past away and thought about less distant mistakes: all he had done for the last two days was offer H around like sweeties. All he had done was draw Johnstone's already antagonistic attention. Dalgleish talked through the thoughts:

"Ah don't have the manpower to organise an escorted visit tae a GP, but there's a guy in E-Hall wi' a nursin' qualification if ye..."

"Ah'll live." Jas raised his eyes...

Last night's wet intrusion into his body tugged at his mind.

...and met gunmetal scrutiny of his face:

"That lip looks nasty..." Frown. "...but ah take it there's nae lasting damage done?"

He tried not to think about the dull ache inside, which immediately flowered into a jabbing, psychosomatic heat: a vision of tiny, viral cells beating his into submission was something no one could do anything about.

Ian Dalgleish took and refilled his glass from a bottle of spring water which stood on top of the filing cabinet, then handed it back. "Can ye identify ony o' them?"

Jas stared at the glass. Faces blurred in the face of last night. Even if he could... he couldn't – for the same reason no prisoner could. He placed the glass on the desk. "Ah think you should maybe reconsider if giein' Neil Johnstone even more clout than he's awready got's such a guid idea..."

"Ye're no' in the Force, noo..." Low baritone. "...ah – Hadrian – ken whit we're doin'."

He raised his eyes from the glass and looked at the face of the ex-police officer with whom he had served six months of his probation. The man who had taught him chess almost two decades ago...

...the man who had listened, when his own father's face twisted and turned away...

...the man with whom he had arrested and restrained Alan Somerville.

Gunmetal stared back. "Lea' it tae us: forget aboot the drugs – an' Neil Johnstone: ye're ainly makin' trouble for yersel', whit wi' the grudge he's awready holdin'."

It was the truth, and he knew it.

Grudges...

The thought came from nowhere, unwanted in its sudden clarity. As the arresting officer, he'd only been doing his job. Marie's betrayal had been rewarded by the arc of a Stanley knife.

How far did a Johnstone-grudge extend – through sister...

...to brother? Had Neil been intimidating Paul, more punishment by proxy for Marie?

"Sure ye canny put names tae faces? Ah'll gie ye as much protection as ah..."

"Did ye offer protection tae McGhee?" The thought formed in his brain, tripped from his lips seconds later.

Exasperation. "Whit ye talkin' aboot?"

"Ye ken there's old scores tae be settled, between me and Johnstone – an' ye must ken aboot McGhee's sister an' her part in puttin' Johnstone in here." In his grip, the water shivered.

Ian Dalgleish turned to the filing cabinet, opened a drawer. "Whit wis the name again?"

Jas frowned at a broad, grey back. "McGhee... Paul McGhee – in fur possession, got early release..."

"Twenty-seventh o' September..." The sentence ended for him. Turning. Folder lowered, gunmetal eyes raised. "...C-Hall.That him?"

"Aye – wis he Hadrian's grass?"

Eyebrow raised.

"Wis Paul McGhee battin' fur both sides?"

File closed, returned to cabinet. "The snitch system ainly works wi' long-termers, – you should ken that."

He placed the glass of water on the desk and began to collect upturned chessmen. Grey legs edged into his line of vision. Jas looked up at the ramrod figure.

"Dae yersel' a favour: forget aboot this... McGhee – an' try an' keep oota Johnstone's way."

Jas stood up. His legs felt like they belonged to someone else.

"He's..." Eyes on his swollen face. "...made his point. Keep yer head doon, an' this'll be the end of it."

He stared. "So Paul wisney gettin' ony hassle fae Johnstone?"

Pause. "McGhee's oot, noo..." Thoughtful. "..an' Johnstone's got – what, three brothers?" Gunmetal stared back.

Jas considered the implication, watched ex-sergeant Dalgleish do the same..

Then the eyes looked beyond him. "Hadrian were aware o' the... relationship between McGhee an' Johnstone, but it seemed amicable enough an'..."

"Whit relationship?" The word echoed in his head.

The question ignored. "If ye won't identify faces, there's no' much more ah can do..." Large fingers pressed a small button on the desk.

Behind, sounds of a door opening.

"...want tae take the day aff cleaning-duties? Git some rest?"

"Whit relationship?"

Ian Dalgleish frowned. "Ah've no' got time fur aw' this, Anderson – dae ya want the day aff or no'?" Impatient – and back on the opposite side of the fence, with a second Hadrian-presence now in the doorway.

Frustration tingled on his skin. Jas sighed, remembering the reason he had taken duties in the first place. And what went through his mind when it wasn't otherwise occuiped. "Ah'll keep on the move."

Tight smile, then a nod beyond him. Another voice:

"Come on, Anderson..."

Flanked by Brodie-clones, Jas left the room.

On the ground floor of B-Hall, a tall, tangle-haired figure made its way towards him. "Okay? Ye didney...?"

"Ah didney lag, if that's whit ye..."

Scowl. "Ye didney see a doctor, ah wiz gonny say!" Stevie edged around the metal trolley, eyes narrowed. A hand on his shoulder.

Jas closed his eyes. "Ah wiz wi' Dalgleish."

Snort. "Whit did that bastard want?"

Good question...

Relationship.

...his conversation with the ex-polis flapped about in his mind, neither taking flight or settling to rest. "Whit wis goin' oan between Johnstone and Paul McGhee?" Eyelids opened.

Stevie stared straight ahead, ignoring the question. "Listen, ah wanna ken, Jas-man. Ah wanna ken why ye're attractin' aw' this trouble."

He almost laughed.

Stevie. Head cocked, expression a mixture of curiosity and annoyance.

Jas shivered.

The hand tightened, trying to absorb the shakes.

He remembered Dalgleish's words of warning. His mind wouldn't leave things alone...

...Paul McGhee...Neil Johnstone...grasses...Hamster...

Sigh. "We're oan tray-collectin' . Come oan..." The hand lingered, then removed itself. "...tell me while we look busy."

The trays were from prisoners confined to cells.

New prisoners.

Old, athritic prisoners.

Ill prisoners.

Stevie pushed the increasingly heavy trolley. Jas walked beside him and talked.

About old news... Neil Johnstone... Marie.

About Paul.

About why he was in here...

...and the price of his release. He stopped talking, as they approached a locked gate.

Stevie waved at a red-eye.

The gate slid open.

They walked through.

One of the trolley's wheels developed a squeak. The sound punctuated Stevie's silent thought processes.

Jas sighed: he had to trust someone. Despite Stevie's reputation, the man who'd bathed and cleaned him earlier seemed a better bet than most.

He could be wrong.

He'd been wrong before...

...the squeak fell silent. Stevie leant against a yellow-brick wall and stared at him. " Ah thought Johnstone arranged last night cos he thought ye were dealin' – or cos he jist disney like polis."

Jas scowled. "So did ah." He looked at Stevie. "Noo you tell me more aboot Paul and Johnstone..."

Last night.

The gymnasium.

No *stay off my patch.*

No *this is for being polis.*

No *this is fur putting me here.*

Just...

...keep yer nose oota whit disney concern ye...

He listened to the squeaky wheel. Then Stevie's low voice:

"Dunno much, Jas-man – dunno there's much tae tell. Wee Paul served his time as Johnstone's cunt. Four months..." Brown eyes narrowed. "None o' onywan's business..." The pale face reddened, looked away. "...but their's."

Neil Johnstone and the brother of the woman whose testimony had put him here?

His own uncertain future, and Marie's ability to alter it pulsed in his brain. "If ah'm gonny get oota here at aw', it's ma business." He wondered if Marie knew her beloved brother had been taking it up the arse from the guy who had scarred her for life.

Three brothers. Two on the outside...

...he considered the other implication of an ex-Gorbals sergeant's words. "Mebbe Johnstone arranged a Welcome Home party fur Paul, efter they let him oot."

"So ask him." Head still averted.

"Ah asked everywan but Johnstone..." Along with flashing heroin around, every second word from his lips in the past two days had been either Paul or McGhee.

...keep yer nose oota whit disney concern ye...

Jas frowned. "...an' he let me join his mates in their wee work-oot last night an' telt me tae keep ma nose oot."

Angry voice. "So take the advice, Jas-man."

...keep yer nose oota whit disney concern ye...

He couldn't – not if he wanted to walk free from the Sherrif Court on December 4th. Rocks and hard places filled his mind. Something occurred to him: maybe he and McGhee had attracted Johnstone's unwanted attention in the same way. "Wiz Paul tryin' tae deal?"

"Get real, Jas-man!" Snort. "Wi' Johnstone an' Dalgleish workin' hand in hand?"

Jas seized the trolley. The squeak stopped, echoed around him. He stared into amber eyes.

The shaggy head shook. "Fur ex-polis, ye're affy stupid sometimes, Jas-man..."

His throat was dry. He continued to stare.

"...how dae ye think the H is gettin' in here?"

Jas remembered Marie, and her pains. "There's dozens o' ways..."

"Aye – an' the easiest is if ye're no' wanna the wans that gets searched!" Scowl.

He remembered an ex-Gorbals sergeant's innovative policy. "Mebbe Hadrian are turnin' a blind eye tae Johnstone's dealin' but..."

"Ye're no' listenin', Jas-man." The trolley was wrenched away from his grip. The squeak disrupted his thoughts. "Ah'm no' talkin' aboot Hadrian allowin' stuff tae happen: ah'm talkin' aboot Dalgleish floggin' heroin, cos it flushes oot yer system quicker than the hash, an' disney fuck up their precious drug tests..."

Jas blinked.

Stevie's face was a thunder-cloud. "...an' strong-armin' onywan who disney buy fae his pal Johnstone!"

Jas stared. His brain ground into gear. Amidst the other implications of Stevie's words, an unwanted thought surfaced. Drugs...

...he'd given the last of Marie's H to Hamster. If the kid was caught in possession of...

Jas gripped the trolley and heaved.

The door to David Hamilton's single cell was unlocked. And empty.

Stevie's presence and four cigarettes confirmed none of the men returning from breakfast had seen David since lock-up last night. Jas didn't question screws.

They didn't pass any to question.

The squeaky wheel increased in volume. As did his frustration. Then no squeak:

"Hold oan – ah need a piss." Stevie veered left, into C-Hall's showers.

Jas lit a cigarette, stared down then up a deserted corridor.

The reason for the relationship between Paul McGhee and Neil Johnstone was semi-explained.

The reasons for the relationship between Ian Dalgleish and Paul McGhee tossed and turned in his brain, refusing to lie down.

Snitching still seemed the more probable motivation: every police officer knew the value of a grass.

Paul: inmate under both SPS and Hadrian-rule. Small-time, first conviction, good behaviour, early release.

Hadrian:taking over from the SPS. Eager to make their mark in a new environment. Eager to find out Johnstone's source of supply, the extent of the dealing.

There was logic to Dalgleish's denial of Paul McGhee as a paid informer.

Just as Paul wouldn't want the fact made public...

...amongst inmates, at least.

If Paul had been integral – via his status as Johnstone's cunt – in securing information for Hadrian on exactly how the man was organising his drugs deals...

"Oi! Jas-man?"

An urgent voice cut through his thoughts. He followed it into the shower block.

Stevie stood at a urinal, still zipping up. He nodded towards the last, doorless stall.

Jas stared, then walked past nine cubicles. He paused at the tenth.

A crouching back.

A crouching, padded back.

Step-cut hair.

Ears hidden by expensive headphones. Jas leaned in towards the shape which cowered beside the toilet bowl. He tapped a shiny, nylon shoulder.

Hamster shrieked, tried to burrow further into the corner.

Footsteps behind. Stevie pushed past, grabbed a thin neck and hauled David Hamilton from the stall.

A games console clattered to the floor.

One headphone dangled blaringly from a naked ear. A rodent face stared up at him, eyes taking in the facial injuries. Fear fading to horror at the state of another face.

Hamster's mouth opened. Then closed. Then opened again.

Jas stared at wordless lips, then grabbed a padded arm and hauled the small boy out into the corridor.

"Dalgleish is after me, fierce man!" Once the talking started, it was hard to stem the flow.

Back in his cell, Hamster fiddled with the games console, vainly attempting to fix the unfixable. Badly concealed panic burbled up from the lowered head.

Stevie stood in the doorway, eyes on the corridor.

No mention of the heroin. Jas stared at the top of a step-cut head and tried to make sense of garbled words:

"...wants ma computer – bastard goes oan an' oan aboot it. Ah thought he wanted me tae grass fur him! He jist wants tae..."

"Yer play-station?"

The babbling stopped. Hamster glanced up.

"Aw' this is over a fuckin' games console?" Jas eyed the cracked plastic at present between small, trembling hands.

"Naw! No' this – it's fucked onyway..." Cracked plastic thrown on the bunk. "...ma pc."

Jas blinked.

"The Epson."

Jas frowned. "Whit ye oan aboot?"

Sigh. Slow words, like talking to a child. "Ma personal computer."

"Whit's he want wi' yer computer?" Jas ran a hand through his hair. This wasn't making sense.

"Fuck kens – fierce thing's worse than useless, onyway ..." Scowl. "...see some folk an' technology? See idiots? Bet it wiz insured onyway, ah..."

"Start at the beginnin'." Jas tried to focus his ears.

"Right at the beginnin'?"

Jas noddied "An' go slowly." He sank to a crouch.

Deep breath. "Me an' ma best mate did Hadrian!"

Jas stared.

"We did Hadrian's headquarters in Livingston an'.."

"When?"

"Fuckin' ages ago – last year sometime."

"Okay... and?"

Laugh. "We hud a van, clip-boards...fake 'taches an' ID... jist waltzed in an' cleared an office fae right under theirs noses!" Headshake. The step-cut hair flopped and flitted around the rodent face.

"Ah thought you wur oan remand fur joy-ridin', no' deception an' theft?"

"Ah am, man! We got away wi' it!" Giggling. "Telt the doorman we wur takin' them tae git serviced: two photocopiers, coupla laser printers, a scanner still in its box." Hand through step-cut hair. Shrug. "Did it fur a laugh – we didney hurt onywan, an' they're proabably insured tae the hilt..." Serious. "..fierce, ya shoulda seen us – in an' oot in minutes!"

"Very clever, ah'm sure – but if Mr Dalgleish wants the stuff back somewan obviously saw yous an'..."

"Naebody recognised us, man! Only me an' Fierce Paul kent aboot it..." Frown. "...goat a guid price fur the resta the stuff, but ah wiz wantin' tae upgrade onyway, so ah kept the pc..." Frown. "...dunno why, noo: fuckin' thing's fucked – tried tae load Windows 98 onto it, hard drive wiz fulla shite..."

His brain stared to work. Marie's information, concerning a friend in Longriggend. Black Bill's words, about the friend Paul intended to visit, when he got out.

Same age... even the same hair-cut. Jas raised an eyebrow. "Paul McGhee?"

Eyes alight. "You ken Fierce Paul, man?" Beaming. Voice increasing in volume. "Ah, Jesus! Whit's he up tae?" A hand through step-cut hair. "Christ, ah heard he got early release. Fierce Paul an' me ur mates, yeah? Best mates – ah've kent him since ah wiz a kid..."

Jas smiled at the teenage Methuselah. His head hurt.

Hamster continued to talk.

Jas let him, pausing to clarify terms and names. Early last year: TV and newspaper coverage of the break-in escaped him. From time to time he glanced at Stevie.

Head averted, eyes on the walkway for unwanted interruptions.

After a while, David stopped talking.

After another while, Jas's head ceased to hurt. He peered at the rodent face. "Dalgleish wants this stuff that you an' McGhee stole fae Hadrian?"

Head shake. "Naw, just the pc."

"How diz he even ken ye've...?"

"Accordin' tae Paul, he'd hud a hand in everythin' fae the Ice-Cream Wars tae stealing Shergar!" Stevie's sceptical voice.

Jas looked up.

Stevie was frowning. "Paul telt onywan who wid listen..." Pupils narrowing towards Hamster "...but he never mentioned ony partner."

Offended. "Ah wiz wi' Fierce Paul – ah wiz there! Ask him, man! He'll..."

"Paul's no' here tae tell onywan onythin'!" Jas stared from Hamster's half-open mouth to Stevie's scowl and back again.

The unravelable was beginning to unravel.

Paul McGhee: first offence – eighteen months. A second offence – even for the lesser crime of breaking-and-entering – would mean a longer sentence. Amid lies and fictions, and in his attempts to impress more experienced men – like Neil Johnstone – had Paul's boasting brought the boy's crime to Hadrian's attention, giving ex-polis Dalgleish the leverage he needed to persuade McGhee to act as Hadrian's snitch?

Jas stared at the skinny figure in the padded jacket. "You were in Longriggend wi' Paul?"

Nod. "He turned eighteen three months afore me..."

"Wiz Paul grassin', in Longriggend?"

Horrified. "No way, man! Fierce Paul's straight up – always! He widney..."

"Well, he wiz grassin' in here."

Stevie: "Ah don't believe it!"

Jas glanced up at the doorway: Black Bill had no reason to lie, but there was logic to Stevie's ignorance, given the status of grasses. "Paul wiz friendly wi' Dalgleish. How ye think he got oot early – Brownie points?"

Vociferous, rodent denial. "Naw, no' Paul – he widney grass up his mates tae save his ain skin."

The conclusion was inevitable. " If you an' Paul wurney spotted doin' the job, how come Dalgleish kens you've got this pc?"

Sullen, rodent stare.

Stevie: "Ah canny see it, Jas-man. Wee Paul wiz sussed: he kent whit wid happen onywan found oot he wis grassin'..."

"Mebbe it's in the genes: his sister grassed up Johnstone." Jas frowned. "An' Johnstones tend tae haud grudges." He thought about the gallus, bullet-headed kid he'd met three years earlier. He thought about the screams of the boy three cells down, and the silence which had followed...

...maybe grassing to Dalgleish was a similarly desperate act? If his sister was anything to go by, Paul McGhee's instinct for survival would break all other supposedly iron codes of conduct.

He let possibilities germinate in his mind. Neil Johnstone: only one of four Johnstones. At least two of whom were in a position to finish whatever retribution job their baby brother had started when he took the brother of the woman who had put him here as his cunt...

"...eh, Jas-man?"

His attention returned to amber eyes and a rodent face.

Stevie. Frowning. "Ah wiz tellin' the boay he'd be better aff jist avoidin' the bastard – he's ainly on remand..."

Rodent lips quivering. "An' ah keep tellin' ye, he's no' said nothin' aboot ony snitchin'. He jist wants ma pc." Close to tears.

Jas sighed. "Gie Dalgleish the fuckin' computer, if he wants it that much."

Sniff. "Ah canny."

"Why not?"

Another sniff. Fiddling with an ear-piece. "Ah don't huv it ony mair – ah selt it oan." More fiddling. "Help me oot, eh man? Get him aff ma back." Hand into jeans pocket. Small package removed. "Yer pal Telly telt me ah'm too... high-risk, whit wi' aw' the heat fae Dalgleish."

Jas stared at the last of Marie's H, and cursed her again for causing not one but two problems. A memory of the cell-search... and later...

...stirred in someone else. Stevie lunged forward, gripped a fistful of padded nylon and pulled.

Huge trainers feet dangled three inches from stone floor.

"Did you tip Dalgleish the nod, fuck-face? Did you tell him the Jas-man wiz dealin' tae save yer ain skin?"

Hamster tried a headshake, failed and bobbed marionette-like instead. "No' me – honest!" The voice was rodent shrill.

"Put him doon, Stevie."

Limp figure gently lowered to the bed.

Hamster frowned, smoothing nonexistent lapels. "Watch the gear, eh pal?"

Jas almost laughed. Then sobered. "Dalgleish mention drugs, last time he cornered ye?"

Headshake.

"He mention Paul?"

Headshake. "Said he wanted the pc. Said he'd..." Adam's apple doing the marionette act. "...break both ma legs if ah didney gie it tae him." Suddenly terrified again. "Man, ye gotta help me..." Fidgeting wildly. Voice from behind:

"Whit wiz oan the hard drive?" Voice from the doorway.

"Eh?"

"Ye said ye tried tae load Windows 98: did ye see whit wiz oan the hard drive?"

Jas's eyes flicked to Stevie.

Self-conscious blush. Then explanation. "Ah did part o' a computer course, in the Shotts..." Back to Hamster. "...whit operatin' system? Mac?"

"Naw, DOS, an' ah did access summa the stuff – nae programs, jist files, like some eejit hud saved them tae the C drive 'stead o' A." Snort.

"Gonny shut up an' lemme think?" Jas closed his eyes.

"Whit should ah dae, man?"

He had no idea. Jas opened his eyes. "Stay here – if Dalgleish appears, stall him." He strode from the cell onto an empty walkway. Behind, the trolley's squeak nagged his ears like questions nagged in his brain.

The relationship between Paul McGhee and Neil Johnstone as a three-way?

Neil Johnstone: maintaining his power position with drugs and settling old scores.

Paul McGhee: desperate to get out, and willing to do anything to get there.

One factor in common...

...Ian Dalgleish – trying to control the Bar-L by controlling the drugs supply. And controlling Neil Johnstone.

Stevie's voice cut through his speculation: "Ah thought wee McGhee wiz makin' it aw' up..." Low laugh. "...ah widda loved tae huv seen they Hadrian guys' faces when they wur tellin' the polis whit got past their fuckin' security an'..."

"Where's the phones in this place?" Jas paused, turned.

Eyes raised from the trolley.

Jas frowned. Doubt tugged at his brain. "Ah need tae check somethin'."

"Nae calls oot fur..." Brodie-speak. "...the duration o' the strike, Jas-man." The squeak continued, then stopped. "There's a mobile in D-Hall, but..."

"Can you set it up? Get a price?"

Stare. "It's Neil Johnstone's mobile, Jas-man."

He scowled. Devils and fathomless blue oceans floated before him. But maybe it was time he took a swim: as a man who had known Paul McGhee intimately, Jas knew his own passage to the outside was dependent on information Johnstone could give him. "Set it up."

Blink.

"Do it!"

"Okay, Jas-man. But ah'm comin' with ye." Turning.

The squeaky wheel faded.

So did his nerve.

Maybe the prey coming to the hunter would catch him off-guard...

Jas fumbled for cigarettes like a condemned man.

...but there were all types of hunters.

And all types of traps.

Twenty

On his way to collect bucket and mop, he passed three Hadrian uniforms. Jas peered beneath the grey, tried to see through the facade to the man beneath.

Neil Johnstone had facilitated last night.

Neil Johnstone had access to keys...

...he waited at the gate, under the gaze of another red eye, a gram of high-grade H once more snuggled against his balls.

Peace offering?

He stared down the empty corridor. Guts turned to slush.

If past and recent experience were anything to go by, Johnstones were hard to appease...

...was the future a different matter?

The slush froze, churning in the pit of his stomach, a block of semi-liquid ice.

Three years ago, Neil had threatened him from this prison, left interesting messages on the Eastercraigs answering machine.

Jas leant the mop against a yellow-brick wall and rubbed his hot face.

Three years was a long time.

A lot of water under the bridge, since then...

...bridges could be burnt. Or built.

Bootsteps. Minus trolley-squeak. His eyes flicked right.

Stevie sauntered towards him, mop and bucket in hand. "Okay, Jas-man?" The greeting echoed in the stone tunnel.

He attempted corresponding enthusiasm. "Aye."

"There's somethin' goin' oan, ower in C-Hall – ah passed six o' Hadrian's cowboys an' no' wanna them asked me where ah wis aff tae." Lop-sided grin.

Jas frowned, mind elsewhere. A hand on his shoulder, fingers massaging:

"Ye sure ye wanna dae this?"

The temperature dropped. The slush ball in his guts solidified. Jas mirrored the hardening in his mind, shrugged a shrug he didn't feel. "Ah jist wanna use his mobile – this is business."

Last night had been business.

Four years ago, arresting Neil had been business.

Three years ago...

...Leigh.

Neil Johnstone's brother – Jimmy Mygo – had slit Leigh Nicols's throat, left his signature in blood on Jas's bedroom wall.

Not business – pleasure?

The ball of ice was spreading outwards. There were old scores on both sides...

...he watched Stevie patiently wave a hand in front of a blinking red eye.

Time healed some wounds.

Others, it closed prematurely, sealing infection inside.

A click. The sound of metal on metal. The gate slid open.

Jas lifted his mop and bucket, followed Stevie through two sets of security gates. They left B-Hall.

Cold, November wind blasted between the weave of the scratchy jumper. He glanced at Stevie, who still wore the bikers' jacket, in breach of all prison rules.

Jas frowned: maybe Hadrian had other things to think about. Like he did.

They walked quickly. Stevie talked nervously:

"Never met him, masel', but everywan kens Johnstone – ye hear stories..."

Jas quickened his pace.

"...ma first year here, he blinded a guy – the screws couldney prove nothin'..."

A sudden gust of icy air rippled over his skin.

"...last year, ah heard he kicked somewan fae A-Hall tae death – somethin' tae dae wi' somethin' somewan said aboot his brother – stomped oan his heid that hard there wur bits o' the guy's brain embedded in the fuckin' floor."

Jas thrust hands deeper into the pockets of his combat pants.

"Got fifteen years added tae his sentence, fur that – been a bit quiet since."

Last night had been quiet? Dealing inside on a larger scale than he'd ever considered outside was quiet?

D-Hall loomed ahead.

Paul McGhee. Eighteen months for possession.

Neil Johnstone. Technically, a long-termer. Here for the duration, with little more to lose...

...McGhee's need for release burned inside him, an echo of a dull ache. Last night...

Jas stared at barbed-wire topped walls. Icing on a stone cake, escape that way was impossible, and pointless. He thought about the egg-yolk warrior at breakfast.

Other places to escape to. Safer places. Permanent places.

Tempting places. Jas listened to the sound of their boots over the howling wind and concentrated on the here and now.

Ahead, the gate to D-Hall stood ajar. Three shapes framed the doorway. The only grey was the sky above their heads.

Jas lowered his face against icy air.

He was expected.

The denimed men led them along more corridors, up more metal stairs onto more metal walkways. Yellow brick had become comfortingly familiar.

No grey anywhere.

Fingers tightened around the mop. His guts were knitting a densely stitched straitjacket, which stretched from throat to groin.

Music... faint music....

His ears strained.

...a low, vocal melody...repetitive...haunting...

And a smell.

...fruity... waxy...

Ahead, the blue escort halted and parted.

Jas dumped the mop and bucket on the metal walkway and strode into a cell. Behind, Stevie did likewise.

The music was louder, but still low, emanating from a small, expensive-looking cd player on a shelf above the piss-pot. Two candles burned slowly on the window-sill, either side of a seven-inch stone phallus.

Jas blinked, looked around. He didn't recognise either of the two men present.

Both had completely shaved heads, both wore the regulation denims.

He stared at a short, middle-aged man with skin like a baby and the body of a miniature Schwartzenegger, searching the memory of last night for a matching body type.

And found none.

Too small.

Too bulky.

Arnie met the stare with complete detachment.

Gaze moved slowly from the man on his feet to the man on the bunk.

Age?

Hard to tell. The sallow face had a lived-in look. Eyes lowered. Stubby hands in lap, stubbier fingers flexing and unflexing the intricate strings of a cat's cradle. Light from the candles shone against the top of a gleaming skull.

Neither man resembled the seventeen-year-old kid Jas had last seen in the dock, in Glasgow's High Court, glaring angrily at himself and Marie McGhee as the judge passed sentence.

Maybe Neil was too important to handle Jas himself – he had been, last night.

Then he looked closer...

...met and held a familiar stare.

Neither of them spoke.

This wasn't about words. This was about actions.

And reactions.

In the background, the soothing hum of some kind of digital

incantation mirrored the movement of other, string-draped digits.

A scowl twitched his injured bottom lip.

Neil Johnstone stood up, the cat's cradle flexing slowly, gaze or rhythm never faltering. "You're deid, Anderson..."

Lightning-like, Stevie was at his side, fists clenched.

"...sooner or later, we're aw' deid."

Jas held a hand in front of Stevie. Tensed muscle flexed against his arm.

"Life is the flight o' a sparra through the feastin'-hall o' eternity." Pupils like dark stars raised to his. "Gone in the blink o' an eye."

Arnie moved fluidly left, taking his place as right-hand man beside the strangely serene Neil Johnstone.

"Lea' us, William." Dark stars darkened further.

Jas turned, watched as the small man began to usher Stevie towards the door. Mohamet moving the mountain.

Stevie remained still.

Jas focused on mahogany eyes, then flicked his head walk-waywards.

Disbelieving frown.

Jas nodded.

Reluctant. "Okay, but ah'll be jist ootside if ye..." Mohamet got his way.

Two men, one at least six-one, the other no more than five-six, made their way from the cell onto the walk-way.

As the door closed, the small space filled up with the sound of the stringed eastern instrument and the musty scent of candles.

"Sit..." Neil Johnstone resumed his previous position on the bunk, fingers flexing.

Jas remained on his feet. Sounds, smells and uncertainties crowded into his head. He focused on the top of a shining skull.

"...or stand. Ah bear ye no harm, Jas Anderson."

The words had an archaic quality, like dialogue from a bad film. The baby of the Johnstone family had either found religion...

...or lost his marbles. Jas wondered if he'd get anything approaching sense out of the man. "If ye bear me nae harm, why did ye send four guys tae ma cell last night?"

Shaven pate tilted back. Eyes at odds with the face – blank, yet full of something unreadable. Small smile. "Polis never could get their facts right..."

He debated correcting his status. Thin lips talked through the internal debate.

"...ah've taken vows – wanna which prevents me inflictin' or bein' party tae the inflictin' o' violence on any livin' creature – includin' ex-polis, Jas Anderson." Eyes on the facial bruises. "Ma hands only touch flesh in love."

The truth? His mind was read.

"Ah huv a past, ah'll no' deny that – we ur all the sum o' oor experiences. Ah got tae atone fur whit ah done."

Jas watched dark pupils expand, then contract. The man was something else: half-fakir, half-faker? "So ye're dealin' H as an offering tae Shiva?" He scowled, thrust a hand into the combat-pants and threw the cellophane package onto the cell floor. "Well, say a fuckin' prayer fur me!"

A tiny smile stroked the outline of thin lips. The cat's cradle contorted into an intricate lattice. "Shiva thanks ye." Strings twisted again.

"Tell her ah don't want ony trouble."

Silent nod.

Jas blinked. The eastern music, the smell...

"So what dae ye want, Jas Anderson?" Eyes to the cellophane package. "Ye workin' wi' Dalgleish?" Eyes raised.

He sensed suspicion for the first time. He risked the truth. "Ah'm workin' wi' somewan, but it's Marie McGhee." He scanned the sallow face for a response.

Dark eyes expanded.

So did Jas. "Paul's sister?"

Fingers flexed. Strings shivered. "Ah ken who she is."

More to the point, he knew who Paul was. "These vows don't include celibacy?"

The cat's cradle pulled tight, then deftly twisted. Eyes to the curving stone phallus. "Sexual energy is wanna the maist positive forces in the universe – Shiva kens that. Paul kent it tae." Eyes back to the cellophane package. "How's he doin'?"

Jas stared at the most reliable source of Paul McGhee's whereabouts, the reason he was here at all. At the moment, it was the least of his concerns. He leant down, lifted the square of heroin and sat it on the bunk. "So you didney arrange ma night visit?"

The question ignored. Eyes still on the heroin. Cat's cradle drooping. "We aw' huv oor ain demons."

Jas frowned. Lines of communication as tangled as the cat's cradle.

Small smile. "Didney think it had sunk in yet."

He inhaled lungfuls of waxy, too-sweet air. His head swam with the sitar's sliding strings.

"Wi' Dalgleish behind me, ah don't need ony physical stuff tae stay at the top, Jas Anderson. Whitever demon's efter you, it's no' wanna mine."

The man sitting cross-legged on the bunk before him was a million miles from the sullen-eyed boy he'd seen sent down for two years...

...but the passivity was more distracting than any aggression.

Jas needed answers. He needed the truth.

He needed...

...voice to his left:

"Ye wanna use oor mobile?"

His eyes flicked to the stocky man with the impassive face, who had reappeared in the doorway, then beyond to Stevie's shaggy head. Jas nodded abstractedly.

"Where ye wanna call?"

Jas frowned.

Impassive face became explaining face. "Ootside the UK'll cost ye mair..."

"Local."

William blinked agreement, then walked to a small, custom-built locker in the far, right-hand corner of the cell. Crouching, he produced a key from his pocket.

Humming....

Jas's eyes flicked back to Neil. The man was rocking gently, fingers flexing rhythmically in time to the sound which escaped slightly parted lips. Voice at his side:

"Ye ken how tae work it?"

He took the mobile. An Oki. Parent company somewhere in the Far East, the cellular phones were manufactured just outside Glasgow. It seemed appropriate. Jas nodded.

Brief bow. "Next door's empty – ye've goat ten minutes."

Shuffling behind told him Stevie was edging towards the doorway. Jas nodded again to William, then glanced at Neil.

The strings of the cat's cradle draped stubby hands which were now united in prayer position. Eyes closed, still humming, the figure continued to rock.

The movement was hypnotic. Jas stood mesmerised. Sound behind him.

More humming... different pitch.

There was a sense he was now interrupting something, would continue to interrupt as long as he remained in the cell...

...and a sense his presence no longer even registered. The mobile slick in his grasp, Jas moved out onto the walk-way.

"The piss-artist formerly known as Neil Johnstone..." Stevie was shaking his shaggy head. "But the way he runs this Hall's got less tae dae wi' trances..." Frown. "...an' more tae dae wi' his pal there: Johnstone's maybe taken a vow, but Wullie husney – ex-middle weight, he wiz sayin'..."

Jas walked into the adjacent cell. He didn't want to know...

...nothing anyone in here told him made any sense. Contradictions twisted and tangled themselves into an unintelligible knot.

Johnstone... drugs... McGhee... the Hadrian break-in... Hamster... the Hadrian break-in... Dalgleish...

Speculation.

Rumour...

...everything was unreliable.

One detail he could clarify. Jas sat on the bunk and punched in the number of London Road Police Station.

DI McLeod answered on the second ring.

He identified himself, unnecessarily.

Silence...

He could hear faint noise in the background, over the sound of breathing: typing, the low hum of a laser-printer – distant, muted voices. "If ya canny talk, ah can..."

"Sigh. "I'm alone – and I know where you are..."

"Last year. Before the summer." No time for pleasantries. "Hadrian Security's headquarters in Livingston had a break-in..."

"What?"

"Hadrian..." Jas sighed. "...ah need tae know whit was taken..."

"Slow down and say all that again."

Jas frowned, did as he was asked.

"Hold on..."

Eyes flicked to Stevie's leathered back. As he waited, time played its usual Barlinnie tricks. The mobile grew warm in his fist. His bottom lip began to ache. Eventually:

"You sure you've got this right?"

He moved the phone closer to his ear. "Maybe it wiz earlier – or later – in the year, but there canny be that many break-ins at..."

"According to the PNC, there were none."

He tensed.

"There's no record of any break-in at any premises belonging to Hadrian Security Solutions last year... or the year before... or this year. I checked. Have you got your facts right?"

No recorded crime: either Paul McGhee and David Hamilton were consummate con-artists and were making the whole thing up, or the break-in at Hadrian headquarters had purposely gone unreported. He patted pockets for cigarettes.

Stevie stuck a limp roll-up in his mouth, lit it and turned to resume sentry-duty.

Jas grabbed a leathered arm. He needed someone else to hear this.

Stevie sank to his hunkers, brown eyes shining with curiosity and suspicion.

Jas held the mobile between them.

"Sounds like someone's been having you on, Jas. Maxwell Fulton runs a tight ship, down there in Livingston..." Pause. "...you should know – you're at present part of his... cargo."

"Who the fuck's...?"

"Head of Hadrian Security Solutions – and a couple of other thriving commercial ventures, if the financial pages of *The Scotsman* and the FT Index are anything to go by..."

Commercial ventures...

...Pioneering Security Solutions and mission statments.

A skeleton staff.

No resident nurse.

No resident governor.

No basic human rights.

Hadrian were using the Bar-L as a guinea pig.

"...and doing a good job, from all accounts."

Penal innovation slid into another strategy, and gave a whole knew meaning to insider dealing. "There's mair drugs in here than fuckin' Possil..."

"Par for the course..." Pause. "Hard to eradicate that, Jas – you know how things..."

"Hadrian officers are supplying the stuff!"

Silence.

He didn't want to believe it either, but Neil Johnstone and Stevie had no reason to lie. The security company, on the other hand, had a share price at stake and a reputation to protect. "Hadrian are bringin' heroin in here – ah'm no' sure if it's some radical strategy tae keep things quiet, or fur the cash, but..."

"You're serious?"

He gripped the mobile. "'Course ah'm fuckin' serious! Ah..."

"You have proof?"

Jas frowned.

"Names, dates – how the stuff's getting in?"

He had nothing concrete.

"Has this anything to do with that... drugs dealer you were interested in – Paul...what was his name?"

His lips tightened around the cigarette's filter. Nothing to do with Paul McGhee...

...and everything to do with how Hadrian were running the Bar-L.

Movement at his side.

Stevie left the crouch, darting to the cell door.

"Jas? You still there?"

"Aye..." Proof.

Proof.

He stared at Stevie's broad back, then the motion of a large palm.

Ann talked on, voice lower now. "Get me hard evidence of Hadrian's complicity in any drug dealing and I can..." She was mid-sentence when he severed the connection. Jas stared at Stevie.

Brown eyes glowed chestnut and ebony by turns. Apologetic. "Think they're wantin' their phone back."

He got up from the bunk.

"So whit happens noo?"

Jas glanced down at the mobile.

Drugs were part of prison life.

He was part of prison life.

The word of a prisoner was nothing...

...without proof. And there were other matters at stake here. He looked at Stevie then the phone. "We get this back tae Buddah next door – an' we get back tae B-Hall."

As they walked through gate after gate and across a darkening courtyard, Jas watched the way Stevie's deltoids moved beneath the bikers' jacket. He tried to concentrate...

...Neil Johnstone's denial of last night refused to gel.

Why should the man lie?

He had nothing to lose...

...or prove...

...he pushed the thought aside and focused his mind on the other reason he had visited the eerie cell.

Hamster... Paul... break-ins...

DI Ann McLeod was right: he had no evidence, concerning the drugs rackets.

The Hadrian break-in was another matter.

The past two years of company searches and absentee fathers receded in the face of eight years of police training.

Paul McGhee had obviously brought himself to the attention of Hadrian officers by bragging to other prisoners about the Livingston job.

A job the security company had failed to report.

Not worth the hassle of reporting?

Ahead, Stevie had paused.

Jas broke into a jog.

The pale brow furrowed in concentration. "Whit's really goin' on here, Jas-man?"

Breath condensed in the air between them. He shook his head. "Nae idea..."

The brow furrowed further. Then a hand on his face.

Jas flinched.

The hand remained where it was, then gently traced the still swollen outline of his bottom lip. Low words. "Wullie sez Johnstone hud nothin' tae dae wi' whit happened tae you."

Jas seized a wrist, thumb brushing white scar tissue. Dusky air froze on his skin. He released the wrist and moved back, staring at the man wearing his bikers' jacket – the only man he'd known who filled it the way he did.

Mumbled words. "If ah find the bastards who took you fae the cell ah'll..."

"No' your problem, pal!" Stevie's anger was both touching and dangerous. Neither reaction was useful, right now. Jas scowled. "C'mon." He strode towards the entrance to B-Hall, pushing last night to where it sat most easily.

If there had been a wheel, Hamster would have been on it.

Jas watched the small figure in the padded jacket pace for another circuit, then walked into the cell.

Eyes widening. Headphones ripped from ears. "Well? Is he aff my back?"

A sour laugh. “Naw, but ah think we ken why he’s oan it!”

Jas shot Stevie a warning glance. He sat down on an untidily made cot. “Ah want ye tae go an’ find Mr Dalgleish...”

“No way, man!” Horror scuttled across the rodent features, dragging panic in its wake. “Ah’m no’...”

“Shut up an’ listen! Go see him, an’ tell him ah’ve got the pc.” He glanced from a rat-like relieved face to a pale, angry one. “Tell him Paul’s bin in touch wi’ me, an’ ah’m handlin’ negotiations.”

“Whit ye...?”

“If he wants it that bad...” He fingered his bottom lip.

“Ah...” Understanding. “Fierce, man! “ A hand through step-cut hair. “You an’...” Nod behind. “...the big guy set tae sort him oot?”

“Jist dae it!” Jas glared at Hamster.

Rodent confusion. “Whit ye gonny...?” Head shake. “...this is aw’ beyond me.” Rodent-panic. “Ah’ll no’ need tae own up tae onythin’, will ah? Ah’m in enough shite as it, whit wi’ the...”

“Has Dalgleish mentioned turnin’ ye in ?”

Uncertain. “Naw, but...”

“He wants the polis kept oota this, Hamster. Whit diz that tell ye?” Answer from an unexpected source:

“The hard drive wis full, ye said? Oan this... affy valuable pc?”

Rodent-nod.

Jas let Stevie run with thoughts already forming in his own head.

“The hospitals ur always doin’ that – ah read in the paper aboot all these pcs they dumped? Folk bought them at car boot sales... fulla medical records an’ personal details – confidential-stuff...”

He glanced left.

Stevie’s eyes glowed. “...an’ that tells me Dalgleish’s goat somethin’ else, apart fae a break-in, tae hide.”

Twenty-One

Two bells later:

“Ye said we!”

“Ah meant me!”

Stevie’s brown eyes an unconvinced, burning ochre.

Jas stared. The memory of last night smouldered, stoked each time clothes came into contact with his body. Stevie's fury was an ignition he couldn't risk: the man had already had a final warning, from Ian Dalgelish.

Burning ochre sparked. "This is aw' wrang, Jas-man – ye canny dae deals wi' a bastard like him!" Flaring. "Ye've no' even goat the fuckin' pc!"

He looked away from the eyes. "He disney ken that."

Stevie's fists were clenched, his broad body rigid.

Jas tried a smile. "Ah ken whit ah'm doin' – ah ken the way his mind works, ah ..." Marie's words. "...can talk the way he talks."

Sceptical snort.

His eyes flicked up.

A scowl twisted Stevie's features. "Wance polis always polis?"

Jas mirrored the scowl, wondering about the truth in the words. "Ye really believe that?" He stared into burning eyes.

One fence...

...straddled?

Stevie snorted again, turned and stalked to the window. "If ye're lookin' fur proof..." Low words. "...ah think ah...ken where he keeps his stash."

Jas blinked at a leathered back.

"His drugs." Stevie turned. "There's a big freezer at the back o' the kitchens, wi' a padlock. Only wan guy huz the key – only wan guy ever goes fuckin' near it." Striding forward, Stevie stopped an inch away. "Either Dalgleish huz a fuckin' frozen food habit, or..."

"Think he'd be stupid enough to keep drugs in a public area?" Jas almost laughed.

An angular face flinched as the words struck its surface.

One fence.

Two sides.

He glared, body needing the exercise, mind needing the rest. He pulled off the scratchy jumper.

"Ye don't believe me? C'mon – ah'll show ye!"

He felt heat from Stevie's body... then a hand on his bare arm.

His guts turned over.

Too close...

Too close..

Too...

Jas grabbed a scarred wrist, wrenching the hand away. "Get

oota here! If Dalgleish turns up ah..."

"But..."

"Lose yersel', Stevie!"

A ripple of anxiety flexed in his guts. He needed to be alone, needed to think, to plan...

...and didn't need the distraction this man's presence provided. He sank to a crouch, then braced himself parallel to the floor.

The turn-up of jeans inches from his face.

Silence. Then obedience. Then booted feet striding past his eyes.

Jas sighed and began the push-ups.

Paul McGhee.

Early release.

Low profile.

Staring out of the small window, Jas frowned. Hands gripped the bars. He gazed over the stone wall, down into Riddrie.

Where the fuck was Paul McGhee? Maybe Neil Johnstone's vow of non-violence, but Jas doubted this would extend to his brothers.

Paul McGhee: early release. No one had seen him since.

Neil Johnstone – via the mobile – arranging a reception committee to finish what he had started?

A shiver rippled through his right biceps. Jas frowned. His body still ached... when he let it.

This wasn't about last night...

This was... business.

Not merely the business of informing Marie of her brother's whereabouts, and securing his own, at-present insecure future.

But business concerning tenders and contracts... bigger pictures. He closed his eyes.

An image projected itself onto his eyelids: an image of Hadrian shares... of investors... investments...

...of break-ins which should have been reported to the police... of Hamster... threats and coercion... of snouts and small-time dealers like Paul McGhee...

...of prisoners with keys to cells... four faceless men beating and...

Jas opened his eyes and frowned. This wasn't about last night.

His mind skimmed back to decades ago, when he and Ian Dalgleish had played chess together.

Chess players were rarely team players...

...a team of two? Experienced sergeant and green probationer.

Alan Somerville...

...he pushed the past away and concentrated on the present.

Hadrian Security Solutions. Strategies, goals, long-term financial forecasts.

Chess...

...and an ex-sergeant in the Gorbals who knew how to use his pawns. Jas regripped the bars, hauled himself up to the small window, then straightened his arms...

...and let a brew of disparate ingredients ferment in his mind.

He was on sit-ups when:

"Why you not in the dining hall, Anderson?"

Jas grabbed a T-shirt and wiped sweat from his chest. Eyes focused on a pink face sprouting from a grey Hadrian blouson. A surprised pink face. He stared at Brodie, who was hugging a sheaf of blue folders. "No' hungry..."

Snort. "Well, you're wanted, Anderson."

"Whit fur?"

Frown. "Don't ask questions..." Brodie moved back. "... just get dressed."

Jas grabbed the scratchy jumper. As he pulled it on, eyes on his face.

"McStay an' you not gettin' along?"

He frowned, ran a tentative finger over his bottom lip. "Ah fell in the showers." He watched Brodie's features run a gamut of expressions and finally settle on a manufactured disinterest:

"Try to watch where you're goin', in future."

Jas searched the words for a hint of understanding, the give-away shadow that Brodie either knew what was going on in the prison, and accepted – or was ignorant.

He settled on the latter. From the walkway, the sounds of feet and buckets and trolleys. Frowning, Jas moved towards the door. "How long will this take?" He turned.

He needed to talk with Ian Dalgleish.

He needed to know about the pc.

"In case you've forgotten..." Expressionless face. "...an illegal weapon was found in your cell, Anderson – we've got to make out the report, for headquarters."

Jas turned away and strode out onto the walkway. Pen-pushing... the removal of privileges. From the other end of the block, the squabbling sounds of another petty argument...

He scowled.

...and all Hadrian could do was fill in forms. Listening to the thump of boots on metal, he stared down into the empty recreation area. Voice behind:

"Get a move on, Anderson – Mr Dalgleish hasn't got all day!"

Brodie knocked on the door of a familiar office, opened then stood aside.

Jas walked into the room. Behind, he was vaguely aware of a door unclosed. Brodie's voice:

"Want me to get McStay now?"

Gunmetal eyes acknowledged him, them aimed themselves over his right shoulder:

"No' at the moment."

A grey arm brushed past his shoulder, delivered the pile of blue folders onto the desk between them:

"Right, Mr Dalgleish!"

Jas looked from the handsome face to the chess board, filling its usual place on the desk between them.

Few pawns left. The black knight was a move away from checking the white king.

Dalgleish got up from behind the desk, strode past him.

The sound of a half-open door closing. Creak, but no click.

Jas stared at the chess board. "He's got ye." Grey moved into his vision.

"Ah've got him, ye mean..." Long fingers lifted the knight and executed the move. "...forgot ah always take black, didn't ye?"

Jas raised his eyes.

"You huv access tae property which belongs to Hadrian Security Solutions." Dalgleish sat down behind the desk.

Straight-to-the-point. He hadn't exected anything less. Polis training returned like a bad dream, unwanted but familiar. Jas tried to make his face expressionless. "Aye, so ye can stop hasslin' Hamster – he kens nothin'."

"How did you find oot aboot it?"

He hadn't expected this. Jas's mind clutched at plausiblities. Then one was provided:

A frown. "Same place you got the heroin?" Dalgleish was staring at the chess board, eyes fixed on the helpless white king.

Jas blinked, seizing the prompt. "Paul telt Marie everythin', afore he got oot." The lie came easily. Using the man's own assumptions against him came easier still. But gave little gratification.

Sigh. "Your visitor." Dalgleish raised his eyes, gunmetal blank. Large fingers gripped the top folder. "McGhee's sister – ah shouldda worked it oot. You eyeways did keep strange company."

Jas watched large fingers tighten around the blue folder. "Nae mair strange than you. Sometimes it pays aff – like your arrangement wi' Johnstone pays aff. Dae you buy his road-tae-Damascus act?"

Eyes narrowing. "Ye've seen him?" Disapproval.

Movement between halls was prohibited...

...but so was the dealing of drugs. "Aye, me an' Neil had a wee chat."

Disapproval deepening. "Ye've nae idea whit's at stake here."

"Oh, ah understand all right..." He pushed his respect for this man away, seized the edge of the desk. Fingers tightened. "An' it's..." The phrase circled in his head, then dropped to earth. "...none o' ma business." Jas moved his gaze to the folders. "But that is – whit aboot the weapon an' the condoms?" He refocused on the grey face.

Large hands picked up a blue folder, thumbed it open.

Jas stared at the small bald spot on the crown of a grey head.

"Ah see nae record of ony charges against you." Gunmetal raised.

A vision of Paul McGhee standing here, two months ago, uttering a similar question and receiving a similar response flickered on the wall behind an iron-grey head.

Privileges.

Favours.

Arrangements...

"Noo, ah want that pc..."

"Ye'll get it." Jas strained to keep his face expressionless. "Satisfy ma curiosity, though: did Paul come tae you wi' the... proposal, wantin' away fae Johnstone, or did ye make him the offer efter ye worked oot whit he hud access tae?"

A shadow of a flinch. Then impassivity recloaked the face.

"Come oan: ah ken aboot the whole thing – the McGhee/Hamilton break-in, the single cell – the favours the wee bastard got aff ye. Why did ye no' jist turn him over tae the polis?"

Folder closed, replaced on the desk. "Hadrian ainly wants its property back – Maxwell Fulton's prepared tae waive criminal charges if..."

"Is this an example o' the Hadrian philosophy? Private deals withoot polis involvement?"

"Nothin's ever black and white, Anderson – you ken that..." Pause.

Something in the voice pushed the years away.

...black and white...

Alan Sommerville.

Nearly twenty years ago.

...black and white...

...Jas glanced down at the chess board, then raised eyes to the man on the other side of the desk.

Large hands rubbed the rugged face, then removed themselves.

Jas stared into gun-metal eyes.

Long nights in the Gorbals.

Flexibility. Adaptability...

"Jist tell me where ah can pick up the pc, and ah'll see you git an easier time of it – if ye get sent doon fur the drugs charges, ye'll be back in here fur a while."

Jas raised an eyebrow. Bribe? Or threat...

...two sides of the same coin.

"Don't be naive, man." No flicker on the thick-set face. Gunmetal eyes fixed him, safeties off. "You of aw' people should understand the way things work."

Eyes flicked down to the threatened white king. Heart pounding, Jas let the man talk.

"This is aw' merely temporary." Ian Dalgleish sat down. "Hadrian's goat a big future – the Scottish Prison Association couldney organise a blow-job in a hairdrier factory!" Elbows on the desk, hands clasped."We're the future, man..."

"The future that had their ain security breached by two kids an' a delivery van?"

Forced laugh.

Something began to make sense: not grassing, but...

...blackmail. "Paul worked oot there wis somethin' important oan that hard drive, didn't he?" His mind was racing. "Did ye bend another o' Hadrian's rules tae get him early release, in exchange fur the pc?"

Expression frozen. Dalgleish moved out from behind the desk.

"Bendin' the rules is part o' everyday life – ah telt ye that, years ago."

He stared.

Alan Somerville.

Rules...

Gunmetal returned the stare. "Ah could huv you an' McGhee's sister fur handlin' stolen goods – oan toppa the dealin' charges..."

Jas blinked. Rules could be bent either way.

"...but whit guid wid that dae either o' us?"

Blackmail... worked both ways.

Dalgeish pulled the telephone towads him, lifted the receiver and held it out. "Phone her – phone McGhee's sister an' tell her tae bring the pc tae a... spot o' your choice."

In the sudden silence, Jas listened to the burr of a dialing one over the sound of a bluff being called. He scrabbled for plausible stalls, then remembered he held an equal number of cards..

...or so the man before him thought. Jas took the receiver, replaced in in its cradle. "We dae this ma way." The dialing tone died. He stared at Dalgleish.

Confusion, badly hidden. And the beginings of something else.

The bruises on his body pulsed. "Ah need tae be sure ye'll keep yer word – somewan's already hud a go at me!"

Frown. "That'll no' happen again – no' inside a Hadrian prison." Dalgleish stood inches away. "You have ma word."

Inches stretched to miles. Jas scowled, recalling share prices and long-term projections. "Diz Maxwell Fulton ken aboot yer drugs rackets? Or is that your way o' showin' initiative?"

The face was ashen, powder-burned.

Jas seized the advantage, followed his line of thought. "Diz he ken his officers dae deals wi' cons tae get this pc back?" He gripped the edge of the desk, pushing away the past..

Dalgleish was staring at him.

Ears strained beyond the unlocked door, to sounds of keys and trays rattling. "Why didn't Hadrian report the break-in tae the polis?" Jas released the desk, stared at Dalgleish. Something was making sense. "It wisney jist damage limitation on bad publicity, wis it?"

Pause, then: "There's sensitive information on that pc – nae use tae onywan else, but Mr Fulton would like it back, nae questions asked."

"McGhee worked this oot?"

Silent assent.

"He strung ye along fur it?"

Sigh. Nod.

Jas stared. A bullet-headed teenager had bought his early release, then welched on the deal: no wonder Paul McGhee was keeping a low profile.

"Hadrian huv the chance tae make a difference – a real difference. This is a crucial time for the company."

Jas looked up from the chessboard.

Dalgleish stood ramrod straight. "Justice, man – that's whit it's aw' aboot. Visible justice – we have tae be seen tae be dealin' wi' oor criminal population. If the courts continue tae award custodials at their present rate, we'll need a new prison every three weeks. Hadrian already huv the contract tae build four over the next two years – we're the maist competitive security company around – wi' a good track record..."

His mind was elsewhere, back in a holding-cell, nearly twenty years ago.

Dalgleish talked on. "We can build them, and we can run them – have you ever seen Barlinnie so in control?"

He thought about last night...about the night before and the nameless kid screaming three cells down...

"Things are very competitive in the private security business: Hadrian canny risk the information some..." Scowl. "...moron saved ontae the hard drive fallin' intae the wrong hands..." Gunmetal stare. "...you're a fair man: ah ken ye'll want tae do the right thing. The pc is, after all, oor property."

Jas blinked.

A bell rang...

He ignored it.

...again...and again...

...until the sound was obliterated by an unfamiliar but instantly recognisable siren.

Buzzing.

Ian Dalgleish moved swiftly round to the other side of the desk and lifted the telephone. The baritone was low, barely audible over the siren's whine. Jas tried to hear the words. Failed.

The call was brief.

Dalgleish opened a drawer, removed a set of keys and a mobile phone.

The door behind burst inwards. The room was filled with

shouting grey. Gunmetal eyes caught his. Booming baritone over the shouting:

"Back tae yer cell, Anderson – we'll continue this conversation later!" The eyes darted away.

The huddle of grey looked scared and unprepared. And preoccupied.

Thoughts of his own safety returned. Taking advantage of the confusion, Jas scooped the contraband froom the top folder. The Bic dropped to the floor. The condoms went straight into his pocket. He moved towards the door.

Beyond, the siren's howl continued to announce the outbreak of a disturbance somewhere in the prison.

The corridors were devoid of denim and peppered with swiftly moving grey uniforms, all of whom advised him to return to his cell but made no effort to accompany him there.

Regardless of how far Dalgleish had gone to try to gain control of Barlinnie, it hadn't worked.

Jas knew whatever was happening was happening in another hall.

He also knew Hadrian would need most of their meagre staff to handle it.

Reaching the end of a corridor, he looked both ways.

Right: cells...

Jas remembered Stevie's information.

...left: an opportunity? The powerful odour of over-cooked vegetables told him the dining-hall and kitchens must be somewhere close by.

Jas inched along yellow-brick wall, following his nose.

No cells in this part of the prison. Storerooms. He quickened his pace, turned a corner.

No security gates in this area:..

...he could smell the outside, a damp, frosty smell. Jas broke into a run.

Ahead, a caterpillar of figures in white overalls and hair-caps straggled out of a room and walked away from him, a grey figure bringing up the rear.

The kitchens..the freezer...

DI Ann McLeod's request for evidence.

...sweat poured down his face. This part of the prison was warmer than the cell area. A rumble beneath his feet told him the boiler-rooms were directly below. He reached the doorway from which the kitchen workers had emerged, glanced in. Some sort of food preparation area.

Empty.

As he strode past stainless-steel cutting tables and an enormous cooking range, his brain raced ahead.

Even if he did find drugs, there was no proof the drugs had been brought in by Dalgleish...

...another rumble – not below his feet, this time. And distant voices.

Jas ignored the sound, veering past a bank of sinks. He gazed at two doors.

One marked *Refrigeration Room – authorized personnel only.* The other unmarked...

He seized the handle.

...and unlocked.

Jas pushed opened the door, fumbling for a light switch.

The room was lined with chest-freezers.....

...banging. In the distance.

He glanced over his shoulder, then turned back and opened the lid of the freezer nearest.

Misty air. Frosted joints of meat glistened up at him. Rolling up the sleeves of the scratchy jumper, he plunged elbow deep into rigid animal flesh and began to heave.

Three plunges later his arms were numb and the floor was littered with ossified haunches.

Jas wiped icy sweat from his eyes.

Nothing... pointless...

He turned and strode back into the main food-preparation area. Eyes scanning...then locating the object of their scan.

In a corner. Not a chest-freezer. One of the upright variety...

He ran towards it.

...and locked. Fingering the small padlock, he glanced around for something he could use as leverage.

Nothing.

All utensils were locked away.

Jas sank to his hunkers.He stared at the freezer, suddenly struck by the silence. No bells... no footsteps..

...just distant rumblings... and voices. He scrutinised heavy steel preparation tables for anything he could use...

...then paused. Following the legs of the structure nearest, he noticed it wasn't bolted to the floor.

The scratchy jumper stuck to his skin, making him itch. Jas pulled it over his head, wrapped it around both hands then gripped the far edge and...

...pushed.

The solid table crashed into the freezer with a satisfyingly damaging thud.

He pulled...

..then pushed again.

And again...

...after four impacts, he stopped, listened.

Bootsteps... running...

Jas shoved the table against the freezer one last time.

Sounds of splintering metal...

...and the breaking of a vacuum seal.

He stared at ripped hinges, then at the still secure padlock holding the door shut.

Bootsteps... nearing....

He frowned, hauled the table back and gripped the freezer's hinges with both hands. If he was lucky?

A drugs cache: the key to which only a Hadrian officer was likely to possess.

Jas pulled...

If he was unlucky? A fridge full of cheap margarine and an advancing posse of Hadrian-booted feet demanding to know what he was doing here and why he had demolished a piece of Her Majesty's property.

...more snowy condensation.

He gritted his teeth and pulled again. Jas peered through the two-inch gap he had made, then tugged harder.

Something clutched at his guts.

Jas stared at the frozen face of a bullet-headed teenager, eyes zeroing in on the large tongue which protruded from the open, frost-etched mouth.

Twenty-Two

Wisps of white curled around the icy face, tendrilling towards him.

Jas backed away.

Paul McGhee had got early release, all right.

Thumps from above. And a crash.

He tore his eyes from the stiff, lifeless body and glanced over his shoulder.

Sounds of running... distant running... getting closer.

Marie's brother wasn't going anywhere, but he was...

...eyes barely registering a snow-covering of small white packets, Jas closed the freezer door. A lingering chill licked the back of his neck. He picked up Telly's scratchy jumper and ran from the kitchens...

...straight into a helmeted grey form. "What you doing down here, Anderson?"

He stepped back, staring at the visored face but recognising the voice. Brodie was holding a large transparent shield. "Ah want tae make a phone call!" Fingers gripped his bare arm:

"Change the record, eh?" Bravado less convincing than usual. "Get back to your cell!" Pulling.

A rumble. Then the sounds of running... and shouting.

Jas twisted away. "There's..."

"Just get moving, Anderson!" Brodie re-gripped and pushed him along the corridor.

Jas gave up and complied. Rumblings above were increasing in volume.

Behind, he could hear bootsteps. He walked towards metal stairs, mind sifting through contradictory accounts...

Ian Dalgleish.

Neil Johnstone.

The former was doing more deals with more prisoners than he'd thought.

The latter had killed at least twice....

...and had known Paul McGhee intimately. The vow of non-violence flickered in Jas's head, ephemeral as candle flame.

Two sets of boots clattered on metal stairs and joined echoing voices and more bootsteps from above.

Jas paused. Something tingled in the air around him...

...he opened his mouth. "There's a body in wanna yer freezers!" The shape of a riot shield against his spine:

Information ignored. "I said get a move on, Anderson!"

He was pushed through a doorway and into a sea of shielded Hadrian grey.

And banging. From behind locked doors.

The smell of panic and confusion twitched his nostrils. Jas

scanned the group of officers for faces...

...all obscured beneath helmets and face-guards.

"Ah'm serious! Go look fur yersels..."

"Shut it!" Brodie pushed him towards a bulky figure. "Get him back to his cell!"

Helmetted nod.

He felt himself pushed towards more metal stairs. Jas turned back to the faceless Hadrian officer. "Where's Mr Dalgleish?"

"Never you mind, Anderson, just get back tae yer cell – we'll handle this!" A fist pushed again.

Jas frowned and walked on past rows of locked doors.

B-Hall seemed in control...

...for the moment.

When they reached the cell, the metal door was trembling under the force of blows from inside. He knew it was the safest place to be – during a riot, at least. Jas waited while the door was unlocked.

On the other side, Stevie's fist raised, mid-thump. A look. Then thumping resumed.

Behind, slamming. Then locking.

He moved past Stevie. The cell resounded with vibrations from inside and out. "When did this start?" Jas turned.

Amber eyes glowing, adrenalin-tinged. "Tea time – over somewan borrowin' somewan else's radio... C-Hall's bin sealed aw' ready..." Fist raised, another two thumps on the door. "They're gonny tear the fuckin' place apart!"

Jas sat down on the lower bunk. Paul McGhee... dead...

Over thumps: "Where were ye, onyway?" Pause in thumps. "Did Dalgleish turn up? Did ye...?"

"Naw, ah didney find oot onythin aboot the fuckin' pc!" Jas rubbed his face. His head hurt, his mind was racing. Paul McGhee... Neil Johnstone... Ian Dalgleish ...

Thumps again.

Rules bent...

...and broken.

Neil Johnstone... a man kicked to death a year ago.

Neil Johnstone... settling a very old score, with the brother of the woman whose testimony had put him here?

Were Hadrian so desperate to demonstrate their ability to run an efficient prison they would cover up murder?

Thumps... louder...

Jas looked up. Stevie was kicking the door now, large boots impacting on solid metal. He stared at the heavy shoulders, felt the same tension in the cell he'd sensed downstairs...

...and would probably feel all over the prison. "Quit that, eh?" Jas rubbed his face. He needed to think...

Alan Sommervile.

...needed to...

Stevie kicked harder. "So whit happened?"

Jas scowled into his hands. Irritation crawled over his skin. He leapt out from the bottom bunk and grabbed a leathered shoulder. "Will ye quit that racket! Noo!"

Under his fingers, the shoulder was rigid. Stevie spun round, fists clenched. In the background, the banging had increased in volume. Over the noise, the heat of breath on his face, he could feel the hammer of his own heart.

They stared at each other. Paul McGhee's frozen features melted in the face of Stevie's glowing eyes.

A twitch in his groin.

Not now, not...

...the movement was razor-quick. Pushed backwards by the force of Stevie's bulk, he felt his body continue to respond. Jas tried to control what was between his legs with what was between his ears...

...and failed. He could smell the man, feel...

...guts churning he stood rigid as fingers fumbled at his zip, gripping then hauling combat pants and underwear down over thighs.

Then hands on his waist...

...and a furious face against his groin.

Jas flinched. Breathy stubble on his shaft. Then vibrations. Mumbled curses.

He pressed hands to the sides of Stevie's head, held him loosely. Unheard vied with unspoken words. Fingers tensed. Five o'clock shadow rough against his balls and thighs. Hips bucking instinctively, he thrust into Stevie's face.

Cock said fast.

Heart said slow.

Brain screamed no.

Hands slipped to the back of his thighs, gripping painfully.

Mind short-circuited by the pressure of lips and tongue on his prick, he moaned.

Stevie sucked awkwardly, with none of the skill of other men who'd used their mouths on him, over the years.

He sucked eagerly. Anxiously. Angrily.

Jas inhaled sharply as teeth glanced off his shaft, then hurriedly hid themselves behind lips.

Stubble rasped against bruised balls, which throbbed further under the friction...

...then Stevie's mouth was everywhere, leaving a desperate, frustrated saliva trail over belly, cock, thighs, balls.

Jas shoved a hand into tangled hair, drawing the wet tongue upwards, over stomach and chest hair.

Stevie settled on his right nipple and began to nuzzle like a furious child.

Something knotted, unknotted then retied itself in the pit of his stomach.

Last night...

...fifteen minutes ago.

The frozen, dead body shimmered in his mind.

Around them, banging from other cells became rhythmic, pounding in his head and syncing with his heart.

Frustrations released themselves...

...twining the fingers of one hand into thick brown hair, Jas reached down, tearing at Stevie's shirt, then jeans.

A moan replaced the curses around his stiffening nub. Stevie's cock leapt free, flexing in his fist. The shaft was damp against his palm. Sweat broke out on his balls, joining the spit.

A shiver racked two bodies.

Jas traced the outline of Stevie with a rough thumb.

Teeth clamped over his nipple.

Jas gritted other teeth, dragging down his cell-mate's jeans.

Stevie groaned, mouth leaving nipple and burying itself in his neck.

Jas leant forward, pushing until Stevie's spine connected with the cell wall...

...and pressed himself against the shaking man. Sweat cemented chest to chest, thigh to thigh...

...skin to skin. Mouth stabbed at mouth, missed and settled for ear.

Another prick flexed against his own.

Jas pulled away. His guts ached for the man.

Stevie reached between them, ran a shaking finger up the shaft, then down again. Fingers tightened around him.

His brain told him no. His body said yes with every glide of his cell-mate's fist. Tightening the grip, fingers sank into the warm flesh of Stevie's shoulder. His other hand lingered at the root of the man's prick, ring finger rubbing the underside of the tight ball-sack.

Stevie's hand faltered, lost rhythm for a second.

Jas stared, continued to finger the furry skin. His fingers moved lower, felt Stevie tremble as he massaged the puckered skin behind the man's balls.

"Oh fuck..."

His own cock was throbbing, Stevie's fingers almost painfully tight around his shaft. His right hand began to move faster.

Stevie's body stiffened.

Jas slowed the motion of his fist.

Stevie groaned, head lowered in frustration.

Brain said no.

Body said...

...Jas clenched his teeth, fist dragging up and down his cell-mate's prick. He pulled away, gripping shoulders. Balls drawn up hard against his body.

Brain said no.

Body said...

...hands slipped down over shoulders, coming to rest on two icy buttocks.

The fist remained stubbornly around his prick, which pulsed painfully in the iron grip. And tightened.

Jas inhaled sharply, fingers spreading over the cheeks of Stevie's arse. He felt the response, the thrust against his open palms, grinding back into his hands.

In the cold, damp cell, panting echoed over distant shouts.

Thumbs dragged the length of the warm crevice.

A moan... and two solid mounds pressing back.

"Nae condoms..." His voice sounded strange.

"Ah'll risk it..."

Last night was a cold, burning memory, but one part of it could still be with him. "Ah'll no'." He grabbed a handful of hair, stared into flaming eyes. They almost melted the burning ice. Hoarse words and an aching need did the rest:

"Pull oot, then! Ah don't care whit ye dae, but ah want yer prick inside me. Noo!"

A reckless confirmation ground against his thigh and spurred his brain into action. Fumbling in the pocket of the discarded combat pants, Jas located one of repossessions from Ian Dalgiesh's office.

Stevie's breath singed the back of his neck. He tore at the packaging with his teeth. Then fingers were tree-trunks, clumsily rolling the condom into place .

The latex was thin, unlubed. Barely adequate for fucking women and smuggling white powder.

Body rigid and mind blank, Jas grabbed Stevie's shoulders and pushed him in the direction of the lower bunk. Skull impacted with the frame of the bed above. Desire cut through shock. Manoeuvring heavy legs, he hooked pale knees over his shoulders and seized his prick. Beneath the condom, the shaft was tacky with Stevie's spit, slick with the sweat of the man's grip.

Soft curses, fingers digging into shoulder skin.

The banging from the other cells faded away, replaced by a distant shimmer in his ears.

Jas stared down.

Pain framed the closed eyes.

His fingers located the moist opening. Shifting position, he gasped as the head of his latexed prick dragged on delicate skin.

"Don't stop..."

Bitten-down nails on his back told a different story.Tensed and unlubed, Stevie was difficult to enter.

Fingers uncurling, Jas stroked the iron rosette.

A moan. Rigid muscle flinched.

His fingertip circled a pucker of tension. Jas lowered his head, spat onto the quivering hole and massaged more vigorously.

A nail's length slipped in. Breath caught in his throat. A shiver of need swept the length of his prick.

Another moan.

Jas removed his finger, gripped sweating shoulders. Positioning the aching head of his cock, he bucked hard with his hips.

A sharp inhale. Fingers scraped the skin on his back. Muscle quivered...

...then Jas mirrored the gasp and slid forward. As he pounded into the rigid, frustrated man something pounded out...

...of them both. Prick half-buried inside Stevie, Jas paused. Hands down, thumbs dug into Stevie's spine and arched the quivering back. He wanted deeper...

...nails ploughed parallel furrows into his shoulders and he knew Stevie wanted the same. Elbows braced against the soiled mattress, he withdrew...

...then thrust again. Eyes closed, he tried to shut out Stevie's grunts and his own thoughts of tearing latex.

It didn't work. He increased the speed of the fuck.

That worked. The warm tunnel of muscle was tight and ridged against his shaft. Sensation flooded his body, blocking everything else. Below, movement told him Stevie was jerking his own prick furiously.

The knowledge brought him close... too close.

Fists clenched under Stevie's back, instinct pulled him out, gasping. The force of the orgasm took the breath out of his lungs, sent it fizzing in his ears. He opened unfocused eyes, watching a shower of spunk fill the tip of the condom.

Panting... cursing...

Guts on fire, sweat drenching them both, Jas pulled the writhing body up from the bed and trapped a fist-wrapped cock between them.

...shouting... then wetness.

One arm slung around his neck, Stevie clung to him.

Another heart hammered against his chest.

Another wetness. Jas pressed his face against a damp cheek, held the man until two salty liquids dried and sealed two bodies together.

Eventually, he lowered them both back onto the bunk, fumbling one-handed for a blanket.

Stevie's breath was low and shallow. The smell of their sex filled the small, cold cell.

Jas shivered. A sob against his neck...

...when his breath returned to normal, the banging had stopped. Or maybe he no longer registered the sound.

Stevie was clammy against him.

Jas eased himself free of the condom, knotted and tossed it away. Wrapping his arms around the bikers' jacket, he pulled the man closer and closed his eyes.

Paul McGhee's frost-etched features flickered once, then faded.

In sleep, freed and unsettered, his subconscious pushed back the years and held them there.

Summer... July... the usual winds and rain.

The seventh of an eight-hour night shift. The holding-cells full of drunken, Glasgow Fair revellers. Minor offences. Most sleeping off the results of too much exuberance.

An on-going chess game interrupted for the umpteenth time by four undercover Drugs Squad officers...

...barely managing to restrain a 6'4", thrashing dreadlocked form.

Alan Sommerville. Address somewhere in Westbourne Park, London. Arrested in Central Station, on possession and suspicion of supplying: specifically, of acting as a drugs courier.

Alan Sommerville. A powerfully built man...

...and extremely annoyed at having to spend any time at all in Gorbals Police Station.

The drugs squad wanted him processed and held until they could check his known associates. And until he calmed down.

All the holding-cells were full. Busy night.

It had taken all six of them to get Alan Sommerville into an unused side office.

It had taken one of them to track down the leather restraints, to keep him there...

Sweat poured down his forehead. Jas mumbled in his sleep.

..."Tighter, Anderson!" Sergeant Dalgleish's baritone boomed in his head.

The Drugs Squad guys had departed quickly.

A size 12 baseball boot caught him above the right eye. Blood pouring from the cut, Jas hauled the restraint past the fourth notch, threw Alan Somerville into a corner, where he continued to writhe and curse.

The use of restraints were strictly governed, following accidents in other parts of the country. One-hourly checks on the prisoner.

His responsibility.

His responsibility.

His...

Scraping.

Eyelids shot open. Remembering the previous night, he rolled from the bunk, tripping in his half-undressed state.

More scraping. Not key-scraping.

It took seconds to clear his mind. Jas stared at the door hatch.

Pale face. Brodie-clone. "Roll-call..." Behind, low, baritone: "Anderson?"

Jas frowned, the dream fresh in his mind. "Whit happened tae Paul McGhee?" He moved closer to the door hatch.

Behind, a snuffle. Then Stevie's shallow sleep-breathing resumed.

Words from beyond the door hatch. "Finish off up here, then get back to the control room, Stewart." Quiet, authoritative baritone.

The response was a set of departing footsteps.

Jas blinked, repeated his question.

Frustrated whisper. "Whit dae ye mean?"

Jas moved towards the voice, lowering his own. "He's dead in wanna your freezers! Whit dae you ken aboot it?"

Seconds after that, more scraping. The cell door opened.

No torch this time.

And silence..

He focused through darkness. The rest of the Hall was silent. Jas repeated the information, eyes finally making out the bulky shape in the cell doorway.

"Is this some sorta joke?"

"Paul wisney laughin'."

The shape moved into the cell, closing the door.

He could make out features now, make out a mixture of shock, curiosity and... something else.

Baritone whisper. "McStay..." Sigh. "He huz access tae the kitchen – he shared a cell wi' the McGhee-boay fur a couple of nights before his release..."

The voice was very close. The implication unmistakable.

Jas frowned. "Who signed the release papers? Is there no' some record that Paul never left Barlinnie?"

Unexpectedly, the light flickered on.

He stared at Dalgleish.

Gunmetal stared back, ignoring his question. "Ah tried tae warn ye aboot McStay..."

In the background, a groaning snuffle.

"...tried tae warn McGhee, but he widney listen. No wan should be sharin' wi' McStay. He's in here fur kickin' the shite oota queers. The way things work in prison fucks wi' his brain: he's either offerin' his mooth tae ony prick he can find, or tryin' tae off himsel' – an' them! Disney ken if he's comin' or goin' – it's aw' in his psych report. It wis ainly a matter o' time before he..."

"Ya bastard!"

Something pale and naked launched itself at the Hadrian-grey back, roaring like an animal. Then Stevie was on top of Dalgleish, thumbs digging into the man's windpipe.

Barlinnie Standard Time stood still...

He watched Hadrian grey and the black leather of the bikers' jacket roll together on concrete. Stevie was howling something over strangled, rasping breath.

...then speeded up. Jas lunged into the Dalgleish/McStay struggle and seized a tensed, leathered shoulder.

Another roar...

...then pain. Stevie threw him backwards. Spine contacted with the bunk's metal frame.

Thudding... in his brain...

Jas stared.

More thudding.

Hands pressed to temples, he levered himself upright. Fuzzy shapes waltzed before his eyes.

Thudding... then a sickening crunch...

He shook his head. Vision cleared...

...just as the back of Dalgleish's skull impacted on the stone floor for a third time.

Jas threw himself forward, hooked and tightened an arm around Stevie's throat. And pulled.

Dalgleish's face pulsed blue-white, eyes rolling back in his head. A thick, sticky pool of red was spreading outwards from beneath his body.

Jas grabbed one ear, twisted viciously.

Stevie's grasp slackened.

Dalgleish's head dropped to the floor one last time.

Stevie was still shouting as Jas wrenched an iron grip from a badly damaged windpipe. He elbowed his cell-mate aside and searched for a pulse.

Amazingly, Dalgleish was still breathing.

Fingers moved over damp hair, examining then raising the head. Red seeped over knuckles. Jas frowned. Scalp wound: a lot of bleeding, no real damage. "Gimme yer hand!"

Behind, the shouting had eased to low curses.

"Yer hand, Stevie. Now!"

A trembling palm appeared at his left. Jas grabbed fingers,

pressed them against a long cut on the back of Dalgleish's scalp. "Keep it there!"

The hand quivered against his. The mumble became audible. "Let him fuckin' bleed!"

He stared at the inert form. Dalgleish was breathing – just. But unconscious. A dangerous state, given the head injury. He scanned the cell, then reached for the piss-pot. Stevie yelled, darting back as Jas hurled the icy contents over the Hadrian officer's pale face.

A cough.

More coughing.

Beneath the now-retching head, he watched ketchup dilute to burgundy under flickering fluorescent light. The blood-piss soup coagulated then stretched, separating into tiny concentric circles within circles.

"Finish the bastard aff – or ah will!" The words were low, rigid with anger.

Jas ignored him, grabbed yesterday's red, contraband underwear. Fingers tightened on damp fabric. Deftly, he removed a bootlace, eased Stevie's hand away from the scalp cut and fashioned a makeshift pressure-pad. He stared.

Adequate, but the man needed medical attention. He glanced up.

Brown eyes glazed with rage. Skin flushed with exertion. "Whit's goin' on, Jas-man?"

He frowned: he had to ask. "Whit wis a meant tae find in that freezer?"

Eyes alight. "Ye looked? Wiz it like ah thought?" Eyes to the unconscious form. "Ah knew that bastard wiz as bent as fuck! Ah..."

"Who's bent, Stevie?" Words with a multitude of meanings fought in his brain. Jas stared at Stevie's scarred, naked body, remembering an hour earlier...

...Dalgleish's implication and the reaction that implication had generated.

Amber eyes flicking to his. "There wur drugs in that freezer – right?"

Jas nodded. It wasn't a lie. "...an' a body."

Colour drained from the angular face.

"Paul McGhee's dead, Stevie – did you kill him?"

Horror. "Me? Whit ye – me?" Stunned silence, punctuated by rapid, shallow breathing.

Jas scowled. He was stupid to doubt Stevie: most of the man's violence – whatever the cause – was directed inwards, at himself.

"Wee Paul's deid?" Disbelief. "But why would...?"

"Ah've nae proof o' who killed him, or why, but ah ken who fuckin' covered it up!"

Confusion on the pale face.

Jas talked – about the understanding between Ian Dalgleish and Paul McGhee... about devils you knew and could work with... about pcs and Hadrian and a company's desperate attempts to be seen to be in charge...

...but not about a Gorbals custody sergeant who had covered-up a green probationer's stupid mistake. He stopped talking, stared.

Understanding condensed on the angular face.

Jas watched the expression change, the rage return:

"The fuckin'...!" Stevie lunged past him.

Preventing a second attack, Jas released Dalgleish's head and grabbed bare shoulders.

The head lolled back against bare brick. Damp, deeper scarlet briefs saved the skull from more damage.

Spittle flew from Stevie's lips onto ashen skin. "It wiz him!"

Jas stepped between his cell-mate and the prostrate form. "Whit wiz him?"

"He kent ye wur askin' questions aboot wee Paul..." Stevie's eyes blazed. "...he let those guys in here! He organised yer rape – he's goat mair tae lose than onywan if ony bodies ur fun' aroon' here!"

Jas stared.

...keep yer nose oota whit disney concern ye...

Something twisted in his guts.

"Lemme finish the bastard aff! Lemme....!"

"No!" The word came from somewhere other than his guts. He pushed Stevie back, turned.

Two ex-polis.

One fence.

Two sides...

...a chess player who knew how to use his knights. And sacrifice his pawns for greater victories.

Jas glanced at the half-open door into darkness, then down at the semi-conscious form of Officer Dalgleish. The sound of Stevie's breathing throbbed in his ears, over low moans from the floor. He nudged Dalgleish with the toe of a boot.

A groan...

...and rattling.

Crouching, he slipped a hand into the right-hand pocket of badly fitting grey trousers.

Metal.

Over lolling protests, Jas removed a large set of keys. Staring at the slumped, helpless man, he found himself laughing. "Will ah open a coupla cell doors, Mr Dalgleish – see whit creeps oot?" Last night's powelessness scythed through his mind..

Stevie moved closer.

Reason cut through. "Ye don't touch him, right?" He kicked Dalgleish again. "Naebody touches him..." Eyes flicked over shoulder, met brown, smouldering embers. Power carried certain... responsibilities.

Slow nod. "If ye say so, Jas-man."

He threw the keys into the air, caught them one-handed.

A spluttering flicker. Then darkness.

The black cleared his mind.

Hadrian handled security inside Barlinnie. Beyond Hadrian's walls was a different matter.

In the gloom, piss and warm blood singed his nostrils. Jas hauled the man to his feet.

Dalgleish was heavy in semi-stupor.

Jas slapped the squat face once. Then twice. "Ah trusted you." Low words:

"Ah didney ken onythin' aboot any... rape. They were ainly meant tae rough ye up. Ye were rockin' the boat..." Fear, badly hidden.

Voice from behind. "Fuck him over, Jas-man – or gie him tae the poz guys in F-Hall!"

Jas shivered and thought of his own possible fate. Fist tightened around a handful of grey. "Wid ye like that, Dalgleish?"

The fear flowed freely now.

Behind, Stevie fed on it...

...six blocks of abused men would gorge themselves on it, given the chance.

"Fur pity's sake, man..." Babbling. "...onythin' ye want – jist name it. Onythin'!"

Jas shook Dalgleish. "Ye really wanna ken whit ah want? Ye really need tae ask?"

A tremble swept the body in his grip. The response felt rather than seen.

Jas pulled the quivering Dalgleish-shape closer. His voice was low. "Did Neil Johnstone killed Paul McGhee, cos he thought his cunt wis grassin' tae you?"

Dalgleish coughed, shook his head. Denial or an attempt to clear it? Behind:

"You're deid, ya fucker!"

"Shut it, Stevie!" Jas scowled.

At his feet, Dalgleish coughed again. The man was losing consciousness.

Another cover-up pushed itself to the front of his brain, distracting the primal need for mindless revenge. "But he wis wrang – cos your only interest in McGhee wis a fuckin' computer." Jas leant down, slapped the lolling face. "Whit's on the hard drive o' that pc?"

Nothing.

He slapped again, harder.

Choking sounds. "Copies o' letters fae Maxwell Fulton tae the Scottish Office..."

"Whit else?" Letters could be explained away, faked, denied.

Bloody snot dripped onto trembling lips. "Records o' transactions. Statements o' the payments..."

Jas gripped grey shoulders.

A cough. "Maxwell Fulton bought the prison contracts..."

Bingo! Bribery was a prosecutable offence; financial details couldn't be argued with. "Ken whit ah want noo, Dalgleish?"

Snuffling.

Jas released the shoulders. "Ah want this wee speech tae huv a bigger audience!"

Dalgleish slumped against him. More coughing. "Get me tae a doctor! Please..."

He frowned.

"Who cares aboot pcs?" Disappointment behind. "Ye're wasting yer time, Jas-man. Fuck him over – fur whit he did tae you an' all the other poor bastards..."

Dalgleish's breath on his face.

Power was nothing...

...without control. Jas sank to a crouch, slung Dalgleish over his left shoulder and stood up.

"Ye're mad – where ya gonny take him? In case ye huvney noticed, there's a riot goin' oan oot there. Ye'll be in solitary afore ye can tell'em onythin'!

Jas focused on sceptical brown eyes. He'd forgotten where he was...

...what he was. The word of a prisoner against the word of a screw.

The keys were heavy in his hands...

...then sudden lightness. "Oi!"

The back of the bikers' jacket and his passport to the control room disappeared out of the cell and merged into blackness.

"Stevie!"

No response... no sound...

...then metal on metal... metal in metal...and low voices.

He had to get Dalgleish out. Alive. Jas scowled: at the end of every corridor, cctv cameras. With or without keys, if he could get the man down three flights of stairs and...

Twenty-Three

Movement was difficult enough. He sloughed the semi-conscious form from his shoulders and pushed.

Dalgleish stumbled.

Jas grabbed a wrist, twisted.

A yell of surprise.

He wrenched the grey-clad arm further up the grey-clad back.

A hiss of pain from between grey-sounding lips.

Somewhere ahead, laughter. "Hey, boays?" A shout to no-one in particular and everyone in general. "Guess whit the Jas-man's got oot here?"

The sentence resounded against rows of locked doors.

In front, Dalgleish flinched.

Jas paused.

This wasn't about tit for tat.

This wasn't about settling old scores and grudges.

He pushed the trembling body forward, quickened his pace.

Ahead, the scraping of metal on metal, keys gripped in fingers unused to control, keys in locks. Another key...

...unlocking another cell. His own fingers tightened around Dalgleish's wrist.

Tightened, and raised.

A scream split the dark.

Jas felt bone shift. Dislocated, not broken. But painful nonetheless. Enough to keep the man conscious – for both their sakes.

Dalgleish was whimpering now, staggering.

Jas pushed on.

Behind, the whispered spread of information.

Pupils expanding in the gloom, he stared ahead at the outline of stairs which led to landings above and below.

The noise behind grew in strength. Stevie worked quickly and efficiently, opening doors, opening more than doors.

Jas shoved the bulky body hard against the metal railing and turned. And watched.

Movement in the dark. Furtive. Like rats scurrying from traps, unexpectedly free. Random, disoriented...

B-Hall flooded with light.

...but not disorganised. Jas frowned down the walkway.

Stevie stood at the opposite end, fist clamped around the main security light switch.

His cell-mate's eyes glowed copper. Jas heaved Dalgleish upright, spun him round.

The man's face was a mask of blood and bruises.

He glared into pinpricked pupils. "Stay with it..." His voice was hardly audible.

Head lowered. Muttering. "Ma wrist... ma fuckin' wrist – ye've broken ma..."

"...don't pass oot oan me..." Voice lower still.

Muttering into formless mumbles.

Jas wedged an index finger between two displaced bones.

"Okay!" Screamed more than said.

Whirring above his head. Jas looked up.

A red, electronic eye slowly swept the area.

He pushed his burden closer to the cctv camera's blinking lens and held him there. Over the man's shaking shoulder, floors below, he could see more denim swarming from behind open cell doors...

This wasn't about tit for tat.

This was about corruption, cover-ups and drug deals.

...out for blood was an understatement. And getting to the control room by that route was now out of the question.

"Please..." Ragged whisper.

Jas lowered his face.

"...please – they'll kill me."

"Why did ye cover up the death o' a prisoner? Why did ye no' report Paul McGhee's murder? Easier to keep his body here than risk fuckin' up Hadrian's precious public image?"

"...you an' me, we can work somethin' oot if..."

"Oh, we're gonny work somethin' oot..." Jas clenched his fists. If he couldn't get to the control room, the control room could come to him. He gripped piss-soaked hair, hauling the broad face back. "...but first, we gotta make sure yer mates get yer guid side!" He held the head directly in front of the red eye. "Aye?"

A howled assent.

He waited for the electronically controlled gate to open.

Around them, the noise of more cells unlocking, the sound of more voices.

And waited. He watched the group of semi-denimed men inching along the walkway towards them, then flicked his gaze back to the red eye. A shiver of irritation grew to a throb in his fists. Jas frowned.

Remaining here wasn't an option: Hadrian weren't about to open gates when a riot was in progress.

Down was no longer an option, for similar reasons.

Jas looked up, stared at a small metal door then scanned the walkways. Eyes zeroed in on a pair of broad shoulders in a familiar bikers' jacket. "Geez the fuckin' keys, Stevie!" The shout only just audible over the growing sounds of cell-destruction.

Head cocked, Stevie followed his gaze to the door on the landing above. Metal hurled through the air.

Jas caught the keys. The sound of pounding footsteps. Then a breathless voice at his side:

"C'mon, then."

Jas shook his head at Stevie. "This is between me..." A flick of his fingers.

A low moan, this time.

"...an' him!" Keys wrenched from his fingers. Jas made a grab for them.

Adrenalin gave his cell-mate speed. Half way up the metal stairs, Stevie turned. "C'mon, Jas-man!" Stevie quickly unlocked the small door, then tossed the bunch of keys into the air.

They landed in the middle of the suicide net.

From each side of the walkway, a denimed figure threw itself onto reinforced nylon mesh and struggled towards the prize. Behind, low angry words:

"Bastard – ye're gonny fuckin' pay fur... c'mere, ya..."

Jas heaved Dalgleish upright, hauled him away from the approaching mob and towards the stairs.

Barlinnie Standard Time had suddenly sprouted wings. Everything was moving too fast...

...and not fast enough.

In five seconds they were on the upper landing.

In what seemed like hours, they were through the door, and back into blackness.

Jas pushed Dalgleish towards Stevie's urgent voice.

Less dark.

But icy coldness.

And near-silence. From the roof of B-Hall, Jas gazed up at the November sky, then flicked his eyes to the glittering sparkles which outlined Riddrie.

"Great view, eh?" Stevie crouched at his side, bikers' jacket zipped against night frost.

Sub-zero air erected every hair on his bare chest. Jas glanced to where Ian Dalgleish crouched, silently nursing an injured wrist. "This wan's better."

The man had shrunk in stature. The uniform seemed to hang on him, something he could no longer fill.

A low laugh from Stevie.

He watched huddled Hadrian grey try to blend in with roof slate-grey...

...and succeed all too easily.

Jas frowned: visibility was all. The police – or the army – would take control soon.

After pushing Dalgleish through the small skylight in Barlinnie's roof, he'd wedged it shut. A dead Dalgleish was no good to him...

...but this needed visibility. He glanced at Stevie. "Got a light?"

Curious smile. "Funny time fur a fag, Jas-man." Hands patting the bikers' jacket, nonetheless. Pause. Something located, withdrawn. Fingers extended.

Jas took the complimentary matchbook.

Stevie was still fumbling. A laugh. "Nae ciggies..." Something else withdrawn. "...unless ye wanna smoke this?"

He stared at the unopened, unread Rule Book Officer Brodie had ceremoniously given him, on his first day.

It seemed appropriate. Jas aimed a foot at the Dalgleish-shape.

Gasp of panic, then howl of pain as one good and one not-so-good wrist tried to snatch purchase on frosted slate tiles.

Stevie caught Dalgleish by the collar, hauled him back up the sloping roof.

Staring into the night, Jas searched for the snake of blue-white lights which should be making its way from Blackhill Police station.

Nothing.

He waited, shivering.

More nothing.

Jas frowned along Smithycroft Road, towards the patch of unlit ground which was Barlinnie's car park.

Nothing...

He narrowed his eyes: would Hadrian be stupid enough to try to handle the riot themselves?

...then a red glow. Looked like a brazier.

The SPA's unofficial picket-line.

Drawing cold night air into his lungs, Jas yelled.

His voice evaporated into darkness.

He shouted again.

Another voice joined his.

Jas struck a match, igniting the first page of Hadrian's rule-book.

The cheap paper caught easily, burned brightly. He hurled the flaming booklet from singeing fingers, watched it fall inside Barlinnie's walls like a shooting star.

His wish was silent. Jas glanced from Stevie's impassive features to the distant, glowing brazier. His skin glowed in unison as the low temperature seeped through into his bones, stemming the warming effect of adrenalin.

Nothing.

More nothing.

Wind whipped around his shoulders. From below, in B-Hall, distant rumbles.

Then through the night, low shouting. Voices audible... distant voices:

"Whit's goin' on up there? Whit ye...?"

"Get the polis!" Jas cupped freezing hands around his mouth. "Ah've got a hostage up here an' ah wanna talk tae the polis!" Reached down, he grabbed a shoulder, pulling the slumped figure to his feet.

The man was heavy.

Jas propped him up, felt Stevie do likewise.

Shouted words drifted through the night, followed by the weak beam of a torch. "Go back inside, son, ye..."

"Don't ye believe me, pal?" Jas gripped Dalgleish's arm.

A howl of agony. "Dae as he sez!" The baritone trembled.

"Jist phone the polis, pal..." Something occurred to him. "... an' ask fur DI McLeod. London Road!"

Silence. Thoughtful silence.

Jas pulled his gaze from Dalgleish to Stevie. "Get back tae yer cell – this is nothin' tae dae wi' you!"

Scowl. To a heap of Hadrian-grey and back again.

Jas mirrored the expression. "Want yer sentence increased? Cos that's whit'll happen if you – or onywan else – lays a finger oan him!" Jas wondered if common sense stood any chance against Stevie's palpable hatred of the third man on the roof.

The scowl flickered.

"Do it!" Stevie's eyes bored into his.

Jas held the stare, then watched the back of a leather jacket move over the roof as Stevie clambered reluctantly back towards the small skylight.

One problem down...

He thought about Daligeish.

...one to go. A low growl broke through the thought:

"Thanks..."

He shivered. "Ah dinny want yer thanks..." Jas watched Stevie pull the crowbar wedge from the skylight. He refocused on the now-standing Dalgleish. "When the polis git here, you're gonny tell them everythin' – includin' the cover-up of Paul McGhee's death..."

"Where's yer proof?"

Jas frowned.

"There's nothin' in that freezer noo, cept frozen chips – an' your fingerprints." Gunmetal eyes sighted his. "Ah left a coupla bags o' smack behind, jist tae be oan the safe side."

The frown froze. The implication shimmered. On remand for dealing, any further drugs involvement would only muddy the waters.

Dalgleish seized his confusion. "Come on, Anderson – who's

gonny miss wan mair bit o' double-crossin' junkie scum, onyway?"

...double-crossin'...

...double-crossin'...

The phrase rang in his ears. A shiver colder than than the frost on a bullet-headed boy's teenage stubble swept his skin and focused his mind. Jas grabbed bulky grey shoulders.

"Whit huv ye done, man?" He pulled Dalgleish closer.

"Grow up, Anderson!" Scowling answer to another question. "Did yer years oan the Force teach ye nothin'?"

A muscle pulsed in his forehead.

Laugh. "Jist another bitta rubbish – like that black bastard Somerville!"

Something colder than the night air formed in his head. "You killed Paul..." He tightened his fists. "You sent guys tae fuck me over, you let them..."

Last night was a hole deep inside his mind...

A Dalgleish-shaped hole.

A hole he wanted to to close with his fists.

Gunmetal glinted, inches from his. "Ye wur eyeways a stupid fucker, Anderson – Paul McGhee hud mair o' a clue than you ever hud...." Mocking. "...but even he wisney as clever as he thought he wis!"

His heart pounded, threatening to burst out of his chest.

"Ah knew it, back then. Ye were soft, Anderson – yer game wis soft... ah could use yer ain men against ye, every time."

Jas blinked.

Dalgleish seized the advantage. "Nae strategy, nae long-term goals, nae overall ambition."

Jas gripped handfuls of grey Hadrian uniform, twisted the fabric between his fingers and tried to ignore the contempt in the voice. "Ye killed Paul cos ye're... ambitious?"

Footsteps behind.

Muscle quivered in his arms. "Cos he wouldney hand over a fuckin' pc?"

"You canny prove ah killed McGhee, Anderson an' efter ye've bin charged wi' incitin' a riot an' assaultin' an officer ah doubt the judge at yer trial will..."

Face wet with Dalgleish-spit, mind reeling, Jas lowered his head.

A hand on his arm.

He turned his head slowly, stared at Stevie and a rodent-faced shape. The former held the crowbar he'd used to seal the roof door:

"Ah found this wan cowerin' in a corner, thought he'd be better aff up here wi' us than..." Words fading. Eyes to Dalgleish. "...did he jist say whit ah...?"

"He killed Fierce Paul?"

Jas looked from Stevie to Hamster. Rodent-eyes refusing to believe. Wetness convincing them.

"Bastard!"

Jas pushed Stevie away, foiling the lunge towards the Hadrian officer.

"Murderin' bastard!" On his back, Stevie glowered from wet roof tiles. "Bastard!"

"Bastard.... bastard... bastard... bastard... bastard... bastard..."

Stevie's shouts were echoing...

Jas glanced over his shoulder.

...not echoes. He stared at the procession of denimed men clambering through the skylight onto the roof. At their head, a shaved skull. The sombre figure held a flickering candle and made its way towards them.

Dalgleish, turning: "Johnstone! Git this mad bastard away fae me!"

Neil Johnstone continued to approach.

Dalgleish, panicking. "Come oan, man! We hud an arrangement – ah took care o' things fur you, ah..."

"You...." Pausing. Holding a candle directly into a sweating, grey face. "...murdered..." Flame flickering. "...ma ..."

"It's lies, Johnstone..." Backing away. "...your brother killed Anderson's wee boyfriend: he'd say onythin' tae see you add another twenty years tae yer sentence fur killing me!"

The words hit his skin like blows, stinging with logic. His right arm ached with a wound which still smarted.

Candle turning.

Jas felt its heat in the cold air.

Spectral eyes gazed.

A logic he could use. "He's right aboot wan thing." Jas met the stare. "Hurting him's no' gonny dae onywan any good."

The spectral stare never wavered in its conviction.

Jas frowned. "He killed Paul over a stolen pc, but he's no' gonny get away wi' it." He glanced beyond Neil Johnstone to the growing group of men, spotted Telly's mottled pate. His gaze moved to Hamster.

Padded jacket edging forward. The rodent-face was blotchy, eyes red-rimmed. "It's straight-up, man.." Mouth twitching towards the candle. "Dalgleish threatened me tae – telt me Paul hud given him ma name..."

Neil Johnstone continued to stare. Dark stars had become black holes, sucking everything in.

Jas clenched his fist. "Let me... handle it..."

Powerful lungs blasted up from the car park. "The polis ur on their way, son – jist take it easy..." The voice sounded like Billy McKinley's.

At Hamster's side, Stevie was rigid.

Voice from below. "...an' stay calm..."

He held Johnstone's gaze, balanced on a horizon between order and chaos. "Remember yer vows, Neil: let me handle it...."

Black holes closing in on themselves. An almost imperceptible nod. In the background:

"Bastard... bastard... bastard... bastard..."

The unearthly figure of Neil Johnstone turned away, eyes lowered. The chant resounded around him. Jas watched the scourge of the Bar-L rejoin the stocky, muscular man. He turned to the criminal at his side...

...and glanced beyond an ashen Dalgleish to Stevie's angular face, lips moving with dozens of others.

Gay-bashers.

Cop killers.

Rapists.

Armed robbers.

Drug dealers...

...petty thieves, kids caught with half a tab of E... alcoholics... TV licence evaders... the homeless... the disturbed...

A society within a society...

...at the corner of his eye, a blue flashing serpent. Relief relaxed his mouth. Sinking to a crouch, Jas released his grip on Dalgleish and hugged his chest. He focused on the line of police cars writhing through the darkness. A dull ache in the pit of his stomach told him this was far from over.

"Is anyone injured up there?" DI McLeod's artificial articulation was distorted further by the electronic bullhorn.

Jas hauled Dalgleish onto rubber legs. Cupping a hand around mouth, he mentally phrased his demands.

Bullhorn tones cut through his thoughts. "James Anderson is not to be harmed. Release your hostage and we can..."

Laughter from behind obliterated the end of the sentence.

He filled his lungs. Ah'm fine, Ann."

An amplified intake of breath.

More laughter, ebbing into silence.

Jas focused on the blue/white flashes below, eyes skimming the edge of the roof. Pushing Stevie back, he grasped Dalgleish's quivering arm and dragged the Hadrian officer forward.

"Is your hostage unharmed?" Amplified inquiry from below.

An icy gust buffeted his face. Boot toes wedged in ancient Victorian guttering, he looked at the man he had respected – the man who had provided the nearest thing to a role model he'd ever known, in the Force. "He's fine."

Ian Dalgliesh flinched in his grip.

"Good – that's good. We want to keep it that way, Jas – we don't want anyone hurt and neither do you."

Hurt... hurt...

Her voice filled his head. He stared...

...at a man who had killed in cold blood, organised at least one beating and rape in colder blood, conspired and plotted with Maxwell Fulton.

Two sides...

...of one man. Resolve and anger took wings. Jas cleared his throat, feeling eighteen again. A probationer. Green. Awkward. Confused..

Dalgleish stared at him.

Jas moved closer, heart faltering...

Dalgleish braced himself.

...and stopped. "Ah worshipped you." Jas stared at the pale, sweating face. "When other guys said you wur oota date in yer methods, ah defended you..."

Under his fingers, shivers fled up and down the officer's arm. Eyes stared back into his. Message unreadable.

"...when ah hud doubts aboot the job, whit you'd telt me kept me goin': wan rule fur aw'..." Jas released the arm. His fingers felt stained, contaminated.

Dalgleish inched away, backing along the narrow roof-edge.

Jas followed. "...when ma ain faither widney look at me, you said ma ability tae dae the job wis aw' that mattered."

"Now, is there anything we can get you?" Somewhere in the

distance, a bullhorned voice talked on. It was miles away...

...and he was back in Gorbals division, sitting on the other side of a night sergeant's desk, spilling his eighteen-year-old heart to a grey-haired night sergeant.

Dalgleish took another step backwards.

Jas continued to walk. "When ah made ma mistakes, you wur there fur me. When ah made ma first arrest, you bought the drinks..." Something wet on his face. Jas brushed it away. "...an' goat tickets fur the Celtic/Aberdeen game." He hated football – always had. Memory soured in his stomach. The stands at Parkhead football ground. Roaring 'You'll Never Walk Alone' with tens of thousands of others. Smugly reading past the words, to their sham-application for himself, and every other gay cop who wore the uniform. Tears coursed down his face.

He always walked alone.

Always had. Always would.

"You taught me respect fur masel' an' repect fur the job – when ah applied tae CID, your report goat me the post..." Icy wind froze the tears. "...you knew Alan Sommerville choked on his ain vomit cos ah'd restrained him too tightly an' didney dae the second hourly check. You put yersel' oan the line fur me..." Words more sobs than syllables. "..if ah wis that much o' a stupid fucker, why did ye dae that, Sergeant Dalgleish?"

The face on the man inches away was an unreadable, fear-sealed mask.

"...why?" Jas reached out, touched a shoulder and tried to close the gap and the hole inside himself.

Dalgleish wobbled precariously, shrieked.

Jas barely heard the sound.

Gorbals Police Station.

An unfurnished side office.

Staring at the black, lifeless face of Alan Somerville – a prisoner in his custody, whom he had allowed to die.

A gust of wind tore through the self-pity. Jas wiped his eyes on the back of a goosefleshed arm. And saw clearly for the first time.

...black bastard...

A desk sergeant's two unaccompanied visits to Alan Sommerville's cell, Jas himself dispatched to the toilets to wash blood from his face and smoke endless cigarettes.

...black bastard...

A desk sergeant who had been sympathetic, conciliatory beyond the call of duty and uniformed camaraderie when Jas had thought his career was over.

...black bastard...

A desk sergeant who had arranged for Jas to be elsewhere, when he'd returned to Alan Sommerville's cell alone for a third time, removing and returning the restraints to the locked cupboard...

...black bastard...

...and swearing under oath that they'd ever been used. Something snapped in his mind. "Why did ye let me believe in somethin' that didney exist?"

Dazzling light.

Jas took a step back, out of the path of sudden, powerful illumination from below. Vision sparkling, he stared at the up-lighted shape that was Dalgleish.

His guts churned. For twenty years he'd carried the guilt of one fatal mistake. For those same twenty years he'd borne a burden of gratitude...

Jas looked at the silhouetted face, then pushed the man to his knees.

...which was as much of a sham as the uniform he'd worn for an equal number of years.

A cover-up. A desk sergeant's cover up. Not to save the career of a green probationer. To save his own.

Silence...

...below, even the traffic seemed to stop.

Fizzing in his ears. Jas lowered his voice and stared down. "You're... scum."

Gunmetal eyes stared up, no ammo left. Grey lips moved. Jas didn't hear the excuses, didn't want to. Sound whooshed around him. He stared at the grey face, watched it grey further as he gripped a pair of broad shoulders. His own face glowed scarlet.

A scream through the night.

He thought about the man he'd counted on as fair, honest and decent: one of the few genuine apples, compensating for all the rotten fruit he'd ever had to work with..

He thought about two nights ago, shaking and terrified, tied to a vaulting horse, on one man's orders.

He thought about Paul McGhee, strangled over a missing pc...

Jas swayed.

...and Alan Somerville, not the first black man to die in police custody. A sudden gust of wind swirled up from the courtyard, thirty feet below and carried baritone pleas with it.

He thought of roof-top scuffles, of accidents...

Tears ran from gunmetal eyes.

He clenched fists, his own vision blurring. Fingers tightened around grey fabric...

...bullhorned words cut through something worse than pain:

"Jas? Jas Anderson?"

Different voice. He wodered vaguely what had happened to Ann.

"...this is Billy – Billy MacKinley..."

He drew the broad figure up towards him. Grey knees left the roof. Booted feet dangled. Icy gusts howled around them.

"...he's no' worth it, Jas. C'mon doon, pal..."

He stared at Dalgleish. Not worth it... not worth it.

"...they stupid bastards in the control room huv fucked their state-o'-the-art automatic entry-exit. Gonny open the gates fur us, wi' the manual override? Ah'm freezin' ma arse aff oot here!"

His right arm trembled, fingers uncurling. Legs melted. He slumped down. Somewhere to his left, he was aware of movement. Jas raised his head.

Dalgliesh was scrabbling over sloping tiles, hauling himself back up the roof.

An opportunity gone. The moment had passed.

Then more movement. Closer. And the warm leather of his own jacket draped around shaking shoulders. Behind, Stevie's hands trembled against him.

The moment had passed. Something approaching satisfaction coursed through his veins...

...only approaching. One last request: the reason he was here at all. Jas eased himself upright, numb hands cupped around mouth. "Ann? Phone Marie McGhee an' tell her ah've found her brother. We're comin' doon!"

As he picked his way through the sea of damp denim, a voice at his knees:

"Ye did aw' right, Anderson..."

He peered through the flickering candle at the cadaverous face.

"...fur ex-polis."

He held Neil Johnstone's blank, luminous stare for a few seconds, then continued towards the skylight.

Dalgleish's keys had ended up fuck knew where, but all the gates were open anyway...

...barring the large security door which separated the outside world from the world of the Bar-L. Jas gazed up at the small metal box, six feet above his head.

A couple of circuit-boards and some wiring.

He glanced to where Stevie stood with Hamster...

... then beyond to the sorry figure which was what was left of Ian Dalgleish.

Waves of denim had parted to let them through, ebbing away from the Hadrian officer, trusting to justice.

Jas raised the metal crowbar, swung it behind his head then brought it down on the fuse-box.

Instant darkness...

...then the smooth grate of a door opening.

And voices.

Twenty-Four

More bare brick. More bars.

Different bare brick...

...his eyes moved from the small window. In the interview-room, Jas stared across the table at DI Ann McLeod. His final sentences of explanation hung in the air between them.

In the distance, the sounds of order reasserting itself. SPS and police order.

Jas glanced at Stevie, then Ann.

Three a.m. eyes animating.

He sighed. "Diz that make clear why ah started the riot in B-Hall?"

DI McLeod smiled. "I don't think you realise what we've got here, Jas." She fingered the edges of a notepad. "If what you've told me pans out, there's going to be a lot of red faces in a lot of high places." Smile shrinking. "Hadrian can kiss goodbye to any corporate aspirations they have, as far as prison security is concerned." Frown. "I'll be surprised if anyone will hire them to run as much as a sack race, after this!"

He leant back in the hard plastic chair and tried to feel a sense of achievement. "Whit happens noo?"

"David Hamilton's given us the approximate whereabouts of his pc. If the hard drive corroborates what you've told me, we can start proceedings against Hadrian."

"Whit aboot Dalgleish?" Stevie voiced an echo of his own discontent. Ann's professional tones:

"We should be able to persuade him to cooperate, regarding dates, places and names more important than his own..."

He watched Stevie's frown harden.

"...but I don't think he'll be pressing any charges, Mr McStay, if that's what's worrying you: his injuries could have been sustained any number of ways." Eyes to Jas. "It's thanks to you two he wasn't more seriously hurt. Clever move to get him up onto the roof and out of harm's way!"

No mention of the few icy minutes, when the man's future had hung in the balance on the edge of B-Hall's roof. Jas rubbed his face. He didn't feel clever, he felt...? A snort at his side:

"That bastard murdered wee Paul an' dumped his body in wanna the incinerators – whit ur the polis gonny dae aboot it?"

Jas could hear the familiar anger and frustration. He watched DI Ann McLeod bristle:

"That will be looked into, Mr McStay – our main priority now is getting this place back under control."

The Bar-L had never been more in control than when twenty men had climbed out onto the roof in protest at the treatment of another. He glanced from Stevie's sullen face to Ann's police mask and back again. He knew she was right...

Paul McGhee would be mourned by his sister, Hamster and maybe Neil Johnstone, but as far as Strathclyde Police were concerned, his death was mere paraffin on Hadrian's already blazing funeral pyre.

...but it didn't make him feel any better. "When dae we give oor formal statements?" Maybe seeing the words in black-and-white would help.

Scraping of chair legs. DI McLeod stood up. "Tomorrow..." Notebook clutched tightly. "...you'll be taken into the custody of Stewart Street, Jas, as a crown witness." Professional smile tilting downwards. " I can't say what'll happen after that, concerning your own... er, trial, but I'm afraid you'll need to spend what's left of tonight in this..." She glanced around, then at her watch. "...place. Sorry, but..." Forced smile. "...don't suppose another four hours is going to..." Sentence cut short.

How many hours had it taken Dalgleish to strangle the life from Paul McGhee, or the Bar-L to kill the nameless boy who screamed all night, three cells down?

How many minutes had it taken a Gorbals sergeant to to vent racist anger on the helpless body of a restrained prisoner?

How long had he been unconscious, two nights ago, in the gymnasium?

She read his expression wrongly. "Again, my apologies – red tape. But tomorrow, we'll get this whole mess cleared up. I'll contact your solicitor and..."

"Jas-man?"

Stevie's voice was soft. Jas cocked his head.

Brown eyes burned. "Tell her."

"Tell me what?" Impatient. "Can't it wait til morning?"

He locked eyes with Stevie. If the police weren't particularly interested in the death of one prisoner, how much less interest could they show in the beating and rape of another? He shook his head.

"Tell her, man!" Insistent.

"Won't it keep, Jas? I've got a lot to do and..."

"It'll keep."

Brown eyes narrowed to an ominous glint. Then Stevie looked away.

"Good!" DI McLeod walked towards the locked door. Then turned. "Your cooperation in all this will not go unnoticed, Mr. McStay. I'm sure the Procurator Fiscal..."

"Ah didney dae it fur the fuckin' Fiscal!" Words exploded from the furious face. Stevie leapt from his chair. "Ah did it fur..."

The door burst open. Two burly SPS Officers. "Everythin' okay, ma'am?" Two sets of eyes suspiciously scanning.

Jas gripped Stevie's arm.

Ann stared at them, expression difficult to read. "Everything's fine." Then a shrug. "Put it all in your statement tomorrow, Mr McStay." To the officers. "Take them back to their cell, please."

Them.

One fence.

Two sides.

Them...

...no longer ex-polis, even as far as polis was concerned. The gulf between himself and DI McLeod was miles wide.

Criminal?

Not quite...

...his fingers tightened on a tensed, denim-encased biceps. Jas watched Ann nod briefly in his direction, before leaving the room. He released Stevie's arm.

As the two screws escorted them along too-familiar corridors, his identity blurred, refocused and blurred again.

No-man's land...

Stevie's boots thumped on the metal walkway behind.

...always a dangerous place to be. He slowed, approaching the open door of their cell.

Their...

...them...

Jas paused, eyes flicking over his shoulder. Shared grievances and enemies created bonds...

...but how strong were bonds forged from flawed metal?

Stevie was still scowling.

"In ye go, boys."

As he entered the cell, he studied the face of another man...

A man who had tried to beat him to a pulp.

A man whose skin was decorated by reminders of feelings – of a world – he couldn't control.

A man who had stayed by his side through everything, bathed his damaged body.

A man who had lain beneath him, fucked with him.

A man who was doing time for an unprovoked attack on two innocent men.

...a man with an estranged wife. And two children.

The slam of the heavy metal door resounded in his head. Jas continued to stare.

The alliance between Stevie and himself was convenience-based.

Necessity-based.

His eyes followed denimed shoulders to the far wall. Tension rippled in the cold air between them. He focused on the loop of tangled hair at the back of the man's neck.

Stevie stared at brick. "He's gonny get away wi' it, isn't he? That bastard murdered wee Paul, near hauf-killed you an'..."

"He'll no' get away wi' it..." The lie tripped off his tongue, stumbled then fell. "...okay, he will get away wi' some o' it, but no' murder. Ah..."

"Shouldda fucked him ower when we had the chance, Jas-man ..." Fist raised against bare brick. "...shouldda pushed him aff that fuckin' roof an'..."

"He'll pay, Stevie..." He sat down on the lower bunk, groped underneath for cigarettes. Denied his precious job and promotion prospects was probably the worst punishment Dalgleish could be given. Or losing the respect of an eighteen-year-old probationer? Jas wanted to believe it.

Stevie sank to a crouch. "Aye, he'll pay – bastard!"

Jas could smell the man, taste him, feel the familiar rage...

...an anger they shared.

An anger which damaged only themselves. He spun round, gripped heaving shoulders. Fingers under a stubbly chin, Jas tilted the lowered head up to his. Fluorescent light exaggerated every line and crease on the angular face. He stared into dilated pupils, then released the chin. "We'll talk aboot it in the mornin'."

Words wouldn't cut it.

Not now...

He began to undress. Bikers' jacket...

...boots...

...fingers paused as he lowered zip. A twitch against his thumb made him look up.

Stevie was watching, fists clenched.

The gaze met.

Stevie looked away, began to undo his own boots.

Jas continued to undress. The last two hours swayed drunkenly in his head. Shadows of adrenalin continued to gallop through his veins, chasing rational thought beyond his reach. He grasped at it, needing to think about something other than the hardening in his crotch.

"Jas."

The word sent a low shiver over his scalp and made his prick stiffen further. He kicked feet free and raised his head.

Stevie. Inches away. Naked. Shaking.

They stood silently, eyes on each other's body. Two pale skins under yellow fluorescent flickers.

His gaze travelled down from amber eyes, past parted lips and bristling stubble to the hard white torso, and the information carved there. Jas tossed the combat pants onto the lower bunk, stretched out a hand and traced the outline of a particularly knobbly scar.

Skin flinched under his touch. A sound, somewhere between a growl and a whimper, brushed his cheek. Then a head on his shoulder.

He looked down between them. Transparent liquid was oozing from the small slit in the head of Stevie's hard cock.

His guts twisted. He wanted to catch the droplets, rub them into the silky skin.

He wanted to...

...once was a mistake.

Twice would be...

Something wet brushed his stomach.

He recognised it as a mouth, rubbing a hand over Stevie's tangly head. A warm fist gripped the root of his prick, holding the shaft steady...

...then enveloping warmth. Prick flexed as Stevie's tongue rolled around the head. Fingers dug into the back of his thighs.

The man kneeling before him trembled. Jas savoured the skin contact, then reached down, fingers settling loosely on heavy shoulders.

The mouth on his cock moved down. A tongue lapped at his balls. Jas moaned, feeling nipples or ridges of scar tissue contact with his thighs.Hands moved to Stevie's head.

The tongue flicked around and under his ball-sack.

Jas inhaled sharply, fingers digging into tangled hair.

Flinching. And the sound of air rushing into lungs as Stevie pulled back.

The smell of sweat and a salty odour hung in cold, inhospitable air. Jas stared down.

Breath and five o'clock shadow rasped against his thighs.

A low moan...

...then one hand removed from his thigh, and a mouth replaced over his prick. Stevie's nose pressed against his belly, the rough chin dragging against his aching balls.

Jas listened to the sounds, shivered at the movements and tried to hold back.

Once was a mistake.

Twice was...

...spreading palms, Jas gripped his cell-mate's scalp with both hands and did what he should have done after their fight. He fucked Stevie's face hard and mercilessly, ignoring the choking sounds as an all-too-efficient gag kicked in and sent shivers of pleasure up through his body.

Nipples tingling, he gripped Stevie's ears and thrust faster, pounding himself past spasming throat muscle and into the warm, tight tunnel...

...balls clenched against Stevie's chin, Jas threw back his head and tried to pull out.

Two strong hands wouldn't let him.

He jerked forward, pushing with his hips.

Stevie sprawled backwards panting, choking, sobbing.

Once was... cunt. A series of holes, to be fucked when there was nothing better to fuck.

Twice would be...

...under dull yellow gloom Jas gripped heavy shoulders, pulled Stevie to his feet and kissed him, pushing a lock of brown hair back from the reddening face. Arms tightened around his waist.

Jas pushed the world away and slipped his tongue into Stevie's mouth. He felt the shiver in his own body, felt the corresponding moan in his own mouth as another tongue explored the inside of his gums.

Two feet below, another prick flexed against his own, anger mutating into something else.

Holes were for cocks... not tongues.

Staring at closed eyelids, Jas tried to read Stevie's face, then gave up and read what the man's body – and his own – was painting in letters six feet high...

...then they were on the bottom bunk, mouths moving less gently as frantic hands explored and caressed two very different bodies.

Jas seized scarred wrists, pinning Stevie's arms above his head.

The sound of shallow breathing filled the cell.

He straddled thighs and stared down.

Amber eyes hidden behind screwed-shut eyelids.

Jas watched the way the man's prick bucked, stabbing the air between them as Stevie thrust up with his hips...

...then he regripped wrists with one hand, covered the prick with the other and heard the corresponding moan.

Desperate.

Angry.

Awkward...

...he watched Stevie fuck his fist like it was an opponent.

He watched the man struggle in his grip, lunging upwards off the soiled mattress, contorting his body in an attempt to get free...

...and only thrust himself deeper and harder into Jas's curled fingers.

It was a fight Stevie couldn't win.

A fight he wanted to lose.

Sweat dribbled onto closed eyes.

Jas leant over, licked it away...

...and began to drag his own cock up and down Stevie's thigh.

In a writhing morass of skin and sweat, he lost the rhythm of the hand-job, then lost it completely as balls clenched unexpectedly and his mind shattered. Fingers tightened on wrists, then relaxed as he shot against Stevie's thigh...

...and his cell-mate's spine arched up from the bunk.

Warm wetness filled his fist.

Panting filled his head.

Jas blinked back shock, opened his mouth...

...and met the returning kiss head on, holding the damp face between spunk-sticky palms. Rib-cracking arms wrapped themselves around him. Bristling stubble rasped against his hands as he winced and sucked Stevie's tongue into his dry mouth.

A thigh edged between his. Then arms pushed him over onto his back.

A body covered his. He groaned into the open mouth. His softening prick flexed against the leg. Stevie was heavy, took his breath away...

...again... and again...

A low moan. Not pleasure. Something else.

Sweat and spunk cooled rapidly on his burning skin. He eased out from under the bulk, stared at the spent force.

Eyelids shot open. Enormous pupils stared up at him.

Stevie's breath was low and shallow.

Jas shivered, groping backwards with one hand. Finding the blanket, he dragged grey woollen scratchiness over his shoulders.

Once was a mistake.

Twice was...

...something he didn't need.

Flinching. And the sound of breath rushing into lungs as Stevie pulled away:

Hoarse. "Man, ah gotta say something."

Jas frowned: you and me both. He reached for a large hand, laced fingers with his own and watched Stevie stare towards the small, barred window. All sorts of sex... all sorts of pillow-talk.

Fingers rigid in his. Jas watched his cell-mate's lips, watched the man try to form words from thoughts still beyond him...

...in a world beyond Barlinnie's stone walls, guys like Stevie peppered cruising grounds and cottages the length and breadth of Scotland.

Sometimes they watched.

Sometimes they indulged.

Sometimes they beat the living shite out of those whose bodies they craved...

...as if killing the man would kill the desire in themselves.

"Ah dunno why ah..." The words were low, rigid with concentration. Stevie's Adam's apple bobbed convulsively.

Jas remembered the actions of the one man his teenage self had found the courage to approach. He stared at the scarlet face inches from his.

An angry push onto the floor of a seaside public toilet had been the thin end of the wedge.

His index finger lay along the line of least resistance. The raised scar tissue of a scored wrist pressed into his skin.

Was anger turned inwards progress, of a sort?

Was prison the only environment in which Stevie could vent feelings?

Jas tightened his grip on the fingers, staring at a patch of drying spunk, just above Stevie's left nipple and below a long-healed slash. He rubbed with the index finger of his free hand, watching crystals powder under the movement.

Fingers gripped his, crushing.

He winced, rubbing a rough finger over the knobbly scar tissue which ringed Stevie's wrists like handcuffs.

"...ah dunno why ah feel... oh fuck..."

He raised his finger, licked the tip and tasted the results of another unwanted encounter.

His spunk, or Stevie's?

"...ah, forget it!" The voice broke. Stevie didn't have the words.

Jas thought about the woman in the photograph yards above their heads.

A hand grabbed his arm. He looked down.

Brown eyes glazed with confusion. Stevie glanced away.

Jas stared at the hand on his arm.

"...ah widney hurt you..." Fingers were digging in painfully. "...fur aw' the world, ah widney..."

"Ye're fuckin' hurtin' me now, pal!" Humour: the great diffuser,

Low laugh. The fingers removed.

Jas could still feel their imprint. Other words crouched at the back of his own throat.

Convenience-based.

Necessity-based.

He wondered vaguely who Stevie would team up with, for the remainder of his sentence...

...more than vaguely. Jas edged way, disentangling their limbs.

Not his problem. None of his business.

A spluttering flicker. Then darkness.

The timer switch gone haywire...

...breath on his face. Jas scowled in the darkness.

Movement.

He flinched.

Stevie edged out from his side.

Jas watched the hulking outline pad across the short distance to the piss-pot. The lower bunk suddenly felt very empty. He tried not to listen to the sounds of pissing. Or the footsteps. Or the pause.

His stomach lurched...

...then tensed as a chilled body eased itself back in beside his.

"Gimme some o' the covers, eh Jas-man?"

He lifted the blanket, draping it around the shivering shape.

Stevie snuggled down, face buried in Jas's chest.

The sounds of slowed breathing...

...then sleep breathing.

One leg was numbing with the weight of the man. His brain raced under the weight of other things.

Glancing shards from a voyeur moon illuminated two arms.

One reaching back, the other stretching forwards.

He wondered what Stevie dreamt about.

Then gave up wondering.

Twenty-Five

With the dawn, he edged out from beside the gently snoring shape and dressed in half-darkness.

He had no idea when the police escort from Stewart Street would arrive.

It couldn't come soon enough. Pulling on boots, Jas braced

one arm against cold bare brick and stared down.

Asleep, Stevie looked younger, softer. Rage and frustration overcome by exhaustion.

Jas tied his lace.

He had lain awake, holding the man's relaxed body, listening to the sounds that body made, smelling the fading odour of their sweat and spunk...

...and pulling part of himself away.

Inside was one thing: outside was something else.

Too many questions he wanted to ask and knew Stevie couldn't answer...

...until he questioned himself.

Soft snuffling.

Jas watched the blanket-draped shape shift position.

Hairy arms reached for then gripped the soiled pillow, holding it tightly.

Dragging his eyes away, he looked around the cell. Wallet, keys and watch were in the office safe. Everything else he'd come in with had been traded or used up...

He dropped to a crouch, reaching under the bed. Two packets of Bensons and Hedges. Fingers tightened. Jas stared at his bikers' jacket, draped over the bottom of the bunk.

...or loaned out. He straightened up, unwrapped cellophane from one of the packets and lit a cigarette, still staring at the heap of battered, well-worn leather. He had other jackets...

Jas flicked his fourth cigarette end into the piss-pot and listened to another sizzle.

The door swung inwards.

He stepped forward.

White shirt/black tie.

No grey.

The Scottish Prisoner Service officer stared at him, then nodded, backing out onto the walkway.

Jas glanced at Stevie one last time, grabbed a towel and followed the officer out of the cell.

He showered alone.

He ate breakfast alone.

The white shirt/black tied presence of the SPS was visible everywhere. The grey was nowhere.

In reception, Brodie's SPS counterpart silently returned wallet, keys and watch.

Jas signed for his possessions, ears tuning-in to the sounds of Barlinnie awakening.

His watch told him the time...

6.45 a.m.

...his brain told him Strathclyde police and the SPA wanted him out of the prison as soon as possible.

For different reasons.

His presence had been a spanner in everyone's works, from the start...

...but spanners were tools.

Marie's tool.

Ann's tool...

...everyone's tool, used when it had suited.

Stevie's tool?

His brain told him it was for the best. His heart told another story. Ushered into the empty visiting area, Jas sat down to wait.

He wondered vaguely where, in the vast labyrinth of the Bar-L's boiler-rooms and furnaces, Paul McGhee's remains were located.

He lit a cigarette.

Five cigarettes later, more keys. And radio-crackle.

He glanced up.

Four navy-coloured figures entered the room. Carrying hats. "James Anderson?"

Jas stood up, nodded. The size of the police escort surprised him.

The appearance of a white shirt and a bikers' jacket behind the serge was a bigger surprise.

Stevie moved from beside the SPS escort and pushed his way forward, struggling out of worn leather. "Hey, Jas-man! Ye forgot yer..." To the five men. "...geez a coupla minutes, eh?" Eyes flicking between uniforms. Jacket extended in explanation.

Mouth creased into a smile.

Stevie walked towards him: "They had ye oot quick this mornin', eh?"

He edged back to a wall table.

The uniforms retreated to a far corner.

Between him and them, Stevie. Moving closer, voice lowered. Brown eyes glowing. "Ah saw Mr McLean – the governor? He gave me permission tae come an'..." Wanting to justify? Wanting to...?

Jas looked away. He didn't want this.

Throat clearing. "Listen, Jas-man..." Fumbling for something to say. Falling back on actions.

A grip on his arm:

"...you take care, eh?"

Jas ran a hand roughly over the dark head. "You as well!" Fingers feeling the warmth of Stevie's hair, the hand withdrawn. "Six months an' you'll be oot too." He perched on a table.

"Aye..." Stevie perched beside him. "...it'll go fast, noo – ah'm really lookin' forward tae seein' Sam an' Haley again..." Frown. "...dunno if ah'll huv a job to go back tae, though."

He nodded, grasping for the veneer of easy camaraderie which would make this bearable. Not a skill he'd ever really acquired. Jas stood up. "Aye, well..."

"Er..." Fumbling in jeans pocket. A slip of paper extended. "...here."

Jas took it, read it, then looked at Stevie.

"Gimme a ring, if ya like – that's ma sister's number. Dunno where ah'll be stayin', but she'll ken how tae git holda me."

He took out his wallet. Placing inside a number he knew he'd never call, he withdrew a business card and returned the gesture.

Business card: it seemed appropriate.

Last night they'd done the business...

...if his instincts were accurate, Jas knew Stevie was – at best – on the first stage of a long journey. Maybe, on the outside, he'd eventually get around to paying men for access to their bodies or seeking out the domination services of women like Marie, safe in the knowledge it was just business...

...their fingers brushed. Jas watched lowered brown eyes take in printed words.

A laugh. "Anderson Investigations, eh? Sounds impressive."

Jas grinned. "It keeps me aff the streets."

Grin returned. "An' gets ye intae the jail!"

He maintained the grin, gazing into Stevie's eyes. Behind the veneer, a flicker. Jas ignored it, then found himself pulled into a hug:

"Keep in touch, Jas-man ! Aw' the best!" Words against his face.

"Aye – you too!" Every muscle in his body hurt, the pain in his chest worst of all. "Come an' see me if ye ever need a PI."

Words against his ear:

"That bastard Dalgleish'll rot in hell fur..."

"Seeya, Stevie!" He rubbed the broad back with a clenched fist, then pushed. "Okay, that's me ready." Jas strode towards the serge escort.

He didn't look back.

Only outside, in icy November air, did he miss the bikers' jacket. But the cold helped in other ways.

Fingers in his hair. Tutting, then: "Ye've let it get affy long, Mr Anderson."

Jas lifted his chin. *Clyde FM* squawked from a small radio, wedged between a tub of gel and an ancient Brylcreme ad.

Terry draped the worn nylon cover-all around him.

Jas leant back in the barber's chair. "All the mair fur ye tae cut, eh?"

Hoarse laugh. "Still two-fifty, whether it's doon tae yer ears or yer arse."

"Gotta put they prices up, Terry..."

Buzzing.

"...folk'll be takin' advantage of ye!"

Muffled hoarse laugh. His head tilted forward by a gnarled hand. The satisfying pressure of clippers on the back of his neck. "This wan's on me, Mr Anderson."

He'd never been so popular...

...or given as many statements...

Jas looked down at the dark blond hair snowing gently onto his nylon-covered lap.

...or gone as long without a visit to the barber's.

For the three-month duration of the police investigation and the trial of Maxwell Fulton OBE, he'd been instructed to avoid contact with anyone who might prejudice the case against the power behind Hadrian Security Solutions...

A hand flattening his ear.

...Terry was prejudicial, at the best of times – and the world's worst gossip. Clipper blades followed the contours of his skull.

In Glasgow's High Court, he'd watched the killed-for Epson pc dragged centre-stage, the contents of its hard drive projected onto on a 6' x 6' screen. He'd given his testimony, then listened to ex-Officers Brodie, Fowler aka Pepperpot and finally Dalgleish trot out skin-saving platitudes.

It was amazing how fast the grey merged back into black-and-white.

No blue anywhere. Prisoners' testimony wasn't deemed reliable...

Terry moved round to his left side.

...or necessary. Maxwell Fulton's token five-year suspended sentence was icing on the cake...

...as was the court case: Hadrian Security Solutions had lost all major contracts as soon as charges had been brought against Fulton. The company was now in financial difficulties...

...a justice, of sorts.

"Ah'll tell Billy ye wur askin' after him, eh Mr Anderson?" Shouted over buzzing.

"Aye, dae that, Terry – he keepin' okay?"

"Oh, he's fine, Mr Anderson... hated no' workin' an' wiz affy glad tae git back on the job – pay rise tae, did ye hear?"

Jas nodded. His own business had been on hold for the past twelve weeks. DI McLeod had promised compensation from the Lord Advocate's office would be forthcoming.

A justice, of sorts...

...but he wouldn't hold his breath. Buzzing then pressure against his right ear. Then words:

"Ah wiz sorry tae hear aboot that lassie's brother, Mr Anderson. Terrible thing tae happen."

More justice was at present in progress...

His scalp shimmered under the efficient clippers.

...the trial of Ian Dalgleish.

When the police had dropped murder charges, allegedly due to insufficient evidence, Marie had picked up the gauntlet.

A private prosecution.

He wondered how much justice was costing her. He marvelled at her need for their sort of justice. Leaning back in his chair, he stared into Terry's mid-section.

Every prisoner present on Barlinnie's roof, four months ago, had been summonsed. In the wake of his own statement to the court, Graham Bell, David Hamilton, Neil Johnstone and other men he didn't know gave corresponding low, solemn testimony to the words they'd heard from Ian Dalgleish's own lips...

No buzzing. "Sure ye want it all aff, Mr Anderson? Affy severe."

...Jas had left the court room before one man he knew only

too well was due to give his. "Aye, Terry..." Fists tightened around the arms of the barber's chair. "...ah want it aw' aff."

"Okay, it's your heid!"

Buzzing.

The jury had already been out four days, on McGhee vs Dalgleish. Four mornings in a row he'd gone down to the High Court, sat in the witness room beside a sullen Marie. Chainsmoking Embassy Regal. Drinking watery coffee-machine coffee and weighing up possibilities.

The clippers tracked from the front of his head to the back.

Again.

Again.

And again.

Four days had been enough...

"...ah'd lock'im up an' throw away the key, Mr Anderson!"

To give them their due, the police and Strathclyde's Chief Pathologist's office had cooperated fully with Marie's legal team.

Remnants of charred flesh found in the furnace of Barlinnie's boiler room had been identified as Paul McGhee's left ear-lobe – initially on the basis of the distinctive tourmaline ear-stud soldered to blackened gristle. DNA had done the rest.

An ear and some ashes: not a lot to bury.

There was no doubt in anyone's mind that Paul McGhee had been unlawfully killed in HM Prison Barlinnie...

...by person or persons unknown. Jas shifted position.

The roof-top confession had, predictably, been disallowed. Equally predictably, the confession with which Dalgleish had plea-bargained with Strathclyde police was also disallowed.

Marie...

...a junkie whose only witnesses were classically unreliable. A junkie fighting for justice, for someone the court knew only as another junkie.

Terry removed the clipper-guard. Pressure on the back of his neck, mirroring pressure in his head... in the dark place where he wanted it to stay.

"Think the lassie'll win, Mr Anderson?" No buzzing.

"It could go eether way, Terry." He closed his eyes. A soft brush flicked hair from his face. He flinched.

No 'conspiracy to rape' charges had been brought against Ian Dalgleish. Rape was difficult to prove...

...but he had testified, along with three other inmates, to excessive brutality at the proxy hands of the ex-Hadrian officer, and sexual assault: every little helped.

Then he'd watched Neil Johnstone and Black Bill recount their own relationships with the dead McGhee. The latter spoke of Marie's brother with a strange sort of affection. The former said as little as possible.

Jas wondered if Marie's solicitor had deemed this the best course of action.

He'd watched the faces of the jury.

Eight men and seven women.

Marie had wanted an all-female jury: Scottish women were harder, less prone to sentimentality.

Jas had stared at the faces of eight men, watched their sympathy evaporate as the defence had raised the issue of homosexuality, with its implication of consent.

The prosecution objected strongly.

The judge ruled orientation irrelevant, ordered the jury to disregard the question.

But the seed of unreliability had been planted in the minds of eight insecure men. It grew enough to throw photographic evidence of his and others' injuries into shade.

Clever barristers won every time. Tinny words crashed in on his thoughts. Jas opened his eyes.

Terry was fiddling with the volume control of the ancient radio...

"...scenes of chaos outside the High Court in Glasgow, earlier today, as a verdict of Not Guilty was returned in the almost-unprecedented private prosecution of Ian Dalgleish, recently employed by the controversial Hadrian Security Solutions."

The thumping in his ears obliterated the rest of the report. Jas ripped the nylon cover-all from around his neck and stood up. His guts pulsed.

No...

An ancient, lined face stared at him.

No...

Frown. "Ah'm sorry, Mr Anderson – it's fuckin' crime that lassie's brother wiz..."

"Seeya later, Terry..." He thrust a hand into his pocket, pulled out a five-pound note and left it on his empty chair.

Surprise. "Mr Anderson – haud oan fur yer change!"

Jas grabbed his levi jacket and walked from the barbers' shop.

His own disappointment surprised him more.

No change...

Nothing changed...

...nothing anyone did ever changed anything. He should have taken illegal advice and thrown Dalgleish off Barlinnie's roof, when he'd had the chance.

Pulling the collar of the jacket up round his ears, he walked through watery March sunshine towards home.

Home...

Jas lit a cigarette.

The telephone rang.

He reached over, wrenched the plug from its socket. Staring at the TV, he allowed more information to wash over him.

Some good...

Our Westminster correspondent reported three resignations within the Scottish Office, in the light of the Hadrian Cash-for-Contracts scandal, but no names. At Prime Minister's Question Time, the Leader of the Opposition called for a thorough investigation into the feasibility of turning the running of more prisons over to private hands.

...mostly bad.

The stately walls of the House of Commons faded, replaced by mock-Grecian columns.

'Chaos' was an understatement. The pavement outside Glasgow's High Court was a heaving, jostling mass of discontent.

Jas watched a microphone forced into a small rodent-face. Denied the padding of the Puffa jacket, David Hamilton looked smaller and even younger in cheap suit and tie. As Hamster fumbled his way through inarticulate dissatisfaction with the outcome of the trial, Jas's eyes strayed over the background crowd.

He recognised Marie's barrister, who looked embarrassed, and a middle-aged woman who looked confused.

A faceless voice-over identified her as Mrs McGhee, estranged mother of the deceased. It also informed viewers Ian Dalgleish had left earlier by a rear door.

Marie herself was nowhere in sight.

He aimed the remote and fired. Watching the screen snap into black, he thought about eating, then decided against it.

No appetite.

He thought about ringing Peter, who'd called at least eight

times each week, since his release.

No appetite...

The second HIV test was still two weeks away.

...for anything,

Buzzing.

Jas sighed. No longer merely identified as James Anderson, care of Stewart Street Police, he'd talked to four journalists already...

More buzzing.

...and didn't particularly feel like talking to any more. He aimed the remote, fired again and turned up the volume: they'd get bored before he did.

Pounding replaced buzzing. A harsh voice over the weather forecaster's polished feminine tones:

"Jas? Come oan – lemme in!"

He dragged himself up from the too-soft sofa.

More pounding.

In the hall, pink artexing ripped his arm the way it always did. He half-smiled: nothing changed...

..including Marie's penchant for spontaneity. A frown covered the smile: maybe tonight they both needed company. He wrenched security-bolts back and opened the door.

"Ah see yer Feng Shui's still away tae fuck." She stared at the freezer then barged past into the lounge. "Whit time is it, Big Man?"

He closed the door, glanced at his watch. "Nearly seven..." He made his way back through to the lounge. "... look, ah ken things didn't work oot fur us in court, but..."

"Wiz talkin' tae a mate o' yours, the day." Skinny arms clutching themselves for heat. "Fuck, it's like Siberia in here!"

He looked at her.

"Steven – Stevie somethin'..." She grabbed the Levi from the sofa, threw it at him. "Come on: we're goin' oot fur a meal – ma treat."

He caught the jacket and wanted to ask.

But didn't.

Jas stared at Marie.

The scar blazed red against an ashen cheek. It matched her eyes. She looked away, then strode towards the door.

Questions blistered on his lips...

...he let them fester and scab there. Shout from the hall:

"Come oan!" Urgent. "Ah'm fuckin' starvin' – an' whit the fuck huv ye done tae yer hair?"

Struggling into Levi sleeves, he followed.

The restaurant was expensive.

And busy. Marie seemed to know everyone. And those she didn't were soon made aware of her presence.

He ate silently, watching her watch the clock.

When the brandies and eight-oh-five arrived, she seemed to relax. "Neil Johnstone sent a single red rose tae Paul's memorial-service..."

He lit her cigarette, then his own.

"...an' somewan sent me ten thousand fur the prosecution-fund."

"Did ye take it?"

Laugh. "Course ah fuckin' took it!"

Behind, the sound of diners dining underpinned her lack of further explanation.

Mine enemy's enemy? Jas exhaled and changed the subject. "Ah didney see ye oan the news, fae the court – thought ye'd be in the front row."

She blew cigarette smoke over his head. "Things tae dae." Scowl.

He frowned, brandy glass clutched tightly.

"Oi, son?" Hand waved extravagantly at a young waiter. "...'nother coupla brandies over here!"

He tried to read her mood like he'd tried to enjoy the trout in butter. And failed.

The brandies arrived. Marie slipped a five-pound note into the astonished waiter's hand: she'd already tipped more than any sane or sober person did.

He watched her down the second brandy, pushed his own across the table. "Okay – whit's this aw' aboot?"

Hand into pocket. Large bundle of notes produced. Ten counted off, extended. "Yer fee, Big Man. Go on..." Notes brandished. "...it's ma money, no' the Johnstones'..." Snort. "...an' ah can afford it!"

Flashing it about wasn't her style. He wondered how much the private prosecution had cost, and not just in monetary terms. "Thanks." Jas took a wad of hundred-pound notes from slim fingers, folded and shoved the cash in his wallet.

She'd kept her part of the bargain, securing a suspended sentence and more probation for herself: further payment was an unexpected gesture. He glanced around.

People were staring. Marie was a curiosity, an overnight celebrity. Maybe she was enjoying her fifteen minutes.

He swirled the brandy around his glass, then downed it. "Ye're no' gonny tell me whit's really goin' oan here, ur ye?"

Head lowered. "Ye're right – ah'm no'."

He peered through the veil of hair and thought he saw a smile. Or maybe it was just the scar twitching.

Three brandies later, she paid by Access and staggered off into the night.

The taxi driver had the radio tuned to *Clyde FM*.

The nine o'clock news bulletin reported the death of a man in a hit-and-run incident. Outside a pub in the west end of Glasgow, frequented by ex-police officers. Unconfirmed reports identified the victim as former Hadrian employee Ian Dalgleish.

Jas watched the taxi's meter flick up another ten pence.

Someone had opted for an out of court settlement.

As they cut up onto Cumbernauld Road, he rubbed his face and wondered how much of the ten thousand it had taken.

The bedside clock read 2.03a.m.

Jas closed his eyes and tried to sleep. Then gave up. He pulled back the duvet, slipped out of bed and fell to a crouch.

After the tenth press-up, his mind was racing faster than ever.

After the twentieth, he'd mentally planned out his case-load for the next few months. Publicity never did any business harm, and he was already turning clients away.

After the fortieth, his mind drifted off.

A knowing blond wraith told him what he was doing and why he was doing it.

Leigh...

...Jas gritted his teeth, pumped his arms more slowly. With time, the bad dreams would fade. He frowned: another dead, betraying man to haunt him, another man who'd escaped justice.

With time – and luck – the feel and smell of a very much alive man would merge completely with the nightmare that had been ten days in the Bar-L.

Necessity. A marriage of convenience.

Sex...

...nothing more.

An outlet...

...nothing more.

After the sixtieth, his body was glowing, ears buzzing with blood. He lost count...

...more buzzing. Not in his ears. Arms trembling, Jas grabbed jeans and hauled them over quivering thighs.

Finger held against buzzer.

Jas walked into the hall, brain crackling.

He knew who had probably organised it.

He knew who had no doubt paid for it.

The identity of the driver was the only variable.

Marie's closing statement to the man who had killed her brother spun around his head.

They both had motives.

They both had alibis. Marie was clever enough to cover any other tracks. But motivation was everything...

...he slid back bolts, braced for the all-too familiar uniforms of Strathclyde police, then opened the door. And stared. Early morning air stiffened his chest hair.

Amber eyes stared back. "Ye forgot yer jacket, Jas-man."

A chill more than coldness rippled over his body. He narrowed his eyes, took in the tall, tangle-haired figure wearing bikers' leather and holding a Farmfoods carrier-bag.

"Er..." Uncertain. "...sorry tae turn up withoot phonin' – ah tried tae call ye, but ah couldney..."

Jas stepped back. "S'okay, Stevie – ah wiz already up."

A hand behind his head. Grin. "Hey, check the haircut!" Fingers rubbing scalp-bristles.

Warmth from the press-ups flooded his body. The sound of the man's voice numbed his brain. Seizing Stevie's waist, he pulled him into the hallway. Arms grabbed him in a bear-hug. Words against his neck:

"Ah got the bastard, Jas-man."

– The End –

Also in the new GMP series:

Ulster Alien *by Stephen Birkett*

A poignant coming-out story set amidst the troubles of Northern Ireland.

Meet Matthew Woodhead - a sensitive child with his beloved best-friend Danny; an awkward teenager struggling to fit in with the gang; a young gay man on the brink of coming out. But in Northern Ireland everything is more complicated. Matthew's journey to adulthood takes place against a background of civil rights protests, terrorist bombings and the Save Ulster From Sodomy campaign. A world where young lives are destroyed by murder, and young minds by sectarian bigotry. Closely modelled on his own experience, Stephen Birkett portrays a world where the bonds of male friendship are strong, but a gay identity is that much harder to attain.

price - £9.95

ISBN : 1 902852 01 X

Teleny *by Oscar Wilde*

The only complete edition of this erotic tale.

First published in 1893, this outrageous novel of homosexual love has been attributed to Oscar Wilde with varying degrees of certainty. This edition, carefully prepared from original sources in the British Library archives, is the only one on sale annotated and unabridged. Ahead of its time in its celebration of uninhibited sensual passion between men.

"It is a bizarre book, alternating porn with florid purple passages, a hymn to sodomy with an angry attack on notions of the 'natural'" New Statesman.

price - £9.95

ISBN : 1 902852 00 1

All the Queen's Men *by Nick Elwood*

A revealing account of fourteen years as an openly gay man in the British Army.

"Out for most of my career as a cavalry bandsman, I discovered a gay military world where many squaddies were partial to a bit of cock fun. I indulged in numerous flirtations and affairs. There were no threats and rarely any hostility. Encounters with the Military Police, at first invasive grew into an irrepressible reckless defiance. We banded together, protected by peers and senior ranks alike.

I became engaged to a 16-year-old civilian, lithe and brown eyed Andreas, the summer soulmate of my dreams. Working up through the ranks to Trumpet Major I experienced much during my army career, pride in my sexuality, elation and loss. What a bummer it is to be in love."

price - £9.95

ISBN : 1 902852 03 6

Foolish Fire *by Guy Willard*

The first in a new trilogy of an all-american teenager's sexual adventures.

Guy willard is your all-American boy, a good-looking, popular teenager with only one hidden secret... a flaming desire for other boys. This first book in a trilogy of his sexual adventures is set at Freedom High School, where he inches his way out of the closet through a series of humerous and poignant episodes. From "Physical Education" to "Technically a Virgin", Guy's personal story is thoroughly true to life: always sexy, but very human.

price - £8.95

ISBN : 1 902852 02 8

Growing Pains *by Mike Seabrook*

The sequel to this author's most popular novel "out of bounds".

Mike Seabrook's many fans will remember Stephen Hill, the dashing young cricketer from Out of Bounds, his teacher and lover Graham, and his clever schoolfriend Richard. Two years after Stephen was forced to leave home, Graham dies in a plane crash, and Steven comes into an unexpected legacy, including a large country pub in Sussex. But as well as the strains this new fortune places on his relationship with friend Richard, the pair have to confront the homophobia of a group of the villagers, resentful of the changes Steven and Richard bring into their lives. Things finally come to a head when a young boy is brutally raped and left for dead.

price - £9.95

ISBN : 1 902852 05 2